Prologue :

From nowhere, I saw the gun. Bang.
The pain only lasted a moment, and I gripped the entry
wound, as blood fell. I closed my eyes, one last time.

So the strange gypsy woman was right. My name really was on the bullet that was in the barrel of this gun. I did not want to expect my murderer to be so familiar to me.

My mind raced back over the three years since my parents' deaths and I remembered every one of my lovers in chronological order. Some were more prominent than others because of one reason or other.

Ophelia Mason was the psychotic bitch that scared the shit out of me. Even now with my fucked up belief that she was neither dead nor alive like Schroeder's cat. Even from beyond the grave she haunted me. I met her during my singing days on Canal Street and she literally stalked me ever since. She was one of those mistakes that you kind of shove under a carpet and hope nobody finds out that you did it. Literally. Unfortunately for me, this bitch didn't like to stay dead for long.

Chris Mumford was once my hand fasted husband and he had left me again when I slept with that nurse that kept popping up in my life. We had met on a coach in Mallorca when we were training to be reps, we both had girlfriends and we both relieved each other if there was no sock on the door. I knew that he would never forgive me but there was something about that sexy little ginger with green eyes that made me want to get him back.

I think that I was in love with Daisy when I met her, but after she died during our induction course I transferred my lust to her identical cousin Lana, who I had met in Blackpool soon after. She was that one lady that I could not decipher as a friend or lover and like the others she had been on my journey almost all the way.

I thought that Emily could have been the love of my life at one time, but when I learned that she was my psychopaths' sister; things were never the same again. We had met when she stripped in The Black Orchid and we were briefly hand fasted as well. I loved her different to Chris, but more at the same time.

I had met Anne in Marmaris and we became lovers only last year, and whilst short lived, I think that she could have been the one to make me forget the horrors of my past. In fact my list of carnal partners was extensive, and yet I was destined to be alone for ever. And what about my best friend Samuel Chetwynd? My partner from our days in the band

Crotchless Thong. He had once forged his own successful solo career which was long over. I had banged both his wife and sister recently, and if he knew about the fun I had with his current squeeze, I would not blame him if his hand was on the trigger of this gun. Hell I fucking deserved it.

This is my final chapter, and how I, Connor Sebastian Candlish came to look into the eyes of my killer, and to understand why. I have to take you on a journey, back to where it all started. January 19th, three years ago when I had been singing to a packed bar on the entertainment circuit in Manchester. The night I met... Her!

January 19th ....

ONE

The phone rang, and I panicked. Glancing at the clock on the bedside cabinet, the red luminous lights read 2.34. Who the hell would ring at this time?

I looked over at the sleeping blonde next to me, I had met her in the bar just a few hours ago.

How had this phone call not even awoken her?

Scrambling for the handset, I composed myself, and spoke, "This better be good"

"Mr Candlish?" A voice asked.

"Who is this?" I hissed almost silently, "It's half way through the night"

"Mr Candlish" The voice spoke again, "My name is nurse Hambleton from the Royal Hospital"

This got my attention, something inside me stirred, and I turned away from the now alert blonde next to me, "What has happened?"

"Mr Candlish, I am sorry, but earlier tonight there was an accident on the Motorway. Your parents were involved in a car accident. Your mother was pronounced dead on the scene, but your father has just had to undergo an emergency splenectomy. I think you should come to us as soon as possible" Nurse Hambleton explained.

I nodded. I don't know why I nodded, but it felt natural, "I am on my way"

I replaced the phone, and turned to the teenage girl lying next to me, as she touched my shoulder.

"You have to leave" I muttered, as I hopped out of bed, pulling on my jeans, minus the pants.

"Charming" She retorted, "It's the middle of the night in Manchester, how the fuck do I get home?"

"In case you were unaware, this city is a Metropolis ya dumb bitch" I hissed, my shirt was on the floor and looked wet yet I didn't care, "Use the phone, and fuck off"

Clasping the shirt, I turned momentarily, she had a tear in her eye, "I thought you were so hot tonight, but you turned out to be a total and utter knob like the rest of them"

Anger filled me as I buttoned up my shirt, she slowly moved off the bed. Her pert nipples were aroused, as she failed to cover her modesty. I felt an urge in my jeans once more as I saw her pubis briefly as she clambered out of the bed in a drunken movement.

I turned to her, and clambered back on the bed, clasping her buttocks firmly; she fought me off for a moment, and swore a few times, as I pulled her back towards me. My penis bulging in my jeans, ready to burst through the button up fly any moment.

I used my hand to release my member, and entered her almost instantly, as her welcoming clefts opened for me.

"This does not make up for you telling me to fuck off" She moaned as I forcefully thrust her from the bed, against the wall, my hands reaching wantonly for her nipples, squeezing hard.

"Shut up" I growled, as I concentrated on the wall, a Doctor Who poster glared back at me, peeling away in the top corner, I raised one of my hands and pressed it against the red haired companion, "This is last time I fuck you, then you have to leave"

She groaned, as I thrust deeper, levering her buttocks for my own personal comfort, I remained concentrated on the companion as I thought of her instead of this blonde before me. I did not care, I needed to release soon.

Glancing down on her back, I noticed a small tramp stamp on the base of her spine, I returned my gaze to the poster, and smiled. In my mind's eye, the red head companion was before me, not this teenager that I had bought with a single shot of vodka at Churchill's earlier after my set.

Cheap slut, I thought, as I began to pump harder, and faster, her screams were rampant, and coasted as her hair smashed against the wall, I gripped hard, and pushed deeper inside making her high pitched moan escalate. I was nearly there.

The red head companion was once more there instead, and I shot forth my seed, and slapped her arse, withdrawing almost instantly. A drop of semen spilled from my tip, dribbling onto the floor as she turned to face me.

"What the fuck is your problem?" She cried.

"Get dressed" I muttered, as I tucked myself back into my jeans, glancing at the luminous dials of the clock once more, 2.38.

A wry smile crossed my face as I reached a personal best in ejaculating into some bird I have never met before tonight.

Whimpering, and possibly crying, she scrambled for her clothes strewn across the floor, "I never even came"

"I did" I whispered, "And that's all that matters"

"You bastard" She hissed, as she carelessly dressed, "I picked you up in a gay bar you faggot"

I laughed, "And I bought you with one shot of vodka you cheap slut, now get dressed, and fuck off"

She didn't complete her dressing, as she slipped on her high heels and rushed toward my doorway, "I bet you don't even remember my name"

I shrugged as I searched for the charger to my mobile phone.

She had stopped in the doorway, as she tore open the door, "It's Ophelia"

"Ok" I muttered, as I grabbed my leather jacket, "Fuck off then Ophelia"

I saw the anger raise in her eyes once more, as she stepped harshly towards me, her breasts still pert.

She raised her hand and slapped me hard across the face with her palm flat, the sound reverberated around the room as I almost lost my balance as she continued to swear.

Anger once more raised in me, my penis was erect once more, as I clasped at her ranting arms. I pulled her toward me, and once more our lips met, my tongue darted into her reluctant mouth, as I forcefully guided her back to the bed.

My member forced itself through the unbuttoned fly, and she straddled me.

"You do love me don't you?" She whispered as she lowered herself onto my cock, gripping it with her tight clefts, and began to ride frantically.

I didn't answer. My hand felt the heat against my sore cheek, before darting up to her chest, clasping at the mounds of flesh, bringing her toward me, burying my face into her breasts.

Glancing at the clock once more, I allowed her on top controlling my ejaculation this time.

There will be no traffic today; I knew I would be fine.

I never told her what happened, instead, I just told her I needed to go to work. I don't know how she bought this excuse, but she did. I dropped her off back on the still lively Canal Street where we met, and drove off, leaving her. I think she saw someone she recognised as she joined a group of girls within seconds of me pulling away.

My mind turned onto the nurse's comments as I drove away. I hope I was not too late for my father. He said I should become a singer after hearing me in my amateur dramatic society's production of Our House five years ago. With a few karaoke competitions and lead roles in a number of other shows under my belt, I got noticed. I had landed an agent, a slimy bastard called Thomas Gibbs, but I was also singing in a band with my best friend Samuel Chetwynd. We only did a few pub gigs, but we had a small fan base for our band Crotchless Thong.

Eventually, Thomas persuaded me to move to Manchester, and I left the band, for the best, Samuel went on to have a song in the charts and was last heard of in America. As for me, for the last year I was in the Manchester bars, singing a set for £200 a night, five nights a week. Thomas took £50 per session and I kept the rest. More recently, the new owners of Churchill's were having me two nights a week having met them back at home in Staffordshire, and had helped me find a cheap apartment in Deansgate. I say cheap, I earned enough, and I was 23, living it up as best I could.

I recall it was raining as I drove along the motorway, but that was about it, I seem to have then gone into some sort of trance, as I parked into the spacious car park at the hospital. I walked into the almost vacant reception area of Accident and Emergency. The elderly receptionist took her time in seeing me, although I was the only one in the queue, she seemed more interested in her cup of tea and chat with her colleague.

"Excuse me" I must have asked about half a dozen times, to her raising her finger at me signalling me to wait.

Eventually she sauntered over to her desk, and smiled as though nothing had happened. "Can I help you?" She smiled her toothless smile.

"I received a call from Nurse Hambleton earlier, my parents were involved in an RTA" I spoke barely a whisper.

"Name?" She requested.

"Helena and Ben Candlish" I responded monotonously.

She typed in the names and her face changed. Something within her snapped, as the smile became a mournful grey tinge, "I am sorry"

"What is that supposed to mean?" I asked, as she tapped a few numbers into the keypad next to her.

"Nurse Hambleton to reception please" The elderly woman's voice announced over a tannoy.

She turned once more to me, "Mr Candlish, if you can wait over by the doors behind us, someone will be with you shortly"

I moved toward the doorway, which opened before I got to them. A tall blonde nurse held the door open for me.

"You must be Connor" She greeted, as I nodded, "Your father asked me to give you this"

I glanced down at her hand, as she handed me a brown envelope. I nodded as I took the envelope, gently touching her hand as I did so.

"Your father passed away half an hour ago" Nurse Hambleton responded, "He said you were quite the entertainer...."

I barely slept that night, I checked into an overly expensive hotel in the town centre. Nurse Hambleton lay there next to me, her tunic was hung up neatly on the doorway. I tried to be quiet as I dressed in the same clothes. The envelope on the bedside cabinet just looked at me, I was unsure what it contained. Like a zombie I went to the restaurant downstairs, and bit into a slice of cold toast, and opened the envelope in front of several strangers as they ate their breakfast.

"Connor" It read, "I don't want you to remain in Manchester with that creep Thomas, and I think you are better than that. Think about when you were singing in that band with your best friend. That is when you were happiest"

A tear fell from my eye, as I continued.

"Your cousin Cordelia had the time of her life as a holiday representative, and now she is Head of Entertainment in a hotel chain in Florida, please do this, and make me smile"

I carefully folded the paper, and rested it by the coffee. And smiled. "Yes"

The next few days became a blur of alcohol consumption, funeral preparation and application for a role as a mainline representative for Fantastical Holidays. Then I left this in the back of my mind as I thought I had no hope in getting the role.

The funeral took place on a blustery Friday morning, with both parents being buried side by side in a graveyard, in a church I had not stepped in before. I was under the impression I would set into a ball of flames as I stepped inside the church, as the family I had not seen since moving to Manchester paid their respects, filtered off to the wake. A small gathering they said. I think I counted over 100 people in the room, and could probably name about ten, maybe twelve. My sister Coral was blubbering in the corner with her latest squeeze, some bum that she met whilst in a charity shop apparently. I didn't have time. Thomas had told me I had to sing the wedding song in front of people. I could not believe it, this balding ginger grease ball wanted me to sing *"Mandy"* at the funeral. So I did. I held back my tears and sang to a crowd that really could not be bothered to sing, or dance. Two people had died for Christ's sake. I noticed my old friend, a bald man called Samuel watching me from the bar. He raised his glass to toast my parents, but I did not respond.

The song finished and three people applauded. So I sat down and grabbed a cheese and onion sandwich as I sat alone, with the exception of ancient aunties that would occasionally come over to grieve loudly. The smell of Mothballs and, or urine lingered as they left. I could see Thomas hovering on his phone in the corner of the room, glancing occasionally at me, grabbing his crotch suggestively as he spoke to someone. I cringed. Vile creature.

When my mobile rang, I didn't recognise the number, so I took it outside, in the smoker's area. I had not smoked since I was 15, but I decided I would have one whilst taking the call, it gave me something to do. I smiled as a cute blonde female brushed past me gently letting her hand brush against me for the briefest of moments. She disappeared into the crowd as I answered my phone.

"Mr Candlish, we're very impressed by your resume" An overly excited American woman spoke, and before I could interject, she went on, "You are very impressive, and we would like to invite you to an open day in Stockport tomorrow, you can showcase your skills and if you are lucky we will get you on the next available training course. How does that sound?"

"I am sorry who is this?" I muttered lighting my cigarette.

"Oh forgive me Mr Candlish, I was so blown away by your resume, I was excited to speak with you" She explained, "My name is Olivia Buchannan, Chief Recruitment officer for Fantastical Holidays, it is just that you left your application until the last minute, we have an open day tomorrow and we would love you to come along and see if the life of a rep is for you"

"That's great, it would be a pleasure" I smiled.

"Excellent, I need you do a Math test, English test and a presentation on a sale of your choice, I will pop this in an email" She continued.

"Thank you, looking forward to it" I smiled for the first time in days.

"Perfect. I will email you the directions shortly, have a great day" And with that the call closed.

I pocketed the phone, and took another drag on the cigarette, I didn't savour that taste, and I extinguished it immediately.

My eyes raised, and I watched the vapour trail of a passing plane above. The smile crossed my face, and inside, a dance-like holiday tune came on through as the door opened.

I took one last glance around, and I hardly knew anyone else in there.

TWO

I left the party without notice, and slept for the first time in days in that overly priced hotel in Staffordshire. The next morning, there was ice in the air, as I set off from the hotel, the phone was ringing before I even pulled onto the motorway.

It was Thomas. What the fuck did he want? It was barely 7.00AM and a Saturday. I feigned tiredness as I answered on the hands free, "What is it Tommo?"

"You left early" He responded, I knew from the tone of his voice he was after something, "I had a girl called Ophelia in my office yesterday, she says she knows you"

"One night stand" I whispered, "Look I am on my way somewhere..."

"I thought we had something special" Thomas interrupted almost sarcastically. "Yup" I responded nonchalantly.

He brushed off my comment, and continued, "I don't pay you to get your dick wet with some pussy whenever you feel like it, now what are you doing tonight?"

"I have a meeting this morning" I responded, "So I should be in Manchester by six, where am I needed"

"You know where" His voice hinting of smut "What is your meeting?" " "Personal" I responded bluntly.

His silent response lasted for an eternity, before he continued, "I am not happy with you Connor, I needed to speak with you last night and you just left your own parents wake...."

"I said goodbye to those I saw" I lied.

"So what shall I say to Ophelia?" He teased.

"Look my battery is about to die" Another lie, "I will message you when I am back in Manchester"

I terminated the call, and concentrated on my journey as I saw a turn off sign for Stockport.

There were no cars in the car-park of the hotel, it was still early, we were not needed until 10AM, oh well, it would give me time to work on my project. Grabbing my bag, I walked into the grey marble hotel, and located a sign advising the Fantastical Holidays seminar would be in the Jackson Suite. It was the large hallway at the end of the corridor. So I sat down with my notepad, a coffee, and waited.

Gradually, I saw a bunch of suits arriving, and entering the Jackson Suite, one of the brunette ladies winked as she walked past and as I took a mouthful of coffee, she returned within a few moments.

"You're early" She smiled, as she perched next to me, extending her hand, "Olivia Buchannan, Fantastical Holidays"

"Hello Olivia, we spoke yesterday" I smiled, "Connor Candlish"

The smile across her face was immediate, "I am glad you came"

Something about her lips said come to me, I had to struggle hard to remain calm, "I am too" She whispered, "I looked on your website last night and you made me a little moist"

I felt the colour rush to my face as her hand inched closer to my thigh, gripping it slightly, as another person entered the reception. They didn't notice us in the corner, and disappeared behind the pillar.

"Do you think we could have a one to one before we start?... I would like to get to know you as a person" She gestured her head toward the entrance, "I am parked in a secluded area of the car- park"

I raised my eyebrow as a response, and she soon clasped my hand, and led me out into the car park. There were a few more cars this time.

"I could tell when I spoke with you" Olivia continued, "You were Fantastical material"

She led me to a camper van, and tore open the side door with force. Her skirt revealed her thigh as she stepped inside, turning instantly, to offer me her hand.

Accepting, I pulled the door closed behind me, "So a one to one?"

"Shut up" She smiled, as she clawed at my crotch, "I haven't had a man in months, and you're it... You cannot fuck me yet, I am on, but leave that to me"

Within a second of her finishing her sentence, my erect penis was in her mouth, and her hands were cold against my buttocks, the suction from those lips were like a Henry Vacuum cleaner. Through the window, I could see people arriving. The dampness of my perspiring palm slapped the window for a moment, creating a steamy glow around the imprint. I was aware now that she had two of her fingers inside her fanny, poking away with each suck she gave to my cock.

I felt the semen rush through my groin and shooting into her mouth almost as instantly, she pulled away, and spat the white goo onto the floor.

"Wait five minutes and then go in" She muttered, and wiped her lips with the back of her hand.

She straightened her skirt, and left the camper van without any other word. I glanced at disgust at the saliva covered semen on the floor of her vehicle, and I laughed to myself, 'Dirty Bitch'

I waited. And watched her walk casually back to the entrance of the hotel, and thought to myself, fuck this, and opened the door once more.

The Jackson Suite was laid out in a horseshoe shape with about twenty people eagerly sat poised with their pens and pads, as I entered. Three or four other people followed me through and we grabbed our seats. I sat next to a tall Asian lad who didn't make an effort to talk until he was asked to stand up and introduce himself. Olivia, and two other colleagues eventually came in and took their place at the head of the table.

"Welcome to you all" Olivia announced, as she took her seat, avoiding glancing at me as best she could, "I am Olivia Buchannen, Chief Recruitment officer for Fantastical Holidays, and to my left we have our trainers Andrew Buckman and Jayne Leech"

Together, this comedic duo gave a little wave as they acknowledged the room.

"Ok" Andrew smiled as he rose, tea-potting as he spoke as camp as anyone I have ever met, "Today will be split into three sections, you will have your exams first, and we will assess this information, if you fail this we will send you home at this point and ask you re-apply in six weeks. Then you will have your presentations, and a one to one...."

He carried on speaking as I cheekily glanced back at Olivia. She refused to acknowledge this gesture, and blushed, before brushing her hair, and pretending to write.

Jayne was speaking next, she was an African lady who was talking about her life as a rep.

For the next hour, I watched as everyone stood up to say a little about themselves, and I realised I was possibly the eldest in the room. When it came to my turn, I rose, and spoke clearly, as Jayne, Andrew and Olivia took notes. I could not help but think of Olivia's lips as I spoke.

"Hello, I am Connor Candlish, I am 23, and currently live in Manchester as a cabaret singer..." I noticed Andrew's smile and thought to myself that Thomas would love this, "I've wanted to be a holiday rep since I was 18 but didn't know how to approach it. I graduated from University a few years ago with a First Class Honours in Marketing, and have experience in car sales"

The team applauded as they did for all the others, and I lowered back to the seat. Olivia gave me a glance and another wink.

The morning continued, and we had our exams, the Asian lad and three girls left during lunch. One of those girls did not take it too well, and was escorted off the premises by security whilst swearing, and vowing revenge. We just observed, and carried on with our lunch.

We entered the Jackson Suite once more ready to present our sales pitch, and I thought I would go first. We were allowed 5 minutes to set up our slides, and props. I noticed Andrew and Olivia look at me seductively as Jayne scratched notes on her pad.

Pleased that my poster of the moon and the globe was set up accurately enough, I heard the mutters off some of the audience whisper about the props. They would be in for a surprise.

"Good Morning, and welcome to Stockport" I announced, bringing the attention from my audience, as the gentle tune 'Life on Mars' By David Bowie gently began in the background, just loud enough to hear whilst I spoke, "My name is Connor and I am your rep here for your holiday duration, I am here for two hours in the morning, and an hour in the evening, and you will find my rep times on the notice board in the hall way. If you need any assistance whilst I am not here, I can be contacted on my number, also on the board, or at the hotel next door where I am also repping. So rest assured I am here with my team to help"

I noticed Jayne and Andrew nod in agreement and jot something down, as Olivia   smiled at me in agreement, her lips slightly parted, as she moisturised them with her tongue.

"Of course, we are here on holiday for a short time, and not a long time, so we at Fantastical Holidays believe that you should take home some fantastical souvenirs" I continued, as I pulled a pathetic looking plastic rocket that I had made from a shampoo bottle I had stolen from the previous hotel, and as my audience giggled, I smiled, "So we would like to offer you the chance to try our new day out, as we take you from Manchester Airport to the most amazing, gratifying destination you will ever experience, and you too can be the first to participate in our journey to the moon"

The shampoo rocket slowly raised, and travelled to the poster of the moon.

"It takes just 2 hours to get there, and you can relax in our Lunar Spa, and enjoy a piece of moon pie all gratis in this all inclusive journey for just £25" I placed the rocket to the desk and continued, "The moon has been a destination that only a few would attend since the 1960's and now that this option is soon to be available to the general public, why not take advantage of this first opportunity and say to your friends at home, 'I did that before anyone else' and make them a bit jealous of your holiday"

I reached under the desk and brought out my sister's alien teddy bear, and smiled as I continued, "And you will enjoy this day out with the help of one of the locals, meet Eddie the Alien"

The audience, including those marking the presentation applauded, as I passed Eddie to the nearest participant, and then I answered their questions as best I could.

The remainder of the presentations were just as good, and then we adjourned to reception to await our one to ones. I could not wait to see Olivia again.

Alas, I didn't. The managers decided to do individual interviews to speed up the process from the remaining prospective candidates. I sat with this Scottish girl, Ceri Drewen, a very out and proud lesbian from Aberdeen who was openly lusting after Olivia too.

When Olivia opened the door with her envelope open, we both raised our heads, and waited. She called out someone else, and he strutted his stuff into the room, so we just carried on, heads down on our phones, someone else was playing Sudoku and was moaning that nine could not possibly fit somewhere as Jayne called her in.

The guy that went in to Olivia came out almost in tears, and brushing his now unkempt quiff back into place as Olivia stood once more in the doorway.

"If anyone else tries it on with me, it will be automatic no" She shouted behind him as he rushed out of the hotel, she looked at me, and then muttered the name, "Ceri Drewen"

The blonde haired Scottish lass beside me raised, and raised a knowing eyebrow as she followed her into the room, teasing me that she had a perfect arse as the doors closed.

Then Andrew announced my name.

It was shortly before four when the majority of us that had been asked to stay behind went back. Ceri and I were together for this and smiled as we noticed that there was another eight people that had gone.

"Well, from 27 candidates today, we narrowed this down to you lucky people" Andrew announced, once more tea-potting as he spoke.

We all cheered, and hugged each other, congratulating each other as we did so.

"If I call your name you will be going to Mallorca for your training in March" He continued, as he scanned an A4 piece of paper, "And those that are left will be going to Turkey in April"

"But that is months away" Someone commented, "I thought we would be going soon"

"Season won't start until March or April" Jayne announced, "So please do not hand in your notices just yet"

The list was read and Ceri and I were the last to be called, we were heading to Mallorca in March. Together we hugged, and exchanged our numbers.

I noticed Olivia approach from the side of the room, having congratulated everyone else.

"Congratulations" She smiled, once more, using those lips, "I am pleased you got through, you both really impressed us, Ceri, I know you wanted Mainland Spain, but Mallorca will be the perfect start for you"

Ceri thanked her, and moved onto another girl she had been chatting to earlier, as Olivia turned once more to me.

"I am sorry I won't see you in Turkey" She smiled, "I tried, but Andrew certainly wants you on his team"

I nodded as I turned to face Andrew smiling at me from amidst some men he was also congratulating, "Thanks"

The sun had already set and the rain was coming down heavily as I returned back to my apartment in Manchester. I threw my clothes onto the floor as I entered the bedroom, didn't care where they ended up, and I threw the bag onto the bed, and put my stupid phone back on charge. There were a few missed calls, I knew who they were from, and some messages. They could wait. I needed a shower before I went to my gig.

Naked, I walked into the bathroom, and started to run the bath, the heat from the water soon filled the room with condensation, and I brushed back my shoulder length brown hair, and smiled back at my distorted reflection.

"Right Connor" I announced, "New start, tell Thomas where to shove his job in about a month and go, have a party and live the life of Riley in Spain.... You can do this"

The phone rang again, and I left it to go to voice mail, as I leapt into the warm water of my bath tub, and soaked.

I wasn't in there long when my intercom went off. I sighed as I clambered out of the bath tub and wrapped the towel around my waist, dripping all over the tiled floor.

"Yes" I announced as I pressed the intercom system.

"Connor, you're back, let me in please, I'm horny" She announced.

I sighed again, Ophelia appeared on the scanner, I pressed the button, "Come up"

I dropped the towel to the floor as I heard her walking along the hallway. She entered the room, and smiled, "I've missed you"

"I've heard" My response.

THREE

February 3rd.

I had been waiting for weeks now, and kept my secret as best I could. Only my cousin Cordelia and my sister knew I had got the job, but no one else knew.

Each day that passed, I waited for the letter to arrive to confirm like we were promised. Ceri had disappeared off the face of the Earth and she was the only one I had exchanged numbers with at the hotel in Stockport.

Ophelia was literally at my house daily, with the occasional night off when she was visiting relatives. She was virtually at every show I did. I just didn't have the heart to tell her about Nurse Hambleton or Olivia. Mind you she didn't know about any of the others either. She despised Thomas as much as I did. She called him a letch when he was about.

She had been to college this morning, and was heading down the hallway as the post mistress arrived. My heart sank as I watched her take my mail, and I sat back on the bed as she entered my apartment.

"I have your mail" She announced as she placed it onto the mattress near to my feet.

"I have a gig in Salford tonight" I didn't really pay attention to her, "Why are you collecting my mail?"

She didn't respond, so silently I reached for the two pieces of mail she had placed there, here it was. "Anything interesting?" She asked.

"Bills" I lied, "Are you up to anything today?"

"I was thinking" She smiled, as she lowered herself to my crotch, mimicking a blow job without actually arousing me.

I brushed her away, holding the envelope and rose, heading toward the bathroom, "I have to be somewhere for two o'clock"

As I was in the bathroom, I opened the important envelope and smiled as I read the words, 'Congratulations, we are pleased to offer you a part on the training course for Fantastical Holidays Overseas Rep, your course commences March 19th, please find enclosed your air ticket confirmation, and luggage of 40kilo and a uniform list. Please send us in your measurements before March 1st and we will send your uniform to Palma...'

Reaching for the phone, I typed a message to Ceri, and quickly returned to the bedroom, shoving the letter inside the mirror cabinet on the way out.

Ophelia lay on the bed, seductively. I tried to ignore her, as she writhed on top of the quilt, her fingers were already touching herself, as she licked her lips wantonly to me, "Give me some before you go"

I sighed, and turned back to her, "I really have some stuff to do"

"Do me first" She commanded, I shrugged and approached her. My head lowered down to her vagina, and my tongue went in as I moved her fingers out of the way.

First port of call today, was the hairdressers to give me a new style, the long hair was gone for a short smart style. I haven't been abroad in years and that hair would be a teat in the heat I suppose. I know Ophelia will moan like a bitch when I get back, but I didn't care, she was a one night stand that never fucked off.

Then I was able to tell Thomas exactly what I thought and pass him the most magnificent and creative resignation I could think of. I was looking forward to that more than anything. I also needed to find a temporary bar job until I went to Mallorca. Didn't care about my apartment, which was due to expire the day after I flew anyway.

It was cold as I parked the car outside Churchill's, I could see Justin having a sneaky fag beside the doorway, under the pretence he was sweeping up, as his husband cleaned up inside.

"What do you want slag?" He laughed, as he stubbed the butt in the wall, and quickly chomping on some gum, "And you keep your trap shut about that ciggie"

I perched against the wall, "I need a job for a short term"

"Singing drying up?" He sighed sarcastically.

"Nah" I muttered nonchalantly, "I am quitting the singing, and I got a job in Spain"

He laughed out loud, "So you've banged enough people here, you gonna get yourself a Pedro?"

"Since my parents died, I realised that I needed to something for me for once" I responded.

"Thomas is gonna go ape shit" Justin laughed, "But he's a knob head anyway, so yes, when can you start then?"

"Tomorrow? I have a few things I need to do first" I laughed.

"Like that Blonde bint you have been seeing?" He spat out the gum, and swept it into his dustpan.

I pulled a face, and slapped his shoulder, as I turned back to my car, "Thanks Just, you saved my life"

Thomas's office was in a back street of Manchester city centre, you could see the dog turd and litter strewn in the cobbled pathway as I parked my car in the alley way. Some chavs were smoking hashish openly nearby.

"Fag" One of them laughed, as he saw me push open the metallic doorway to Thomas's office. "Your mother sucks cock for less than a half of shandy" I responded without thought. His friends found it funny although I could tell he didn't get the abuse.

I could hear him shouting abuse outside as I made my way up the dank stairwell; I still found some of the graffiti hilarious after all this time.

I could hear Thomas now talking to someone on the phone, I say talking, he was actually on the phone to one of those dirty sex lines for a change.

The smell of mould lingered in my nostrils as I pushed open his doorway. The dimly lit office was only illuminated by the sun light, as he looked at me once more.

"Don't you fucking knock?" He hissed, as he slammed the phone down. Sure enough, his pants were around his ankles, and his hand covered his cock, as he quickly pulled up his jeans.

"I did" I lied, "You were too busy talking to Busty Brenda or whatever her name is" "What do you want?" He smiled, as he realised I had seen everything.

"I quit" I didn't even think of what I was saying, as I handed him a fluorescent green envelope. The campest I could find to piss him off.

"What?" He hit the roof, "Whose poached you?"

"Fantastical Holidays" I responded, "I am moving to Spain"

He laughed his usual sarcastic laugh, before realising I was telling him the truth, "You're leaving to be a holiday whore? You're gonna split your arse in two for minimum wage?"

I didn't say anything. I just gestured to the envelope.

"No" He muttered, as he shook his head, "You do not quit on me"

"Too late" I smiled, as I turned my back on him.

"You were just a glorified backing singer in that shit band" He announced, "What was it called?"

"Crotchless Thong" I smiled, remembering my old friend Chet, who had gone ahead to have a one hit wonder by shagging the right girl. I continued, "Goodbye Tommo"

Furiously, he leapt over the table, and rushed over to me, slamming the door shut again as I tried to open it, "Nobody walks out on me"

I could feel his erect groin press into my back, as I closed my eyes.

His dirty breath against my neck as he grabbed my arm, forcing me around. His cock was harder now, and digging into my leg.

"You will stay here, and you will fuck me whenever I say" He announced through gritted teeth, "You will not move to Spain"

"I am leaving" I sighed.

He shook his head once more, and tore his penis out of his jeans, "You will suck it and stay like the good slut I pay you for"

I remained stationary, and he tried to force my hand onto his genitalia.

He was beginning to get angry now, his reddened face and the steam was now coming out of his mouth, "Earn your fucking money"

"Ok" I responded distantly, as I slowly lowered myself to my knees. I could sense him smiling above me, as his rancid brie smelling knob loomed in front of my face, steam also coming off his purple head, "I suppose I should give you a farewell present"

I allowed my hands to cup his buttocks, as I cringed, inching closer to his penis.

"Make it a good one and I will forget this moment of madness" He panted, already imagining my pierced tongue around his shaft.
I nodded, as I could smell his sweaty bollocks close to my nose.

Then I drew my head back sharply, and nutted him in his dick as hard as I could, using my hands to keep him from moving back.

His scream pitched in tone, as I let him go, and he coiled into the foetal position, crying like a girl as I rose calmly.

"I'm sorry ginger pubes" I muttered, "No more of your shit, that's me done"

"You'll be sorry" He cried between breaths.

"Sorry I didn't do this sooner" I pulled the door open, and slammed it behind me as I left.

The chav I confused minutes ago sauntered toward me as I stepped into the cobbled street again.

"Give your regards to your mother for me" I muttered, opening the car door with force, aware that he had urinated all over the windscreen.

He muttered something inaudible whilst his face resembled that of a bulldog licking a nettle he'd just pissed on.

"Perfect advertisement for contraceptive" I laughed.

He looked at me gormlessly as he took a moment to think about what I had said, but by the time he realised I was heading off down the street, giving him the finger in the rear view mirror.

She was waiting angrily when I got back to the apartment. I could sense her fury as I saw the torn envelope on the television stand. I could tell she had been crying as she glared at me.

"Why did you beat up Thomas?" She hissed, as I noticed the paper in her hand.

I approached, and reached for the paper, to which she retracted sharply, "I didn't beat him up, I resigned"

"I had to stop him from calling the police" She shouted, "And then he told me what you have done"

What was it I have meant to have done?" I asked, eyeing the paper in her hand, knowing full well I knew what she was on about.

You are moving to Spain to get away from me" She cried.

"I am moving to Spain yes" I agreed.

"What about me?" She cried.

"Perhaps it's time you met someone your own age?" I commented, ignoring her pleas.

"I don't want anyone else" She whimpered, "I want you"

"Fuck off"

"No" She screamed, "I am sick of you telling me to fuck off, I love you"

"Door's that way" I whispered, gesturing to the door, "Goodbye"

FOUR

March 18th.

The last five weeks were filled with parties and sex whenever I could get it. Working in a gay bar, I found it easier to speak to the women, as they all believed they were safe, until I worked my charm. Justin had found me a small couch to surf on at Kyle's, one of the strippers' apartments for a while, and I had sold pretty much all of my possessions in car boot sales, and the like recently. Thomas had tried to press charges, but then backed out when I pointed out that the reason I had nutted him in the balls was because waving his wang in my face was a no. Meanwhile I had no idea where Ophelia had gone. She was still on social media but for some reason did not want to speak with me. Maybe she got the point?

Churchill's had closed the back part of the bar for some reason, like I didn't know, but I had to go along with the secret. My stripper house mate, was crap at keeping secrets and had left his Facebook page open whilst he was getting his chest waxed by his Scandinavian girlfriend Malin. So tonight was my last night in Manchester, and I knew that my friends had arranged a farewell party. I walked into the bar, and could see Curtis the ever excited, overly camp drag queen waiting impatiently at the bar, as he signalled me over.

Here we go.

"Justin isn't happy" He announced, his acting was a poor as his drag skills. I mean everyone knew he was a shit drag impersonator, but that was his forte, I think.

"Oh" I muttered, "I better go see him then, where is he?"

"Over in the small bar" He announced, barely containing his excitement, I knew that he was dying to squeal as he followed me.

I pushed the diamante curtains as I entered the bar, and as I did so, the music began to raise, *Peter, Paul and Mary's 'Leaving On a Jet Plane"* started, and everyone chorused.

I feigned the shock as I promised myself, as I saw Justin and his husband Ryan on the stage, microphone poised.

"Ladies, the slag has entered" Ryan laughed, causing a massive applause, and cheer from all my friends. I saw Coral and her different man over in the audience, with a banner wishing me luck, there was people I had not seen for a while, and even a few people from the training day, who lived close and were flying out tomorrow with me.

"What a surprise" I laughed, as Kyle and Malin offered me a drink.

"As you all know, our little Connor Candlish is making a new start for himself in Palma, which means he's gonna be sticking his thing in any hole that comes his way in Shaggamuff" Justin announced over the mike, "Well, he's done the entire of Manchester"

Everyone laughed, as I blushed. I worked hard for this reputation.

Then I saw her. Ophelia stood near to the bar, with a cocktail in her hand, and gave me a knowing wink as the music crescendoed into the chorus of the song.

The toilets in Churchill's were the perfect place for a farewell screw. And she knew it was the last time. But she wasn't as angry as I expected. Or wanted.

After I came, she sat on the toilet, and casually dressed without speaking. "Well" I muttered. "Bye then"

"Adios" She announced, as she brushed passed me, putting her knickers in my hand, "Something to remember me by"
She pulled open the door, and left without saying a word.

I screwed up the panties and tossed them into the bowl, and followed her out, and into the party. I have no idea where she went as she disappeared into the crowd.

March 19th

I hardly slept last night, I took home some random girl that was in the bar, and although nothing happened, mainly due to the alcohol consumed, and the Ophelia incident in the toilets, I didn't have any energy. Kyle and Malin drove me to the airport, and as I struggled with two oversized suitcases, I located the Fantastical Tours desk in terminal one. There were a few faces I recognised in the queue, but Ceri was still not there.

The cheery, enthusiastic Olivia stood at the desk ticking off our names, and supplying our tickets as like sheep we waited. I kept watching those lips remembering it around my penis.

"You guys are going to be amazing, make sure you have a good time, and remember, it's all work hard, play hard" She announced.

I accepted my ticket, and tried to glance at the list to see if there was anyone else I recognised. "Excuse me Olivia" I enquired.

"Connor" She smiled back, "I haven't seen you since Stockport, pity you didn't stay in touch"

"Thanks" I smiled, "I am wondering if Ceri Drewen had changed to Turkey I haven't heard off her since that day in Stockport"

She checked her list, and shook her head, "Was she the Scottish girl? Bit of a rug muncher?" I laughed, as I nodded.

"Let me check, you two were friends weren't you?" She answered, as she pulled out her phone, "Olivia here, I have Connor Candlish asking about Ceri Drewen...."

I smiled as two lads from the course signalled to me that they were heading for caffeine, as Olivia spoke. I acknowledged with a nod.

"I'm sorry" Jayne sounded sincere, "Ceri passed away the day of the training course. Her car went off the road in Lancaster...."

Something inside me broke at that point. I had only known her for a few hours. And I had text her a few times. Now she was dead. I didn't hear the rest of her explanation.

I nodded as I accepted this news. And slowly walked over to the two lads, who were pondering over the drinks machine.

"Apparently they had another induction day" The shorter guy announced, as he pressed a few buttons on the machine.

I grunted an acknowledgement, as I thought back to Ceri.

We landed just two hours later. The pilot announced that twenty six new holiday reps were on the flight, and we received a cheer by a bunch of total strangers, which made us all smile.

As we entered the arrivals lounge, the scouse holiday rep stood proudly with her clip board, and a sign that said 'New Reps Here' the heat from the Mallorcian sun was a lot hotter than it was in the UK. Gloomy old Manchester was well behind me now.

We approached her and she gave us all envelopes and directed us to coach number 6. As I boarded the coach, I quickly grabbed the front seat behind the driver, as groups of people slowly filled the coach, chatting away as though they had known each other for years. The shorter guy and his friend sat behind me, and offered me a small bottle of vodka they bought at customs.

"Better hide it" He announced, "Did you see that woman Hitler that directed us here?" His friend laughed, "Since you turned gay you hated all women Keith"

I twisted open the vodka and drank it neat, as they started to play fight behind me. The coach was filling up fast, as the scouser returned to the coach. Keith groaned under his breath.

"Alright team Fantastical" She cheerfully announced, as she checked her clip board, and everyone on board cheered heartily, "My name is Sian, and I've been repping here for three years, so I know what you are feeling right now, and you guys are gonna love it, but I am sorry but there is another flight with three other Reps coming in from East Midlands"

Someone groaned from the back and announced in a broad cockney accent, "Fricken Northerners"

Almost everyone on the coach jeered at him, as Sian glared at him, "Alright dick head, this is my coach and I have a bigger gob than you"

We all cheered, the poor geezer must have wanted the ground to open up and swallow him whole.

"And I probably have a bigger cock than you as well" Sian continued as she gestured with her little finger at him.

"Prove it" He shouted in defence. She smiled, "Sure will" She smiled, as she flashed her massive tits at us all, causing everyone to cheer. The image lasted a matter of seconds, as she covered herself up without embarrassment, "What's your name pee wee?"

"Chris" He laughed.

"Good" She winked at him, "Keep it up soldier because we can have some fun this week, or I can make your life hell.... whatever makes you hard"

I wolf whistled, as another blonde girl thought she would join in, flashing her smaller breasts at the stranger next to her, causing more of a cheer, Keith and his man started to kiss passionately, as I watched on. Sian noticed the empty vodka bottle in my hand.

"Ok smartarse" She announced, "Pass it over"

I felt myself blush as she held her hand firmly out, sternly glancing at me. I passed it almost instantly.

"Not that one, the full one" She insisted.

"I don't have any" I announced, as I gestured to Keith, "This dude passed it to me"

"Puss" She muttered, as she leaned over to Keith, "Now man slut, pass me some vodka, and we will forget all about this"

Keith smiled, as he pulled out some more miniatures of vodka and passed one to her. She opened it and poured the entire content into her mouth before tossing the empty at me, "Put that in the bin bell end, I will go check on this flight"

She leapt off the coach and I watched wantonly as her ass looked fine as she ran toward the automatic doors.

"Wow, still hate her then Keith?" I asked.

He paused for a moment, as he followed my gaze, "I think I just turned straight"

His boyfriend gently slapped his arm. The girl who flashed her boobs to the stranger rose, and walked to the front of the coach.

"Alright Team Fantastical" She mimicked in the poorest Liverpudlian accent I have ever heard, "Welcome to Mallorca, and the first annual Miss Tits competition, I clearly only got my job because I am massive slag"

"Oi, that's my shag for the night" Chris announced, brushing his ginger quiff back in one swoosh, flashing his emerald eyes, "And her baps are better than your fried eggs love"

"Naff off ball bag" She smirked, as she clambered off the bus to light a cigarette, soon joined by several other people.

"I'm gonna have her tonight" I giggled at Keith, as he passed me another bottle. "I thought you were on our bus" He laughed.

I laughed out loud, and opened the whisky this time, as we saw Sian and three people emerge from the automatic doors.

"Shit the wife's back" Chris shouted, loud enough that she heard from outside.

Two girls boarded the coach and went straight the back, as the third nervously stepped on board. For a tall girl she seemed out of place as she glanced around the bus for a vacant seat from behind her glasses. I smiled as I offered the seat next to mine.

"Thank you" She accepted the offer, and smiled, I almost melted at her Glaswegian voice, "My name is Daisy"

"Connor" I smiled, "Wanna share my bed tonight?"

She laughed the sweetest of giggles I had ever heard, "Unfortunately Romeo I am a taken Juliet, but you know what, I like you"

I didn't even bother hiding the blush.

Sian began to get impatient with the girls outside the coach, as she conducted a head count to confirm how many people were on board.

"Alright saggy" She shouted through the door, the girl seemed genuinely shocked by the announcement, "If we leave now, we can get to the hotel in time for breakfast"

She didn't respond, just flicked her cigarette as she led the group back on board the coach, and the demonic glare exchanged between them made me laugh out loud, as did Daisy.

We arrived at The Bellevue Hotel less than half an hour after we left the airport. Daisy and I laughed as we sat together on the marble floor of the hotel, as Sian read out a number of names to check us in individually.

Daisy smiled and hid a blush as a waiter passed us, "That's my baby"

I realised at that point that Daisy had been a holiday fling that followed her dream.

"I was here just a few months ago, and Marco treated me like a princess" She smiled, "And that is when I said, 'come on Daisy, get yourself out there, and be with him"

"So you applied to be a rep?" I responded.

She nodded enthusiastically, "I know it sounds like something you read in *Take a Break*, but this is real"

"Connor Candlish and Chris Mumford?" Sian announced interrupting our conversation a little.

I acknowledged and smiled to myself as Cockney Chris also did, accepting the key cards on my behalf.

"Do you fancy a drink at the bar later?" I asked.

"I would love to" She smiled, giving me that cute giggle again, as she heard Sian announce her name, along with someone called Beverley.

She rose and accepted the key card, as fried eggs Beverley approached Sian. Again that glare echoed anger throughout the reception.

"I will see you down here in half an hour" I smiled, as Hockey Chris rushed over to me, passing me the card.
"Dude, we gotta get pissed" He announced, "That Scottish bird seems hot" "Yes" I agreed, "I think we will be good friends"

"Yeah" He laughed, "I bet you will be eating her haggis by the end of the day"

"No" I smiled, as I watched her and Beverley enter the elevator together, enthusiastically chatting together, "She's a friend, and that is all"

Within fifteen minutes, I walked out into the poolside bar. I had changed into my jeans and white shirt. Daisy was already there, alone. I ordered a lager and by the time I sat next to her, three more girls, and a male had arrived. They must have been at the bar before me.

"Guys, this is Connor, and he's lovely" Daisy introduced, "He's a singer from Manchester"

We exchanged pleasantries, there was Northern girl Clare with the curly hair, who had the biggest blonde perm I have seen this side of the 80's. She was a Fantastical Holidays Travel Agent from Gateshead who was looking for a different side to her career. Her roommate was Julie from Kent, who didn't really want to be there, but had recently left her boyfriend. Then there was another Scottish girl, a flame haired tall girl, Shannon, who was fresh out of jail according to her, she was trying to get over her past. Then there was Matty from Birmingham with the broadest yam yam accent ever.

"Apparently there is more reps arriving from Birmingham tonight" Clare announced, as she bit into her cheese toastie that already on the table, "Two more arriving"

Daisy smiled as she leaned in closer, "Can I have a chat with you?"

"Sure" I responded, I gestured that we left the table.

"No it is ok, it's just that Beverley's boyfriend works over in Magaluf for a night club and she wants him to come over tonight, so can I have your bed?" She announced precariously.

I smiled, as I touched her arm, "Any time" Something inside us made us laugh once more.

The evening saw almost the entire new reps gather in the bar for a drink, and a getting to know you session. Matt was also a singer, and was interested in locating a karaoke bar nearby but was soon canoodling with Clare with the curly hair. Daisy and I seemed inseparable, as were Chris and Sian who disappeared on multiple occasions returning looking flustered. Keith was on his own as his boyfriend was tired from travelling all day. Wuss.

It was just after 930 when Beverley introduced us to her boyfriend Ben, a meathead who took instant dislike to male reps, stating that we were all faggots and the girls were glamour slappers who opened their legs for a phone card. Charming, considering Beverley was now one of those slappers opening her legs for a phone card.

Then as the night wore on, the plane from Birmingham had landed, and Andrew arrived with the new arrivals. One very familiar person stood at the reception, in her mini skirt, and small white jacket that revealed her back to the room.

That tramp stamp once more on show.

"Hello Connor" She smiled, as she flashed her room key at me.

"Ophelia?" I did not know whether my eyes were playing tricks on me, or whether the Estrella Dram was affecting me more than the others.

"Why should you have all the fun?" Ophelia announced proudly, "I'm in room 616 and I fancy a replay from last night, I hope you bought my knickers with you, apparently it can get cold in the evening here"

"Why are you doing this?" I whispered.

Ophelia smiled, as she inched closer to me, her hand cupping my penis within a second, "Because I own your cock, and it does what I say, now meet me in my room in five minutes"

She released her grip, and clasped her suitcases, as Andrew who had been oblivious to the scene before him walked towards us, with a wide smile on his face.

"Ah, the newbies" He announced, "I hope to see you all at 9AM sin hangover, as tomorrow is going to be a hard slog"

Ophelia licked her lips at me, mouthing the words hard slog again without Andrew's knowledge.

"Oh, and whilst you're here, this is our new trainer Ophelia Mason, she speaks highly of you Mr Candlish" I could not sense if he was disgusted or turned on but he had his eyes firmly in my penile area.

"Yes" Ophelia added, "I do plan on making this week hard"

Chris and Sian were busy pleasuring each other in the bed next to mine as I entered the room in the dark, they seemed oblivious to me and Daisy's arrival soon after midnight. Silently Daisy clambered into the bed having undressed in the moonlight, and I watched as she pulled the cotton sheets above her breasts, before I removed my clothes and lay on the hard floor of the balcony. The cool air felt great against my skin.

It was the longest night of my life. Inside that room this wonderful lady I had just met was sleeping in my bed, and I was outside. Upstairs somewhere my crazy weird stalker ex one night stand that never fucked off waited for me.

I was erect, and I allowed myself to touch my shaft, tugging hard for long moments as I thought of what was going on in that room, and I felt the orgasmic sensation as I stroked the hardness of my cock, starting off slow, and smooth, I soon gained rhythm and began to speed up my pace. Steaming pre-cum would soon seep into my palm as I shafted myself knowing my own movements. In the dark moonlight, I glanced down at my own manhood, and at that moment I felt that urge of spasm, I bucked, and thrust my hips in the air with the flowing movement of my hand and rhythm, I watched as the first shot of sperm shot from my japs eye. That volley of my jizz followed by bursts of my own ivory coloured juice covered my chest, and I bit my own lip as I tried to stifle my moan, I felt the sensation diminish as I allowed it to fall off my body and onto the cold floor.

I waited. I don't know what for, I just needed to feel the cool air against my now sweaty body for long moments.

I don't know how long I waited, but I suddenly became aware that she was watching me. I wasn't shocked, I just smiled as she stepped out onto the balcony, and lit her cigarette.

"I could have helped with that" Sian whispered between inhaling and exhaling her smoke, "Looks more impressive than two pumps and a squirt I just experienced"

"I needed some release" I whispered, still not moving from the ground.

Sian smiled as she walked barefoot toward the edge of the balcony, slipping momentarily on my spunk, maintaining her balance expertly, "Why didn't you join us? You and that Scot?"

"Just a friend" I whispered.

"Reps can't be just friends" She announced, as she fixated her gaze to my now flaccid cock, "But you will learn this"

FIVE

I remained silent as I sat at the breakfast table earlier than anyone else, Sian sauntered into the restaurant, pouring a coffee from the urn, and pulling the seat opposite me.

"I stole some of your deodorant" She took a sip of the caffeine, "You don't mind" I didn't even respond.

"You want Daisy don't you?" She muttered, in her worst Scottish accent, as she lifted her foot, pressing calmly against my leg, rising as she spoke, "You want her steak bake, her sticky toffee pudding"

"Fuck off" I bit into the cold toast, cringing as the toes reached the tip of my penis, stroking it expertly under the table.

She retracted instantly, and sighed, "You won't last, it's all about the fucking in this game, you see a girl you like, you bang it, you see a fit looking mother, you take it to bed, and you let her ride your cock til she screams, you lick any minge you can find, young, old, smelly, dry, wet, flabby... you see a bloke with an impressive package, you put your mouth around his dick and you swallow, you bend over and open your chocolate starfish and you scream loudly, and fake every orgasm it takes until you receive your commission"

"I don't think so" I protested.

"You lie naked under everyone and anyone, and you make them say that they enjoyed this holiday, you take their money, and you make Andrew and your supervisors smile" She explained, lighting a cigarette as she spoke, Beverley and Shannon had now appeared in the restaurant, I watched aware that they may hear, as she continued, "You do whatever it takes to mark that excellent on the all-important questionnaire"

"You know nothing" I whispered.

"Four years I have done this" She smiled, "If those mother fuckers don't pay up after you fuck them, take up smoking and extinguish your fag on their minge or ball sack, teach them a lesson"

"You're sick" I whispered.

"If you piss off Andrew, you put that cock in your mouth, and you make him cum" She continued, "If he doesn't shoot in your mouth, you turn over, and you open your hole and let him put it in you. It's the only way that you will save your.... career"

I once more failed to respond.

"I checked you all out when you got here, and I can categorise pretty much all of you, who will stay, who will buckle. Take that stupid cow you let sleep in your bed last night..." She flicked her ash into the coffee cup.

"Leave Daisy alone" I whispered.

She shook her head, "She will realise that her Spanish fling is a man slut, and she will go, Chris will probably get syphilis before the end of season, and saggy will fuck off out of resort with some customers money" She counted on her fingers, as Shannon and Beverley sat as far away as possible. I could see Shannon looking over at me, Sian continued, "You won't last the season because you will fuck up something big style, and you will end up on the flight home with your flaccid dick in your pocket if you are not careful Connor, take it from me... you are now a whore, and you will enjoy it"

I took a sip of my own coffee, "Just because you open your flaps for a bit of cash doesn't mean we all will"

She laughed, alerting the attention of the others, as more reps started to enter the room, her tone lowered, "They pay shit in this job, and I give you three months max"

She rose, and tapped her cup loudly with her spoon, once more alerting the attention of the now almost full restaurant.

"Hello new reps" She announced, barely taking her eyes off me, "Good luck today, remember, listen to Andrew, he is one of the most amazing team leaders you will meet, and he knows his stuff"

I noticed then, Andrew was behind me, as the new reps listened attentively. I also noticed Daisy had arrived, with her sweet little smile, she calmly sat next to me with a bowl of fruit salad in her hand.

"I will be here for you if you need me" Sian continued.

I smiled back at Daisy, and Chris collapsed in a heap where Sian had sat within a   second of her moving away, scratching his groin.

"What do you think of this I heard?" He asked, "All reps fuck each other nightly... men and men, women and women?"

I shrugged.

"If a dude comes near me with a hard on I think I will rip the fucker off" He laughed.

We entered the largest room on the roof of the Bellevue, Andrew and Ophelia had already set up the room for the week's training, and I knew that Ophelia was giving me the stink eye for not turning up in her room last night.

I took a seat next to Daisy, as Ophelia handed out reams of documents, including pens and paper, and she paused at me.

"Where were you?" She questioned, barely audible to anyone but me, "I waited for you like I told you"

"I went to bed like a good boy" I responded, "Andrew did tell us we needed to be ready for 9AM"

Ophelia smirked, as she moved away, still whispering to me, "You will do me tonight, or I will purposely make your life hell"

I ignored her comment, as I turned my gaze back to Andrew, who observed the room.

"Welcome to Mallorca" He announced, as Ophelia returned back to his side, perching her buttocks on the desk before him, "For those that met me in Stockport, you already know me, I believe that some people from the South had their interview with Jayne and Olivia. Anyway, I digress, my name is Andy Buckman, and this lovely lady is Ophelia Mason from Manchester"

"I thought Jayne would be here" I called before Ophelia could make her introduction.

"Jayne has met with a small accident back home, and Ophelia here comes highly recommended from her previous job in England" Andrew announced.

"An accident?" I questioned, directing my eyes at Ophelia.

"Nothing too bad" Ophelia smiled, "She broke her ankle last week, and I offered my services, very kind of you to be concerned over our dear colleague"

"A trivial matter" Andrew brushed aside, surely he was aware Ophelia was looking at me, "Ophelia here graduated with a first class degree in tourism last summer, and has been working in our Sun Centre in Leeds, but we will have all introductions throughout the week during our team jollies, now firstly, we will introduce each other with two truths and a lie. As a team we will try to see which one is the lie. I have taken the liberty in putting your names in a hat, and my lovely assistant will draw partners"

Ophelia smiled excitedly as she grabbed an upturned fez from the desk, a high pitched squeal leapt from her mouth as she buried her hand into the hat. Andrew sat at the desk, and placed a pencil onto the pad in front of him.

"First couple" Ophelia announced, as though in a show room, "Is.... Shannon McBain and..... Keith Brown"

Keith rose and took a seat next to his new partner.

"Connor Candlish" Ophelia announced, teasingly, as she opened a second piece of paper, her smile increased, "Me"

I nodded, in disgust as she read the remaining names, and gradually everyone went to their new partner. I watched as Daisy moved over to her new partner, and awaited my fate as soon Ophelia sat in the vacant seat next to me.

"We have five minutes" She announced to me, as she licked her lips back at me, "Can I blow your horn?"

"We have stuff to do" I announced, circling the pen between my fingers.

"I know everything about you baby" She whispered, "And you will come to my room tonight"

"I don't want to fuck you" I announced.

"Oh you will" She whispered, "Three things, I am a Libra, I ran naked through a street in Dublin and I am a black belt in Karate.... which one Connor?"

"The black belt" I whispered back, almost unconcerned.

"Good" She smiled, as she forced her key card into my palm, "I have a lot of power here now and can get you thrown off the course in a heartbeat, so I know tonight, you will screw my brains out, and make me gush all over those cotton sheets"

Her hand disappeared under the table, and clasped my groin again, forcing it to become hard in her hand, "Stop this"

"My vagina feels empty without you, it's like an almost aching feeling, and it's deep inside me, wanting you. Sometimes, I feel wet, sometimes I don't. Being here with you now, I have butterflies, starting in my chest, going straight into my pussy, and the heat is intense, I want to extinguish it. Sometimes sensations turn into electric shocks through my body, I want to feel you grind against me, I could die happily with you pinning down, kissing me.... grinding" She continued.

"What did you do to Jayne?" I questioned, trying to change the subject.

Her smile widened, "When you took this job I knew what I had to do, and I had to get this job, so I did what any normal woman would do"

I glared at her widened eyes, "So you broke her ankle?"

She tapped her head, "I knew what I had to do, I did my research and tracked her down, seduced her tight ass, and Daddy bought her out"

"You bitch" I whispered.

"So she went skiing with her money, and she didn't see that danger sign, she's very lucky to have survived her fall" She whispered, "But when you are in love, it conquers everything"

She placed the crumpled paper on the desk, clearly visible I had been partnered with Shannon, I glared at her.

"Ok" Andrew announced from his desk, "Who is first?"

Ophelia's hand shot in the air, I tried to protest for a moment, "As the new trainer, I would like to go first to show how it is done...."

Andrew agreed with a hand gesture, and Ophelia grabbed my wrist, dragging me to the front of the room.

Daisy's eyes sparkled back at me as I glanced over to her.

"This is Connor Candlish from Manchester, he tells everyone he's 23 but really he's going to be 30 in May, he's a singer, and he once had a threesome with someone who offered him a job and her husband"

The audience gasped, and Chris cheered from the back of the room, I felt the colour rush to my face.

"I have never had a threesome" I panicked.

"Connor, they're supposed to guess" She jokingly protested, "And that is how it's done..." I wanted to die right there as everyone laughed.

"I'm confused" Andrew announced, "You are actually 23, so which is the lie?" The redness returned.

The embarrassment did not last too long, as one of the girls got emotional and asked to leave because she missed her mother. I believe she was flying home later. Meanwhile, I knew what I needed to do today, as I fingered her spare key card in my pocket. They announced that she was only here for the week, and I suppose I could handle her for that long. This time, the one night stand really will fuck off, back to another country and I will be rid of her.

Andrew gave us an assignment to work on in the afternoon, and we were sent off to different parts of the hotel to work on a presentation to put on later that day to the rest of the team, excursions we offered on the island. We received the programme for the event and were told to sell the idea as creative as we could.

I waited at the elevator doorway, my finger poised over the number 6, as I thought about my ideas.

Without thought, I pressed 6, and waited for the long journey just 10 storeys down. The elevator made a sharp tinging sound as the doors opened, and a metallic voice announced floor 6.

I saw her doorway opposite the elevator doors, and opened it with minimal struggle from the plastic card.

"I'm here" I announced, forcefully.

"I am in the shower, the Spanish heat is too much" She announced from the marbled bathroom.

I obeyed, as I knew what she wanted, I started to remove my clothes, as I pushed open the doorway. The steam from the hot water hit me in the face as I pushed aside the plastic shower cover. I grabbed her waist, and forced her hard against the wall, turning her around swiftly, her face pressed hard against the wall, as I penetrated her from behind. The way she liked it. No foreplay, no kissing, just in, and firm.

"Yes" She cried, as I pumped hard, wanting it to be over as quick as possible, her body was slippery under the water that poured freely over us, and I felt the enjoyment increase in my loins.

She arched her back as she twisted her head toward me, forcing her lips onto mine, and I allowed my tongue to dart into her mouth, before forcing my hand against her head and turning her away again.

My hands cupped her soaked breasts and I squeezed hard, knowing I was about to explode inside her. My spasm uncontrollable, as I began to slip in the water at my feet. Her screams of orgasmic lust satisfied my own, as she writhed her hips in an oval form, forcing me deeper inside her, soon I felt her clench the tip of the head of my penis, twitching internally, and sucking my juice from inside.

I groaned as I emptied my semen inside her.

"That was a good starter" She sighed as she turned back to me, assuring she nodded, "Oh you made me cum"

She lowered herself down my smooth body, and put my semi-erect penis into her mouth, sucking her cum, and what was left inside me from the tip, before she rose, and pushed me away from her.

"You have an assignment to do, now be good, and come back after dinner" She commanded, as she pulled the plastic shower curtain back.

I smiled as I backed out of the room, and dressed without drying. I needed to get out of her room. The key card deliberately left on the floor.

SIX

Gradually, we gathered into the large room again, shortly after 4PM that day. Daisy was quiet as she sat with her back to me, scribbling something down in her note pad. Shannon and Clare with the curly hair raced in giggling to themselves, and making some sort of apology as Andrew and Ophelia sat impatiently at their desk.

"How would you feel if we were your guests at your hotel waiting for you?" Andrew asked, tea-potting again as he did so well in Stockport.

"The lift took its time" Clare with the curly hair sarcastically responded, as she pulled up a chair to the side of Daisy, "And guests can fucking wait if I have to"

Andrew shook his head, "I can see someone else going home today if you have that sort of attitude"

Clare muttered some sort of apology and then flicked her wrist insinuating a wanker when he turned away.

Ophelia glanced at me, and shook her head, mouthing the word, 'key' silently, Chris noticed the gesture.

"Have you banged her?" He asked casually silent enough only for me to hear. "Long story" I muttered.

"She's hot" Chris whispered, adjusting his crotch obviously to the whole room, "I would stick it to her all night you son of a bitch"

"Have her, she's in room 616" I invited.

He high fived me, which the whole room observed. Ophelia gave me the finger.

Gradually we put on our presentations for the days and nights out on the island as per our choosing, and we laughed as Beverley told us about a bar crawl in Magalluf and demonstrated a wet tee-shirt contest with several girls. Shannon told us about horse-riding in C'an Picafort, emphasising on the sangria, and the chicken meal.

I was last to go up this time, just after Chris had simulated shagging an inflatable dolphin.

I stood before the group, and smiled, "Ok guys, so I want you to trust me on this one, close your eyes...."

I watched as everyone in the room closed their eyes, I pressed the button on my iPod, and the dulcet tone of *Dance Macabre* began to sing through the room, in their minds, darkness.

"Sense the beat in the air as the overture rises, smoke bellows from the stage, the curtain twitches, something moves from the shadows, and twelve dancers move as one, ladies and gentlemen, welcome to Son Amar. Imagine the taste of Chicken in a basket meal, and a glass of wine as you watch 15 shows for the price of one.....open your eyes" I then spoke about some of the acts inside the show, as I think all of the room gasped as they opened their eyes. They cheered my pitch, and I felt relieved that part was over.

Andrew's eyes were still closed, and he was imagining something sexual. I think he ejaculated as I spoke.

"That was..." He stuttered, as he opened his eyes, shaking his head, "I love Son Amar, and if you make me want it more, you're good, and you will go far on this course"

Pleased, I nodded to myself, as I took my seat, noticing Daisy was still quiet in her seat, glancing occasionally at Clare.

Eventually, Andrew completed his paperwork, and gathered us closer to the table, Ophelia continued to watch me.

"Some of those presentations were amazing, and some were shit, now I understand it's a first but I think three of you failed this assignment. You will be informed personally of your feedback in your private session at the end of the week" He spoke, "I think some of you need to consider if this is a career for you, or if I should book you on a flight home... now, some of you will be shadowing airport runs tomorrow and those of you not will watch a full on welcome meeting, courtesy of Sian"

I thought to myself, 'that bitch'

"The night is yours to do what you wish" Andrew continued, "Just be mindful that people know that you are in training and you are now the face of Fantastical Holidays, and don't forget, tomorrow you have the welcome party at Judes which is a pirate theme"

"I just need to speak with you Chris before you leave" Ophelia announced as people started to gather their belongings.

He glanced at me, and passed me a knowing smile, which I brushed off, I turned to find Daisy, but she was hastily following Clare with the curly hair out of the room.

"Shannon" I called, causing her to stop in the door way, allowing the remainder of our colleagues to leave.

"What is it gorgeous?" She whispered, as she thrust her breasts into my body for no reason. I cupped her waist as I pulled her out of the room, closely followed by Andrew.

"No fraternising" He muttered almost disgusted that a man and a woman could even touch each other, disappearing almost instantly into the open elevator.

"Arsehole" She whispered as the door closed, before turning to me, and adding seductively, "So, I think we should go back to my room, and have some naked fun"

"Maybe" I smiled, allowing my hand to stroke her arm gently, "What has happened with Clare and Daisy?"

Disappointment crossed her face, "You want her don't you?"

"Just tell me" I urged.

"During our break, when we were working on our presentations, Daisy caught Clare and Marco in the bar" She spoke, "Clare had his dick in her mouth and Daisy went ape, she smashed a glass on the bar, and then Marco had to calm her down"

I bit my bottom lip, as she continued.

"That Daisy is like a young Shirley fricken Valentine" Shannon continued; as I felt her hand inch closer to my cock, she didn't even try to hide it, "Get yourself a real woman"

"Later" I smiled, brushing her hand away, "I have to go and find her, see that she is ok, but about this naked fun.... I will see you in an hour?"

Excitement filled her face as she slowly backed away to the elevator, "Can't wait, we have to be quiet though, I am sharing with that ginger slapper from Blackpool, and we're in the room next to Ophelia, room 617"

I smiled, as I repeated her room number, aware that the door was opening behind me.

Ophelia smiled as she brushed past me, reaching the elevator, barely acknowledging Shannon, as Chris lingered behind.

"Are you ok mate?" I asked.

"Yes" He responded quickly, and slightly high pitched.

"What did she say?" I asked, concerned that Ophelia had said something about me.

He paused as he glanced at me, "She wants to have a threesome tonight, me and you... but I don't do sword fighting mate"

I laughed, "So what did you say?"

"Lights out, you and I do not make eye contact and we do not touch each other, you in one hole, me in the other... then we swap" He explained, almost as if scripted, "She is coming around after dinner"

I swallowed hard as I watched her wink at me just as the doors closed.

I found Daisy at the bar about two hours later, there was a bottle of wine at her side, with almost half gone.

Without speaking, I sat next to her, as the señorita behind the bar smiled and gestured to the draft lager before her, I nodded.

"Daisy, are you ok?" I asked.

She did not answer, as she ran her finger around the rim of her glass. "He's not worth it" I muttered, attracting a glare from her.

"I gave up everything for him" She muttered, as she took a large swallow from the glass, "I had a journalism job, and a house, and a cat named Kitty"

"You're going to be a great rep" I smiled.

She shook her head, as she refilled her glass.

"Don't give up" I urged, as the barmaid placed the drink before me. "I am going to kill that slut" She whispered.

"Daisy, you're just being silly" I commented, once more attracted the glare from her.

"You don't know shit" She hissed, as she took the drink completely in her mouth. She slammed the glass down on the bar, and clambered off her seat.

"Wait" I pleaded.

"Fuck yourself" She mumbled, as she turned on her heels, and paced away from the bar, attracting the attention of some of the guests.

I leapt off my seat and followed her, pleading, as she saw her target outside by the pool. She must have seen her from the bar.

"Bitch" She screamed, causing Clare with the curly hair to smirk back at her for a moment.

"Get over it" Clare laughed, as Daisy lunged forward, grabbing Clare's mane of hair, and forcing them both heavily into the pool.

Someone screamed, as the water began to foam and some red appeared in the effervescent splashing.

It was over as quickly as it began, as a lifeguard had already intercepted the battle in the water, and someone who was in the pool had restrained Clare.

The lifeguard was shouting something in Spanish, as he pulled Daisy out of the pool with force, and commenced mouth to mouth.

The blood from her head continued to run, and the area was cleared quickly by the hotel staff.

Clare remained calm as she sat down near to the pool edge, still being restrained by the heavy set male, as I raced over to her.

"Leave it be" The man commented.

"Clare?" I asked.

She remained quiet.

By now, Andrew had appeared at the bar area, and glanced over to us both. Slowly he shook his head. I saw Ophelia and Chris, and some of the other reps lingering nearby. They must have come out of their rooms during the commotion.

Andrew placed his hand on Clare's shoulder, "You do realise that this is the end of your career?"

She nodded, still maintaining eye contact with the resuscitation taking place nearby.

I turned back to Daisy, and slowly walked over to the lifeguard, as Sian crouched at her side for a moment, before she rose, and made her way over to Andrew.

She whispered something into his ear.

I turned my head back to Daisy, and felt my heart sink. A towel had been placed over her face.

Andrew shook his head again, and led Clare inside the hotel.

I cupped my hands against my mouth, as I took everything in. Daisy's head had hit the floor of the pool when she had entered the water. That was the last time I saw Daisy, and Clare.

SEVEN

The following day started with a heavy cloud over the room, as six seats remained empty, I had put a single rose on Daisy's seat as Andrew and Ophelia sat patiently at their desk. The room was silent for what seemed like an eternity as Andrew cleared his throat and rose.

"Due to yesterday's incident, we will be giving you all a day off training and will fast track the course, and your supervisors are aware of this. Last night, Daisy was taken back to the UK and Clare will be before a judge today charged with the accidental death of our colleague" He announced mournfully.

"She attacked Clare" Someone muttered from the back of the room, I did not see who spoke, definitely female.

Andrew gestured with his hand to stop, "If any of you need counselling over the incident, then we can arrange this, but please take the day off and we will reschedule the welcome party at Judes for the end of the week"

"Just please don't get too drunk" Ophelia added, as she gave the signal for us to leave. Everyone made their way to the doorway, I did not want to be there now. I had only known Daisy for two days and now she was gone.

As I followed Matty out of the room, I heard him reference that some of the other colleagues from the course had flown home that morning due to the fight. Shannon was waiting by the elevator with a smile on her face, which turned into concern as I approached.

"How are you feeling?" She queried. I shrugged.

"A few of us are talking about going down to the beach, wanna come?" She asked.

"I have a few things I need to do" I responded.

"You still owe me a portion from last night" She teased, "My room-mate went home, so I have a nice room to myself"

"Later" I answered, I brushed past her, and headed to the stairwell. Aware that Ophelia was behind me, all the way.

I managed to give her the slip without her knowing as I entered the street outside the hotel. I ducked behind a bush, and watched as she rushed ahead searching for me. After a few moments, I turned the other way.

I found myself in a bar. Then another, and another. Daytime drinking in the sun. I deserved this.

I was aware that the last bar I was in was a gay bar by the way the customers overly camped themselves up whilst playing pool, and ordering cocktails with umbrellas. Again, I did not really care.

"You are one of the new reps aren't you?" Someone asked from the end of the bar.

I nodded.

"It is a shame about that girl" He continued, I noticed he was now closer.

"I don't mean to be rude mate" I responded, as I finished off my Estrella Dram, and signalled for another to the young barman, "I don't want to talk about it and I don't think I would discuss this with a stranger"

"Sorry" He continued, closer now, his hand outstretched, "My name's Brian, and I work for Fantastical Holidays, I saw you at the airport... I will buy this one mate"

I smiled, as I accepted.

Brian introduced himself to me, telling me how he had lived here for a few years, and was openly gay. I didn't mind this. I told him about me, why I became a rep, what I did, I found myself talking about Daisy to him like I had known him for a number of years.

I told him also about Thomas in Manchester. How he used to force me into some scenarios just to make more money. But the conversation would soon digress to Daisy.

"Sounds like you need something to take your mind off her" He smiled.

"I don't do drugs" I presumed he was offering me some tablet of sorts.

He laughed, as I felt him hand touch my thigh.

"It doesn't make you gay if you don't swallow" He teased.
"I don't think so" I muttered.

"I won't tell anyone" He reached closer up my thigh, dangerously close to my crotch.

I took a drink from my glass, and glanced over at the smiling bar man, he gestured to the toilet at the far end of the bar.

I nodded, and followed Brian into the surprisingly clean cubicle.

He perched himself onto the toilet as I allowed him to undo my own fly. He was gentle as he lifted my penis out of its nesting place in my boxers.

It gained hardness as he licked my flaccid member with his pierced tongue, he forced me to part my legs as far apart as I could in the confined space. I let out a moan as I felt him take one of my balls into his mouth, he allowed it to move inside his mouth, then he switched to the other, then almost instantly put both inside. It hurt for a moment as he sucked hard, but I persevered. He moved away, and then licked my shaft, as he worked his way to my tip, caressing the sensitive underside of my cock, his tongue lashed, and I cupped his long hair, gripping his head as hard as I could. I felt his lips open and then my penis entered his moist mouth, and enter into his throat.

A hand touch my balls, as I groaned more. The other cupped my buttocks, as he exaggerated the length of my dick, I began to buck my hips up and down as he gagged a little for a moment. My thighs pressed against him, my pubic hair was literally pressing against his eye lashes as he continued to suck hard.

My groans soon became intense, he took this as a sign, and grabbed my dick firm with his suction, my penis flexed, my spunk shot forth into his mouth as I screamed in ecstasy, as the involuntary quiver sent my semen out of me.

I didn't wait. I pulled out of his mouth and tucked myself back into my boxers. "My turn?" He asked, wiping away drool from his lip.

I didn't respond, I turned, and unlocked the door. He rose behind me and pressed his erect cock against my back.

"Next time" He smiled, as he stroked my arm, thrusting a little into my back. I nodded. Then opened the door.

I did not finish that drink as I left the bar.

Back at the hotel, I smiled as Shannon sat at the bar. Without speaking I took her hand, and pulled her toward the doorway.

We kissed passionately throughout the elevator ride back to floor six.

We continued to kiss as she opened her door, eagerly assisting each other as we removed each other's clothing.

I lurched forward, and used my teeth to clench onto her nipple for a moment, lowering her gently onto the bed, my hard cock tickling her sex eager to enter.
She arched her back as I entered, thrusting keenly into her fast.

"Say my name" I urged, as I writhed my hips in an oval formation to penetrate her deeper.

"What if the bitch next door hears?" She gasped.

"Let her" I grunted, as I glanced at the wall, hoping Ophelia was in her own room, listening. Shannon obeyed, as she called out my name loudly. I smiled.

Ophelia was clearly in there, as I heard the door slam, I pumped harder.

I felt her hands tour down my back, sliding on my moist back, she cupped my buttocks with one hand, the same as Brian did earlier, and I allowed her to squeeze hard and nuzzled her neck. I felt my loins tighten, and the familiar tickling sensation as my semen travelled through my urethra, and into her.

I stayed with her that night, waking early for a shower. Together, we held each other in the steaming room, I used her shower gel as both a shampoo and a body wash, and we kissed more.

I gently inserted my finger into her cleft as a tease, causing her to twitch with excitement. "I have an idea for this welcoming party" She announced.

She leaned in closer to me, and whispered her idea, causing me to smile. I then clambered out of the shower, and allowed her to watch me as I dried, and pulled on my jeans.

Topless, I walked over to her as she too dried, with my boxers in my hand, I smiled, as I passed them to her, "Something to remember me by"

She laughed, as she tossed them back to me.

Today was the day some of the team would shadow airport transfers and others would be observing a welcome meeting.

I was lucky enough to remain at the hotel for Sian's welcome, as Shannon went off to the airport. Sian signalled me over to her from across the pool. In the sun, I felt out of place in my black trousers, and lime green shirt, with a blazer, but I knew what I was signing up for when I decided to do this. She was setting up her meeting, and was about to put her microphone headset on, as I arrived.

"I specifically asked for you today" She smiled, as she handed me a note pad of names, "When they come in, just tick them off so I know who attended, and then we can chase up the none attendees later"

"You asked for me?" I asked "Why?"

"Because if you get Alcudia, there is a chance you will have to dual rep, and I thought it would be nice for you" Sian responded, as she turned on her microphone, expertly pulling the mouthpiece to her lips, her voice soon became enhanced, as she continued, "Ladies and Gentlemen, welcome to Mallorca, your Fantastical Holidays welcome will commence in just 5 minutes so come along and meet your reps"

She switched off the microphone and lifted the headset, glancing behind me.

"The first guests are arriving, so do as I said, and you will have to stand in for Brian for moment as he's late" She continued, "He's probably hanging out of his arse today, was his birthday yesterday and apparently he pulled"

"Brian?" I queried.

"I have changed my opinion on you Connor" Sian smiled, as she tapped my shoulder, "Maybe you will last after all"

"Hello Connor" Brian's voice announced behind me, "You shot and ran?"

"Fuck off" I muttered.

"Connor.... I would have loved to have smelt your morning breathe" He laughed, as he cupped my cock briefly.

EIGHT

The remainder of the week was spent avoiding Ophelia as much as possible, avoiding Brian and Sian for the same reason, and sleeping occasionally with Shannon. Luckily Brian and Sian did not tell anyone about the dalliance in the bar. Not that I actually cared.

We learned on the last day that Clare was sent back to the UK to face charges in her own country, and two more people left, including Keith's boyfriend James.

On the Saturday morning we awaited in the reception as our names were listed on the reps wall, who was going to stay in Palma, and who was going to Alcudia.

Both Shannon and I were heading to Alcudia on the same coach, with Chris, Beverley, Keith and Matty. We all high fived each other, Shannon grabbed my arse with her spare hand as she did so, it had been obvious we were sleeping together to the team.

Andrew and Ophelia arrived together, and I could see her giving me the stink eye, probably because I never did have that sword fight with Chris and her. Together they commanded our attention. "Well team, I know this has been a turbulent week, with the accident in the week, and..."

Andrew spoke, he paused as he glanced at me, "There has been some serious bed hopping" I glared at Sian in the background, she shrugged.

"I know that reps have a promiscuous nature, just be careful" He continued, "So tonight, we will have the reps welcome party at Judes, remember it is pirate themed, and be ready in reception for 7pm"

He pressed the play button on his CD player, and *Hollerback Girl by Gwen Stefani* commenced loud enough to start a chorus from the new reps, some raised their hands and swayed to the tune, singing.

Ophelia took the opportunity to step into the groups of people to congratulate them; Chris seemed like an eager puppy around her, as they soon joined Shannon and I.

"Congratulations on Alcudia" She smiled, "Connor, I need to have a quick chat, alone"

I could sense the disappointment on Chris and Shannon's faces as she guided me away from them.

"You've been avoiding me" She commented, "I know you were friends with that girl that died, but I told you, I own you"

"Fuck off" I whispered, "You don't own me"

"Really?" She questioned, "Then why did you come to my room the other day? Why did you allow the slapper in the room next door to me to call your entire name out during your little debacle?"

I refused to answer, as she allowed her hand to stroke my arm.

"Chris has offered to quit and come back to the UK with me" She whispered. "Go for it" I urged.

Her hand paused on my groin, stroking it tentatively, ""He has some good moves, but he is not you... Come to my room after lunch, and service me one last time"

"Last?" I questioned.

"Last" She assured, "And then I will forget all about you here, putting your dick in any pussy that comes your way, I will let you free"

I paused, brushing her hand away from my cock, "You were meant to be a one night stand that I fucked, and then never saw again"

"Give me a happy ending that is all I want" She smiled, "And then I will ask Chris to quit and take me home"

I glanced over at Chris, he had his back to us chatting with Matty and Keith, Shannon was nowhere to be seen. I turned back to her.

"One last time" I emphasised the word one, with my finger. She bit her bottom lip and smiled.

I smiled back, and quickly thought of a reason why she wanted to speak to me, as we both mingled in the groups, I was aware Brian was chatting to Shannon now outside the reception area, he glanced at me for a brief moment, and pushed his tongue into his cheek, and then put his arm around Shannon.

I shrugged it off, and approached Chris.

"I heard you are considering going home with Ophelia?" I asked just loud enough for him, and no one else to hear.

He smiled, "She is a beast in bed, I think she might be the one" I nodded, "She's certainly something"

I felt his hand press against my arm, "I know you and her had a history, are you ok with this mate?

I nodded, as I saw Brian return through the doors.

"I am sorry we never got that threesome" Chris continued as though part of a normal conversation.

"No sword fights" I laughed as Brian interrupted the conversation.

"I think you better go find Shannon" He announced, with a sarcastic smile on his feminine face.

I mouthed the word twat at him, and he smiled once more, as I turned on my heels.

As I rushed outside, I saw Sian and Shannon sitting on the roadside, Sian had her arm around Shannon's shoulder. She saw me approach, and whispered something to her.

Her tear stained face looked up at me. "You bastard" She hissed, as Sian rose.

"I think you have some apologies to make" She commented, as she walked toward me.

"What the fuck did I ever do to you?" I commented.

Her smile mirrored Brian's just moments ago, as I took a gulp, and sat next to Shannon.

"What have I done?" I asked.

She cried into her hands, muffling her words, but clear enough, "You slept with Ophelia"

That surprised me. After the way those two tossers smirked, I thought they were going to say something else.

"Well, yes" I stuttered.

She turned to face me, her mascara had run, and her nose was red, "When?"

I struggled to think fast, "I.... I...."

I could see the anger cross her face, "What did she want when she took you aside"

"She wanted to check I was ok over Daisy, she knew we were close" I spoke fast.

"So when did you bang her?" She insisted.

"Before we came here" I wasn't exactly lying.

"They told me it was here" She wanted to believe me.

"Is that what Brian was talking to you about?" I questioned.

She nodded, and I embraced her in my arm, as I continued, "Reps apparently become gossip-mongers when they are sad and past their sell by date"

"I shouldn't have let them get to me" She confessed, as she put her hand in mine, "Let's go and spend the day in bed"

I frowned, "Chris and I decided we were going to have one last lads session here before the party... you don't mind?"

"I suppose" She smiled, "Listen I am going to go back to my room, and make myself look pretty, can you cover me in there?"

I nodded, as I pressed my lips against hers, "Ignore them"

I watched as she expertly brushed past our colleagues as she avoided everyone, as I followed her into the reception area.

Brian and Sian watched and shook their head, as I approached them.

"You pair of pricks" I hissed, aware that Andrew could hear the conversation.

"Don't you speak to us like that" Sian protested, "Or next time I will tell her the truth"

"What is going on?" Andrew intervened.

"Oh come on Connor, tell Andrew" Brian urged. I paused, as I shook my head.

"Life as a rep" Andrew agreed, with a gentle nod to Sian, "It's one drama after another"

I had managed to convince Chris to cover for me, he told Shannon that we were going to a bar in the town to celebrate our graduation, and she bought it. She went off to another bar with Beverley and Ben, and a few of the other girls. Together, we entered Ophelia's room, and removed our clothes, as she watched eagerly, and surprised.

Almost synchronised, our clothes fell through the air, as Chris and I kept secure eye contact as we circled the bed on which she lay.

He leaned down, and commenced kissing her passionately, throwing her roughly onto the mattress, as I lowered myself down her body, gently kissing her body, I slid my hand under her thigh, into her skirt. Chris's hand meandered down her body, and stroked my hair, startled, he pulled away for a brief moment before allowing it to return.

I felt the elastic on her panties with the tips of my fingers, and I pulled them sharply, tearing them apart, and away from her flesh in a swift movement. She yelped, and glanced down at me, I ignored her, as I allowed my forefinger, and middle finger to enter her moist welcoming vagina. I used my other hand to pull at her skirt, tossing it aside, as her blonde pubic hair glistened in the sunlit room.

I heard him tear at her blouse, causing the buttons to explode all over the room.

I held my cock in my hand, and nodded to Chris as he glanced over at me. As I parted her legs with my own, I allowed the tip to gently press against her lips, and Chris straddled her chest, forcing his dick deep into her mouth, he thrust forward, forcing her to lie on the bed, as I pumped hard inside her. Chris kept turning his head to watch me, and smiled, as he realised I was looking back.

He began to lean over to me, his dick still inside her mouth, as he pressed his own lips against mine for a brief moment, he cupped my face, and continued to thrust his member inside her mouth. His ginger hair felt soft in my hand as it brushed past.

I reach over to him, and pulled him closer, forcing him out of Ophelia, and she struggled to watch, I allowed my tongue to dart in his mouth for a moment, then I pushed him aside, signalling to her. I moved rhythmically on top over her, and grappled at her hips, forcing her on her side, my erect cock still inside her, Chris lowered himself down her back, touching me, or her, depending on how we moved.

His cock pressed firm against her anus, and she groaned as he pushed himself into her, I forced my lips onto her moist mouth to stop her from moaning.

We kissed each other, me and him, her and him, me and her. Chris soon felt his own pleasure being reached, as he pulled out of her, and held his penis in his own hand, violently tossing himself over us both. Steaming pre-cum would soon seep out of his slit, I glanced down at my own manhood, inside her, still thrusting with firm, hard movements. He bucked, and thrust his hips towards us, I watched as he shot his load, covering her breasts with his cream and I bit my own lip, feeling the explosion inside my own groin.
Chris collapsed in a heap next to her, and nuzzled at her neck, his green eyes firmly on me, as I filled her. Simultaneously, we both orgasmed.

After that, Chris and I waited in our boxers as she showered. He kept looking over at me, but diverting his gaze as I noticed.

"It is ok" I whispered.

"I have never done anything like this before" He muttered, embarrassed.

"It is ok" I repeated, "We won't tell anyone"

"Thank you" He smiled, as his face brightened up, and involuntary placed his hand on my naked knee.

Nervously he pulled it off, and I grabbed it again, placing it back.

"We are going to be here for six months" I whispered, "If you ever want to do this again, we can..."

He smiled, as he nodded.

"I don't think I can go back with her"

"Then don't" I responded.

"I am not gay" He protested.

"Neither am I" I smiled back.

He leaned in nervously to kiss me again pausing momentarily to glance at the door where she showered.

I cupped his cheek, and turned his head back to me, and pressed my lips against his, just for a moment. I felt him smile.

The remainder of the day, Chris and I did drink, but remained in the hotel bar, as Ophelia threw away the clothes we just destroyed, and packed her suitcase. We watched her as she walked into the reception to check out. She smiled as she glanced over at us, and within a minute, she walked out of the reception doors into an awaiting limousine, without so much as a farewell.

Chris raised a glass and we clinked together, as we enjoyed the rest of the day together.

Soon after five, Shannon and Beverley returned, and joined us for a brief drink. Shannon became amorous, and I could sense the alcohol on her breath as she flirted with me.

"We need to get ready for tonight" Beverley announced, as she grabbed her bag, "What are you two going as?"

"Secret" I smiled, as I tapped my nose.

Shannon urged me back to the room, and I rose, leaving a small amount of foam in my glass. I turned once more to Chris, and embraced him, "See you soon brother"

He nodded, as together we all made our way to our rooms.

Jude's bar was full to the brim of pirates, pirate wenches, and ship-wreck victims, there was even a couple of parrots in the midst as we entered the room. Shannon and I wore a full length white gown each, and masks. Together we made our way to the centre of the dance floor.

"Ready?" She asked excitedly. I nodded in agreement.

Together, we removed our masks, revealing our golden faces.

Sian was nearby, grinding against Matty, her look of disapproval obvious as she asked, "What the hell have you two come as?"

"Ships mast heads" I announced, as in uniformity we opened up our gowns, revealing our naked bodies entirely sprayed gold, as we posed, and then danced together, as everyone cheered.

Almost everyone. Andrew stood before us, in shock, and handed us our gowns. "Back to the hotel" He announced sternly.

We laughed as we retrieved our gowns.

"Now "He shouted, almost over the music.

"Oh dear" Sian muttered, now joined by Brian who was drooling a little, "Looks like someone is on the next flight home"

"Shut your mouth bitch" Shannon retaliated, still reeling over their conversation earlier, and turning on her heels, "Come on babes"

"Remember what I said" Sian announced, as she pushed her tongue into her cheek, and winked, "Andrew likes his wiener sucked"

NINE

Surprisingly, Shannon and I simply got a slap on the knuckles for our naked escapade, Andrew said that too many people had left the course one way or another and could not afford to lose any more. And the next day, we boarded a coach and travelled to the North of the Island, along with Chris, Keith, Matty and Beverley, along with some others that did not socialise with us.

We were all advised that I was to share with Chris, Shannon with Beverley and Keith with Matty as we were issued with apartment keys each along the way.

We sang our songs on the journey, and as we pulled alongside a Burger King on a corner, the coach stopped, as Andrew pulled out his clip board.

"Ok, Keith and Matty this is you" He announced, as he clambered off the coach.

The lads seemed excited as they rose, and high fived us as they left the coach. Beverley stepped off the coach for a cigarette as Andrew took them to the apartment, and minutes later, Matty and Keith appeared on the balcony above the restaurant, and Andrew ordered Beverley back onto the bus.

Chris and I were next off, as we pulled up just outside a bar called Madness, Andrew guided us off the coach along with two other reps, Shannon and I briefly kissed before I left her.

"Your apartment can be quite noisy I'm afraid" Andrew announced, "But knowing you four, you won't let it get to you"

He guided us into a cool hallway, up two flights of stairs, and toward a heavy oak door. The two other reps went into the room opposite us, leaving their door open as Andrew hovered in the hallway. Chris eagerly used his key to open it with force, and we entered the large two bedroom apartment. We could see the coach outside our balcony.

"Don't forget, we are all booked in the Rancho Grande show tonight" Andrew continued, "Coach will be here at six-thirty"

We nodded, as he left, and together we ran over to the balcony, throwing our suitcases to the floor, as we tore open the balcony door, just to see the coach pulling away. We waved at our friends, and enjoyed our view of the mountain to our left for a moment.

"So what room do you want?" Chris asked, returning to his suitcases. "I don't mind" I responded.

He excitedly dragged his suitcases to one of the white doors, and pushed it open with his rear, "I will take this one"

Within a moment he emerged from the door as I started to gather my suitcases. "You ok mate?" I asked.

"Yes" He smiled, "I just wanted to say I am really pleased you and I will be roommates"

I nodded, and made my way to the room opposite the one he had chosen.

"I know you and Shannon are a couple, and I intend on bringing plenty of women back here, so shall we just have a sock on the door code?" He asked casually, before adding almost silently, "And if either of us get lonely, we can just knock on the door?"

"As long as there is no sock on the door" I laughed.

He laughed too, and together, we returned to our rooms alone.

As the evening drew on, we all gathered in Rancho Grande, where Shannon, and most of the others enjoyed a horse ride in the Mallorcian countryside, as myself, Chris and Keith opted to join the Sangria wagon, mainly to have free sangria en route.

Chris and I sat next to each other as a large blonde woman boarded, her hand in a cast as she perched herself opposite us.

"What the fuck are you looking at?" She asked, as she stared at us, without waiting, she grabbed one of the sangria samples.

"Nothing" Chris muttered, "How did you break your arm?"

"Fucking pissed I was" She laughed in her Irish accent, "I fell off a table in Madness last week...so which one of you is Connor?"

"Me" I responded.

A smile crossed her face, as she passed me one of the shots, "I am Kellie, and you see that big white hotel outside your apartment?"

I nodded.

"That's ours, you and I will be repping there for this season and I heard you are pretty good" She smiled, taking a large swill of her drink, "I would love to rape you tonight"

Shock shot across my face, as the sangria wagon pulled off, I could not believe she was so open about it.

She turned to speak with someone next to her as Chris smiled at me.

"Go for it" He urged, "I bet she will make yesterday look like a tea party" "You go for it" I wasn't so sure.

"Mate, I love the big women, you don't know what you're missing out on" He urged.

"I'm scared" I joked.

"Fifty Euros says you won't do it" He whispered.

I knew his game, so shook his hand, "Get your wallet out"

"I will keep Shannon entertained" He smiled as I rose, and cross the wagon, sitting next to her, I offered her yet another sangria which she accepted with a smile.

"So, you will be coming back to mine" She insisted, and she placed her hand on my dick. I could sense Chris was watching, as I leaned in, and pressed my lips against hers.

"Wow that was fast" Someone announced from the other side of the wagon. I extended my middle finger, and carried on lashing my tongue in her mouth.

Once more Chris came through for me as the wagon pulled into the little cement covered park. He leapt ahead and told Shannon I had too much sangria, and had caught a taxi home. In reality, I had ended up back at the Burger King apartments.

She did not even wait for me to get into the room before she had her hands on my fly, pulling my jeans down with one swift movement.

My flaccid penis gained hardness as I felt her wet mouth suck hard onto the shaft, taking me wholly inside in one gulp, and I felt the back of her throat with my tip.

I grabbed her head, and tried to push it deeper into her mouth, as I groaned more, I felt her rough grip on my testicles, pulling hard, I nearly screamed as she continued to suck without allowing me to move. Her plastered hand moved around to my buttocks and she squeezed hard, her fingers penetrated my anus and I felt her tongue lash against the base of my cock. I began to push my hips up and down as I assisted her mouth movement. My thighs pressed against her face, and I tried to force deeper again.

My groans soon became intense, she knew the signal, and grabbed my dick firm with her fast suction, my seed shot forth as I screamed in ecstasy, she removed my quivering member from her lips, as my semen spilled out of me onto her face, her tongue lashing at the salty liquid."Now me" She ordered, as she rose.

Under her control, I allowed her to guide me to the messed up bed, she clumsily stepped out of her large panties, one leg at a time, kicking them carelessly over the room, her legs opened wide, and she guided me toward her open vagina. I created a slow steady movement of my tongue against her flaps, my tongue flat, as I moved between each cleft, and slowly stroked the clitoris, her hips moved frantically as I teased her by not deciding which part to go to next. Occasionally, I allowed a finger to enter her and soon I found myself putting my entire fist inside her.

My wrist jutted out of her as I flexed my hand from palm to fist, and then stretching my fingers inside her vagina, I could feel her insides against my fingers, wet, and her body moved in spasm, as I fluctuated my movements between fast and slow, the intensity inside her increased, as I felt the gush of fluid and her screams increase. She tightly closed her legs, entrapping my face inside her pussy, and I stifled my gag, her grip lifted me a moment, and then she released me.

My face was wet with her cum as I pulled away for a moment, she allowed her perfect hand to stroke herself, my sticky arm draped against my side, not knowing what to do.

"Get out" She muttered.

I did not need to be told twice, as I turned on my heels, noticing the door was open all along.

A shadow in the doorway remained watching me.

"Who is it?" I called.

He slowly inched toward me, and I could sense that he was wearing some sort of PVC outfit, covering his entire body. He placed a gloved hand on my shoulder, and gestured for me to leave.

I was unsure as I gathered my clothes, as I turned back for a moment, he stood between her legs, and carefully lifted them in the air.

"Yes" She called, as I heard the unzipping of his crotch.

I pulled on my jeans, and smiled as I left him penetrating her.

TEN

June 15th.

As the season progressed, we saw each other grow as reps. Shannon and I remained an item, and Chris found a relationship with a Swedish rep called Joanna. Kellie and I worked well together, and we barely mentioned that night, although she did admit she now slept with her door open, and had met her rubber man several times, always elusive. There had also been a few reports that the larger ladies in our unit had met with the same man. He would make love to them and leave them without revealing his face. It was also clear that Keith and Andrew had embarked on an affair recently.

Sian was correct, Kellie and I were often pairing each other up with the occasional single mother, father, granny, good looking over 18 year old, male and female, didn't matter. Give them something they wanted, they paid our commission.

Kellie had thrown a sickie on me, so I covered her in the reception area of the hotel, as she slept off a hangover when it started to rain heavily outside. The rain soon changed into hailstones, and I knew that trouble was about to brew when the tattooed muscle man and wife Gary and Heather Matthews barged into the reception, soaking wet, and stinking of a three day old booze session. They had been pissed since they landed at Palma airport. They clearly had a benefit paid holiday and were enjoying the all-inclusive. Typical scratcher type. Loud, mouthy, full of shit.

"Oi Wanker" He called, as he lurched across my desk, sending my promotional pamphlets to the floor, clasping at my shirt, "What the fuck are you going to do about the weather?"

I cringed as his stale breath lingered in my nostrils, "Sir, I am sorry I don't control over the weather"

"I don't give a flying fuck you homo" He insulted, causing his hideous wife to laugh in a broad snort, "This company will be finished when I am through with it, I was promised sunshine 7 days a week when I booked this holiday, now get the fuck this hail away from me, or there will be hell to pay"

"You tell him Gazza" His wife cheered, attracting more scratchers from around the hotel. The receptionist quickly called security.

"I am sorry Mr Matthews" I apologised, without fear, "But as it's the big man's day off, I cannot ask him to switch the weather to the sunshine channel"

"Oh" He smirked, "Funny fucker eh?" "I like to think so" I retaliated.

"I pay your fucking wages matey" He snarled, "Now sort it out"

"As I said" I responded, fully aware that security had now entered from behind him, "This is something I do not have control over, and if you pay my wages, four hundred pound PCM and commission isn't worth this shit"

Anger filled his face, I could see the steam coming from his ears, and I smiled, as I thought of a way to anger this wanker more.

"If I am of no assistance to you Gazza, may I suggest that you learn to write words with more than one syllable, attach it to a disabled lesbian pigeon with dyslexia, and hopefully it will reach head office in the UK before civilisation is taken over by your family of monkeys"

"Little bastard" He hissed, as he used his force to throw me backward, against the windowed reception, I felt it crack against my back, and I saw two burly Spanish Security guards rugby tackle him to the ground.

I heard his wife argue that her husband was being victimised, and once more, the argument that Fantastical Holidays would be ruined once they had finished. I groaned in agony as a hot first aider came running to my side.

I liked these customers. Arseholes, the lot of them.

June 21st.

As Kellie and I ran The Maharajah hotel, we were used to over 400 people a week, and completed a joint welcome meeting. She would start the presentations, and I would meet the customers, and put in my now infamous Son Amar presentation and as we concluded a particularly crowded welcome, we felt our hearts sink as Andrew entered the auditorium, signalling me over to him, with his colleague Sian to his side.

Kellie continued to talk to guests as I made my apologies to those that tried to talk to me, as I approached Andrew and Sian.

"I need you to cover Beverley's transfer tonight, and possibly the airport tomorrow" He announced as a matter of factly, "Sian has come up from Palma to cover her units for a bit"

Fury crossed my face as I spoke, "You had me on a midnight run last night, and you know I got back at five this morning to do this shit"

Sian laughed, "Can't hack it can you?"

"You have to be kidding me?" I whispered, "Sian and Kellie never do the transfers, and you come down hard on me for no reason"

"If you come back for a second season you will have priority over the first years" Andrew announced, as he brushed aside my comments, "Beverley has handed in a sick note, she thinks she may be pregnant"

"She was fucking necking back vodka last night she is just hung over" I insisted, "I won't do it"

"You will" Andrew warned, "Or I will bring up your illegal raffles on the coaches as a form of disciplinary"

"What?" I asked, aware that I had covered my tracks.

"Last week, when you guided Son Amar, you sold raffle tickets, whilst my mother was on the coach. You gave a bottle of shit white wine for the winner, and a jar of jam from the restaurant for the booby prize winner" He noted, as Sian agreed with him, "That was my mother you gave the jam to, so it did not take too much hard work to figure out who was guiding her coach you stupid knob"

I did not know what to say, as I reluctantly accepted the transfer list and the airport run that he passed over to me.

"That's a good boy" Sian spoke to me as though I was her schnauzer.

I mouthed something offensive to her, and put on my smile to welcome my guests. Kellie smiled as she passed me an envelope.

"I have to guide again tonight" I muttered.

"My mystery man has said he will be at the party tomorrow night" She ignored my comment, the bitch, "I have to find a suitable costume for this party"

The P Party that Keith had arranged for his birthday, I was not impressed, "Look you're going to have to look after this place yourself today, I need a siesta"

"Yeah" She snatched back the envelope, "Wonder what he will wear?"

"He's a man in leather, he won't be too difficult to avoid" I responded, just as uninterested.

Shortly before two I retired to bed, just to get a siesta before guiding the show Pirates, and awoke in the blazing afternoon sun.

As I wandered into the lounge area, I could see Chris sunbathing on the balcony, naked as per usual. I tried to be as quiet as possible as I poured some juice into one of the stolen glasses from the bar downstairs, and sleepily made my way to the bathroom.

As I urinated into the toilet, I heard the door open, and Chris smiled as he walked in, erection first.

"Where's the wife?" I asked, continuing to urinate.

"She's down at the airport and there's a delay" He announced, as I felt his erection press against me now.

I felt him nuzzle against me, "Shannon could be here soon"

"Nope" He responded, "Same delay, and you were asleep when I knocked on earlier.... we had a deal. If one of us gets horny...."

"I don't have long" I announced, I had finished my piss.

His hand pulled down my boxers, and felt his cock press against my anus. I heard the gentle squirt of something behind me, then the smell of coconut tanning lotion soon followed, as I felt him finger my hole. I sprang instantly to life.

I did not stop him, as I let him enter me. The pain lasted just a second, as he bent me over the bath tub. This had become synonymous of our living arrangement, and now he had become more masculine in the role. It was our little secret, and we both loved it.

The night was long, as I returned back to my apartment shortly after 1.00 AM, and I could hear Chris in his room with the ever loud Joanna. I collapsed on my bed, and awoke with a start when my alarm on my mobile went off four hours later.

Three messages from Shannon on the screen, I tossed the phone back on charge, as I wandered naked into the bathroom for the coldest shower. I tried not to scream out at the coldness, but I could not care that Chris or Joanna may be asleep.

Having dressed in record time, I wandered down the street, with my hair still damp as I approached the awaiting coach. Carlos again, he was such a miserable Spanish Bastard, he tapped his watch to insinuate I was too early, and pulled his cap over his eyes again.

I was aware that there were still revellers out and about, this place never slept, and then I noticed someone familiar hanging around the back of the coach.

It was Beverley, dressed in a long flowing dress, and you could still see bits of blonde her in her home dyed hair, the stains still covering her flesh.

"Thought you were ill" I whispered.

It was then I noticed she had been crying, and put my arm around her shoulders, bringing her closer to me.

"You're the only one I could trust" She cried gently, "I need your help"

ELEVEN

I glanced at her feet, and could see a small bag, in her hand she held her passport, and a piece of paper.

"Where are you going?" I asked, now noticing a bulging purse at her side, I could see the corners of some Euro's sticking through the unkempt leather stitching, "You're running away aren't you?"

She nodded and did not even try to defend it, "Ben has been sleeping with other women, and I can't stay here"

I knew Ben was seeing other women, he had tried it on with Shannon recently, but I pretended not to know, "I am sorry to hear that"

"I faked a sick note from a quack in town, and I booked a one way ticket back to Birmingham" She explained quietly.

"And the money in your purse?" I gestured.

She tried to hide it for a moment, before realising she could not lie, "I told all my guests that my card machine was broken, and had all this cash. I have to go, can you get me on your coach"

I didn't even think, "Of course, but you have to hide that money, you know what happened last time someone left"

"I have planned it well" Beverley commented, "I have a flight before my appointment with Andrew, and Shannon is going to say she hasn't seen me since I went to the hospital this morning, my phone is in my room so I cannot be called"

I smiled, as I heard some movement on the coach, "Well, let's try this, you trust me right?" She nodded.

I leaned in for a kiss, and allowed her to kiss me back, aware that Carlos the bus driver was watching. I pulled away, giving her a gentle wink, "Carlos, I need to take this lovely lady to the airport, reckon we can squeeze her on?"

"Si" He smiled, scratching his groin with a smile, as he accepted her small bag, throwing it carelessly into the under carriage of the coach.

The journey to the airport seemed longer than usual, as I was aware I was aiding and abetting a criminal. The coach was not as full as I would have like just in case someone did a stop check, I had not had one in a month, so I knew it was risky. But it was fine. As I stepped off the coach, and allowed the guests through to the departure lounge. Their flight was slightly delayed but I didn't tell them that.

I ignored them as instead of following them into the airport to ensure their check in went smoothly, I turned the opposite way with Beverley, as already her flight had a last call flashing on the screen. We remained slightly hidden from view behind a Fun Travel desk.

"Thank you" She whispered, as I could see she was holding back some tears. "Go" I urged, pushing her away.

She smiled, as she forced a kiss on me for a single moment, "I always thought you were lovely when I met you that first day"

"You have to go" I urged.

She opened her bulging purse, and clasped five hundred Euro's in her hand, forcing it into my hand in their crumpled forms, "Treat that lady of yours"

"No" I responded, as I peeled two fifty Euro notes from the stash, "You're gonna need as much money as possible, I will take one hundred, and treat Shannon to some chips and a few beers"

She smiled, as she shoved the stolen money back into her purse. "I will never forget you" I smiled once more as I forced her to accept she has to leave now.

I watched as she rushed to the desk, and waited as she checked in, trying not to glance at any of her now former colleagues in the airport. I almost felt my heart sink as I saw Brian glance over at her for a second, but he did not notice who it was. Relief set in as she finalised her check in and walked through the gate, without glancing back.

I carelessly shoved the one hundred Euro's into my socks, a trick I had learned early on in my career, and casually walked out from my hiding place, toward the crowd of people.

Brian collared me as I approached the first queue of people, "Where have you been? Gatwick is delayed, and you left me to deal with this"

"When nature calls" I whispered, "One must obey"

He seized the opportunity to lean in closer to me, to avoid a confrontation in front of the guests, who were not paying attention, after all it was early, and they just wanted to sit down or get some duty free in before flying home.

"If you let me suck you again" He whispered, "I won't tell"

"No chance" I whispered back, "I would not let you near my knob if you were offering me a hundred Euro"

He smiled, as he checked his wallet, flashing it at me "Make it two hundred and you are on"

"What is that?" I asked, "Your liquidation?"

"Meet me in the toilet when you can" He whispered, as he walked away from the crowd. I did not respond, and just smiled at the guests.

The delay was not as long as expected. They were through within an hour. It was already 10AM when the new arrivals arrived in the morning sunshine. Brian was less than happy that I did not follow him to the bathroom when he wanted, and scowled at me in the arrivals area. Barely acknowledging me, I loved it.

Soon after, my heart began to sink as I saw Andrew arrive frantically looking for us, with Shannon close behind.

He gathered us together, aware that people were arriving, but he caused us to huddle in together, I knew what was about to come, as did Shannon, but we went along with it.

"You two have been here for a few hours, have either of you seen Beverley at the airport at all?" He asked.

"No" I did not answer too swiftly, "There was a small delay on the Gatwick flight, but that was all"

"She's gone missing" He continued, "With her liquidation, almost seven thousand Euro is missing...."

The cheap bitch I thought, without reacting too over dramatically.

Andrew released us from the huddle, and shook his head, "She is the fourth to do this, and we may have to change the process"

"I am sorry" Shannon confessed, "I did not see her leave, I thought I heard her in her room, but I wasn't sure"

"It is ok" Andrew assured, "Can you cover her units for a few days?"

She nodded, and glanced knowingly at me. I was aware that Brian was still watching Andrew as I mouthed the words, "She got away"

"Well never mind, I have reported her image to airport security, and hopefully we will get her before she leaves the airport" He insisted, as he gestured to the ever increasing new guests, "Please help the people"

Shannon grabbed my hand, her golden skin looked radiant in the sun light, as we walked over to the arrivals, and she whispered, "Thank you for looking after her"

"Welcome to Mallorca" I cheerily announced, glancing back at Shannon with a smile, to the nearest couple, a lovely elderly couple, complete with walking sticks and big hats "Where will you be staying this holiday?"

"This is our first holiday in years" The wife announced, I shrugged at Shannon. "Really?" I smiled back.

"He's had a new bag you know" She continued, gesturing to her husband, who remained henpecked and silent.

"Really?" I repeated, "What type?"

"Colostomy" She responded calmly.

Well, what could I say to that? I held the form out in front of her, "What is your name sweetheart?"

"Pardon?" She asked.

I glanced at her hand baggage, and saw the name "Collins" on the label. "Is it Mrs Collins?" I asked.

"Collins yes" She agreed.

I glanced at my sheet, and eventually found the name, thank fuck they were in Palma, and not in my hotel in Alcudia.

"You're on coach 6" I spoke, I realised I was fighting a losing battle, "I will tell you what, let me take you there"

Together, the three of us slowly made our way out of the airport, leaving Shannon and Brian to handle the others. I am sure I also saw a turd in his bag.

I relished the sunlight as Mr and Mrs Collins boarded their coach, I am sure I could smell urine on them.

I decided to enjoy the warmth whilst my colleagues directed people out to their coaches, I could see the people slowly entering the coach park, and I could see Andrew in the distance, watching the arriving coaches for Beverley.

The morning was turning out lovely. It was moments like this I savoured this job.

I waited as long as I could possibly wait as the coaches became filled with new arrivals, and soon enough I was awaiting outside my own coach, number 8, aware that my own guests would be arriving.

Soon, Shannon appeared at the door way, and I could see her point over to me, nervously I decided to hide from the oncoming as I recognised him instantly, I walked around the coach, as I saw Keith sitting carefree on the tuft of grass at the side of my bus.

"What transfer are you on?" I asked. "Number 9" He responded, "Why?"

Frantically, I clasped the fifty Euro cash out of my shoe, and offered it him, and panicked, "I cannot be on this coach"

He took it, and smiled, "Whoever it is has just bought me some birthday drinks" We swapped our clipboards, "If anyone asks you have not seen me"

I walked away from him, and made my escape behind the coach, as I could see Shannon nearby speaking to the creep.

"He was on this coach, but I don't know where he has gone" I heard her say.

I quickly raced between the buses, and felt an instant shot of relief as I stood outside my new coach, knowing that for now I was safe. I sneakily boarded the coach, and peered through the window into the one adjacent to me, I saw him enter the coach, and I smiled.

"What the fuck was that about?" Shannon asked, as she appeared in the doorway.

Eagerly, I stepped back off the coach, and pulled her to the side of the coach, ignoring the new arrivals, "That man, what did he say to you?"

"He said he is an old friend of yours from Manchester" She announced, "He seemed nice"

I shook my head, "No, he's a vile part of my past, and I never thought I would see him again"

"That's going to be difficult" Shannon confessed, "He's staying at The Maharajah"

Shit.

TWELVE

Furiously I buried my anger in me as I took the transfer back to resort, knowing full well I would have no choice but to confront him again, I knew the last time I saw him he swore revenge on me, and now here it was about to happen. I had no idea what to say, or how to handle it. I even considered repeating what Beverley had just done. But I could not. I knew it was pointless.

We pulled into the resort, and I took a swallow, we were about to drive past my hotel, and I could see Chris and Joanna on the balcony getting over amorous in front of people. Keith's coach had pulled up, and I saw my nemesis get off the coach, with a young man close behind, and then we turned the corner.

"Ok" I sounded loud on the microphone, realising that it was on after all, "We are about to arrive at our first hotel, The Viva Sunrise, and a little bit of news about your rep Sian. She is quite a famous young lady, and a lot of you will not really recognise her with her clothes on, now for legal reasons I cannot say the name of the paper, but it's big, yellow, and there's plenty of it in Mallorca"

A few lads cheered as they got the in-joke immediately, and some of the others had to explain the joke, I glanced at my sheet of paper, and felt my heart sink again, this was the only drop off on this coach.

I willed them to take their time, but once more they were eager to check in their rooms.

I was about to give up, when I heard someone calling for their rep. I smiled, hoping for the first time in three months I would have a complaint that would actually take up all afternoon.

I smiled as I saw a dithering old lady walking towards me.

"How can I help you today?" I asked, willing for the complaint to be a difficult beast for me to control.

"I am a little worried" She explained, "I fly home a week on Saturday, and I am concerned how I will get my suitcase down from the fourth floor, as since my Arthur died..."

"You can just use the elevator" I smiled, gesturing toward the large silver doors to the side of the reception.

"You mean it comes down as well?" She asked, convincingly normal, she turned and shuffled away "I thought they only went up, and I have been using the stairs all fucking week"

And within minutes I was free to make my way back to my hotel. "It's now" I urged myself.

I took my time to walk over the bridge that separated our hotels by with a small dried out canal.

It did not take me long to find them. He was already sitting in the reception area awaiting my arrival.

"Hello" His voice grated on me.

I held out my hand as I approached him, "Tommo"

His look of disgust shocked me, as I noticed the young dark haired man next to him.

"This is he?" The Welsh companion grunted, "You said he was a hunk"

"Must be all this sun" Thomas commented, through gritted teeth, "Making his skin all wrinkly"

"What do you want?" I asked, "You know I don't earn any money doing this job"

Thomas laughed, "You were quite difficult to locate, but then I bumped into Ophelia in the bar, and a few vodkas later, she tells me everything"

"So what do you want?" I asked.

"You" He whispered, "You owe me, and I will make you pay"

"I don't take kindly to threats" I whispered.

"And I don't take kindly to being head-butted in the balls" He announced, as he turned to his companion, "This is my new star, Robin, he's already made me more money than you ever did"

I could sense the pride in Robin's smile, "I'm impressed, he must suck a lot of cock, you wanna become a rep mate, we're all whores"

"Yes" Thomas smiled, "Your female out there was very kind, and told us all about tonight's party"

"You're not welcome" I insisted.

"I beg to differ" He smiled as he waved a paid for ticket before me.

The afternoon commenced, and I rested at Madness bar, and Shannon perched next to me as I finished my meal.

"So what happened?" She asked, as she stole a cold chip.

I shook my head, "He used to be my boss back in Manchester and he used to make me do disgusting things, things I am ashamed to admit"

"Is he the one you slapped nut in the bollocks?" She asked calmly, I had discussed this during one of our first weeks in Alcudia during a game of truth or dare.

I smiled, letting her know that she got it in one.

I felt her hand clasp my thigh, and she leaned forward, "I love that story, it kind of makes me a bit moist"

She raised, and grabbed my hand, together we walked into the cool bar interior, ignoring the sporadic individuals inside. Raul, the waiter winked, he knew what we were about to do.

She knew that Chris would be entertaining and last time we fucked in my place, Chris made a choice to watch, with his dick in his hand, it kind of disturbed her that he didn't want to join in. Just watch.

She used her foot to kick open the door to the toilets, and quickly checked the coast was clear, as she pushed open a cubicle in the gents. She hitched her skirt, and pulled down her knickers, as she forced her lips onto mine. My cock sprang to life again, and she eagerly battled with my fly to release it from its cotton prison.

"I love you" She whispered, passionately her red hair falling over her face as she spoke.

I did not have time to respond, as she lowered instantly, taking my whole shaft into her mouth. I felt my legs weaken as I enjoyed her mouth, but she did not stay there long. She rose, and forced me hard against the door. She used her hand to guide my penis into her vagina, and then straddled me against the same door, her being taller than me had its advantages standing up. Her leg arched upwards, and I clasped it in my hand, as I pushed deeper inside her.

Her hand covered my mouth as I started to groan, and I returned the favour, and it did not take long for her eyes to widen, as I sensed her cumming, and I was still some-way off.

I felt her wetness increase as someone entered the toilets, I could see their feet pause outside the door, and I continued, until I came.

At the party, the theme 'The Letter P' as instructed on the invites that were painstakingly made by Keith's hand weeks earlier, did exactly as it said on the tin. There were Pirates, Priests, Penguins, Prostitutes, Princes, Princesses, Pimps, Porn Stars, even a Pope, Keith himself was dressed in an ankle length flashers mac, and had the word Pervert scrawled onto the back. There were Police, and even Polar bears, and Shannon looked beautiful as a Parrot. I myself was a Punk, I had stolen some paint from the kid's reps across the hall, and recycled a lost property leather jacket, tore my shirt, and put a key in my ear piercing.

Together, we entered Madness for the party that was already in full swing. Sian was dressed as a rather slutty looking Pelican, and was dancing on the table to a wild tune as we arrived, but despite the costumes, neither of us could see Chris. He had disappeared earlier in the day.

Shannon clasped my hand as we saw Thomas and Robin enter the bar, as two camp Police men, but they did not seem to notice us in the doorway.

We approached the bar, and ordered our drinks, and put one in for Keith as already agreed. The night began perfect, with all my friends, with the exception of Thomas and Robin, and Sian, neither of which I would prefer were not there.

Such a small capacity, it was difficult to remain hidden, and Thomas and I crossed paths a number of times. I felt sickened as his eye roved over my body, I knew what he wanted.

Someone, a prostitute, kept passing me bottles of beer, saying someone had bought me the drink, but I could not see where she was pointing on each occasion. Fuck it, free beer was always the best. Shannon had gone missing shortly before midnight when the fun kicked in. The last I saw of her, she was talking to Keith, and the same prostitute passed her a drink, she still had one in her hand.

"Where is Chris?" I shouted, "I miss my friend, he's a ginger... with eyes.... green ones" Another prostitute this time passed me another drink. I laughed as the light headedness increased within me. But I continued to drink. Despite the leprechaun giving me the stink eye from the nearby group of kid's reps.

The beer was flowing to me, and I was hugging everyone I could. Including Robin, I also kissed Sian passionately in the same cubicle I had shagged Shannon in previously, and each time, another person would pass me another beer.

My head started to feel light, but I still continued, Raul tried to offer me water. I pushed it aside.

The karaoke started, and I took advantage to show my poor singing skills whilst drunk. I could see Thomas laughing at me, but I did not care as he came over to me, carrying me away from the microphone, over his shoulder, I saw him place me on a table, and he placed something into my drink. I did not protest, I reached for the beer like a child reaching for a toy.

The man in rubber made an appearance during the evening, and remained elusive in the crowd, making Kellie extra excited that he was here. Another larger rep also showed an interest. I felt my eyes close, and when they reopened, less people were in the bar.

I rose and staggered across the floor, bumping into the chairs and tables that dared to be in my path, I could hear people complain that I had spilled their drinks, but I responded with swearing.

The man in rubber had his back to me, and Kellie and the other rep were speaking with him, and touching him, as I reached them. I laughed at him. As a green fairy ran past, sprinkling something that looked like glitter in the air. I didn't see where she went, probably with the leprechaun that also had gone missing.

"You fuck fat women" I pointed at him with my finger, poking his chest. He grabbed my hand in his own rubber hand, and forced it away. Silent.

"I know you" I smiled, as I remained unpersuasive by his presence, I could barely remain standing as I swayed before him. I felt dizzy, and the man in rubber seemed to feign concern. He reached out to me.

I took the moment to seize the opportunity, and grappled at his face mask, pulling it hard. He could not stop me as he held me in his arms. The mask lay in my palm, and I glanced up at him, and laughed.

Chris's ginger hair, and green eyes looked back at me, almost in fear, as the crowd cheered.

Then I fell to the floor, and he ran.

"Are you on drugs?" Kellie shouted at me, kicking me in the ribs. I knew she was crying.

"I will look after him" Thomas called from beyond my peripheral vision.

"Where is Shannon?" I slurred, barely even completing the words, "And Chris?"

I felt Thomas lift me in his arms again, and hold me tight against his body, I could feel his bulge harden against my slumped body. I think, I am not sure, but I think I touched it.

"This is my friend Tommo" I slurred, as my eyes closed.

"So I'm a friend now?" Thomas asked, his bulge more prominent, and obvious to anyone watching, "Let's get you home"

"I don't want to go home" I protested, more alert now, "I want a drunk and naked pool party" Someone cheered in the distance, and I felt myself guided out of the bar.

The next thing I recall, I was soaking wet. A firm pair of arms held me tight, as the water lapped around me. I could hear people splashing and cheering. Someone was naked next to me and I could see her breasts floating next to me, her hand was gripping onto my soft penis.

I smiled as I noticed Sian before me, as the same arm that was holding me, passed me a small brown bottle.

I grabbed it carelessly, and placed the top of the bottle under my nostril, and inhaled the sweet smelling aroma, and my head once more went light. I felt my penis begin to harden in the water, surprising Sian as she started to furiously tug at me, I felt my eyes close and I turned my head, kissing my holder. Thomas.

I felt his penis harden behind me.

"Buckman" Someone called causing a panic.

Sian released her grip, and made her escape. I did not care. I continued to kiss Thomas's lips, until he pulled away.

"I told you I would get the last laugh" He announced, through gritted teeth, as he turned me around.

The last thing I remember is feeling his hand on the back of my head, as he forced my face into the water.

His dick entered my arse with ease, and I raised my head in drunken protest, and saw Andrew before me, furious.

"Get out" He called.

My eyes rolled to the back of my head and I blacked out.

THIRTEEN

I came to the next morning in hospital, the sun light was harsh on my eyes. I could hear the nurse speaking in Spanish to someone nearby. I felt clumsy as I jolted upright in my sterile bed, my head felt alien to me now, and the pain hit me.

The nurse rushed over to me, along with the doctor, and I could see Sian waiting anxiously at the side of the bed. I was wearing a clinical white gown.

"You must rest" The Doctor spoke in broken English, "You have been very poorly"

"I need to get out of here" I whispered, barely listening to him.

"You have been through a terrible ordeal Mr Candlish" He announced, "Please rest"

"I think you should listen to the doctor" Sian assured.

I thought for a moment, and reluctantly lay back down on the mattress.

"You were bought into hospital this morning by your boss, Mr Buckman" The doctor explained, "You were naked, and showed signs of delirium"

"I was drunk" I responded.

"Mr Candlish, we did a blood test on you, and found a high trace of flunitrazipam in your system" He continued. His English sounded weird to me, but I had not spent much time with a real Spaniard, well, aside from the waitress earlier in the season but she did not speak much with my cock in her mouth.

"What?" I asked.

"It's the medical term for rohypnol" Sian added.

"And you were attacked" The Doctor continued.

I started to remember, I remember seeing Thomas before me again, and I cringed.

"You were raped" Sian translated.

I felt a panic hit me.

"That was not all" Sian took over from the doctor, "Shannon was found unconscious in the toilet, she too had rohypnol in her system, she is across the hall"

"I have to see her" I panicked.

"No" Sian insisted, "You will need to wait, and let the Doctor do his job"

I felt as though she was right, and agreed. My mind was on Shannon as I was asked about what happened, and I tried to piece together how I ended up the way I did. I remember different people were giving me drinks, and I remember seeing Chris at one point, but could not remember him leaving. I remember singing on karaoke, but could not remember anything prior to this.

I felt sick, and tried to close my mind to the questioning.

Eventually Sian convinced the doctor to leave me for a moment. I felt the tears welling up in my eyes, and felt grateful for him leaving me.

Sian placed her caring hand on my shoulder, and tried to make me relax as I began to breathe heavily.

"Connor" She whispered eventually, "You know that you have to take the rap for this"

Concern crossed my face, "You were there, and you saw what happened"

"I was in bed, and I have a witness" I realised she was lying, "I came here out of sheer concern for you"

"You were wanking me off in the swimming pool" I insisted.

"Whilst you had your boyfriend's dick up your arse" She insisted, "And now you are claiming male rape"

"You heard what the Doctor said" I gestured to the closed curtain, "That bastard put rohypnol in my drinks and ..."

"And?" She teased, "There are at least a dozen witnesses, including staff at Madness who confirm that you wanted a drunk and naked party, and you led them to The Maharajah on your own accord"

"You have to tell the truth" I insisted.

"What truth?" She questioned, "That you organised for your friends to get butt naked and fuck you in the pool?"

"This is a set up, you were there" I reminded.

"When you have been in this game for as long as I have, you learn to buy friends and secrets" She smiled, "I have someone to verify I was with him, and you don't have a leg to stand on"

Fury exploded in me.

"You only have one way out of this" She calmly continued, "You give Andrew sex, and you keep your job, if you don't, you will be flying home tonight, especially now that your little friend Ophelia is coming over to hear your case on behalf of HR"

I felt my body shake in anger.

"You're finished" She insisted, calmly.

I screamed, and grabbed her arm sharply, alerting security and the Doctor to the room. She screamed in pain as I gripped onto her arm.

"He's gone mad" She insisted as they released her from my grip.

"This is a set-up" I screamed, the security restrained me, and then I felt the needle enter my buttocks.

I came to again a few hours later, the dusk was hitting the area, I could hear people talking outside my room, and I recognised her voice almost instantly.

"He's awake" I heard Andrew say, and soon I saw him and Ophelia enter the room, closing the door behind them.

"I am afraid to say I have to inform you that this is an official disciplinary due to the number of actions against you" He proceeded, and I saw Ophelia pull out a note pad, and start making notes.

"I was raped" I whispered, still spaced on whatever the drug was they gave to me.

"We have it on record by no fewer than six of your colleagues that you announced that you wanted a drunk and naked party, and it was clear by a number of people that you were in a relationship with the man in question" He continued.

"I only ever had sex with one man willingly" I whispered.

"The man in question has given a statement to the police" He continued, and I heard him unfold a piece of paper, "It reads, that you had been pestering him to come out to Spain as you needed money, and you promised him sexual favours in return"

"Lies" I cried.

"Is it true that you knew this man before he arrived in Mallorca, and did you pay a colleague to take your transfer off you?" Andrew continued.

"No" I lied.

"I happen to know that is untrue" Ophelia interrupted, and she turned to Andrew to explain, "Connor used to sing for Thomas in Manchester, and when he accepted this job he caused an embarrassing incident to him, when he caused a serious groin injury"

"Lies" I repeated.

"Is it also true that you took Beverley to the airport on your coach despite her not being insured to travel?" He continued.

"No" I lied.

"Connor" Andrew shook his head, "I had high hopes for you"

"Give me one more chance please" I cried.

"I am sorry, my hands are tied" Andrew confessed.
"Please" I pleaded, "I will do anything"

Andrew shook his head again, and turned to Ophelia, "Miss Mason, can you give me some time with him. I need to speak with him alone"

"I don't think that is wise" Ophelia protested.

"If you can get the Doctor to supply me with the records, just to see if we can substantiate his claim he was raped" Andrew assured.

Ophelia nodded, and left the room.

"Right" I announced, as I sat upright in the bed again, "Sian told me from the start that if ever I was in trouble, I would need to make you cum"

Andrew smiled, as he approached the bed.

"But" I insisted, "I need you to know that Sian was there last night, and she can support my story"

"Sian was not there" He insisted.

I knew that I was already fighting a losing battle, "And where is my attacker?" "Gone" He answered.

"I was raped" I insisted.

"That's all this is" Andrew announced, taking a seat next to the bed, "A story, and I do not wish to have any sexual favour from you"

"It's true and the medical records will prove it" I insisted.

"No" Andrew sounded stern, "You drugged your partner, in the hope to take her back to your apartment with your fella, and when that failed, you acted on it, and cried rape, and like the boy who cried wolf, nobody believes you"

I sank back to my bed, "I am telling the truth"

"You upset too many people Connor, Kellie doesn't want to work with you, you made Shannon hand in her notice, and Chris does not wish to live with you anymore" He continued.

"Only because I outed him as the rubber gimp that's been banging fat birds all season" I insisted, "And we have been having an affair all season, and it all started after we had a threesome with Ophelia"

"You must stop lying" Andrew insisted, as the door opened, "I managed to convince Sian not to press charges for the bruises you gave to her this morning"

"Tell him about the threesome in Palma" I asked Ophelia as she entered the room. She shook her head, "I don't know what you are on about"

"You bitch" I whispered.

Andrew took the notes, and read them for a moment, "Says here, your bloods were all clear, seems like an open and shut case"

"But" I protested.

"I will have you on the next flight back to Manchester" He continued, aware as Sian entered the room, smiling to herself. I knew also that she was placing my real medical notes into her purse.

June 23rd.

Luckily for me, there was no flights back to Manchester for three days, and I was released from the hospital the following day.

Alone, I made my way back to my apartment. It seemed vacant as I packed. There was no sound at all to be heard, even though the bar was open, and there seemed to be a lot of tourists around. I glanced over to The Maharajah from the balcony, and smiled, as I saw Kellie, and her new dual rep another girl in the reception talking to what should have been my guests.

I hated the fact that Kellie was already enjoying her new partner.

I felt a tear in my eye, as I eyed the lounge area. I had only been here for three months but I had become attached to it. It felt like home. I felt as though I had let myself, and my family down. I thought back to the harsh words that Andrew had said how Shannon had handed in her resignation and that Chris could no longer bear to live with me. I could not speak to them as I no longer had my mobile.

I smiled as I saw a photograph of the three of us at Pirates a few weeks ago. Chris had his arms thrown around me, and I was sitting on Shannon's legs and we were clearly half cut. Joanna sat in the corner of the photo looking bored.

Just as I placed it back on the refrigerator, I heard the door open. I panicked as Chris entered the room in his airport uniform.

"What are you doing here?" He asked.

"I will be out of your way in a few minutes" I muttered, barely wanting to make eye contact. "You embarrassed me the other night" He sounded angry.

"I am sorry, I was drugged" I tried to explain.

"I heard what happened, are you ok?" He changed the subject.

I shrugged, "Shannon has handed in her resignation, and I have been sacked over it" I ignored him as I continued to collect my items from inside the lounge.

"Is it true that you helped Beverley escape?" He asked, still remaining in the doorway, having not moved since he saw me.

I nodded, "I felt it was my duty"

"You have to be the night in shining armour don't you?" He questioned, he had come inside the apartment now, and placed his satchel on the floor.

"I am not going to let a friend hurt" I responded, and then I realised that may not be the best phrase.

"You hurt me" He retaliated, "I did not expect you to remove my mask like that"

"I'm sorry" I repeated, I stopped myself from saying that I was drugged again.

"I did not want people to know it was me" He muttered, "Joanna has split up with me because of that"

"I'm sorry" I repeated, holding back my tears.

"That day when you and me did Ophelia in Palma" He spoke, "You made me realise that there was more to life than just shagging, when I kissed you I...."

Silence proceeded, and I continued to pack, I awaited him to finish.

"Where are you going?" He asked eventually.

I shrugged, "Andrew said you can't live with me anymore, and I understand"

He did not respond.

"I suppose I will head off to Palma for my last few days" I continued.

"I will miss you" He confessed.

I was not going to answer him, but then I realised he was standing next to me, he had clasped my arm, and lowered the bag to the floor.

I turned to face him, a single tear had begun to form in his eye.

"Don't go" His lips quivered.

"I have to" I responded, "I have another three days and I have to go home"

"Please" He pleaded, more tears in his eyes, he pressed his lips against mine. Moments later, our kiss escalated.

I tried to pull away, to look into his eyes, "A moment ago, you said something about that night in Palma"

He paused, and bit his bottom lip, "I only ever loved you"

We kissed again.

FOURTEEN

We spent the day in bed, and made love. Due to my recent experience, it was me in control, and then we held each other in the sticky heat from the Mallorca sun. It felt right that we were holding each other in his room. I actually never wanted the moment to end.

I knew it was going to, so I tried not to think of it, and closed my eyes, and for the first time in a while, I slept.

I heard the shower switch on at some point at dusk, but I wanted more sleep.

When I awoke, it was dark, and I was alone. I felt saddened as I realised he was no longer there. In the moonlight I cried as I showered, and then dressed in some fresh clothes, and took my final glance around the apartment.

Grabbing my bag of what I wanted to take, I made my way out of the place, leaving my key on the table.

Madness bar was loud as I walked through the corridor, and without taking a look back, I walked onto the street.

Lonely, I made my way past my old hotel, and crossed the road, toward the beach. I could hear the life of Mallorca scream its party lifestyle around me, as I sat on the sand, watching the moonlit sea.

I cried again.

It was then I felt a hand on my shoulder. Startled, I turned to see her before me, Shannon offered me a bottle of water, which I accepted.

"I know you are innocent" She confessed as she joined me.

"Thank you" I responded, as I took a long swallow of the water.

"I fly home with you, if you want the company?" She smiled, allowing the wind to blow her red hair wildly in the night breeze.

"No" I smiled, "You have to stay, you are an amazing rep, and you shouldn't quit because of me"

"It is not your fault" She smiled.

"Were you raped?" I asked for the first time.

She shook her head, "I was simply drugged, it looks like Thomas wanted to get you back for what you did back at home"

"Then stay" I smiled, "For me"

Shannon shook her head, "I only got into this game for the fun, and now that is finished. I think we had an amazing three months"

"Dramatic" I smiled.

She nodded, "I remember that day Daisy died like it was yesterday..."

Daisy, I had not thought about her in a long time, I felt guilty about that, I felt guilty about a lot of things over these last few days. I thought back to our first meeting, I remembered that day on the coach. I smiled.

"Do you want me to stay?" She questioned.

I nodded, and followed it with a kiss.

"What I said was" She spoke, "I know that you were set up, so maybe I should stay to take Sian down from the inside. What do you think?"

"You would do that for me?" I asked.

She nodded, "I will do anything for you Connor, I cannot believe that you were raped and I know for a fact that Sian has something to do with it"

I shook my head, "It was Thomas, he wanted revenge and I think she just went along for the ride"

"Know what?" She announced, "I am going to stay, I will get your job back if it is the last thing I do"

I smiled, "If you really want to, I know Sian had, or has my real medical records"

"Then leave it with me" Shannon smiled, "Now, let's get you back to your apartment"

"I don't live there" I announced.

"Chris loves you and you know it" Shannon announced, "He was just talking about you in the office, and told everyone how stupid they are for even believing that you would sabotage your job" I smiled, as I realised I was not abandoned after all, I still had my friends, and lovers.

Together we raised, and made our way back toward the hotel, her hand felt tight in mine, and they swung with our pace.

I noticed then, as we neared Madness again, that there was a banner outside. "Go get them Connor" It read.

And my friends were there, cheering my arrival.

"I found him on the beach" Shannon announced, as Chris handed out a bottle of lager.

"No drugs" He winked, "I promise"

I smiled and accepted the bottle, taking a large swill, Raul approached with a smile on his face.

"My friend" He proudly spoke as he embraced me, "I find that bastard that hurt you and I rip off his balls"

Everybody in the room cheered and I raised my glass, "To ripping off Tommo's balls"

My colleagues cheered and began a chant of 'Rip off the balls of the rapist"

After a moment, Chris took the time to raise another toast, and carelessly clambered onto a table, to make his statement heard.

"This man" He announced, "Has made me realise what love really is, and it does not matter if it is male and female, male and male, female and female, or a variation thereof, but it is friendship, and that is what true love is about"

Everyone, including myself cheered.

He continued, "I am pleased to call Connor Candlish my best friend, and he made me realise that my secret life as the man in rubber, seducing the larger ladies, should be embraced, but..."

He paused, and looked at me direct in the eye, as he lowered himself.

The silence became deafening as he took my hands in his, and he continued, "I would go gay for this man"

He placed his lips on mine, and kissed me once more, in public, causing everyone in the bar to cheer, including Shannon.

"Hands off slut, he's mine" She laughed.

As he pulled away he flashed a smile, and mouthed the words for me, "I love you"

I laughed, and pushed him away for a moment, and then took a seat nearby.

Shannon kissed me, and sat by my side, "This may take some time, but I promise we will get revenge"

I could not help but smile, "This morning, I had nothing, and now I have everything"

Shannon took my hand in hers, "I nearly got a bit jealous by watching Chris kiss you then, but I know how close you two are"

I felt embarrassed by the comment, but brushed it aside, "I appreciate what you are doing for me"

I pressed my lips against hers, and felt her smile

"As long as you love us both" She whispered, "I am happy to share you"

As the night closed, the three of us entered my old apartment, kissing, tearing off our clothes. They clambered onto the bed, and I held my cock in my hand, as he parted her legs, he allowed the tip to gently press against her lips. I soon joined, them, pressing my body against her back, eagerly searching for her anus to enter. They started to kiss, and then he turned to me, kissing me once more. His stubble hurt my lips a little, but I continued. I signalled for him to come behind me, so I could fuck Shannon, and he could fuck me. He obeyed.

As I allowed my own dick to enter her minge, I felt him press his cock against my buttocks, and the pain as he entered was momentarily uncomfortable, his balls started to bang against my arse as I used his force to thrust into Shannon.

I moved rhythmically on top over her, using him as a guide, and grappled at her hips, forcing her on her side, my erect cock still inside her. I forced my lips onto her moist mouth to stop her from moaning.

We kissed each other, me and him, her and him, me and her, she exploded with ecstasy, and

Chris soon felt his own pleasure being reached. He pulled out of me, and then proceeded to masturbate over us, as I continued to pound her hard. He groaned, as pre-cum seeped out of his slit, I glanced down at my own manhood, inside her, still thrusting with firm, hard movements. He strained, forcing his hips towards us, and his ivory semen shot from his dick, covering my back, I bit my own lip, feeling the explosion inside my own groin.

Chris collapsed in a heap next to me, stroking me, as I felt my own release. The sticky remnants of his seed smeared on my naked back.

The next two days were intense, personally, I was semi-drunk spending time with both Shannon and Chris when they were not working. I had a ceremonious burning of my uniform on the beach on the last night, and the three of us curled up and watched the flames lick the clothes until they were nothing but ashes. I then buried the embers with the sand, and the three of us climbed into the same bed, once more, all three of us cuddled, and I slept my final sleep in Alcudia.

That last morning I awoke, and kissed them both on the lips, and showered, leaving them to sleep more.

Naked, I stepped onto the balcony, and watched the morning pass by on my plastic chair. Soon enough, Chris and Shannon joined me, and the three of us celebrated with vodka and bottles of beer.

We dressed a little after two that afternoon, and as I grabbed my suitcase, we made our way down the staircase, and awaited for the coach outside.

"I promise you" Chris smiled, as he embraced me, "We will get you back here soon" "Thank you" I smiled.

"It may be hard, but we will" He assured.

"I know you two will be amazing" I responded, as the coach turned into the street before us. Luckily Shannon was guiding the transfer back to the airport, but this would be the final time I would see Chris.

I reluctantly let go of him, and gently wiped a tear from his eye. "Shannon is going to look after you now, and I will be back on holiday soon. And don't forget, you're coming to mine for Christmas"

He nodded, and turned away, not wanting either of us to see him cry.

"Please" I pleaded with Shannon, as she wrapped her arm around my waist, "Look after him"

"I will" She agreed, as we boarded the coach.

The coach was full to capacity as we set off out of resort, and I sat next to Shannon, watching my home for three months disappear.

Shannon spoke her farewell speech to the captive audience, as I gently slid my hand under her skirt, my fingers strained against the elastic of her knickers, but soon penetrated her vagina, first one finger, then two.

She sighed loudly in shock, dropping the microphone sharply, creating a loud metallic hiss throughout the coach, causing her to blush.

I removed my hand, and licked my fingers, and she laughed.

FIFTEEN

July 9th.

I settled back into the UK with ease, I soon got a telesales job in an insurance team in Manchester, and rented a room above Churchill's, working at the bar occasionally with Kyle and Justin. I often chatted to Shannon and Chris on line, and had already arranged a week out there in August.

Today I had a plan, and needed to pay an old friend a visit, and apply for a new job abroad with other companies.

Justin had allowed me to use his car, and I ran my errands and then I parked outside the cobbled pathway where Thomas's office was. The litter had gone, but the dog shit was still there. The same chavs were smoking the same joints nearby, and once more they remarked on my sexuality as I opened the metallic door that now supported some interesting graffiti on the people inside this very building. Checking my pocket, I felt my cigarettes and lighter inside.

The smell of mould still lingered in my nostrils as I stepped inside the corridor and made my way to his doorway. The dimly lit office was only illuminated by the sun light, and he smiled at me from the dirty desk.

"The wanderer returns" He laughed, not even moving.

Something muffled banged on the table, and soon, Robin rose from under the desk, with a look of disgust on his face.

"Robin, go make me a coffee" Thomas ordered.

"What's this ugly mother doing here?" Robin barked, as he brushed past me, staring evilly at me, barely taking his eyes off me, looking down his nose at me.

I remained stationary in front of the desk, and he straightened up his paper work, and my eyes locked on him. "So they fired your sorry ass" He stated. "That's why I am here" I responded.

"He is not having my job" Robin shouted from the kitchen, clearly eavesdropping into the conversation.

"It's alright" Thomas laughed, "There is no market for washed up whores in my market... I made a mistake taking you out of that boy band you were in with bald bastard"

"Please give me another chance" I got down to my knees, ignoring his comments about Chet. "You made me realise the truth, I should never have left you, and I wish I listened to you like the good little whore you made me"

Thomas raised his eyes, and smiled, "I told you I would win, now tell me why I should take you back?"

I rose, and undid the top few buttons on my shirt, "I remember when you said I was the best blow you ever had"

I waited for his response, aware that Robin was now seething in the kitchen, during the pause I pulled out the cigarettes from my pocket, offering him one.

"I knew you would come crawling back" He smiled, gesturing to his cock, "Now get on your knees you little bitch and let me dump my load in your throat, and only then I will consider taking you back"

I lit my cigarette and nodded. I wasted no time walking around his desk, his legs were already apart, and naked, his erect penis commanded attention.

"Being a rep taught you some dirty habits" Thomas laughed.

I lowered myself to my knees, glancing over to the kitchen behind me, I could see Robin standing there holding a knife in his hand.

I winked at him.

"Take it whole" Thomas insisted.

I leaned forward, and pulled my cigarette out of my mouth.

"I have waited for this day since I came to in that hospital" I whispered, as I stubbed the hot end of the cigarette into the tip of his penis.

His scream was legendary as he bucked, hitting me in the face with his blistering groin, pushing me aside as he cupped himself, I did not care that my lip was split as I rose, and Robin came running in, knife still in hand, and a glass of milk.

I laughed as Thomas put his member into the cold glass.

"You're right" I insisted, "I did get taught a few dirty habits"

"You will die for this" Robin cursed, aware that Thomas was in too much agony to talk. Casually, I made my way back to the door, and pulled it open.

"You raped me in Alcudia" I hissed, "This was just revenge"

It had started to rain as I left the building, and clambered into the car, aware that the chavs were about to follow me again. I flipped them the bird as I started the engine.

Later, I found myself sipping a latte in a coffee bar, it surprised me that I could not get a real coffee in Spain, so savoured the taste, watching the Manchester day crowd go by. I admit, I did cower when a police car went past, thinking that Thomas had reported me. Luckily they just drove on by.

"Do you always shudder when you see the police?" A woman smiled, she looked familiar to me, but I could not place her anywhere in my mind.

"Sonia" She introduced, "I kind of bumped into you at your parent's funeral" "You're the woman in the smoking area" I recalled.

"Dirty habit" She smiled, her lip curled a little in the corners as she did so.

Before I could answer she busied herself with her own mobile and made an excuse to leave. I watched her walk away and I could not help but smile, and I realised that my own cup was empty.

As I was about to leave, I recognised another blonde girl in the queue, her hand brushed back her hair, and I realised it was Beverley.

"Beverley" I smiled with open arms, attracting her attention immediately. A huge smile crossed her face, as she recognised me.

We bought another latte each and sat in the same seat, overlooking the busy high street. "You look great" I smiled.

"I owe you so much Connor" She touched my hand, "I felt for sure I would not have got away with it.

"I prefer you blonde" I gestured, "And I heard it was seven thousand?"

She nodded, "Thank you again for helping me leave"

"I cannot believe you got away with it" I smiled, taking a swallow out of the coffee.

She smiled back, "I know, I moved here last week, and working for Hibiscus Holidays in one of the shops, they know nothing"

"Any jobs going?" I enquired.

She nodded, "There's a recruitment drive next month for winter and next season... but Connor, what are you doing here? They didn't realise you helped me did they?"

"Long story short" I confessed, "After you left, I was drugged and raped, and they said I incited a naked pool party, and that bitch Sian stole my medical notes and I got sacked"

Shock crossed her face, and she apologised to me. But I shrugged it off recalling this morning with Thomas.

"I heard that Sian has recently gone for a promotion, and if she gets it, she will be head of resort for Marmaris next year" She announced, "One of the girls in my office went for it, but she didn't get through the screening process"

"Shannon and Chris are plotting a way to get her back for what she did" I confessed.

Beverley took my hand in her hand, "I know the recruitment officer for Hibiscus Holidays, he's a good man, I have known him for years, ask for Marmaris and get Chris and Shannon to request it for their next season placement"

I nodded, aware that she was glancing at her watch, I did not want her to leave again.

She quickly swallowed the remainder of her coffee, and smiled, "I have to get back to work, but can I take your number? I will get him to make contact"

I smiled, as I quickly jotted my number down onto the coffee receipt, which she took instantly, and placed carefully into her purse.

She rose, and smiled, "You saved my life in Mallorca, so now I will look after you"

She leaned over and planted a kiss on my cheek, I felt myself blush, and smile.

Beverley was true to her word, within an hour my phone rang, whilst I was alone in my room above the bar.

"Mr Candlish, my name is Oliver Duncan, head of recruitment for Hibiscus Holidays, and I have just been passed your number by one of my team members, we're very impressed by her comments about your career with Fantastical Holidays" He explained, He sounded like Chris, as I eagerly listened, "She told me of your experience with them, and I understand that you were the victim of a heinous crime, but she assures me that you would be an innocent party in this"

"Yes sir" I responded, "I was raped by a guest and my records were switched"

"My friend" Oliver spoke, "We at Hibiscus would always start afresh, and we will need someone with your expertise in our company. I am going to send you an application form and get you on the next training course; it will be in Blackpool in September, with the aim for you to start in October in our Winter sun destinations"

I smiled, and gave him an email address. Closed the call, and smiled.

Within seconds I was on line chatting to Shannon and Chris with the news, about my revenge on Thomas, and chance meeting with Beverley, and now this call.

We were not talking long before someone knocked on the door.

"That will be Justin or Kyle wanting some help" I spoke to them, closing Skype with a gentle kiss to them both.

I was still celebrating as I opened the door. It was not Kyle or Justin, but the one night stand that would not fuck off.again.

"What do you want?" I muttered, not inviting her in.

She pushed past me and made herself at home on my mattress.

"I'm horny" She purred, opening her legs expertly, "And now you're back in Manchester, you can scratch my itch"

"I have a girlfriend" I insisted.

"She is in Mallorca" She continued to smile, "And I am here"

I could see that once more she was not wearing any underwear again.

"Now penetrate me with your lovestick"

"No" I whispered, "You got me fired from the job I loved"

She laughed, and rose, "You were not made out to be a rep"

"I told you I was innocent" I announced.

"I know" Ophelia smiled, "And I also know that Sian switched your medical notes, so you were probably raped as you said, but now you are here. I am here. Let's make love"

She did not wait, and forced her lips onto mine, tearing at my shirt once more. "I own you" She bit my lip.

I weakened, and guided her back to the mattress, leaving the door open.

SIXTEEN

I never did tell Ophelia about my phone call, and I went back on holiday without her, I lied and said I was on a training course, in Edinburgh, she bought it. Meanwhile, Shannon and Chris and I shared a bed once more for a week. We collaborated our story, over how to defeat Sian, and both Shannon and Chris made their requests to go to Marmaris for Summer. It was common knowledge that she was leaving Spain to retrain in Turkey ready for the following season, so now our plan was even easier. I just needed these two, and myself to secure Marmaris. Beverley had agreed to pull a few strings with Oliver. Surprisingly, throughout my holiday I did not see Sian or Brian, or even Andrew. That was ok with me, I was happy sunbathing, drinking, and sleeping with the two most important people in my life. I loved them both as much as I ever loved anyone. Part of me also thought about Daisy, and what she would be like today, I could imagine her here in bed with us. She probably was my only regret.

For me, I bathed on the beach, drank in the bars, and enjoying the shows as a guest this time, surprisingly still using my infamous reps discount, people did not even notice I had left. One day, Chris and I were enjoying a date at the Pirates show, when Matty made an appearance, we hid for a moment under the table. Keith almost busted Shannon and me during a Flamenco show, this time we hid in the disabled toilets until we were safe.

Soon enough, our holiday was over, and I once more said farewell to my lovers. Individually. Then I flew back to the UK, and back to work. Also, Ophelia had simply moved into my room during my absence. I explained my tan to the use of sunbeds in Scotland.

Her clothes invaded my closet, and her trinkets were decorating my room, even my television had been replaced by her slightly larger one, and a games console. As I entered my now new room, she lay seductively on the bed, and I lowered my suitcase to the ground.

"I have waited a week for you" She smiled, opening her legs, revealing her bald pussy, "I have also prepared a nice surprise for you"

I walked over to the bed, and allowed my hand to wander up her leg, I thought of Shannon for a moment, and then Olivia, anyone but her, my fingers slowly touched her crotch, and I moved my body along hers, kissing her momentarily. My teeth soon approached her erect nipples, and I bit, she squirmed, and inhaled air between her teeth to control the pain I knew I caused. My hand moved from her pussy, and undid my button, releasing my semi-erect penis from its prison.

I rubbed my own cock, concentrating on kissing her neck, her lips, her breasts, until I knew I was hard enough. Without warning, I lifted her legs, placing them over my shoulders, and I spat onto my own tip, rubbing the saliva down my shaft, she was wet enough, but I needed the lubricant. I guided my dick expertly into her hole, and I carelessly pumped hard, using my hands to squeeze and tease her rosebud nipples.

Our bodies synchronised in rhythm, and her hands shot up my firm body, reaching for my own nipples, that were out of her reach, she bit her own lips frustrated, as I took full ownership of penetrating her.

"Turn me over" She urged eventually.

"No" I began to speed up my pace, I saw Shannon before me, "I haven't shot my load all week, I will cum soon"

She nodded, and clenched a little at that, she knew that was something that would work with me, I gained momentum, and pushed harder, until I felt that all too familiar sensation in my groins, shooting my sweet release through my organ.

I groaned a little too loudly, encouraging her to join in with her own orgasm, I knew that she was faking hers to make me satisfied, and I soon felt my softening cock slip out of her clefts.

I collapsed on top of her, and managed to kiss her briefly on the lips for a moment, before rolling onto my side, "I need a brew, coming downstairs for a pint?"

She did not say anything, and simply rolled away from me, revealing her naked back, covered in beads of perspiration.

"So" She eventually whispered, lifting her long blonde hair, in her hands, to show more of her body, tossing it slightly over her shoulder.

"What the fuck?" I responded, starting at the blackened ink on her back, the flakes of fresh tattoo scab raised, and looked ugly against her white skin.

"Don't you like it?" She pulled a saddened face.
I reached over to touch the sore skin, allowing my fingers to hover over the art, "No" "Well, I do" She insisted, "It means something to me"

I shook my head, as I once more read the words, "Mrs Connor Candlish" across her back. My eyes lowered down her body again to the tramp stamp I first saw.

"So" She whispered, "I think now you're back, maybe you should make the tattoo come true, don't you?"

"I am not marrying you" I responded nonchalantly rolling off the bed.

She rolled onto her back, and stared aimlessly at me, "I think you will find, you will Connor, I have not done this shit for nothing"

I tried not to respond, as I walked over to the doorway, picking a fresh pair of jeans from my wardrobe.

Suddenly, she was behind me, her hand clasped to the back of my neck, and forced me closer to the wooden door of my wardrobe sharply.

I saw a flash of white light, and heard the sickening thud of my head hitting the solid oak wood, as she spoke, "You will marry me, and you will make it official"

I came to a few minutes later, I was aware that my head had a bump the size of a hard-boiled egg forming over my cheekbone, and blood was already drying on my nostril. I slowly rose, dazed, I made my way back to the bed.

"Ophelia?" I called, concerned that I had been bleeding.

She did not respond, but I noticed the doorway was open again.

I cleaned myself up, and allowed my hair to fall over the swelling, and made my way down the staircase into the rear of the bar.

There was quite a few people already in there, Curtis and Justin were serving some early hen party, and waved at me as they noticed me. Justin pardoned himself, and made his way along the bar toward me.

"Slag" He smiled, without even asking my order, he started to pour my lager, "Hope you enjoyed your holiday"

I nodded, "I did not want to come back"

"I see you have a new roommate" He laughed, placing my pint before me, and then gesturing for money.

I opened a scrunched up five pound note from my pocket, and placed it in his hand, "I can't believe she is here, could you not have just told her fuck off or something?"

"You didn't you coward" He laughed. The jovial bastard.

"Touch yourself" I took a sip from the lager, "Is it still ok for Shannon and Chris to stay here for a few weeks when they finish the season?"

He nodded, "How you going to pull this off Connor, you have your wife in your room, your female and male lovers coming over, literally"

I laughed.

"And if I were you I would steer clear of Thomas" He continued, "He came in looking for you last week, and he's limping"

"I will be fine from that cunt" I smiled, unaware that my hair had now began to move naturally.

Justin moved forward, and brushed my hair aside, revealing the reddened lump on my cheekbone, "Oh Connor, please tell me Chris has not hit you"

"No" I smiled, "He would never hurt me, he's in love with me, and this was me being careless"

"Careless?" He questioned with a raised eyebrow.

"I only went and tripped over my suitcase in my room" I lied, embarrassed by the truth. Justin nodded, I think he knew, but remained silent.

I felt her hand touch my shoulder again, and I froze for a moment, as I turned to face Ophelia once more.

"What happened?" She asked me.

I repeated my lie, and Justin moved away, knowingly.

She smiled as she sat down next to me, "That's very good, now buy me a drink, and we will talk once more about this marriage. I knew you would come around to it"

I nodded.

Ophelia had made up her mind, and started to go into bride overload. I started to become weak, and introverted. I remained in the room as often as I could, Chris had vanished off the radar, we were no longer in contact, and he had embarked on a fastidious relationship with Sian, I was not ashamed to admit it offended me, but Shannon seemed to think differently. Even Thomas had disappeared, his offices were closed, not that it seemed any different to when he was there. Beverley and I had our own secrets, as I prepared for a new training course to start. However, as soon as Ophelia would return to the room, I had to give her my attention to put her off the scent.

I once more reverted to lying to her, I told her I had been offered a promotion and would need to go on a course again in a few weeks. I convinced her to use the week to have a hen party abroad, and paid her deposit so that she would not be in the country at the time. Flying from London as opposed to one of the nearer airports. I tried to forget her brute force, but it was always hiding in the back of my mind. I felt weak, what with Thomas and her having the control over me. I hated them both. But as a woman I could not hurt her back. Although there was a time when I wanted to repeat the cigarette stubbing on her. But now she lived here, I could not risk her anger.

How wrong was I? I never realised that she could bear so much rage with me.

September 7th.

She was meant to go to London the night before her flight, she and some of her friends were meant to go to see a musical, but one of her friends had fallen ill, and decided not to go. Nice waste of money there.

She did not tell me that she was staying, instead, I returned home from work, expecting her to be gone. I had foolishly left open my laptop, which I never locked when I was alone, and a habit I failed to lose when she moved in. Idiot.

With her back to me, I could see that she was checking my emails, and had clearly read everything at least once, as she started to recite the email word for word to me, without even turning her head to me.

"Dear Mr Candlish, further to our discussion dated July 9th, and again on August 2nd, we are pleased to invite you to a training course at the Hilton, Blackpool dated September 9th. Please ensure...." She read monotonously, eyes firmly attached to the screen.

"What the fuck?" I asked, as I rushed over to her, taking the lap top from her, tearing the charger from its portal.

She continued, "Please ensure that you bring with you the identification we discussed, and proof of your residency within the UK. The course will last for approximately five days, with the view of you departing the UK soon after. May we wish you a fresh welcome to Hibiscus Holidays, yours, Oliver Duncan, CEO, do I need to continue?"

I could see now that she had been crying, as she glanced up at me with her large eyes, "I was going to tell you..."

"We are getting married in a few months, and you want to go and dip your wick in some tarts abroad again" She announced, her face reddening with anger, "And you get another job abroad, without telling me?"

She rose, and pushed me hard, the laptop fell from my hands, I saw its screen blacken as it hit the wood flooring.

"Yes we fight a lot, but in the end you and I are the perfect match" She almost sang to me, in a tone that I was unsure if she was possessed, "I wouldn't want it any other way"

I felt her hand reach for my neck, and squeeze, I reacted by clasping at her hand, pulling it away sharply, she screamed in pain as I overpowered her.

"You can't do this to me" She cried.

"This was not meant to happen" I insisted, she rose, and shook her head.

My strength surprised me.

"I will not let you leave me" She cried.

"I never loved you" I confessed, "It is Shannon I love"

"No" She screamed, lurching forward, rugby tackling me so hard that our bodies fell through the air.

The last thing I remember seeing was Justin and Kyle in the doorway. The window had shattered through our weight and we plummeted to the street below. I heard someone scream before I closed my eyes.

SEVENTEEN

I knew it was a dream instantly, I felt nervous as I walked Alcudia beach again. All my friends were there, Shannon and Chris were kissing passionately with the waves lapping against their bare legs, but I did not mind. Keith and Matty were trying to entice me to play beach volleyball with some of the other reps. Kellie and my replacement ignored my presence, and continued to eat what seemed like the largest ice cream sundae ever. I could see Raul and some of the bar staff offering me glasses of alcohol, and Sian danced seductively on a floating raft, with Andrew at her side. Clare with the curly hair was also here, holding hands with Daisy. I smiled as I rushed to her side, even in death she was beautiful.

She greeted me with the lingering kiss that I had waited for that first day. I opened my eyes to see Shannon and Chris having intercourse before me, not even noticing my presence. I smiled, they seemed happy.

"You are the best" Daisy smiled, "And you will win"

"What will I win?" I questioned, forgetting for a moment my own mission.

"Sian's downfall will be your awakening" She smiled, her lips still pressed against mine. I nodded, "I am sorry that you died"

"It was my time" She confessed, "It is not yours, now wake up and live"

She faded before me, and as I scanned the area, the beach was vacant, and only my footprints remained as evidence that anybody was there. I knew those few words were burned into my mind.

I came to in the hospital attached to a drip and monitor, with my left arm in a plaster cast. I felt sore, but able to move. My eyes strained against the whiteness of the room, I could make out the figure next to me. It was Justin.

"Where is Ophelia?" I asked, not through concern, more through fear.

Concern crossed Justin's face, "She is in the High Dependency Unit, in a coma, she hit her head hard"

"She tried to kill me" I whispered.

Justin nodded, "Kyle and I saw it all, she attacked you and pushed you through the window.
You're lucky just to have a broken scaphoid and a concussion"
I nodded.

"The police are going to want to interview you" Justin continued, "Kyle and I told them what we saw, and the CCTV footage outside picked up the incident"

I nodded again, "I need to get to this training course"

No sooner as I had finished my sentence, two police men entered the room with a gentle knock on the door. They introduced themselves, and commenced a statement. I felt guilty as I confessed that I had failed to tell Ophelia I was going back abroad, and that I reluctantly agreed to marry her. I felt for sure that they would say I enticed her angry outburst.

They didn't. They agreed that if she came to, she would be charged with common assault. I felt no shame as I cried, and Justin held my good hand.

I was discharged from hospital the following day. I made a small detour to see her unconscious body in the High Dependency Unit, but did not stay. I wanted to be sure she was there. Unable to hurt me. I saw her face and arm covered in scratches from the glass. I smiled, and left her there. The last time I would see her. I was finally free.

I watched her for long seconds as the machine controlled her breathing, the tube that was inserted in her mouth seemed to be almost symbolic of her life with me, controlling. A nurse approached, and offered me some information on her condition. I rejected, and pretended I had the wrong room. I took one more glance, and mouthed the word bitch to her. Now hopefully she will fuck off, and be what she truly should have been. A one night stand. Goodbye you crazy bitch.

I returned to the apartment above the bar, the lap top was on the floor still, and the window was now decorated with a plastic sheet to protect from the rain outside.

First thing I did was to put all of her belongings into a plastic bag, and then took it into the city centre, donating it all to the nearest charity shop I could locate. Then I returned, and packed the remainder of my items into a suitcase, and glanced around the room one last time before walking down into the bar.

Justin and his husband Ryan were awaiting with a pint, and a farewell card as I entered the bar area.

"We will keep you a room open" Ryan smiled, as he embraced me.

"Thank you" I smiled, taking the pint in my hand, "Will you keep me informed if you hear anything about Ophelia?"

"Why do you care if she lives or dies?" Justin asked, "That crazy bitch tried to kill you"

"I don't care" I responded, "She was a one night stand that never left, but if I need to come back to testify against her, I need to know"

"Personally" Justin hissed, "I think you are better off without her, and you need to get back to Shannon and Chris and start living life in the sun again"

I smiled, as I took a long swallow of my pint, "I don't think Chris will be there, but Shannon on the other hand...."

"You'll find some other tart to bang, I am sure of it you big slut" Justin laughed, raising his glass to me one more time.

I had not been to Blackpool in some time, but it had changed when I arrived that afternoon. The last time I was there, I imagined that it would have been the traditional seaside town that I remembered as a child, but now it seemed cleaner, more modern. The crowds of people falling into and out of bars reminded me of a greyer, wetter version of Mallorca. I thought for a moment I saw Chris and Shannon in one of the bars, only on closer inspection I noticed that he was more blonde, and had blue eyes, whereas she was a brunette. They seemed perfect together.

Soon enough, I made my way into the reception area of the Hilton where a smaller group were awaiting their allocated rooms. I checked in at the reception and was directed to wait with the group.

I smiled as I sat in a vacant seat next to a very tall brunette lady, who instantly stuck her hand out to introduce herself to me as Lana Mulrooney, and I instantly picked up her Glaswegian accent.

"I met a lovely Glaswegian a while ago" I announced, remembering Daisy.

She nodded, "My cousin was a holiday rep, and she died on a training course in Mallorca, and when I turned 19 I thought to myself I am going to do what she wanted to do, and carry on her legacy"

"Daisy" I smiled, carefully before I continued, "I was there the day she died"

"You are Connor Candlish" She excitedly responded, shaking my hand again, "She spoke about you loads on Skype, and I think she had a little crush on you"

I felt myself blush, as for a brief moment I saw her once more. Lana had turned her attention to my hand, and commented on the colour of the cast. It was now purple rather than the standard issue white.

I lied to lied to her, telling her I had fallen off my bicycle. I did not really want to comment any further.

A few more people started to enter the reception, and made their way over to us, filling the small area a little more, and Lana and I continued to talk. She advised me that she too was a singer, and had wanted to sing on stage for part of the cabaret. I smiled as I thought how closely she resembled her deceased cousin.

As she continued to talk, I smiled once more, as I recognised a familiar face enter the reception. Instantly, he rushed over to me, and embraced me in his skinny arms.

"James" I laughed, excited over seeing Keith's ex-boyfriend for the first time in a long time, in fact he had left the day after Daisy died, Keith had told me on a number of times that he simply could not handle the fact someone died in his presence, "What are you doing here?"

James smiled back at me, "I regretted giving up repping, and when this opportunity came up I had to try again"

I smiled as I turned to introduce him to Lana, gently approaching the subject that she was related to Daisy. I could sense that this was uneasy. We did not have to wait long as three men in suits soon arrived, the one in front of the others smiled broadly, revealing the whitest set of teeth I have ever seen.

"Ladies and Gentlemen" He announced with the sharp smack of his hands, just once, "My name is Oliver Duncan and welcome to the Hibiscus Holidays Training course"

Oliver was not as I imagined, he was African, he even had the dreadlocks tied back, and spoke with a North London accent although I imagined him Italian if I was honest, his colleagues were soon introduced as Canadian Marcia Little and Welsh Frank Gordon. They did not say much at all. They seemed to observe us throughout the week rather than speak.

I was sharing a room with James and an extremely tall photographer called Sean, who we later found out had left his wife. I continued to tell my colleagues that I broke my wrist coming off my bike, ashamed of the truth.

The first day of training in the Lincoln Suite at the hotel was a fast track life on being a rep seminar, featuring DVD's of reps in their destinations, I smiled when Fatima from Marmaris flashed on the screen, and smiled again when I saw Olivia in the background. I had a flash back to my first meeting with her.

James, Lana and I were assigned to demonstrate good versus bad customer services, for the first day, and we arranged a few sketches during our first break. We digressed from the hotel, and located a small back street café nearby, where Lana devoured a bacon sandwich in record time, and James played with his full English breakfast. I was content with my cheese on toast and ketchup. It was warm outside, and I could see Lana's tattoo through her thin blouse, it looked like Daisy's name and her birth and death year. I was not sure.

Lana explained that she was estranged from a loveless marriage, and James confided that he split up with Keith after finding out he was sneaking off to Andrew's room during that course. They had a row whilst the whole Clare and Daisy incident was going on. I never knew this. Also, Lana confided that Clare had written to apologise for the incident, and had been sentenced to five years for causing the death. I retold my story what happened, and it seemed to give Lana a bit of peace for a moment.

We returned to the hotel soon after two, and overheard a group of other trainees discussing a night in one of the karaoke bars. I thought I would pass.

Oliver, Marcia and Frank entered the room, and took their places at the front of the room, and commenced pouring glasses of water for themselves before announcing that the session had started.

I could sense Oliver watching me, and pondered what Beverley had said to him, but also knew that she had got me the interview and knew that everything would be fine.

The sketches were presented, and I could tell the rookie from the professionals, James and I were the only ones with the understanding how being a rep worked, although in theory James had never completed his training. He still bore the knowledge.

We were the final team to present our sketch, and we received laughs for our version of bad customer service, which saw me, posing as a rep, swearing, and scratching myself, and not listening to the honeymooners, Lana and James. That concluded with me touching Lana inappropriately, much to the amusement of everyone else. The second sketch was that of good customer service, and Lana demonstrated full empathy to James' situation that he had lost his wallet. We received a rapturous applause from all, including Marcia and Frank.

"Now, Connor here has the experience of being a holiday rep" Oliver announced, and I knew what he was about to say next, "Connor was a holiday representative for another company and has joined Hibiscus Holidays after a horrific experience"

I turned to him, and shook my head, "Please, I cannot relive this"

Oliver rose from his seat, and made his way next to me as he spoke, "Being a holiday representative is not all about the alcoholic lifestyle, and sex"

His comment caused a few giggles from the youngest of the room, and I felt my shame bury itself deeper inside me, and he continued.

"Connor, I understand that your personal experience was particularly daunting, and I think personally, the voice of experience can help as a stark warning to those who think that being a rep will be easy" His hand placed itself on my shoulder, "Please can you tell the group what happened?"

I felt my head nod, and I turned to my audience. I took a swallow, and relaxed. I could sense twenty sets of eyes concentrate on me. Plus the trainers behind me.

"Ok" I sounded a little high pitched at first, and I composed myself, to restart, I felt a tear form in my eye as I started, "Being a holiday rep was a dream I had for a number of years, and I put it off for one reason or another. There were two such incidents that made it difficult. First, on my first week in training, a friend of mine, Daisy died in a freak accident. She hit her head at the bottom of the swimming pool"

I could sense I may have upset Lana, as I saw her turn away from me.

I continued, "She was a very lovely lady and I really wanted to be friends with her. She was in love with a Spanish waiter, and he was already onto his next conquest. It upset her and she attacked the other woman, but it was Daisy that died as a result of this accident, and there is not a day that goes by where I do not think about her"

The audience mumbled to themselves, as James made a confession that he too was there at the time to his neighbour.

I continued once more, "About half a dozen people left the company as a result of this, and we were offered counselling for this"

I felt the tear fall from my eye, but had to continue.

"The second incident was worse for me at least" I paused, I wanted to stop right there, but I felt the urge in me want to continue, "I was drugged on rohypnol"

I heard some of the audience gasp in horror, and my vision became blurred.

I continued, freely crying now "I was raped in the swimming pool of my own hotel"

I could not continue, as I felt Oliver guide me to my seat, where Lana placed a caring hand on my leg, whilst James offered me a tissue.

The mournful sense of sorrow crossed the room, and Oliver took the front of the room again.

"I am sorry that you have had to hear from the voice of experience in the repping industry" He explained to the room, "Connor approached us with complete honesty over his experience, and I made the decision to let him do what he loves best. I understand if some of you would be unnerved by either one of these experiences, and if you would like to see me after we can discuss if you wish to proceed with the course or not"

I heard some mumbling from the group, and I dried my eyes, noticing both Lana and James staring at me with care in their eyes.

As the sun set on day one, I felt mixed emotions to hear that only three people had left, and I watched two girls and a boy leave at pretty much the same time. The remainder of the group had gathered in the reception for their karaoke session. A tall bald man approached Lana and I as we waited for James, I remembered his name as Dave from induction, he was from Ireland.

"I thought about what you said in there" He smiled, probably through concern, or maybe even confusion how to speak to a male rape victim more like, "I wish you would consider coming to karaoke tonight, I heard that you are quite singer"

"Thanks" I smiled, karaoke is not really what singers like doing, we need our own music, and I missed that, "But I really don't feel like being gregarious if you know what I mean"

He nodded, and returned to the group, which now included James, who had decided to go along last minute.

Lana and I made our way to the beach, and ate fish and chips out of a newspaper, in the cool night air, watching the party-goers enjoy their evening.

Suddenly, I felt her hand against my thigh again.

"I think this may be some sort of destiny" She smiled, "With you knowing Daisy, and being a former rep, and being there on that day.... I want to request Turkey with you"

"I have to tell you something" I confessed, "I have a girlfriend who will be in Turkey"

"And I don't want any sort of sexual encounter with another man for as long as I can" She laughed, "I am pleased that you are my friend Connor that is all"

I felt myself blush again, which she noticed, and took the moment to steal another one of my now cold chips.

"Ok, but the reason I have asked for Turkey is because I need to confront the bitch who stole my medical records and made me lose my job" I smiled.

"Turkey is massive, there is no guarantee you will get the same resort" She smiled.

"Marmaris, I insist" I smiled.

Her hand tightened on my hand, "Revenge isn't always about making the other person pay for whatever they did"

"I know" I responded, "But I have to make Sian confess to what she did" "Just so you know" She responded, "I will help you"

EIGHTEEN

The evening ended as quick as it began, with Lana and I falling asleep on the beach, awaking only when it started to rain gently soon after 3am. Together we raced back to the hotel, and into the foyer, which was silent this time of the day. Even the night porter was sleeping as we raced through the reception area toward the elevator.

I kissed her goodnight on the lips as she got out on the second floor, and I continued to the third. The corridor was eerily silent as I walked along the dimly lit carpeted runway, and felt for the key card in my pocket. I held my breath as I heard the gentle click of the door latch, and opened the door. I could hear the gentle snore from both of my roommates. Sean was hugging his pillow, and muttering something in his sleep, James was completely under his cover, with just his toe poking out from the far corner. I quietly entered the bathroom, and sat alone on the loo, and I smiled as my penis started to awaken. I pulled down my trousers, and clasped the shaft in my hand.

Tugging hard for long moments, I imagined my own personal X-rated movie in my mind. I often thought of Chris and Shannon together, this time, Lana was there, I could not get over how much she reminded me of Daisy. The eyes, the fringe, I could not really put my finger on it. I felt the orgasmic sensation as I stroked the hardness of my cock, starting off slow, and smooth.

I imagined Lana before me, just standing there, smiling, I soon gained rhythm, and began to speed up my pace, in a motion that I was accustomed to, she suddenly became Shannon, seductively dancing before me, Chris was behind her. I felt the heat of my own pre-cum would soon seep into my palm in the dim light of the bathroom, I shafted myself knowing my own movements. I glanced down at my own manhood, I felt the familiar tingle inside my loins, and at that moment I felt that urge of spasm, I struggled to remain stationary, and in synchronisation to my hand movement I felt my juices release, and I bit my own lip as I tried to stifle my moan, I felt the sensation diminish as I allowed my mess to cover my hand.

In the dim light, I smiled at the glistening goo in my hand, and rose, tucking myself back inside, I left the bathroom, and climbed into my bed.

"Dirty bastard" Sean mumbled.

I smiled to myself as I pulled the cover over my body, and thought, did he see me?

He did. He let me know the following morning that he had got up to use to toilet and I was in there hand over fist. I hid my blushes as we entered the Lincoln Suite. I smiled at Lana as she sat opposite me, and yawned.

The remainder of the week, to me flew by, and as the final day loomed, we learned that only one person had failed the course, a girl names Tara, who disappeared before breakfast. We all waited nervously outside the Lincoln Suite awaiting for our names to be called. Lana had already been in and was pleased that she had been accepted into Turkey with James and Sean, getting ready to go in March next year. In the meantime she and James would be on cabin crew work until the season started. I felt nervous when the door opened, I knew that it was my time, Marcia and Frank were in other rooms calling for their staff, and I smiled as the Irish girl Debs got called just before me.

"Good luck" She smiled.

"You too" I responded, knowing that she and Sean had been making out throughout this week.

I nodded as I pushed open the door. Oliver looked tiny across the room as I allowed the door close behind me.

He greeted me like an old friend as he rose to welcome me to the room, pushing out a chair in front of him.

He lit a suspicious looking cigarette before me, and offered me a smoke, I refused on the pretence that I did not smoke, and I was pleased with this decision as I smelt the hashish in the air.

"I like you Connor" He responded, "And I know that you have asked for Turkey, Marmaris in particular for a reason"

I nodded, trying to ignore the weed.

"Vendetta can be a dangerous game in the world of repping, and Sian and Andrew won't be an easy challenge, I mean, you know that they are uncle and niece?" He asked.

I did not know this as they seemed so different, I thought I would try a gentle lie, "I want to go there because my girlfriend is there next season"

Oliver laughed, "When I was in your shoes, my dick would be in as many bitches I could. I would lick the pussy and leave every one of them wanting more. Connor, why do you want this ginger minge more than any other woman?"

"I love her" I responded.

He smiled, and nodded, "I know all about your career and you are good, I think you will do well in Marmaris, I know you have the gift of the gab, and you can sell ice to the Eskimos? I am right aren't I?"

"Yes sir" I don't know where that came from.

"I should make you ride my cock for letting you get your own way" He spoke with serious in his face, with a pause that to me, lasted an eternity, before he broke it with a laugh.

I joined in the laugh.

"It's all about the pussy" He urged, "I think you want Turkey so you can get your dick sucked by that yank Olivia... and you will no doubt hit that, but if I give you Turkey, I want you to do me the biggest favour"

"What is that?" I asked.

"I will give you Turkey" He leaned in closer, breathing in the drag from his joint, "And you do one season in The Gambia for me, turn the fucker around, make some moolah, and get the fat faggot I have in charge there off his ass to work for me"

He leaned back and blew a perfect circle of smoke, as his eyes remained fixated on me. "Can you do that for me?" He asked.

"The Gambia?" I asked, "Where the fuck is that?"

He laughed, "West Africa, the white ivory coast, I guarantee you the horniest, juiciest pussy you can get your hands on, you go out there, and show them bitches that you are the future of Hibiscus Holidays, and I will give you Marmaris for next season"

I nodded, as I extended my hand, "Deal, and I promise you I will make this the best season you have ever had"

He shook my hand with his firm shake, and tossed the joint into the paper cup before him, "I know you lied to my black ass about not wanting revenge, but I hope for your own sake you teach that Scouse whore a lesson, I think you should pound her pussy so hard she can't walk, make her scream her apology to you brother"

I sensed the seriousness in his voice.

"So when do I start?" I asked.

"I can get you out there in two to three weeks, leave it with me" He smiled, "Sean will be coming with you"

NINETEEN

Within minutes I managed to get online in the privacy of my room, and Shannon was ecstatic over the revelation. She too had recently heard that she was successful on getting Marmaris next season, but was returning back home to Scotland for the winter season. There was still no news on Chris. She ended her Skype with a nipple flash, and I knew that I was getting horny just wanting to be with her. Or Olivia, who if I was honest, I had not really thought of much, but the thought of her lips on my dick again was something I wished for. Then I thought of Lana, in those tight jeans she seemed to like wearing, and once more, all she did was stand there smiling at me, I released my cock from its prison, and felt my hand slide gently down the shaft, as I opened a file on my broken laptop.

I opened the images of Alcudia, and smiled at some of the pictures before me. Sian had somehow made it into some of the pictures, and Kellie too. Also there was the old slapper with an alcohol problem lurking in some pictures, we called her Grace, but her name could have been Mavis, or Gretel, no one knew. She was pretty in an unpretty way. There was now a picture of Chris and I in our shorts, a picture that Shannon took. We had our arms around each other, and I realised that my pace and grip began to quicken, I did not care that Sean or James could return any second now.

I felt my dick harden more in my hand, and I had to pull down my jeans, so that I could allow my balls to slap against my own flesh, otherwise I would never cum.

I closed my eyes for a moment, and frantically tugged at my own meat. I muttered all of their names in a moment of fantasy, unaware of my surroundings.

"I knew it" James smiled from the doorway. How long had he been there?

Before I knew it, he was next to me, his hand reaching for my throbbing member.

His hand felt weird against my erect penis, as he stroked gently down the shaft with his steady movement.

"I knew you and Chris were onto something" He announced, moments before taking my cock entirely in his mouth.

I did not want to touch him, I allowed him to suck me, and tried not to listen to his groans of pleasure. I let out a moan as I felt him pull away for a moment, whilst he admired me, my cock quivered with his suck, He moved away, and as he worked his way to my tip, caressing my dick with loving lashes, I gripped his head, forcing him to take the entire length.

One of his fingers wanted to search for my anus, trying, and failing to enter it. I began to mouth fuck him, up and down, he gagged, but continued. My pubic hair was sodden with his saliva, as he looked up at me for a moment, his hands gripping onto my outer thighs, and his groans of passion became muffled by my thrusts deeper into his throat.

My groans soon became intense, as I felt the crescendo of that point of no return, my penis twitched frantically inside, and as the funny little quiver sent my semen out of me, into him, I watched as he swallowed, and waited for me to go soft inside his mouth.

As he rose afterwards, he smiled, "I waited all week for that"

I laughed as I tucked myself back into my pants, "I got The Gambia"

"Lucky you" He smiled, as he started to throw his clothes into his suitcase.

"Do you want me to return the favour?" I asked, unaware of what to ask in this situation.

"I'm alright" He confessed, "I just had Oliver, swallow my jizz, I don't think I have anything left"

I laughed, and closed the bathroom door behind me, taking off my clothes, and stepping into the hot steaming water. I sighed a sense of relief as I heard him leave moments later.

And so, that evening, we all said our farewells, James and Sean had already left by the time I got to the foyer, we had all added each other to our social media, and Sean and I had already made arrangements to get together before we left, and Lana was awaiting her taxi. Together, we sat on the curb outside the hotel, simply chatting about stupid things.

"What are you going to do until you go on the airline?" I eventually asked.

She shrugged, "Course starts in two weeks, so I am thinking, get drunk, and file for divorce"

I placed my arm around her, and pulled her closer, "Then why don't you and I stay here for a few days?"

"Really?" She questioned.

"Yes" I responded, "I still have my inheritance, and even if we stay just this weekend we can have a little fun"

She smiled, "I would like that, but we have to stay in a cheap and nasty B and B just for the experience"

"Done" I smiled.

"And you will win" She responded. "What?" I responded.

She smiled, "That bitch rep, her downfall will be your awakening"

"Why did you say that?" I asked confused, knowing that I had heard it somewhere before, and then I recalled the dream after Ophelia had attacked me. Daisy had told me that. Surely this was impossible.

"I dreamt it" She confessed, "I saw Daisy on a beach somewhere, and she told me to say this.... I meant to tell you earlier"

I smiled, and remembered Daisy once more.

We found a small two bed roomed bed and breakfast near the Central Pier, we could see the tower through the tiny window. Lana had gone to the shower, which was across the hallway. I searched through my suitcase for my phone charger, as my phone had died earlier in the day. I waited impatiently as the green battery highlighted that a charge was taking place, and it slowly charged to one percent.

I used my thumb to switch the phone on, and waited. I could hear Lana in the shower two doors away, singing a random song, words mismatched and everything. I smiled to myself.

My screen flickered on, and I flicked through the messages that appeared, Justin had messaged me three times, but some other messages came through forcing his messages lower on my screen.

Automatically, the call back service I had set up for voice mail kicked in, and I answered the phone immediately.

"Why didn't you wake me up?" Her voice croaked down the phone, and I felt an instant fear shoot through me, I stared at the vacant screen, as she continued, I heard her moan a little, "You left me lying here in hospital, and now I am lying here naked, all alone, without you.... I am touching myself as I think of you....My vagina feels empty without you inside me, and I have this aching feeling deep inside me, wanting you. I know I get wet as I think of your man meat inside me, and those butterflies are back in my chest have gone straight into my pussy, and the heat is intense, I want to extinguish it, sending electric shocks through my body, I want to feel you grind against me, I could die happily with you pinning down, kissing me.... grinding.... you and I Connor are the perfect match and I would not want it any other way, I will have you again"

The voice mail closed with the time and date of the recording, 18.37 today. Frantically I searched my messages again, and located Justin's messages.

The first one startled me.

"She's out" It read, I read his next message, "The police can't charge her, she has claimed insanity"

I panicked, as I loaded the next message. "I am coming to get you, Ophelia"

My hands shook as I removed the back of the phone, and pulled out the sim card.

"Is everything ok?" Lana smiled, as she returned to the room, in a towelled dressing gown, "You look like you have seen a ghost"

I smiled, and placed the sim card into my pocket, "Phone is broke, I think I dropped it earlier"

That evening, Lana and I celebrated our week of training in the karaoke bar, and I conveniently left the sim card in a broken pile on a bar on the promenade. Lana was singing a fast number, which surprised me for her, but the men in the room really took to her, and I could tell that she was enjoying the attention. Her soon to be ex-husband must have been some sort of cock to let her go.

I really did not want to compare her to Daisy, but the similarity was remarkable. I felt comfortable as she joined me with a young Welsh man that introduced himself as Cameron, or something similar, the accent was too thick. I made my excuses, so that I could use the bathroom, which was situated upstairs. I narrowly avoided the aftershave salesman who had perched himself near the sink, whether to ensure we were washing our hands after our piss, or to perve. One of the two. I took a small sample of some exotic sample, then pretended I had left my wallet with my wife at the bar, promising him I will be back shortly.

As I opened the door, I saw a familiar face before me, and did not know whether I wanted to laugh, or hide. Old Grace stood before me, with her toothless smile. The same old one I remembered from Mallorca.

"I knew I recognised that arse" She smiled, gently touching my arm.

"Fancy seeing you here?" I commented, "I thought you would still be in the sun in Mallorca"

She began to get dangerously close to me, "I had to fly back to Lancashire for a family funeral, and I don't go back for another week, so I thought I would come back to my old haunts"

"I am on holiday" I lied, "I have to get back to my friends" "You do know that I have something for you?" She asked.

I froze with fear, as I felt her hand inch closer to my groin, "I really have to go" "I think you will like what I have to offer" She announced.

"Grace, I am sorry" I began, before I realised this may not even be her name.

She laughed, "I used to know a Grace, she was the bike of Benidorm, but my heart was in such a younger resort, so I went to Mallorca for the fun and the young spunk, and honey, tonight it's your lucky night"

"I am sorry, I am with someone now" I lied again.

Her hand now rested on my penis, "Now are you on about the red headed Scottish lass from Alcudia? The lad, or the bimbo downstairs?"

"Please" I urged.

"You do know that Sian is my Granddaughter?" She continued, as though part of an on-going conversation.

I was silenced.

A smile crossed her leather face, as she stared into my eyes, "She gave me some documents to destroy, and I may just have them in my hotel room"

"Documents?" I questioned.

"The ones that exonerate you over your little pool party fiasco" She continued, "Maybe you can come and pleasure me, and in return I will pass you the documents and tell the spoilt little whore I destroyed them as per her request"

I swallowed, and nodded.

"Good" She smiled, as she withdrew her key card, "I will be ready and waiting for your knob in ten minutes. I promise you the documents"

I nodded, as she leaned forward, planting a kiss on my lips, I cringed, and accepted her mouth for a moment.

She turned, and walked down the staircase, as I paused for a moment, thankful that no one saw this. I saw another shadow on the wall downstairs, it moved as I did and I realised I could be in and out quickly, so decided to tell Lana a little white lie. I found her in the same place as I had left her, the Welsh man was laughing at her jokes, and I knew this would be easy.

She raised her head, "You were gone for some time"

"Sorry, I realised I was out of money when I went to tip the perfume guy, I really need to find a cash point" I lied, "Are you going to be ok here for half an hour?"

She blushed, as Cameron smiled back at her, "I will be fine" "I have not got my phone, so please stay here" I smiled.

The rain was quite heavy as I raced through the back of the karaoke bar, I knew that Grace's hotel was not far, I could see the fluorescent sign as I turned away from the central pier.

I quickly entered the hotel that resembled an end terrace of sorts, and ran up the threadbare staircase. I saw her room just metres away, and inhaled deeply, as I inserted the key card into the slot.

The door opened loudly, and I bit my bottom lip as I entered.

She lay on her back on the bed, waiting, naked, her body was firm for her age, and without a change of mannerism, she opened her thighs, and I could see her aged shaven quim before me.

"Before I do this" I muttered, "I need to know you have what I want"

"On the table" She gestured, without raising her head, "Why don't you get your dick hard, and show me what I missed in Mallorca?"

I glanced at the paperwork on the table, and could see my name clearly on it, with some Spanish writing on it. I could just make out the diagnosis, and smiled, "I need a condom"

"I am not getting pregnant baby" She smiled, as she stroked the length of her pussy with her finger, "Everything in there died a long time ago"

I nodded, as I unbuttoned my wet jeans, and released my cock from my boxers, already hard.

My shirt open, but on, I held my member in my hand.

I clambered onto the bed, and allowed my tip to rub neatly against her receptive opening, and she reached around, clasping my arse cheeks, pulling me closer, I entered her with ease, it felt loose as I entered her clefts, and she started to writhe. I soon maintained equilibrium and started to pump hard into her.

"I may cum quick" I warned, as she clenched hard onto my pounding member.

"It's been so long since I had cock, I could not care if you cum in a minute or an hour" She urged, "Feel my tits"

I leaned forward, still pumping hard, losing concentration for a second, as I felt my head press against her saggy mounds of flesh, my teeth searched longingly for a nipple, eventually finding it soft and off putting. I thought for a moment of Lana before me, I wanted my erection to last long enough to shoot without her thinking I faked it.

I licked her areola and bit into it, causing her to yelp a little with pain, and I stopped, before she forced my head back to the same spot.

I felt her hand move down my body, it clasped at my cock as it pushed inside her, and she stroked her clitoris, her hand touching my dick every time I pushed in.

Once more, Lana lay before me, not this old hag, but I needed that paperwork, and I had to cum. For some reason, Sian came into my mind, and I could see her enjoying my fucking. That helped.

She could sense I was about to shoot. I tensed, to deliver my semen into her depths, she arched her back, and groaned as her vagina held me tight, but I held back. I feigned the ejaculation and quickly withdrew before I could release my fluid.

She sighed deeply as she collapsed back on the bed. "Thank you" I whispered.

She muttered something to me, as I pulled on my jeans again, I smelt of sex and shame, I spotted some aftershave on her table.

"May I? "I asked.

She used her hand to wave it off, I accepted this as a yes, so I sprayed my crotch and surrounding area with it, before covering my body in the spray. I grabbed the paper work, and smiled at her, as she lay motionless on the bed. Revealing her mossy bank for all and sundry.

"I am off now" I whispered.

She did not respond. I decided to pocket the aftershave too, and made my way to the door. "I will take the key with me" I smiled, "In case I want to come back"

She remained silent, and I felt my dick begin to press hard against the denim again. For an older bird she really was not as saggy as I thought. I opened the door, and made my way down the staircase, and back into the pouring rain.

I made my way back to the bar, I felt myself cum as I walked, the friction between my cock and jeans gave me a sensation of pleasure, and without touching myself, I felt the orgasm I should have had a few minutes ago incur in my pants, I bit my bottom lip as I felt the liquid drip down my leg, and around my balls. I felt the aftershave in my hand, and sprayed again, and I noticed the key card still in my hand. I spotted a trash can close by.

"Goodbye Gracey" I whispered, as I posted it through the slit, into the darkness beyond.

I smiled, as I saw the karaoke bar before me, and entered through the back door again, as Lana and Cameron were doing another duet on the microphones.

I raised my eyebrows at them in acknowledgement as I approached the bar, and ordered our drinks. I smiled as I felt the paperwork in my pocket.

The night continued with the three of us, Cameron had left his friends to come with us to a newly opened drag bar called Murtis on the North Shore. We were wet as we entered the overly bright bar, greeted with a random insult from the female impersonator behind a DJ box.

We celebrated our night, drinking, and dancing, Cameron and I even had a strip of down to our pants for a dare from the drag queen. I stopped at a seductive bend, as I pretended to pull my boxers down, only Cameron went on to actually fully remove his pants, and toss them into the audience.

Needless to say, he won the strip off, and the drag queen treated him to a bottle of cheap wine.

Meanwhile, Lana and I danced to forget the image we just witnessed.

We were aware soon enough, that the sun began to rise outside, Cameron had fallen asleep in our booth.

"You really like him?" I questioned.

She shook her head, "It's nice to have the attention"

"I would give you more than attention" I smiled, as I leaned in closer.

I did not wait, and pressed my lips against hers for a moment, she paused, before continuing with a lingering kiss.

"Can we go back now?" She whispered, barely pulling away from my lips.

I nodded, thinking back to earlier in the evening. "But I will need a shower first"

Like naughty children, we quietly left the table, and left Cameron snoozing with his bottle of wine. And we left.

The rain had stopped as we crossed the road to our hotel. I glanced down the road back to the hotel where Grace had stayed as we turned a corner, and saw the flashing blue lights outside. Several people had gathered as the paramedics bought out a stretcher, with a blanket covering the face of someone that had passed away during the night.

"Looks like we have missed some fun" I tried to jest.

"Wow" Lana gasped, as we neared the ambulance.

The blanket covering the face blew gently in the breeze, and lifted it enough off the face, and I felt sick.

Grace was under there, I only saw her for a second, but I recognised her instantly.

The paramedics were carelessly talking to each other about her, and I felt ashamed as one of them referred to her as an "Old slapper who had taken an overdose"

Hauntingly, I watched as they closed the doors to the ambulance, and I felt the paperwork once more in my pocket. I knew I was in that room.

"Such a shame" A voice spoke behind me. I turned on my heels, and faced her.

"You" I whispered.

TWENTY

The tension between Ophelia and I must have been obvious to anyone, Lana released her grip from my hand, and seemed to take a step backwards.

"I need to talk to you about something" Ophelia announced, as though Lana was not there, "I tried to call you, but it seems your phone is off?"

"I lost my phone, and I don't think I have anything to say to you" I announced through clenched teeth, "The last time I saw you...."

She interrupted, "I was not a well woman, and I am sorry for what I did, but please Connor, I need to talk to you in private, please allow me just five minutes"
She seemed sincere, and I turned to Lana, "This is an old friend of mine"

"I am tired, and I need some sleep" Lana smiled without acknowledging Ophelia.

"Can we meet later?" I asked, "We have had a long day"

Ophelia nodded, "Ok, let's meet tomorrow morning, on the Central Pier.... about ten?"

With no further provocation, she walked past me, and I watched as she disappeared around the same corner that we had just turned.

"Who was she?" Lana asked.

"Long story" I responded, "Bad news"

Within minutes we were back at the hotel, and Lana took to her bed, barely speaking she pulled up her blanket over her head, and asked me to switch the light out, and close the curtains. I did, and then left the room for a shower. I stripped in the bathroom, locking the door behind me. The steam from the water misted up the mirror immediately, and I allowed the warmth to envelope me. I wasted no time in rubbing the shower gel into my hair, and over my smooth body, washing the dirt I felt off me. The water seemed a grey colour as it circled the drain by my feet.

I felt myself weep a moment, I was not sure if I cried for old Grace, or that Ophelia was back. It could have possibly been that only a short time ago, I was about to sleep with Lana, and now it seemed a pipe dream.

Moments later, I embraced myself with an overly large towel, and made my way still wet back to the room, my body made a silhouette against the curtain, and I dried, not caring that Lana was still in the room, and still slightly moist, I clambered into my own single bed, and allowed the coolness of the sheet to press against my body. I closed my eyes, and fell straight to sleep.

I awoke about an hour later, I turned to face the vacant bed opposite, and sighed, as I realised I was not sleeping any more today. I swung my legs over the bed, and quickly dressed in fresh clothes. Moments later, Lana returned to the room having freshened herself up with a shower herself.

"Sleep well?" She smiled.

I nodded, "I need some coffee"

"Me too" She smiled, as she showed no fear of releasing the towel before me, her pert breasts made my penis awaken, my eyes widened a little, "I was thinking, let's do all things touristy today"

"Yes" I nodded, my eyes fixated on her boobs, and yet she remained unaware, care-freely dressing before me in a tight fitting tee-shirt, and jeans torn at the knee and just below the buttocks line.

"I have never done the tower, or the fair" She smiled, as she tied her hair back in a bun with ease, "So, can we?"

"Sure" I nodded, as I raised, aware that I was erect, but luckily, my shirt fell over the front of my jeans, and I took her hand.

Together we walked out of the room, to all and sundry we must have seemed an ideal young couple on holiday.

The day was filled with the tourist agenda. After a mug of tepid coffee in a back street café, we made our way up to the tower. The glass floor had Lana screaming in fear as I tried to hide my own worry. Soon after we went to the dungeons below, and enjoyed our guide placing me in a torture chair for fun, and then she herself got accused of witchcraft in a mock court.

We laughed throughout the day, and enjoyed a tram ride down to the South Pier. It took me a while to persuade her to have a go on the bungee ball, and her screams deafened me as we shot in the air. I bought the DVD of the event, before we enjoyed the remainder of the day on the Pleasure Beach, eating hot dogs, and candy floss in between rides.

Throughout, we held hands. I longed to kiss her again, but something did not seem right.

As the sun began to lower in the horizon, we walked slowly along the beach front towards our hotel. We saw Cameron walk past with the same friends that he neglected last night. She blushed as she pretended not to notice him, but it was too late. He seemed annoyed at us for some reason.

We returned to our hotel shortly before one the following morning, and with a friendly peck on the lips, Lana turned her back to me, as she undressed, and clambered into her bed alone. I sighed, and silently moved to my suitcase that was tossed carelessly on the floor. I stared for a moment at the stolen paperwork, and smiled.

"She's your ex fiancé" Lana announced from the bed.

I knew that she was talking about my forthcoming meeting with Ophelia, I nodded, as I perched on the edge of her bed, "She's part of my past, and I don't want to see her"

"She said that she was not a well woman, what did she mean?" She questioned.

"She attacked me" I wanted to spare her the details, "I will meet her in the morning, to hear what she has to say, and then I am rid of her"

"So" Lana smiled, moistening her lips, "You don't love her?"

"I never did" I assured, "She was meant to be a one night stand, and she never went away"

"I can't figure you out" She muttered, I could tell lethargy was setting in.

I decided not to respond, and rose.

"You say you never loved her, but you also have Shannon and that man in Mallorca" She continued, "Yet you told me how much you liked Daisy and me?"

"It's complicated" I responded.

"I think I will go back to Scotland tomorrow morning" She responded, "I would have slept with you, but I have now seen a different side of you"

Words began to fail me, and I removed my shirt, and jeans, before climbing underneath my sheets.

"I will pay you back for today" She continued, "I wish I had gone with Cameron"

I closed my eyes to shut her out, and silently wept.

The alarm on my new phone went off soon after eight the following morning, and Lana was already gone.

Naked, I crouched at the paperwork in the suitcase, and slowly read the Spanish notes, it made no sense to me, I could barely make out my own name in the scrawl.

I dressed in the same jeans and shirt from last night, and used Grace's spray once more, before I turned to the vacant bed on the other side of the room. I noticed a piece of paper folded neatly on the pillow. Cautiously, I moved closer to her bed, it still smelt of her sweetness, my hands shook as I reached for it.

It opened neatly in my hand, as I read, "Dear Connor, I am sorry I cannot stay, I am sure that you are genuinely nice, but I cannot forgive you. You should be in Mallorca with Shannon, and not in a back street hotel with me. I don't think I will accept the job and I will care about you, and thank you for being there for Daisy. Kind regards, Lana. Xx"

I folded the paper back in half, and threw it into the metal bin near the door, and I pulled the door closed behind me.

I finished breakfast in minutes, and as I stepped into the sun, I felt sorrow in my heart that I was not with Lana. Glancing at the time on my phone, I made my way to the promenade, and still surprised over the lack of tourists in the area, the entrance to the Central Pier appeared in view.

The wooden board walk had gaps between them, and I could see the brown ocean below. The staff on the game stores tried to entice me into playing their stall, which I brushed aside. The bar at the end of the pier was cool as I entered, and a young man at the bar welcomed me with a smile. I ordered a lager and a vodka and tonic for Ophelia, and I went outside, perching myself on a table overlooking the length of the pier, and waited.

I drank her drink as well, and had got through another three pints before she arrived, late. She smiled as she made her way to me, and cupped her hand around the vodka and tonic. I noticed she still had abrasions to her face, and arms. She made no effort to cover them. With her denim jacket sleeves rolled up to reveal.

"We said ten o'clock" I responded, glancing at the phone to see that it was after 11.30.

"I said about ten" She remembered, "And I have been watching you for a long time, it took me all my time to pluck up the courage to come over to you"

"You said you wanted to talk" I announced, "Then talk"

"Firstly, I wanted to apologise over my behaviour, when I threw you out of your window" She announced, "But I think that I have more than made up for that"

Shocked, I laughed, "By leaving me that crazy message about why didn't I wake you up?"

She smiled, "The nurse told me a very hot looking young man came to see me, and I knew it was you"

"You're sick" I retaliated, "I don't even know why I am here"

"You're here because you know you have to listen to what I have to say" She insisted, "Now be a good boy, and get me another drink"

"Why should I?" I retaliated, taking the largest mouthful of lager I could muster.

"Because I know for a fact you went back with that old cow the other night" She smiled, playing with the lemon slice in her drink, "Bit of a strange coincidence that she died after you fucked her, don't you think?"

Fear shot through me, "Tell me what you know" "Drink first" She smiled, "Conversation after"

Nervously, I rose, and made my way back to the bar, the same man served me again, and those few moments seemed to last an eternity.

By the time I returned, she was half way down a cigarette, and waiting. She made a show of opening her legs, showing me her mossy hill in the process, and she smiled as she noticed my groin twitch a little.

"Talk" I insisted, pushing her the drink closer to her.

She took her time, taking a savouring sip from her drink, "I remembered your dates of training, and location, and I knew you would stay on once you saw a piece of pussy you liked. All I needed to do was find you and like I said, all I wanted to do was to talk over what happened"

I raised my eyebrow, "I accept your apology"

"I found you" She continued, neglecting my comment, "I got here about half past four on Friday night, and I saw you with that girl in the karaoke bar. I was going to come up to you then but I saw you with the old woman. Kissing her on that staircase, it disgusted me"

I thought back and remembered seeing the shadow on the wall. I shuddered. The image started to play through my mind.

"I followed you back to her hotel, and knew that you were in there putting your dick into her ancient cavern, and I waited outside" She continued. "I was going to talk to you outside but you left so quick, I followed you back and saw you dump the key card in the bin. So I decided to pay her a visit"

"So you killed her?" I questioned, "You hurt Jayne, and now you killed...."

"I did not kill anyone" She insisted, "I made my way back to her room, and she was weeping on her bed when I went in. I told her I was married to you and she confessed that she was lonely"

"We are not married" I insisted. She laughed, "I know that silly"

She paused, as she took another drink out of her glass. "What did you do?" I urged.

"I owe you so much" She whispered, I felt that she was beginning to weaken, "I know you never loved me, but I had to make it right. She told me that she had given you those medical records from Mallorca, She told me that she was lonely since her husband died, and she was living out her life as they used to. In the sun, hanging around with youngsters. She told me she was ready to leave. So I handed her the tablets from her bag, and sat with her whilst she took them"

"You gave her the tablets" I muttered.

"And I cleaned the room to ensure none of your finger prints were in the room. She told me you did not ejaculate in her so I knew you would be safe that way" She continued, "It was just pure luck you were walking past when they found her"

"How did they find her?" I asked.

She smiled, and finished her drink, "Can I have another?"

I nodded, as I took a sip from mine.

"I made a call to the police, and then threw my phone away" She confessed, "I did this all for you"

"Thank you" I smiled.

She allowed the tears that she was holding back to fall.

"I appreciate your help" I smiled, as I stroked her hand.

"Can I have a hug?" She asked.

I nodded, and walked around the table to her, embracing her. "I still love you" She cried, "And I know I can't have you"

I did not want to answer that comment, I rocked her body, swaying momentarily. "Please give me one more chance" She sobbed.

"I cannot" I whispered soothingly.

I felt her nod, "Ok, can I have that drink then at least?"

"Sure" I nodded, and released my grip around her.

I smiled at her as I walked past her, back to my drink, taking the final swallow, as she composed herself, "I will always care you for"

I realised I was repeating the lines from Lana's letter at that point, and smiled.

"Thank you" She smiled.

I turned my back on her, and entered the bar once more. The same man smiled at me, gently stroking my hand as he accepted my cash, I smiled back at him.

"I finish at five if you're interested" He flirted.

I winked, and smiled back, tipping him, "I may be"

As I walked back into the sunshine, Ophelia was gone. I scanned the area, expecting to see her walking along the pier.

"Goodbye Connor" She called, "Her name was Hillary by the way, not Grace"

I span on my heels, almost dropping the glasses from my hands, as I saw her at the far end of the pier, standing on the benches.

"I forgive you" She whispered, as she clambered onto the end of the pier.

Without a second thought, she dropped over the edge before I could reach her. I leaned over the edge, and spotted her denim jacket dancing wilfully along the waves.

"Ophelia" I screamed, attracting the attention of the few people nearby.

TWENTY ONE

Ophelia was reported missing, and searches were implemented immediately. Her denim jacket was retrieved and taken away, and I was interviewed by the police. CCTV had seen that we were talking before her leap of faith. She even hit the local news, her image was plastered on the screen, and I was interviewed over our last moments. I told them about her attacking me, and hunting me down, and how I forgave her, but I omitted the part about Hillary.

As soon as I was free to go, I drank the rest of the day away, in different bars on the Golden Mile, enjoying my freedom. I really wanted Lana here, but I kept thinking of Ophelia disappearing. Those last moments kept replaying in my mind. Even late that afternoon, from the same pier, I watched a police boat out in the Irish Sea searching for her.

My feet made the hardest sound on the wood floor as I walked, unsteadily back along the pier, and onto the promenade.

There seemed to be more people in the resort now, maybe the news had attracted them to the place. I had no idea.

I remembered what she had said about Hillary, and how she had cleaned up after me, still uncertain if she was telling the truth, but she did know a lot about that night. I decided that I was going to make my last night in Blackpool one to remember. Starting with more beer, and some fun.

Entering the karaoke bar, the barman from two nights ago acknowledged me, and commenced pouring my lager. I sang one of my token tunes, and relished in the applause from the minimal crowd. I noticed Cameron and his friends had entered halfway through my song. Cameron seemed embarrassed to see me, probably still angry at Lana and I walking out on him.

I waited at the bar to be served again, as he approached me just minutes later.

"Cannot believe you two abandoned me" He whispered, clearly annoyed, and avoiding eye contact.

"We were tired" I defended.

"You made me look like an absolute bell-end" He retaliated, getting the attention of a barmaid.

"Sorry" I whispered.

He turned back to face me, "To see you both last night fucking hurt me, I had to tell my friends that I had my way and left you, instead you embarrass me by letting me awaken in a gay bar with some tranny trying to get in my pants"

"You were teasing him all night" I defended, as the barmaid passed him his pint, plus an extra one for me.

"I did it so that I can get into your friends knickers" He responded, as he pushed me a pint closer to my hand, "And maybe yours"

I smiled, as I took a sip out of the glass, "I don't fuck on a first date anymore"

"Technically, this is date two...." He whispered, and I sensed his erection form in his trousers, "Drink up and we can go back to my hotel"

We were kissing as we entered his hotel room soon after, and the sun was just setting outside.

He was clawing at my shirt, unbuttoning it carelessly, kissing at my pierced nipples with his wet mouth, leaving behind a string of saliva as he pulled away.

He threw me passionately onto the bed, as he eagerly removed his shirt, and belt to his trousers. He stepped out of them expertly, as I too undressed, down to my shorts.

He slithered along my body, concentrating on my smooth chest with his lips, as his hands wandered down into my pants, clasping firmly onto my stiff dick, pulling back painfully hard, as I removed my pants slowly.

His wet lips now touched mine, and forced my hand to his own member, I clasped it nervously, and began to mimic his movements on my own penis. He was groaning something into my mouth as his tongue darted into mine, as I began to feel my balls tightening, and I knew that my own pre-cum was about to escape. No sooner as I did, I felt him groan into my mouth and I felt the familiar wetness from his bulbous head spill into my hand.

"I want you to be my bitch" He whispered, almost aggressively.

I did not respond, I just wanted to shoot my load, and quick. I could feel the speed of his wanking fluctuate between fast and slow, and I urged him by thrusting my hips to aide his movement.

He pulled away and stared into my eyes, and I felt the point of no return escalate in my loins, as did he. We shot our hot semen at the same time, and we both let out loud groans of passion.

His hand remained firm on my softening member as he bucked, and allowed his juice to spurt a little more over my stomach.

"You have to go" His hand still clasping onto me, "And this never happened" "Fine by me" I whispered.

I pulled my cock out of his hand and grabbed my clothes.

He dropped onto his bed, his naked arse glistened with the perspiration of his own passion, and I dressed quickly.

He smiled at me as he closed his eyes, and for a moment, I remembered Hillary. I spotted his antiperspirant on the bedside, and I sprayed myself, concentrating on my groin area.

"Thank you" He whispered, as he drifted off.

I could not help but smile as I pulled open the door, and made my way back to the night life of Blackpool.

I left Blackpool the following morning, having liaised with the police about where I would be living in case there were any questions needed over Ophelia. As the coach pulled out of the open air coach station, I watched out to the ocean once more, and thought of her. I hated her for having this spell over me.

September 30th

The following few weeks went by in a blur, with police coming and going from my room at the bar, and I slowly accepted that Ophelia was gone. I know I never loved her, but I only wanted her to leave me alone, and not to kill herself. The lack of a body meant that her family could not bury her, or grieve for her. I did not even know anything about her family. Shannon also was no longer in touch. She was due to return to Manchester earlier in the week, but she was not on the flight, and her number was now dead. She had also removed herself from Social Media.

I had received my flight details earlier that week and was due to leave the day after tomorrow, and Sean had arranged to travel over from his home to mine in order for us to fly out together.

I had something to do for her though first. Justin and Curtis thought I was mad when I announced my idea, but as nothing had happened over Hillary, I thought maybe I should owe Ophelia one last farewell. Besides, it was her birthday.

I made my way to a lake nearby, and smiled, as I lit a Chinese Lantern for her in the evening.

I watched as the lantern lifted into a spiral movement into the air.

"Goodbye Ophelia" I whispered, "And thanks for saving me"

A collage of her ran through my mind, I saw her from that first night I met her, from across the bar, she seemed to have been eyeing me throughout my set, I remembered the row in my room when my parents died, and then I saw her with my mail, turning up at my apartment after my bath. I saw her in Mallorca, and with Chris. I saw her anger as she pushed me through the window, and then again in the hospital bed. Then I saw her on the edge of the pier once more. I felt a tear form in my eye as I realised maybe I would miss her.

I composed myself, and watched the lantern dance into the distance, and I forced a smile on my face.

As I got back to the bar, Sean was already there with a bottle of wine waiting, he had already made himself at home in my room, and was ready to start his new life abroad.

"Let's get the party started" He sang over the music that was playing as I entered the bar, "Let's get out of the gay bars and find some pussy"

I clasped the glass of wine he offered, and smiled, "You clearly have not been a holiday rep"

"I plan on getting all kinds of diseases" He smiled, cupping his groin, "Betcha all the milfs, gilfs and clunge are gagging for some young rep cock"

I laughed, "Someone said to me that it's all about the sex as a rep, you see a girl you like, you bang her, you see a fit looking mother, you take it to bed, and you let her ride your cock until she screams and creams, you lick any minge you can find"

Excited, he started to touch himself more, "I can't wait, and my mate said the girls in The Gambia want white cock like no one's business"

"I know nothing about The Gambia my friend" I responded, "But it also works the other way, you see a bloke with an impressive package, you put your mouth around his dick and you swallow, you bend over and you scream loudly, and fake every orgasm it takes until you receive your commission"

Disgust crossed his face, "Nah mate, my arse is exit only, nothing goes in that"

I laughed, how his life will change when he realises how broke he will be in the African sun.

"Hey" He continued, as though forgetting our conversation, "I saw you on the news about that missing girl in Blackpool"

"Let's forget about her" I whispered, snatching the bottle and free pouring my own glass. His hand touched my shoulder, "She was fit"

TWENTY TWO

The following morning it rained heavily as Justin drove us to the airport, although he looked as rough as we did, he swore he had not touched a drop of alcohol the night before. He left us at arrivals, and Sean and I raced out of the rain, and made our way through to the elevator with our suitcases.

We made our way over to the departures lounge, and located the Hibiscus Holidays desk, where Oliver stood waiting, with a young looking brunette lady at his side.

"Look at the tits on that" Sean whispered as we made our way towards them.

I laughed too loud for my liking, and held out my hand to Oliver as we reached the desk.

"Ah, Connor" He smiled, as he shuffled through his paperwork, "I need a chat with you before you board, Sean, I have an issue with your ticket, can you check in with the other desk?"

I felt my stomach flip, as I watched him pass Sean his ticket, and direct him to another desk nearby. I volunteered to look after his suitcase whilst he made his way to the other desk.

Oliver watched him stony faced for a long moment before bringing his attention back to me, I noticed the brunette smiling at me almost uncontrollably, "Right Connor, remember I told you about the fat fucker I have in Banjul?"

I nodded, daring not to answer.

"This is my good friend Sandy, she's going to help you get him sacked" He commented.

I felt relieved, as he passed me my ticket, and I noticed she was trying to look younger than she really was. The pig tails she wore seemed sexy in a school girl kind of way.

"I could not let Sean know about this, I have to be careful, so I need you to be professional about this" Oliver continued, "Sandy will be your room mate in The Gambia, and you will get him out by Christmas, are we clear?"

"How?" I asked, paying attention to Sean in the queue, ensuring he would not return soon.

"Leigh is only there for the black cock" Oliver smiled, "And you're going to catch him out"

"And I know how to do it" Sandy whispered, as she gestured over to the queue where Sean was, he seemed to be experiencing some issues, "I think you're needed"

Oliver nodded, and walked away over to the desk as Sandy grabbed my hand.

"When I give you the nod on the plane" She smiled, "Follow me to the toilet, and I will reveal everything"

"Why not tell me now?" I asked.

"That fat bastard fucked my husband and he needs to pay" She smiled, "Oliver told me what happened to you in Spain, and I think we can use it again"

"I don't want to repeat that" I panicked.

"You want those notes translating from Spanish, and I can do that" She smiled, as she eyed my body, pausing at my groin, "I have not sucked a dick for some time, and I think the mile high club needs a new member"

I felt the colour rush to my face, and my dick began to spring to life. I moved uncomfortably behind my suitcase to hide my package.

Sean was inconsolable that his ticket was incorrect, but Oliver agreed to put him up on a hotel for the night to follow through the next day, and Sandy and I took our place behind two over-romantic hippies that looked as though they smelt of piss and hemp. His hair was greasy and easily longer than hers, and when they were not kissing each other making over-loud smacking and groaning noises, they were groping each other too passionately. Sandy and I both cringed at them, but she too allowed her hand to wander down my back, cupping my buttocks for a moment, before pulling away with a cheeky smile.

We boarded the plane, which was a small air bus, different to the ones I had caught before, and we took our seats, which coincidentally were behind the passionate hippies who were still snogging too much. I nearly wanted to tell them to breathe a bit. Within half an hour, we were taxiing down the runway.

The in-flight movie was about to start when she climbed over me, pressing her firm breasts into my face, deliberately, making my dick awaken again.

"Count to ten" She smiled, as she gestured to the bathroom at the front of the plane, attracting the attention of the hippies. He gave me a knowing smile, as did the old man next to him.

I watched as she sauntered down the aisle. That count to ten was either the longest, or the shortest count dependent upon how fast it was I moved down the aisle. The hippies must have thought it was fast, but the old man next to them who has also heard must have thought I was the slowest of slow.

I nervously knocked on the door, and she released the latch from inside, I squeezed into the room, and she sat precariously on the toilet.

"So what's the plan?" I asked, desperate to get the information as fast as possible.

"You were brutally raped in Spain, and there is nothing more that Leigh wants is a bit of young ass" She explained, "I want you to be caught with your pants down, and him in an inexplicable position"

I nodded.

"Luckily he does not know my married name, so I will be the last person he is expecting" She continued, "When we get to Banjul, you will say I have had a dodgy curry or something and I will make myself known when the time is right"

I nodded again.

"And in return, I will tell you what is in those medical records you have" She smiled, as she began to unbutton her blouse. I allowed her to undo my own fly.

"Here?" I gasped, almost nervous.

"Three hundred people saw you follow me in here" She smiled, "Give them something to remember us by"

It gained hardness as she licked my flaccid member and she forced me to part my legs as far apart as I could in the confined space. She allowed one of my testicles to fall loosely into her mouth, and she expertly used her tongue to move it inside her mouth, then she switched to the other, and instantly put both inside. It hurt for a moment as she sucked hard, pulling downwards as long as she could. She then licked my shaft, as she worked her way to my tip, I found myself gripping her pony tails like a horse, and I guided her mouth back to my dick, guiding it into her open lips, and then my penis entered her moist throat.

I felt her hand touch me firmly, as I groaned more and her tongue was frantically lapping at my member. I began to shake and moved my hips up and down as she gagged a little for a moment as the sound of my length inside her mouth echoed in the small room. My thighs pressed against face, and she adjusted herself to sucking a more comfortable way.

My groans soon became intense, and I struggled to control myself, she realised, and stopped, she slid up my body.

"I like to be bitten" She smiled, as she forced her nipple into my mouth. I obeyed, and gently chewed onto it.

"Harder" She urged.

I obeyed once more, she did not stifle the pleasure, she screamed, and I felt the colour rush to my face. She grabbed my groin, and guided it into her pussy.

"Two pumps and a squirt" She ordered, as someone knocked on the door.

I nodded, I knew I was about to shoot. I thrust into her several times, I managed at least half a dozen thrusts before I felt my own sweet release.

I felt her moist insides suckle on my tip, driving me into a spasm. Someone knocked on the door again.

"That was good" She smiled, as she pulled away from me, quickly pulling up her knickers, I tucked away, and smiled, "Next time, I mean two thrusts"

I laughed, as I pulled open the door to the toilet, and smiled as the hippies stood before me, desperately looking into the cubicle to confirm she was still in there.

We landed in the intense warmth, that was different to the heat in Spain, and the smell of sweat seemed rife in the small airport.

Sandy expertly manhandled the carriers as they tried to assist us with our luggage.

My eyes took a moment to adjust to the new light and heat, and I felt myself already perspiring.

"There he is" She hissed, almost venomously as she guided my eyes toward the humongous overweight sweating man in the parking lot outside.

He had slumped over the rear of the car, with the boot open, his arse crack more prominent that the overhang in his stomach when he moved.

"How did he screw your husband?" I questioned.

"Mehmet was easy, a couple of wines and anything happened" She whispered, "I should have known really"

With that she seemed to move away, and I found myself walking toward the fat man with my suitcase.

"You Connor?" He questioned, spitting as he spoke. I nodded.

"Where is the other one?" He scanned the area.

"She had a dodgy curry" I remembered, "She said to make our way, and she will meet us later"

He swore, as he snatched my suitcase from my hand, and threw it carelessly into the boot, taking a moment to grab a coffee stained binder, that he flung into my hands, before slamming the boot closed.

He wobbled as he moved, "You start at The SeneGambia tomorrow, there's the things you need"

I nodded as I opened the folder, something was sticking to the pages.

"Come on" He mumbled, as he awkwardly clambered into his seat, "Too fucking hot to fuck about"

I nodded, and scanned the car park, I caught Sandy gracefully getting into a beat up old taxi.

I slid in alongside the fat man, the window was open, but I could still smell arse, and sweat, and the seatbelt refused to move as he drove off into the road, sounding his horn to move the passing Gambians in the area.

The SeneGambia was a beautiful modern hotel that led from the dust ridden street, directly onto a white sanded beach. Leigh led the way to the reception, where a small male receptionist greeted him with a mocking homosexual undertone. He passed me my key and clicked his fingers to an eagerly waiting Gambian man who silently rushed to my side, taking my suitcase in a swift movement.

"You read that folder, digest it, and make the sales" Fat man announced, barely looking at me in the eye.

He turned on his chubby heels, and smiled politely at the arrivals entering the hotel, I noticed the hippies amongst the crowd, who gave me the thumbs up. Then fat man stopped in his tracks.

"What the fuck are you doing here?" He asked, as Sandy gracefully made her entrance from the taxi, the driver mauling her luggage.

"Bet you did not expect me to turn up as your new assistant" She smiled, "Mehmet and I have divorced because of you, and I intend to make your life a living hell"

With no further words, she brushed past him, and approached the desk, past the customers, including the disgusted hippies.

October 3rd.

Sandy and I soon settled into our two bed roomed hotel suite, had separate rooms, but in a bizarre blast from the past, she too incorporated the sock on the door rule. I didn't see her take a man back, but she often burst open my door, pleasured me, and rode me in the hot nights. We had only been here for three nights, and she spent two of them on top of me. She luckily did not start in the offices the same time as me, as her predecessor was working her notice, so she spent the days naked on the balcony, or barely dressed by the pool. I even mastered her two pumps and a squirt command, with her assistance of her mouth action beforehand. Have no idea why she wanted this, most women like a period of time.

Fat man had reluctantly arranged a team get together tonight at an outdoor Mexican Restaurant called Weezos, where he openly flirted with the Lily Savage looking owner from Liverpool, and one of the waiters. Sean was already there when he arrived, as he had a room directly above this place.

Sandy watched him with interest, and I enjoyed watching him squirm. The two other reps from other areas soon arrived with their Gambian boyfriends, Michelle was easily pushing fifty, flaunted her barely legal husband to be as she took a seat next to me. The other girl was a shorter, plumper dark haired girl named Tracy, she was a lot younger, and her boyfriend would have been more suited to Michelle age wise. They did not even acknowledge me, as they bickered about who would be guiding a bar crawl. Fat man took it on himself to announce that I would be doing it. Gee thanks. Sandy's predecessor did not bother to turn up.

The night ended with Sean heading off first to be sick after overdoing the lager, fat man paying the bill, and leaving with the girls and their men before midnight. Sandy barely touched her Julbrew Lager until that point. As soon as he left, she took a large swig of the lager, and she opened her clutch bag.

"Are you ok?" I asked.

She tossed my paperwork at me, and placed a cigarette into her mouth, lighting it before she spoke, "I am just dandy"

I carefully opened the paperwork, and smiled as I saw her perfect writing highlighting some of the translations.

"You were brutally raped with a date rape drug, and he caused anal tearing" She explained on the drag of her cigarette, "That doctor should be struck off for hiding the truth"

It took a moment for me to register these words, knowing that I was right all along.

"I think you knew all of this?" She questioned, "I cannot believe that you were subject to that kind of behaviour, if you were a woman, you could easily be forgiven for hiding away, but look at you"

"I got revenge" I smiled, "I stubbed a fag out on his dick, I can still hear the screams"

"You don't have to be brave" She smiled.
I felt a tear form in my eye, those few words had finally given me some closure. I smiled at her, "I will help you get revenge, what do you want me to do"

She placed her hand on mine, and smiled back at me, "I am tired, but let's discuss this in your massive, warm bed"

She leaned over to me, and planted a kiss on me.

"Let's go" I smiled, eager to get back now with this promise.

Together, we rose, and she finished her bottled lager. We made our way to the gateway exit, and I accidentally bumped into a passer-by.

"Excuse me" I apologised, barely taking the time to register, until our eyes met.

It was the honeymooner, but she was with a young Gambian waiter from my hotel. She shook her head as if to plead for me not to say anything. I nodded in acknowledgement.

October 4th.

Her husband was already waiting for me at my desk the next morning. His tear stained eyes told me that he knew something was amiss.

I placed my satchel on the chair, and offered him a drink of vimto, he brushed his hair out of his eyes, and spoke barely above a whisper.

"It's my Moonbeam" He took a drink of vimto, leaving his upper lip stained purple, "She did not come back last night"

I tried not to react to the name, as it did not surprise me that she would have a name like that, "Perhaps she has fallen asleep somewhere?"

"That waiter" He whispered, "He was pawing at her all night during dinner, and at the bar afterwards. He had known we were out here to look at some schools to work on as part of our charity work, and he told us how poor his was, and offered to take us to his compound. She seemed eager"

"A lot of Gambians are poor" I agreed, having remembered an article in the grubby binder that Fat man had passed me.

"No" He insisted, "Moonbeam and I were soul mates, and she is fucking a black man, and I need you to get me the next flight home"
I nodded as I reached for my mobile phone, "You understand that this may be quiet expensive?"

"I don't care" He announced, as he withdrew two passports out of his pocket, "Get me on any flight home, I could not give a flying fuck if it is Manchester, Birmingham, Luton, just get me home"

I nodded, as I dialled the office, I watched him seemingly go off in the distance as I relayed the story. As I did, I took the two passports, and located his, Maverick "Pan" Sunshine.

I mean come on, clearly this was a deed poll pot smoking wank stain if I ever have seen one. Moonbeam and Maverick fucking Sunshine. Once more I kept this within me.

I eventually got him a flight back that evening to East Midlands, and he paid in cash instantly. "Tell me something" He asked distantly, as he pocketed both passports, and the hand written receipt I made,

"That bitch will pay for it, I am taking her passport back to the UK and she can grovel, but is it true that women just want men with massive dicks?"

"I am sorry I don't know the answer to that" I smiled sympathetically.

He rose, "She never complained, we met just seven months ago at a gathering in the woods near Chester, and she was just a secretary in a run-down hotel. We had an amazing time, and got hand fasted by a river by a head witch who promised us a long and happy year"

I realised that he was now unbuttoning his dirty jeans, as I responded, trying to maintain eye contact. "If she has left you, then I think that she will deserve everything that is coming her way"

"She came almost every time we made love" He continued, as he pulled out his schlong, which was erecting with each passing second, "She said it was the biggest thing she had ever seen"

He was not wrong, it was quite large, but also looked like a pulled pork piece of meat that looked as though it needed a good wash, and not just in the swimming pool which I thought he would favour rather than an actual shower.
He posed with his hands on his hips, proudly allowing his unwashed smelly shaft to reach out to me.

"Maverick" I whispered, "This is a family hotel, if anyone sees you do that you can be escorted off the premises"

"My dick is big" He announced, as he put it back into his jeans, still hard, and showing, "She should only worship my penis, and she chose a waiter"

I struggled for words.

He sat back down, and stroked his crotch before me over his jeans, "Would you worship something like this?"

I cringed, as I remembered Tommo and his rancid cock, "I am sorry I have a girlfriend"

The change that crossed his face, forced his hard on to fade at the same time, "Women are fucking slags"

He did not say farewell when he left just a few hours later. He stood by his word and took Moonbeam's passport with him as he boarded the coach to leave. I don't even think he showered to go by the smell of him.

The heat from the sun was so intense at the moment, and I returned to my room to shower and change again. As I showered, I heard Sandy return from her duties, cursing Leigh, or as she affectionately called him 'Fat Fucking Arse Bandit'.

Dripping wet, I wrapped the towel around me as I entered our shared lounge area. She sat open legged on the stool directly under the ceiling fan.

"I have to do it tomorrow" She sighed, "I have phoned Oliver and he is coming in on a Gatwick Flight tonight"

I allowed the towel to slip, as she smiled, opening her legs, showing me her mossy bank as she wore no underwear in this heat. I too had already resorted to this act.

Erect, I approached her, and lifted her legs carefully, she wrapped them around my waist, and guided me into her hot creamy channel, her wetness and tightness made me eager to please, and she used her muscles to grip hard onto my dick, she rose dangerously high, and I struggled to maintain my balance as I lifted her off the stool. I wanted to control myself, as I felt her squeeze, making herself virginally tight.

Soon enough I collapsed to the floor, and took her with me, she remained on top, and rode my member, forcing myself deeper into her chasm.

For a moment, she was no longer Sandy, as I saw Shannon for a second on top, then Ophelia.

I shook the vision away as I reached up at her blouse, unbuttoning her, feeling her milky white flesh. She reached around her back, and I felt her touch my scrotum, squeezing my testicles together. The pain shot through me in a heat of passion, and I screamed. She squeezed hard, and clenched with her vaginal muscles, and within seconds I was releasing my juice inside her again. And she returned the favour. The wetness from within her gushed over my softening member, and the perspiration began to pour off us both.

Without words, she raised, and wiped her minge with my towel, before throwing it back at me, it landed softly on my chest, and she walked out of the room, grabbing her blouse en route, "Tomorrow, I take over"

TWENTY THREE

October 5th.

The following lunch time, Sandy called me into the office for a disciplinary over a balance discrepancy in my liquidation as part of the plan we had discussed over wine and kebab last night.

She sent a taxi around to the hotel, and as I made the thirty minute journey through the dust roads of The Gambia to the office in Kolili, I glanced Moonbeam at a roadside café briefly, in a Gambian dress, and she was being fingered by her new male. The taxi driver made a rude comment about her being a "boss woman" which I learned from the dirty file was a derogatory term for white women in the area. I chose to laugh off the comment as to be honest I thought this of this woman too. I watched as a family of monitor lizards made their way through the sandy roadside, amongst the locals as though a normal everyday occurrence.

Moments later, we turned into a beautiful green area, with rich white houses, and mango trees in almost every garden. The taxi pulled up outside the office, where Sandy waited anxiously puffing away on a cigarette.

I paid the fare, and approached her.

"Oliver is on his way, remember the plan?" She asked, as I tore the button off my shorts, sending it flying into the bushes nearby.

I nodded as if I did not have to go through it for like the twentieth time.

"Remember, I have to do this" She smiled with a hint of caution in her voice.

"I have been beaten up before" I announced, as I braced myself, "Remember Ophelia?"

She nodded, "I will make up for this, I promise"

"You have done more than enough for me" I responded, with a nod, "Do it"

With a moment's pause, she forcefully raised a fist, and punched me square on the nose, to which I screamed, and collapsed, in a heap on the floor.

"Are you ok?" She asked.

In pain I nodded, and rose, my nose was bleeding heavily, and already had stained my pure white Hibiscus uniform.

"Let's do this" She urged, taking her arms around me, before whispering, "I am sorry if that hurt more than it should"

I did not answer, as I allowed her to guide me into the office. I could sense that Leigh was in the office, as he spoke loudly to someone on the telephone.

She nodded at me, as I took my seat, aware that a second taxi had just pulled up outside.

We heard Leigh complete his phone call to the take away place. Sandy waited a moment, and the door to the office opened setting off the alert.

"Help me" Sandy screamed in terrifying fear.

The door to the office I sat in burst open, as Sean entered the room quickly, alerted by the screams.

"What the fuck?" He asked, as Leigh gasped for breath as he too joined the commotion.

"It's Leigh" She cried, "I caught him attacking Connor"

"What?" Leigh panicked.

I feigned tears myself, as I lifted my head in the sun light, "He told me I had to suck his cock or he would set me up for stealing my liquidation"

Leigh frantically began to panic as I rose, allowing my unbuttoned shorts to fall slightly.

"I had to pull him off" Sandy insisted.

"You bitch" He screamed as Sean instantly went to stop him from lurching.

"It was like history repeating itself" I cried, realising I really was a great actor after all.

"Enough" A new voice interrupted from the doorway.

Together, we turned, as Oliver stood in the sunlight.

172

"I have heard enough" He announced, with a sharp tone to Leigh, "This is the end of your career with Hibiscus Holidays if Connor issues me with a statement"

"I want him away from me" I insisted, as I gave Sandy a knowing glance.

"This is a set-up" He insisted, as Michelle entered the room as well.

"Not again Leigh" She sighed.

October 9th

Those next few days were intense as fat man tried to defend himself from our lies, but Sandy and I remained adamant that I was assaulted, and my act as the scared young vulnerable rep was bought by Oliver, who knew that the set-up was far too fast, but I simply used the whole, "He knew what happened in Mallorca" and before we knew it, Sean, Michelle and Tracy, had bought the story as well, and a heartbroken Leigh was on a flight back to the UK with minimal warning. He spent his last few hours in The Gambia drinking to excess, and with some random male prostitute that he could afford.

To celebrate, Oliver treated us all to a night out on him, in a nightclub called Atlantis, which he hired with his own money for just us. He had a reason to. He had his eyes on a pretty young barmaid there, and when he locked the doors to the nightclub, he was soon getting his bell-end sucked by her, as the DJ played. Tracy and her man kissed in the corner, and I watched as his hand slid passionately under her skirt. She leapt a little with the entrance. I smiled, as I helped myself to the flowing alcohol, aware that Sandra and Sean were kissing on the dance floor.

Michelle made her way over to me, and clinked the bottom of her Julbrew bottle to mine.

"Congratulations" She announced, "Pretend we are friends, and listen to me"

I obeyed, and took a swig from my bottle.

"I know that Leigh didn't do anything like what you said" She confessed, and added before I could argue, "The cunt deserved what he got, and now I want you to fuck me so hard that I forget what I know"

"What about your boyfriend?" I asked, aware that she now had her hand on my arse.

"Screw him" She whispered, as she used her other hand to pull a condom out of her pocket, "Scratch my itch, and let's get the party started"

I barely had time to respond, before her lips pressed hard against mine, her tongue was wet and well used to kissing, as her saliva seemed to spill over my mouth, and she pulled my zipper down sharply.

With my erection already prominent, she removed the condom from the wrapper, and placed the bulbous end into her mouth, before lowering herself down, and in one swift move, she used her entire mouth to place the johnny on over my cock, she used her hand to smooth out the latex glove, and then she rose.

I noticed the barmaid, and Oliver watching intensively, as Michelle used her pussy without her hands to guide me into her, whilst still kissing passionately. A little too wet for my liking, and I still ached with my not broken nose.

She began to writhe my dick which felt small inside her chasm, and without warning, I noticed Oliver make his way over to us, his black mamba firm in his hand, his eyes constantly on me. I admit I panicked a little. His barmaid disappeared, and he lifted up Michelle's skirt, and allowed his hands to rub roughly over her body, and mine. His eyes still fixated on me. By now, Sean and Sandy were pounding away on the floor nearby, and Oliver used his manliness to pull Michelle and myself closer to them. Together, we choreographed a lie down near to the others, who had now changed position, with her now bouncing her pussy on his cock.

"You need a password to get inside" Michelle muttered between our kisses, and then she flinched, and I knew he had entered her anus, I could feel his force inside her, making me feel inferior. His massive balls occasionally bounced next to mine as he thrust.

His eyes still remained firmly fixated on me, I had no idea if I was to be scared by him, or if he was deliberately trying to intimidate me, I sensed that Tracy and her man were now on the floor, she was on her knees being penetrated from behind, and she had her lips around Sean's testicles, who was enjoying the orgy.

Sandy reached over to us, and squeezed my sweaty bollocks as I was fucking Michelle's well used fanny. She fondled with them frantically, before her wet tongue lashed at them, occasionally touching Michelle's flaps, but I could not see her I just knew that it felt good. Even the DJ was now banging away the same barmaid that been noshing off Oliver earlier. The music stopped.

Tracy's boyfriend had moved now, and he offered me his penis, which I graciously, and politely rejected, still aware that Oliver was watching me. Not taking it personal, he offered it to Michelle, and I watched in awe as she took the entire length in one fast swallow. I began to fuck harder, and was slightly off-put by the black man's arse inches away from my face. Twitching angrily. Sandy had stopped playing with my nuts, and I felt my cum explode into the condom, I noticed the man with his dick down my partners mouth pull out and he sprayed her face with his hot drink.

It kind of excited me, and I took a moment to remove the johnny, and tossed it aside not caring who had to clean it up, as I noticed Sandy crawling toward me.

She took my flaccid member into her own mouth, and sucked the dregs of jizz out of my urethra, sending me into a spasm of additional orgasm.

175

And as fast as it began, it stopped. I could smell semen, and shit all over the place, but no one cared. Oliver wiped Michelle's bum remnants onto her skirt, and slapped her arse so hard the echo reverberated around the room.

"This is a celebration" He cheered, attracting the cautious laughs from us all.

The next few weeks passed in a blur of alcohol. Oliver left the day after the orgy, and I found myself alone, as Sandy and Sean became an item, and I did not want a repeat as condoms were sparse out here. I did not care. I entertained myself with my hand when I needed it, or the occasional young girl that took my fancy. We learned that Leigh had failed in his appeal at the end of October.

I loved everything about this life now, I had simply forgotten about my friends from Mallorca. I could not trace either Shannon or Chris, but the omnipresent Sian had taken to social media around mid-November to announce her promotion to Head Rep in Marmaris. Fucking Bitch moving on with her life after what she did to me. I fantasised screwing her for revenge, but knowing she was with, or the last I heard, she was with Chris, I knew I could not hurt him. I also found out that Lana had celebrated her divorce, and announced that she was heading to Marmaris too for next Summer. I wanted to make her understand I was not the monster she seemed to think I was.

All in all, The Gambia, was amazing for sun, but as December hit, I knew I had already been here too long, as I grew weary of the same old routine. On Tuesday I would run the Bar Crawl, and nurse a hangover on day off Wednesday. Sandy soon stopped coming back to our shared apartment as she set up home with Sean in his bedsit near the Mexican restaurant so I spent my spare time naked in this heat, and sunbathing on my balcony unaware if anyone could actually see me.

Apart from the one time, my male cleaner Lamin, came to my room and stood there watching me. I had no idea how long he had been there, but I was not nervous. The next day, I caught him sniffing my underwear, but again, like him I never said anything, and he did not know how long I was there. Lamin even had to come to my rescue one evening when a bat had nested in my wardrobe, and I was screaming, and dancing like a girl. Never mind the monitor lizard that had adopted my front door, I named Eric, the bat was another story. I was convinced I would become a vampire.

It turned out Lamin wanted to have me, and as Christmas approached, he bought me small gifts, which he carefully laid out for me. I had not bought him anything as I did not understand his language. Our friendship was based purely on silence. He then moved in for a kiss, which startled me. I had seen Oliver's massive mamba at the orgy and there was no way I was allowing that near me. I backed off and Lamin never came back to my room. In fact he did not return to the hotel. I felt guilty, but I had no way of explaining to him that I was in a relationship, or at least I thought I was.

Michelle fell ill on Christmas Eve, and took herself out of our equation. A few days later she went back to the UK without notice. Sandy reported to us that Michelle had found a lump in her breast and did not trust the Doctors in Africa to diagnose her. It turned out to be the worst. She did not return, and the last sighting of her was as she walked through the automatic doors at the airport.

December 30th.

Winter sun surely was my life, and I barely remembered we were about to enter a New Year, as Tracy and I met to guide the coaches from resort to the airport outside Atlantis. It was 9am, and the heat had already caused me to have pit stains which pissed me off.

Tracy was sucking on an ice lolly and was clearly showing signs of pregnancy as her stomach bloated out. She had not told anyone but earlier in the week I caught her being sick in the airport toilets. It turned out her boyfriend had gone to the UK with another woman without telling her. She said that she was ok, but she had now turned bitter against the Gambian men, even the kind bus and taxi drivers.

She even turned against me as I simply informed her that she had a dribble of vanilla on her tee-shirt. And patiently, we still awaited our coaches.

In the distance, coming from the bush land, I heard the terrible engine roar of a quad bike, and what seemed like a war cry from a couple of young Gambian men.

Tracy took my hand as if it would protect her as the bike carelessly bounced along the road, and I recognised the unhelmeted waiter furiously driving, with his hapless companion gripping on the back of him, screaming for her life.

He came to a sharp stop before me. She fell forwards, and shot past him rolling in a heap in the dirt, screaming.

"You take her home" He pointed at her, "She is dirty, and her fanny is like a hippopotamus yawn"

I glanced over at Moonbeam, as she painfully rose to her bare feet, she had lost a lot of her almost none existent weight, and her gaunt expression left her a shadow of her former self. Blood was pouring from her leg, and thigh, and I noticed track lines in her arm.

"Please don't do this" She pleaded to the waiter.

Without response, he forcefully started his engine, and sprayed the three of us with dust from the roadside. Tracy swore as she tossed her ice lolly to the floor in disgust, and Moonbeam collapsed in a heap.

"You have to help me" She pleaded.

I noticed then the blood was pouring from her vagina heavily. She closed her eyes and dropped to the floor.

She was still asleep when Sandy and I visited her after the airport duties, which I had to do covered in sand, and probably stinking of crap.

Sandy scanned the paperwork before us, having spoken with the doctor just minutes before I arrived.

"This is that hippy from the flight right?" She asked, and then responded without giving me time to respond "What kind of a name is Moonbeam Sunshine?"

"I chose it" She croaked, "Where is my husband?"

"I'm sorry" I whispered, I don't know why I whispered, "He left a long time ago, and he took your passport with him"

I saw her regret come storming through her, "I was such a fool, I should not have left him, but I was swept off my feet"

"First rule of marriage" Sandy announced, almost monotone, "Never let anyone come between you"

"I love Maverick" She responded, "I cannot believe I was so stupid"

"You were too pregnant to be carrying that other man's baby" Sandy continued. She shook her head, and cried "It wasn't his baby, I need to get home"

"It is going to take some time for you to get a new passport through the British Consulate, and the flights back to the UK are expensive this time of year" Sandy explained.

Moonbeam nodded, "Can I ask that you call my father?"

I nodded as I rummaged through my bag for my mobile phone.

"Wait" She whispered, "I think I want to try Maverick first"

"He was very angry with you" I responded.

She held out her hand, and gestured for the mobile.

Cheeky bitch last time I saw her she was getting fingered by the man she had left her husband for, now she wanted to use my mobile? I reluctantly passed the phone over to her.

Sandy and I stepped outside into the corridor as we heard her crying for a moment as we tried not to listen into the conversation.

"Cannot believe the season is over soon" Sandy announced trying to change the subject, "I think you will love Turkey"

"There is still 2 months left of season" I responded.

Moonbeam had stopped screaming and it had now gone almost silent in the room.

"I may come to Turkey to you, I have to serve Mehmet with some legal documents" Sandy laughed, "See what this Shannon has that I don't"

"I think I love her" I smiled.

"Yet you shag anyone who offers it to you?" Sandy smiled, using her thumb to point to the room where Moonbeam sat, "You're no better than her in there"

I had to agree with her, "I think after next season, if she and I are still an item, I will call it a day and settle down with her, make babies...."

"And what if the psycho ex turns up again?" She interrupted.

I had not thought of Ophelia for some time, with the Wi-Fi being poor out here, I was not up to date with the reports of her, and Justin never mentioned anything in our telephone conversations.

"And Chris?" She continued, as though she was trying to break me.

I did not have time to answer as the door opened, and Moonbeam passed me my phone. She did not say anything, and closed the door.

The next morning, I barely recognised Maverick as he returned to The Gambia. His hair was shaved almost completely off, and he was clean shaven, and actually wearing a suit. Dare I say it he smelt like he had finally found out that water was made for bathing as well?

He stepped into the hotel, and approached my desk with force, placing the two passports before me.

"I have come for my wife" He announced.

I felt a smile cross my face. I could not tell if he had come back to take her home to start afresh or if he felt a debt of gratitude for her. He had not destroyed her passport so there must have been something still there.

I put a call through to the room that she had been staying in, and she wasted no time in racing through the hotel grounds, barefoot, but clean. Sandy had given her some clothes, which on her were slightly over sized. But she wore it well.

Together, their eyes caught each other and that pause between them seemed to last an eternity.

I waited without speaking.

She began to walk back towards him, and he remained motionless.

"You came" She announced, barely believing herself.

"You hurt me" He responded nonchalantly.

"I am sorry" I wanted to slap her, she made it look so fucking easy.

She was closer now, and he still remained in the same position, only his hand had moved enough to be touching one of the passports.

"I want to come home" She responded.

His hand moved over to her, clasping the passport.

She cautiously took it from him, and bowed her head, "I understand"

He turned away for a moment, and I noticed that he was crying again, sensitive bell-end.

"Perhaps I can get you both something to drink?" I suggested.

"No" He responded, his hands placed either side of my desk, he hid himself from her, "I told you I have come for my wife, and I am not leaving without her"

She inched closer toward him, and soon she embraced him. Her touch excited him, as it was back erect again, forming hard in his suit, he damn near almost knocked over my table.

Before I knew it, they were kissing once more.

"You have to tell him" I felt like a right twat for interrupting the moment.

"Tell me what?" He announced.

She pulled away from him, biting her bottom lip.

"Tell me what?" He repeated, with more command this time.

"I was carrying your baby when I left you" She confessed, "I lost it"

Great. I knew what was happening next, he broke down in tears again.

January 4th.

I have to admit, I watched them over those last few days enjoying life. Her confession seemed to have built their relationship back to that sickening one they had before. As the sun set on that day, Sean arrived on his transfer coach to take them home. He told me on his return they spent the entire coach journey kissing again.

TWENTY FOUR

March 12th.

I spent the remainder of the Winter season enjoying The Ivory Coast, learning more about the culture, and slave trade, and continuing with one night flings with passing guests, until the season closed down. Tracy had flown home last week, and Sean was due to leave on the first flight today, before Sandy and I. Sean confided that he no longer wished to be a rep and had already secured a journalist position in his local newspaper.

We closed the resort down, and flew back to the UK from the African Sunset. Of course we were drunk all the way back, having smuggled on board our flight some cheap vodka, and as we landed in Manchester, I embraced her for a long moment at the departure point.

I could see Justin and his husband, and Curtis, waiting for me with an overly camp banner through the doors, I wanted to put off myself going out as long as possible.

"Thank you for such an amazing season" Sandy smiled, "You made me realise a lot of dreams out there"

"You accomplished your revenge, and I am happy to be part of that" I laughed, allowing the other passengers to go their merry way.

"It was not just that" Sandy smiled, "The way you helped that hippy girl get back with her husband, showed me there is such a thing as true love, and I promise you, Oliver has received a glowing report on you, which will secure you the Marmaris gig next month"

"He scares the bejesus out of me, the way he stares at me..." I began.

She giggled, "You're an enigma, he could not figure out if he should fuck you or not" I laughed out loud with her, and she soon placed her caring hand on my arm.

"In all serious" Her tone changed, "Go find Shannon, and get Chris away from that bitch that set you up, because you know she will hurt him"

With that, she moved away, through the automatic doors, and the three faggots outside caught me in their sight. They started to sing some terrible version of Circle of Life and I blushed as I moved through the doors. Sandy had already walked through the crowd, and was heading into the night outside. Her ass certainly looked fine in those jeans.

"Come on Princess" Justin laughed, as he embraced me, "We have a surprise for you at home"

The snow was freezing as I got out of the car outside Churchill's, the 'For Sale' sign shocked me, as I glanced up toward my old bedroom window.

"Is this the surprise?" I gestured to the sign, as Curtis struggled with my suitcase, I let him.

"Nope" Justin teased, searching his pockets for the house keys, "But we are selling up, and retiring to Gran Canaria, but we can talk about this later"

Curtis lumbered past me, accidentally of course, touching my arse, and smiling back at me.

"Come on whore" Justin announced, pushing open his door, "It's fucking cold out here"

The empty bar seemed dark with no action within, and we made our way to the counter, where I sat as Justin's husband disappeared behind the bar, and free-poured a glass of lager, and a rose wine.

"You stay here" He smiled, as he placed the drinks before me, and I realised that Justin and Curtis were nowhere to be seen.

I took a drink of my lager, as he ran up the staircase behind me, and I waited. "Hello stranger" She spoke, startling me.

I almost leapt to my feet as I turned on the stool. She was a vision even in her black jeans and red jacket.

"Shannon" I gasped, as I raced over to her.

She froze as I tried to kiss her, she pulled away, and shook her head.

Without speaking, she walked past me, and took a place at the bar in front of her glass of wine. Confused, I walked over to her.

"What have I done?" I questioned.

"Nothing" She seemed cold, as she stared into the vessel of wine. "I missed you" I responded after a moment's silence.

"I came here last week, I had to talk to you" She monotonously continued.

Confusion now set in with me, as she was so cold to me, "You didn't return any of my messages...."

"I took myself off the radar" She replied. A tear fell down her face, "I have something to show you"

Placing a tissue in her hand, I did not know what to do.

She accepted, and withdrew a mobile phone out of her pocket, her hands were shaking.

"Before I show you this" She composed herself, "I wanted to tell you everything but I was too frightened"

"You're scaring me now" My mind was preparing for a whole host of revelations.

Then she began, "She warned me that she would kill me if I said anything"

"Who?" I asked.

"And the monster you see in this video is not the Chris you knew" She pressed the play button on the video she had loaded.

The shaky camera action was blurred to start with, as a gathering of sorts in a bar I did not recognise came into focus.

I heard Shannon's voice whisper on the video, "Connor, you need to see this"

Then I saw Sian dancing erotically, almost riding Chris in public. His head was shaven now, and he was different, he seemed more angry at life, than the fun loving Cockney I first met last year.

He responded to Shannon's video by telling her to fuck off, which angered me more. Then I noticed the girl in the background, sitting behind him.

"When was this filmed?" I asked.

She shushed me, and gestured back to the screen.

Chris rose from his lap dance, and rushed over to the camera. Rage filled his face, "If you are filming this for that bastard Connor..."

"No I...." Shannon began.

He had grabbed her arm, and violently forced her to the floor, the camera still concentrated on the girl in the back, who had now turned to face the brawl, "Tell that cunt I will kill him if I ever see him again"

Shock hit me twice in one scene. First Chris's anger toward me, and then the blonde girl in the video.

The camera was then forcefully thrown to the floor, and then blackness.

"When was this filmed?" I repeated.

"September 30th" She responded, "I had to get a new phone, he thought he destroyed the evidence"

"That Ophelia is still alive" I second guessed.

"He changed so much when you left" She explained, switching off her phone, "I'm sure he was taking some sort of drugs, his moods kept changing, and he hated you"

"Did he tell Sian about our plan?" I became concerned.

She shook her head, "Not that I know of, but any time anyone mentioned you, he would smash things up and tell them how much he despised you"

I wanted to touch her, but her flinch previously offended me, as she continued.

"When Ophelia turned up in resort, I confronted her about what you said happened at the pier, and she told me that she owns you and told me about your plans to marry her"

"You know I was never going to go ahead with that" I responded.

She nodded, "She told me that she was going to make you pay, and that is when she told me about old Gracey in Blackpool. She warned me that she was going to kill me if I said anything...."

"She won't hurt you" I reassured, and I realised that I was holding her hand, when did that happen?

She nodded, "I have loved you since we started seeing each other, and I did not care about you dalliances with Chris, or your love for Daisy before me, and I knew that you had a past, but she scares me"

"I promise you I will make this right" I smiled.

She shook her head, "She's dangerous"

I smiled at her, "When we report this to the police, she will be arrested and out of our lives forever"

"She was shacked up with some Spaniard" She explained, she was closer to me that before now.

I wanted to kiss her, but held back.

"I don't understand why you did not make any contact" I questioned.

She sighed, and pulled away sharply.

"Shannon, I am worried about you" I begged.

Her tears flowed more freely now, "The reason I stopped contact was because of what happened after the video"

"What happened?" I pressed.

She paused, and I waited for her. The pause seemed to last an eternity.

"Chris and Sian wanted to make sure I was scared of them as well as Ophelia"

She explained through shallow breaths, "Sian bashed me"

"And Chris?" I asked.

Another pause, "He...."

I placed my hand back on hers, which she accepted.

"He raped me" She confessed, "And the girls watched"

Fury erupted within me.

TWENTY FIVE

Shannon and I grew closer after her revelation. For days we lay next to each other, naked, but not touching each other. She told me that she feared she could never have a sexual relationship with me, or any other man. She also spoke of how she worried she was pregnant with Chris's child when she was late, but it turned out to be a false alarm. She had been through counselling and was finally moving on, and wanted me to be her future.

I was in love with this flame haired beauty. But she needed time. I put Ophelia, Sian and Chris to the back of my head. Where they fucking belong.

Ophelia had faked her own death to punish me for daring not to love her. I had wasted a lot of time on her. No more.

I knew that Sian was about to get her just desserts when I got to Turkey. I did not know what I was going to do, but she was going down.

And Chris? I could not believe what he had done. I despised him for it. If I ever saw him again, it would be too soon.

March 24th.

It was a crisp morning, the sun was unusually bright, as I kissed her in the same room that I was thrown out of last year by the psycho bitch. Justin and Curtis were taking her shopping for some new clothes for our forthcoming relocation to Turkey.

I felt my penis harden as I watched her walk out of the room. I instantly dropped my trouser, and I allowed myself to touch my shaft, tugging hard for long moments, thinking of her, just Shannon, smiling at me, nothing more. I felt the orgasmic sensation as I stroked the hardness of my cock, starting off slow and smooth. I soon gained rhythm and began to speed up my pace. Steaming pre-cum would soon seep into my palm as I shafted myself knowing my own movements. I wanted to scream with pleasure.

"I forgot my...." Shannon interrupted.

I panicked as I quickly stopped pleasuring myself.

She shook her head, as she approached me, "Allow me" She clasped my dick in her hand, and tugged.

Perspiration was soon dripping off my brow, as she expertly and rhythmically pounded my meat with her firm grip.

"Say when" She smiled, looking into my eyes.

I bit my bottom lip, and nodded, as I felt the juice inside me gather in my balls, "Now"

She stopped wanking me, and lowered her head to my purple head, and took it in her mouth, sucking hard.

I felt the jism inside my groin shoot through my dick, and I sighed out too loud for my own liking as I released it into her.

She continued to suck, sending me into a moment of madness as she drained me.

She rose, and smiled back at me, "I know you have a high sex drive, and I promise you we will make love soon"

"I'm sorry" I apologised, still with my trousers around ankles.

"I love you" She responded, as she gathered her mobile phone from the bedside cabinet. And again, she was gone.

March 30th

What seemed like tradition now, Justin and Curtis drove us to the airport in the evening. Shannon was flying out five hours before me with Fantastical Holidays, and my flight was tomorrow morning, but we wanted to spend our last few hours in Manchester together. I treated us to the first class lounge, and we sat in comfortable leather chairs overlooking the runway of terminal one, smiling and holding hands.

It was shortly before 8 when the screen flickered signalling her flight was ready to board. Holding hands again, I walked her to the departure gate, where we kissed for the longest of times. She tasted perfect to me.

"I will meet you at Madness Bar tomorrow evening" She smiled, as she gathered her passport and ticket from her handbag, "I love you"

"I love you too" I responded, as I watched her make her way to the tunnel.

It pained me to see her leave but I knew that I will see her soon. We knew that Sian was yet to leave Mallorca so she was not yet in resort. We did not know, or did not want to think of the day when we meet.

I made my way back to the first class lounge, and watched her plane taxi down the runway. At least I presume it was hers.

After a while, I opened my satchel, and pulled out a book. Opening it, I found the photograph of Chris, Shannon and I at Pirates in Mallorca. I was sitting on Shannon's legs, and Chris had his arms thrown around me. I smiled as I saw Joanna looking bored in the corner again. This was taken at the time when we were all happy.

"What happened to you Chris?" I questioned, as I stroked his image. I was still angry at him.

About two hours later, it was black outside, and the rain was coming down heavily, and I could see lightening in the distance. I sighed as I noticed the screen state my flight was delayed by three hours, which I did not mind too much, as I had all inclusive alcohol and snacks at hand.

I made my way to the bar, and ordered something different, a brandy this time, and at this time of night, something about a bowl of cornflakes called out to me. I made my way back to the window, and once more weather watched.

I did not notice the girl reflected in the window at first. She cleared her throat to get my attention.

It took me a moment to recognise her, the brown hair was tied back into a single pony tail and those lips were exactly the same.

"Connor Candlish" She smiled.

"Olivia" I rose to greet her with a kiss on her cheek.

She took a seat without invite, and placed her vodka and tonic before her. "You had a rough time with Fantastical" She commented.

"I take it you heard Andrew's version of events" I guessed.

"He's a massive prick" She laughed, "If I would have had you on my team, you would be team leader by now, I wish I fought for you last March"

I shrugged, "Up until that point, I enjoyed my life as a rep. Now I think one last season and I am out of it"

She nodded, and took a drink out of her glass, "Hibiscus are a terrible company" "They gave me The Gambia" I commented.

Surprise crossed her face, "It was you that ousted Fat bastard?"

"My reputation preceded me?" I asked.

Her smile widened, "It was about time he got what was coming to him. Now I have a wide on for you all the more"

I felt the blush burn in my face again, her foot was now stroking my groin, I strained, but the hardness soon returned.

"Some men are born lucky" She licked her lips, "Connor Candlish was born a fucking tripod. I loved sucking your cock in my camper van last year"

"I have a girlfriend" I announced, although I would love to have them lips wrapped around my cock one more time.

"Yes" She responded, her foot still stroking my meat. "Shannon McBain, I read her file... She had a rough time too"

I responded with a nod.

"I admire her balls" She smiled, finishing her drink, "Like you, she is fighting on.... tell me something Connor"

I awaited.

"Sian is out in Marmaris" Olivia announced, "I know what a poisonous bitch she is"

I did not answer.

"Are you out to get revenge on her for what she did to you?" She asked hauntingly.

"What do you mean?" I asked.

"That bitch is going to get everything she deserves and more" Olivia spoke, I could not take my eyes off her hypnotic lips, "Lick my pussy and I will help you"

"I have a girlfriend" I repeated.

"I have a husband" She responded, "I will see you in resort"

With that she rose, and made her way back to the bar.

"Connor" She called, "Same again?"

TWENTY SIX

April 1st

The sun was already high in the sky as I made my way through the military airport at Dalaman. I noticed the horseshoe arrangement of travel agent desks outside with a chorus of people announcing their company names. Ahead of me, I saw the Hibiscus representative looking camper than a row of pink tents eagerly greeting customers. I stood behind a tall brunette lady who seemed also to be joining the team.

Overly camp was with an elderly couple, directing them to a coach, and I recognised them as Mr and Mrs Colostomy Collins I once met in Mallorca, and I smiled, wondering if he had yet another new bag. They were even carrying the same luggage, and I could tell that my colleague was having a problem with them.

"Mr and Mrs Collins" I called out from the rear of the queue.

"Collins yes" She repeated.

I made my way to the guide, "I know these two lovely people from Mallorca last year"

The old couple smiled, I could tell that they did not recall me, bless them they probably could only remember their name.

I smiled at Overly camp, as I glanced at his manifest, "Are you staying in Fetiye this year?"

"Yes" She agreed.

I located the name on the piece of paper, and smiled, "Coach 4" Glancing quickly over the car park, I could see it nearby.

Then as I passed him back the paperwork, I walked back to my place in the queue.

"You had to show off" The brunette responded, as she turned to me.

"Lana" I gasped, "Good to see you"

She smiled, "Still the same old super friendly bloke I see"

"I am just doing my job" I responded, smiling back at her.

"You start tomorrow" She laughed, "Look I want to apologise for that night in Blackpool"

"I take it you heard" I responded, aware that we had not spoken since that day.

She nodded, "It was all over the news, I wanted to make contact with you but I forgot everything about you, full name, number, I just kind of knew I was going to see you here"

As she spoke overly camp had completed his guest list, and made his way to us, he clearly was not happy with me.

"You two must be the new reps" He spoke in a Southern accent that I could not place.

"Lana Mulrooney and Connor Candlish" Lana announced, and I realised she had lied about not remembering my name.

His face lightened up, "Lana, you are on my coach, number seven, I will take you there"

"And me?" I asked.

He thrust the paperwork into my hand, "You seem to know what you're doing, figure it out yourself"

I smirked, as I glanced at the manifest and I soon located my name. Next to it was the letters LB, I passed him it back, "I don't understand"

"LB" He muttered matter-of-factly, "Lei Belle, you are to report to her" "Great" I smiled, "Who is she?"

Overly camp did not bother answering me, he just whistled loudly and rudely used his thumb to gesture that I was here.

His whistle signalled a black soft top convertible to drive toward me from nearby. I marvelled at it as it stopped expertly at my side.

The driver, a beautiful blonde inhaled sharply on a cigarette nodded at me, "Connor Candlish?"

I nodded.

"Get in dickhead" She responded, pressing a button on her dashboard, popping the boot of the car, "I am not your chauffeur or your maid"

I smiled to myself, as I carried my suitcase to the boot, throwing it in, I noticed a lot of vodka stockpiled inside.

I rushed back to the passenger seat, and clambered in. "Name's Lei" She introduced, "I'm your house mate"

"Pleasure to meet you" I put my hand out to shake, but she ignored, looking at me as though I was an alien.

"Oliver has praised you up something chronic" She responded, driving off without giving me time to put my seatbelt on, "And did you mouth fuck that Olivia Buchannen from Fantastical?"

"Long story" I responded.

"Thought so" Lei smiled, "She fucking loves you"

I smiled to myself.

We drove through the green countryside, into the mountains, for over an hour, the heat from the sun was cooled down by the breeze from the speed we travelled.

Soon we glided effortlessly down the final roadside, into Marmaris. Lei seemed more interested in getting home than making small talk, but she pointed out a number of bars and restaurants as we ventured deeper into town. She also identified the Hibiscus Holidays office, which looked like a shed, but as we passed, I saw a swimming pool in the rear.

Moments later, we reached an immaculate apartment building that resembled one of the American buildings I had seen on television. The courtyard opened into a large underground garage which housed three other cars, and a tree of sorts, which grew through the building, reaching out into the sunlit rooftop that seemed to have been cut to fit the said tree.

Without waiting, Lei leapt out of her car, and raced to the rear, she took a few bottles of vodka, and waited for me to pull out my suitcase.

"Right house rules" She explained, leading me to a large oak door, "No customers what-so-ever, I cannot stand scum in my house, and if you do I will tell Oliver you have less than a day to move out"

"I have a girlfriend" I responded.

"Sure you do" She did not believe me, "I have a dog, you will respect his wish to curl up on your chair, bed, piss up your leg, I don't care, he lives here, you rent his space, you understand?"

I nodded, unsure if to believe her.

"And finally" She opened the door, and the instant air conditioning hit me, and I think I shivered a moment, as I entered the marbled mansion before me, "Don't ever leave your dirty pants on the bathroom floor, because I will knock you the fuck out"

I smiled, I liked this girl. Not like Shannon, or anyone else I had met, but she was tough. A bit like Ophelia in a way. She did not hold back.

April 10th

The next week flew by in a plethora of intense training, Turkey was much larger than the smaller resorts I had been used to. Lei and I got to be drinking partners, and her dog Gucci loved me. He only pissed on my leg once. Lei had given up the repping game last year, and was her own business woman, and was leasing her spare room to me as a favour for Oliver. She never divulged their friendship.

She introduced me to her best friend, an older rep called Angie, she was also my supervisor, and had been in resort for years, and Angie and I also became friends, she gave me plenty of tips on the place which helped me with my sales. Which in turn impressed her.

I started off with my own couple of small units near the beach which were conveniently next to the Fantastical Holiday units, which Shannon was working. But by the first liquidation session I impressed Angie so much that she had arranged for me to take over a larger hotel unit near to Lei's apartment. Full of kids. I grinned and bore it.

Lana and I were the headline act for the Rep's Cabaret in a hotel between Marmaris and Icmeler, singing an array of modern and old songs. We had reformed that brief friendship, and I loved it. I think she did too.

The whole resort knew that Shannon and I were a couple, and we spent the time we had together, still celibate so to speak.

As today was my 25th Birthday, I had the day off, and Lei, Shannon and I enjoyed the tourist life, para-sailing, scuba diving, and enjoying a day booze cruise.

It was early evening when we made our way to what had become our hangout, a drag bar called Cheers, where Lei had pre-arranged some drinks ready for us upon arrival. The compere was waiting for us with the drinks as we arrived, and four men dressed as women serenaded me with a rude chorus of Happy Birthday. Lana and Angie were already there, and a few other reps I had met recently. Overly Camp was dancing manically to the music not even associated with the singing, but he had his eye on a group of young men that were encouraging him, as James and Sean arrived. They had just flown into resort today. I had to restrain Sean from announcing our orgy in The Gambia, which he did not like.

The night continued with the show inside Madness, which saw a series of amusing drag acts, and Lei sportingly got up on stage to participate in a humiliating dance act with a random pulled from another part of the audience.

I myself was called on stage for an equally embarrassing act but I laughed the whole thing off, drinking as much as I could.

As the evening closed, we made our way back out to the external area of the bar, and then we moved further down the beach to a karaoke bar nearby.

Overly camp got up and serenaded us, and then we noticed the same group of lads were now in this bar.

The whole evening seemed to be flowing freely.

Until Shannon disappeared for a long while. It was Angie that realised she was missing after Lei went to the bar for the third time.

Frantically I tried to call her on her mobile, as Lei and Lana went to the ladies which was inconveniently situated downstairs.

"Where are you?" I left a voice mail.

I genuinely was worried, we had spent every spare moment together.

"I have her" Lana announced suddenly.

I turned on my heels, and raced to her, as Lana and Lei escorted her toward me.

"I found her crying downstairs" Lana continued.

I lovingly placed my hand against her cheek, as I felt her shaking face. She had stopped crying recently, and I could still see the tracks of her tears, "What's wrong?"

She shook as she spoke, "Chris"

She raised her hand, and gestured outside.

I glanced in the direction of her shaking fingers, and I saw them.

Both Sian and Chris were kissing passionately outside, as though they were in private. His shaven head looked disgusting to me and made him look a lot older than his 23 years.

Lei placed her arm on me to stop me from moving, and shook her head, "No"

Anger roared through my veins as I watched him man handle her, but she seemed to like it.

Then the bitch laughed and led him away from us talking about the nightlife in resort. It was clear that he had only recently arrived.

"They have not seen you yet" Lei continued.

April11th

I barely slept when I got back to Shannon's apartment that she shared. Her flatmate was on airport duty, and I lay naked on the hardened floor next to her. She told me that she saw Chris briefly when she was entering the bathroom, and was sure he didn't see her.

When I did sleep, I dreamt I punched his ginger face in whilst Sian watched. When I awoke, it played over in my mind.

I poured a sour tasting coffee as Shannon made her way into the kitchen moments later, and I offered it to her.

She quietly took the drink, and wrapped her hands around it. "I am sorry I reacted so badly last night" She apologised.

"That's ok" I soothed.

"I want to kill her" She confessed.

Shock crossed my face, "You don't mean that"

"I do" She responded instantly, without pause, "She may as well raped us both. She was with you that night in Mallorca, and she watched Chris attack me, along with that psycho ex bitch of yours"

"I can't kill someone" I panicked, unsure if she meant me to do the deed.

Her blank expression scared me, "When we first met, I told you I had been in prison" I recalled that meeting in Mallorca, we never spoke about it.

"What did you do?" I finally questioned.

"I was sixteen when I crashed her car" She went into a trance as though remembering, "My cousin was teaching me to drive, and I panicked, and we hit a tree, I had to do 18 months in a young offenders"

"So it was an accident" I was thankful.

"I want that bitch out of our lives" She continued, "Then maybe we can have Chris back in our lives, and I won't be as scared of him"

"You're talking crazy" I did not want to say that.

"I know Olivia wants to fuck you" She responded, and then continued before I could interject, "When I caught you wanking the other week, I realised I am unable to give you what you want, let her do it.... I want you to fuck her and then you can find out where the bitch lives"

I could not believe what I was hearing.

"Then leave the rest to me" She finished her coffee, and moved into the shower room, closing the door behind her, "I love you, I will kill you"

"What?" I wasn't sure what I had heard. "I said I will kill for you" She muttered.

TWENTY SEVEN

Dazed with her words, I waited for her to emerge from the shower.

The wet towel gripped at her curves as she stood before me, her red hair clinging to her skin. "You still here?" She asked.

"I'm worried about you" I whispered.

"Olivia wants you to repeat what you did in her camper van last year" She continued as though it was a normal everyday experience, "She lives in one of those maisonettes in Icmeler, it's right on the corner as you go into the area"

"Shannon...." I began to argue.

"No" She screamed, cutting the air, "You owe this to me"

I put my hands onto her to calm her down, which seemed to work for a moment, and I rocked her soothingly.

"I want to make love to you" She confessed, building my hopes in a moment, "But I need you to make Olivia happy, and find out where that bitch lives.... I want to do this for you"

Her words echoed through my mind for the rest of the day. I had a late morning airport run, my own fault for having my birthday off. I knew I should have booked the day after off. Dick.

The coach journey to Dalaman airport was almost two hours long, each way, and customers can be absolute idiots both coming and going. You literally had to walk half of them through to the desks, hand their tickets over, and remind them where they lived. Something I learned last year in both Mallorca and The Gambia, just smile.

Luckily this was a military airport, so reps did not enter the airport, and these numpties were pretty much on their own, so as we pulled up the ramp-way, I allowed my passengers off the coach, and soon the last one, a sloppy romantic blonde bimbette who was kissing her Turkish man far too much for my liking, she tearfully said her farewells to him.

I literally followed him down the ramp-way to the arrivals lounge. He stood there waiting at the horseshoe desks, and as my new customers arrived, he romantically repeated the kissing process with another blonde that could easily pass as the others sister.

I smiled to myself, as I took my position next to my coach, welcoming my new arrivals, lots of young stags, and hens, a few families and the odd lone traveller.

As the coach pulled out of the airport shortly before two, I saw Sian walk down the pathway to where I had stood just moments before. Once more Shannon's cries echoed through my head, and I nodded to myself.

The journey back to Marmaris and Icmeler took that long arduous two hours, and the final lone traveller got off at a small back street hotel.

The driver did not want to wait for me, and drove off as I was checking in lonely old Miss Sanders I found myself stranded about half a kilometre out of the resort, with my suit and clipboard.

The intense heat of the sun made my suit sticky.

Within minutes I had located the main street of Icmeler, full of shops selling clothes, and restaurants, where the Turkish men tried to entice the tourists inside their bars and restaurants with the promise of the most exquisite foods.

I swore as a dolmus shot past me ignoring me, and I glanced over the road, smiling as I noticed the maisonettes before me.

I remembered that Olivia lived in one of these, and I smiled as I noticed a Fantastical Holidays uniform drying on the washing line of the third floor.

Instinct took over, and I ran up the marble staircase. I double checked I was on the right floor, as I paused at the door.

I knocked, and waited.

Moments later, she smiled as she opened the door, "What took you so long?"

"I owe you something" I spoke without thinking.

Olivia smiled as she grabbed at my shirt, pulling me inside the coldness of her air conditioned house.

"I know that you are only here to find where Sian lives" She smiled, "I want you to satisfy me, whilst my husband is at work" She guided me to her bedroom, and perched on the bed.

"I have been thinking of your mouth around my cock for over a year" I confessed.

"I want you to lick my pussy" She purred, "And if I am satisfied, I will turn a blind eye on whatever happens"

"How can I trust you?" I asked, my penis already hard in my sweaty trousers.

She moistened her lips, "I hate reps, especially Sian and as for the cockwomble she is knobbing right now, I have never met anything more pathetic and whiny, and pussy whipped than he. Wasn't he a former fuck buddy of yours?"

I nodded, "I have nothing to hide"

"My husband will be in London until tomorrow" She smiled, "Time is running out"

I kissed her lips, and I felt her bare knees press against my body, she brought my hand up to her breast, and forced me to clasp it as we kissed long and hard. She was not wearing a bra, and her breast felt heavy in the fabric of her blouse. The longer we kissed, the more intense our groans became. Her hands rushed down my body and we helped each other to undress, not caring where our clothes ended up.

She squeezed firmly onto my nipples, and the ball from the piercing popped across the room, again, I only heard it hit something in the distance.

I soon stood naked, and erect before her, and she scuttled along the bed, using her back and legs as support, her wet pussy seemed to call for me. I leaned my face closer to her vagina, I could smell her muskiness and I liked that I could turn her on like this.

"Lick it" She urged, using her thighs to force my head closer into her gaping crevice, "Use your tongue to fuck me"

I began to lick her lips, licking each one, and penetrating the hole, the taste seemed to develop more and more as I fluctuated between fast and slow, and long and short whips. Soon I found myself moving naturally back toward her clitoris that seems to harden and as I teased it with my tongue, I began to suck on it a little, sending her into a spasm that I had too frequently recognised in myself. My fingers gently slid into her clefts, and I soon felt her pussy clamp down on them as the flows of orgasm rushed through her.

As I felt her sticky cum flow, I continued to play with her clitoris with my tongue. I realised as I did this I was pulling at my own dick enjoying the sensation. She was gasping my name, and I rose, still erect.

I stroked my penis over her writhing body, and within several sharp movements, my cum shot through the air and over her tits, and chin.

I cried out in passion, as I forced the remnants out of my urethra and I lay on top of her, still seeping a little.

"That was amazing" She panted.

I did not want to answer. I waited a moment before I peeled my perspiring body off her, my spunk was already drying in the heat, and I stuck to her for a moment.

Naked before her, I wiped my body with a towel that lay on the side of the bed. I did not even care if this was not correct. I smiled as I noticed a photograph of an attractive young man on her bedside cabinet.

"Who is that?" I asked.

"My son" She smiled, "He lives in America with his grandma"

"He's handsome" I smiled.

She sighed as she clambered off the bed, and tried to change the subject, "I have waited for that since last March, in that fucking dirty old van"

"Should have fought for me" I joked.

She nodded, "Go get in the shower, I will wash your clothes"

"I don't have time, I mean your husband...." I began.

"Is in the UK and trust me, your clothes will be dry in no time in this heat" She smiled.

Why not? I thought, and followed her direction to the bathroom.

No sooner as I felt the refreshingly cold water hit me, I heard the washing machine commence nearby.

Two hours passed, and having sat on her balcony in her husband's boxers, and a long island iced tea, my clothes were dried by the heat Turkey's sun offered. I could hear her on the telephone to her husband, and I could sense that their conversation was heated. I ignored them, and glanced over at the beautiful town of Icmeler.

As I dressed later, Olivia smiled, and passed me a folded piece of paper.

"I don't care what you do to her" She smiled, "Just teach that Scouse Slag a lesson" I opened the paper, and memorised the address.

"Shannon is a lucky woman" Olivia smiled, "And this will be our secret"

I nodded.

TWENTY EIGHT

April 17th

I confided in Shannon as soon as I got back, and she smiled as she took the paper from me.

She promised that she would arrange some sort of accident. For some reason, it bought us a lot closer, and she would often stay over at Lei's house with me. Still naked, no touching, but kissing more.

I had never felt more loved, and this no touching was killing me. Every so often when I knew I was alone, I would tug one off. I am sure she knew. Lei and I also grew closer as friends, and Lana would often make excuses to rehearse for our cabaret shows. I knew that she harboured feelings but she buried them, and when things would get intense in rehearsals, she would make an excuse to leave. It was Lei and Shannon that noticed this. Me being male missed it.

Today was cooler than it had been, and Lei and I watched a storm linger over Marmaris harbour drinking vodka, neat from stolen tumblers. The night fell fast, and before I knew it the gigantic white moon was looming over us. I had arranged to meet Shannon in Cheers after her airport run, but she was delayed by three hours. I decided to take Lei up on her offer of a night out with her friends.

We started off in a bar on Bar Street, where the beer was overpriced, and the open air venue seemed to be filled with people looking a lot younger than me.

As we made our way to an indoor bar with thumping music, I felt my heart sink as I saw him in the corner. His hair was still shaven, and he was laughing with his arm wrapped around a girl, that I knew was not Sian.

For ten minutes I managed to avoid him, until Lei and her friends spotted a table nearby.

Without acknowledging him, I sat with my back to him, but I felt his eyes burn into my back.

I turned to him, and for a moment he smiled, his beer bottle rose in greeting.

I returned the gesture, and then turned my attention back to Lei, who was laughing over- dramatically to one of her friend's stories.

His hand touched my shoulder.

Fear hit me as I turned to face him, I wanted to punch him for Shannon, but I was scared of him at the same time.

"Can we talk?" He asked sincerely.

I made an excuse to an oblivious Lei that I needed to get some food, and left without her acknowledging my departure.

We soon found ourselves walking alone along the bustling taverns, we remained about a metre apart, as we spoke, and for a while I forgot what he had done.

"Things changed after you left" He explained, "Andrew had it in for me. He knew we were in a relationship and put the pressure on me to satisfy him. Apparently we were seen in Pirates, but I lied to save you"

"Why did you stop contact?" I asked.

He sighed, "It was the safest way to keep you safe. Sian felt guilty for abandoning you that night in the pool, and she lived in fear that you were going to drop her in it, I had no choice but to shag her to keep her on side"

I smiled, as he explained, I missed this guy.

"Remember that day when I told you I only ever loved you?" He did not really ask a question, but more of a point made, "I am not sure if I ever got over you"

I noticed that his hand was now reaching out for me, and nervously, I took it. His grip felt so relaxed in mine. Together, we walked hand in hand, as he continued.

"I knew that I had to convince her that I was in love with her so that she could trust me" He spoke, and I could tell he was trying not to cry, "Every time we made love, I had to think of those times with you and Shannon, mainly just you"

I did not respond, as I listened to him.

"I stuck with this plan, and then your psycho ex turned up" He continued. "Ophelia" I hissed.

"She is some nut job" He agreed, as he turned to face me, "When I heard that she pushed you through that window, all I wanted to do is to get on the next plane back to you, to make sure you were ok"

"Why didn't you?" I asked.

"Because Sian could not know that I had feelings for you" He confessed.

"And where is Ophelia now?" I questioned.

He shrugged, "Last I heard, she was in Mallorca still"

We walked for a little while longer, barely talking.

"I want to kiss you" He confessed after what seemed like an eternity.

I pulled as he reached over to me "Did you attack Shannon?"

Panic hit him, as he refused the statement, "The worst I did was throw her phone to the floor when she filmed Ophelia"

I did not know what to believe, and I pulled away again as he tried to kiss me again.

"You're right" He nodded, "Come back to mine for old time's sake"

I thought for a moment, as I looked into his eyes. Sincerity.

I smiled, and nodded.

We kissed as soon as we entered through his door way, and as we stood face to face, I felt that familiar hardness form in his shorts, the anger in his face changed, and he frantically pulled away my clothes, kissing me, and gently biting my nipples. I felt him reach for my cock, and guide me to his bedroom by it. We kissed more, and then with force, he span me around, and I felt my trousers fall down to my ankles. I stepped out of them.

I felt his hands roughly stroke my thighs, and perineum.

"Wait" I panicked for some reason.

I genuinely feared this bald version of Chris.

Looking over my shoulder, I saw him take some lubricant from his table, and he smeared it over his swollen member, before taking two coated fingers, and inserting them gently into my ass.

Groaning, I allowed him to probe my sphincter for several minutes, before removing them, and then he guided his slippery cock between my cheeks, until the head pressed against my hole.

"Are you sure about this?" I asked.

"Are you sure about this?" He repeated, almost mockingly, as he pulled me onto him.

I yelped as I felt the sharp pain and he stopped.

He pulled me back onto his cock, he pushed again passed my sphincter, and allowed me to adjust to him inside me. Soon I realised that he was entirely in me, and his balls were almost against mine.

He began to thrust, pulling almost all the way out, and then back in, and as I adjusted to his motions, I allowed my hand to wander between his legs to play with his balls, and he used his hand to sharply pull down on my shaft, hurting a little, as he tugged.

His thighs began to slap hard against my cheeks as he continued to thrust hard into me.

"I have missed you" He gasped, and I believed him.

I felt myself spill in his hand, which excited him, he began to pump harder, and less than a minute after I had shot, I felt him pulsate inside me, and he began to fill me up.

As he finished, he pushed me away from him, and together we dropped onto the bed. "

You have to go" He announced, as I admired his golden sun kissed skin.

"We need to talk" I responded.

"No" He announced, "Sian will be home soon and I need you to go"

Without a second glance, he rolled over, and roughly gathered my clothes, and threw them at me.

"Get out" He whispered.

As though scared, he rallied around the room gathering evidence of his indiscriminating act of lust, and I pulled on my trousers, daring not to talk.

He quickly washed his dick in his sink, and panicked when I was still not dressed on his return.

"Shit" He panicked, grabbing me with force, pulling me onto the balcony, as I heard the jingle of the keys in the door, "Forgive me"

He leaned in for one more kiss, and gestured to the fire exit. I obeyed, and clambered over the edge, carrying my clothes. I moved quickly down one storey as I heard her enter the balcony above, and as I peered through the grated slats of the metal balcony, I saw them kiss.

"I thought you were delayed" He smiled.

"And I thought you were partying" She spoke as vindictive as ever.

"Let's go to bed" He suggested, and pulled her back into the apartment.

I smiled, as I put on my shirt once more, and made my way back down the stairwell, at least five storeys.

I caught up with Lei and her friends, and Overly camp at Cheers later that evening, as the show inside finished. Shannon messaged me to say she was still delayed as Lana soon joined us, still full of ideas for new songs for our show.

The night continued in an alcohol fuelled frenzy, Overly camp was copping off with someone all night and was the first to leave, and Lei's friends all but abandoned her swiftly, and shortly before four, Lei disappeared with one of the bar men, in the bar that did not want to seem to sleep.

Hand in hand, Lana and I made our way along the beach as the sun was already beginning to rise. She lived in an apartment near to Shannon's and as I felt the lethargy hit me, she seemed full of life.

I really needed my bed. That, or Shannon's whichever one is closer.

TWENTY NINE

I slept the whole of that day, I heard Shannon move about the apartment, and each time I awoke, there was a fresh glass of water for me. As the humid night air came, I felt her snuggle against me.

I felt her hand wonder down my body, and it soon rested on my flaccid member, gripping it, making it hard. Without words, she clambered astride of me, she lifted her hips, still gripping onto my shaft, and nestled it in her pussy lips.

She started to rub up and down my rigid pole, as her warm slit enveloped it, I felt the purple head push the pinkish hood of her clit back, and she began to contract her muscles making her pussy suck on my cock, the wet echoes reverberated around the room. Unable to take the teasing any more, I grabbed at her hips, and penetrated her in one stroke.

"If you want me to stop...." I whispered under her.

She ignored this, and started to ride up and down, feeling her own breasts as she allowed me to plunge deeper into her. Her thrusts became harder, and deeper, I felt as though I was climbing through her body through her minge. She moved her hands down onto my chest, and our strokes became as one, in tandem we moved.

She slowly moved one of her hands down towards her clit, and she stroked as she rode, and my cock was beginning to sensitise to every move, and I wanted to release. In the moonlight, I saw her manipulate her pulsating bead, and with two expert fingers, she rubbed. I felt her pussy pulse, as she let out tiny gasps, I felt like a moist velvet glove was clamping down on my cock so tightly it was becoming more difficult to move.

As her wave of orgasm shot through her, I continued to pound my length more, until my own release began to peak. She rode down the wave, and I released my special cream into her twitching pussy.

Laughing softly, she snuggled back onto my chest, and I allowed my pole to soften before letting it fall out of her.

"Thank you" She whispered.

I could not speak. I smiled back, and stroked her wet hair.

April 18th.

As the sun rose the next day, I made Shannon a hearty breakfast whilst she showered. She seemed happier now. She sat naked before me eating and drinking a hot beverage for the first time in ages.

"Last night was wonderful" I commented.

"I'm back baby" She teased, as she teased a sausage into her mouth.

I moved over to her, and kissed her full on the lips, caressing her naked breast passionately, "I have missed you"

She pulled away, "I know I have been a frigid bitch these last few weeks since I got back"

"Now I have you back, let's plan our future" I smiled, "I still have some inheritance left, we can buy a little business somewhere?"

"And raise two beautiful kids" She agreed.

"I say we hand in our resignations today and go home" I proposed.

"No" She smiled, almost controlling, "At least let's finish the season"

Soon after, I made my way to my hotel, Angie was meeting me today to take me to yet another new unit she wanted me to take over. She was waiting with two of my elderly guests. They seemed to enjoy her company. Initially they complained about missing a boat trip, but now she had calmed them down and was arranging for them to go to Rhodes for the day.

As they left to meet the coach, Angie and I hopped into her car, and made the short journey to Icmeler. I smiled to myself as I passed Olivia's apartment, and caught a glance of her and an overweight bloke, I presumed was her husband.

The mountainous area became dense as we meandered alongside a dried out canal, which I also remember walking past the day I munched out on Olivia's mossy bank. Angie continued to talk about Overly-camp who had complained about my success, again I smiled at the fact.

Soon we arrived at a large modern hotel, and as we walked into the reception area, I noticed that it was his hotel I was taking over. He was mid-welcome meeting as we appeared at the back of the bar, which distracted him for a moment, and then for some reason he was promoting our show, wearing a dress.

Angie shook her head, and watched the shambles of a presentation, "You're gonna be a massive success here"

I agreed, I gave up counting at about fifty people, aware that there were more.

Approximately forty minutes later, Overly-camp introduced me to the owner of the hotel, and said his farewells to the staff and some customers he had befriended. Including a young male, that I am sure I recognised from Cheers on my birthday.

A point that was proven minutes later when he asked me if I enjoyed myself.

"Is it true that you used to be a gay porn star?" He asked.

Knob. I thought, instead I smiled, and remembered how I get people to attend welcome meetings, "I guess so"

Angie took me back to Marmaris soon after, with the arrangement that I would be taking over that hotel the next day. I had already arranged to meet Lana at the Geordie bar behind Cheers, knowing that she was an avid Magpies supporter. I preferred Liverpool, but she had her heart set on meeting there. Plus I believe she had a crush on the barman Idris who often made a rush to us when we arrived for a chat.

She was already waiting as Angie let me out of the car, and best of all, she had a cold bottle of Efes waiting for me.

She greeted me with a friendly kiss on the cheek, Idris also joined us for a moment, before spotting a table of young ladies who attracted his attention.

"I have so much to tell you" She smiled, as she withdrew a note pad from her handbag, "We are concentrating far too much on duets that everyone knows, but my idea is to sing a number that everyone sees as a solo, but together, that way we can harmonise"

"Sure" I agreed.

"I wanted to tell you on your birthday but you were so drunk" She giggled.

"I slept most of yesterday" I confessed, "But I had the most wonderful evening" "For your birthday" She presumed.

"Shannon and I made love" I smiled dreamily.

A forced smile crossed her face, "You only really loved Daisy"

I smiled as I took a drink out of my bottle.

"I know I am not her" Lana smiled, and I felt her hand touch mine, "But give me a chance and I will make you happy"

Confused, I slowly placed down my bottle.

"I should never have left you in Blackpool" She confessed, leaning in closer for a kiss.

"No" I whispered, as our lips were a hairs breadth apart.

"Such an idiot" She gasped, as she hastily put her notepad back into her bag, taking out some lira, "I have to go"

"Wait" I pleaded, too late as she rushed into the crowds of tourists.

Stupid woman, I thought, she had a chance back in England but chose not to trust me because of Ophelia.

I barely had time to complete my beer as I noticed Sian and Chris walking towards the bar. I rose.

Anger was back in Chris's face as he paused just inches away from me. Last time we were this close, he was banging me, I nodded to him.

"Well faggot bollocks" Sian announced, "I am surprised that you went back to repping after what you did"

"Nice to see you Sian" I responded as calmly as I could.

"Nice to see you Sian" She mocked, "You throw a drunk and naked drugs and pool party, and accuse that lovely man of hurting you because you were caught out"

"Caught out?" I asked, aware that Chris was too close for comfort.

"You know what I mean" She laughed, "You wanted to ride his cock and when you got scared you cried rape"

"Shut up" I insisted.

"No" Chris insisted, angrily interjecting her, "You shut the fuck up gay boy" "Chris...." I was confused.

He began to circle me, and we were attracting the audience of the tourists in the bars and from the nearby beach.

He mouthed the words, "Trust me" which confused me all the more.

"Teach him a lesson" Sian commanded.

With that, Chris lurched forward toward me, his fist clenched, and punched hard into my stomach, sending the wind out of me. I collapsed in pain, and turned back toward him.

"You tried to make me gay you homo" He spoke through gritted teeth, then he mouthed the word "Sorry"

He raised his foot, and buried it into my stomach hard.

I cried out in pain, my eyes watered and I felt blood spill from my lips as I hit the ground again with force.

As I tried to rise, I noticed Idris had grabbed Chris, and was pulling him away as he abused me, and Sian was laughing at the situation. Passers-by started to disperse, and then I saw Shannon nearby, watching. Scared.

Then I noticed something else. Sian seemed intimidated by Shannon's presence.

Almost synchronised, they turned and ran away from each other, and I scrambled to my feet. Idris had reappeared with a first aid kit to tend my wounds, but I needed to leave, and find Shannon.

Blood spilled from my lip as I raced along the side street, to try to find Shannon, she had disappeared in the crowds, just like Lana did before her.

Frantically, I scanned the people and failed to locate her, as Idris caught up with me with his first aid kit.

"Stop being a dick" He ordered, and pulled me back to the bar.

"I need to find her" I cried.

THIRTY

Shannon was not at her apartment when I got back later in the evening. Her phone was off, and I panicked.

It took me a moment to think straight, as I caught my bruised face in the mirror above her bed.

Trust him? Those were his last fucking words to me. Just a few days we were shagging on his bed, and now he was punching my lights out. I reached over Shannon's make-up that was scattered across the cabinet nearby, and quickly dabbed myself with her concealer.

"Shit" I realised.

I knew where she was.

I quickly changed into shorts and a tee-shirt that I always kept there, and raced through the resort to the apartment that Chris had taken me to earlier in the week.

The communal entrance was decorated with fountains and plants that I did not remember seeing previously, but as I approached the doorway, I recognised it instantly.

I banged on the door, and waited for long moments, until an amused Sian opened up. I barged past her into the room, to which she protested instantly.

"Where is she?" I asked.

Still with the door open, she gestured for me to leave, "You're fucking crazy, now get out before I call the police"

"Where are Chris and Shannon?" I asked.

As though she found it entertaining, she closed the door, "Walk into my parlour said the spider to the fly"

Fear began to hit me, but I think I hid it well, "I know what you did to me in Mallorca"

She shrugged, "So what? I needed to keep my job, you were indispensable, and I remember sitting with you in the hotel telling you that you wouldn't last"

"I did nothing to you" I insisted, "And you got me fired from the job I loved"

She began to step toward me, "And yet here you are, in another uniform, licking minge wherever you can get it, sucking cock if it is offered to you"

I remained quiet, as I scanned the room for signs that someone else was there, clearly there was not.

She continued, "I heard you fucked my Gran before the old bitch died"

"She gave me the medical records and I had them translated" I began to explain.

She brushed aside the comment, "That old cow left me with less than ten thousand pounds in her will the selfish whore, but you put your dick in her rancid pussy and fucked her to death"

"No" I whispered remembering the whole incident in my head.

"Yes" She smiled, "And now, you have come for me again"

She pressed her body against me, and I began to fight the urge to be erect in her presence.

"So I had to let you take the rap for your own discrepancy" She continued, her hand now pressing against my shorts, cupping my penis, firmly, as she lowered herself, I felt her lips against me, she bit gently into the fabric of my clothes, and I forcefully grabbed her by the hair pulling her upwards.

"I fucking hate you" I hissed.

"That's right" She cried through the pain, "Treat me like the bitch that I am, I want you to fuck me raw as punishment"

Despite my grip in her hair, she forced herself closer, and planted a moist kiss onto me, as she used her hands to loosen my shorts.

My bulge soon erupted, and she stroked it gently. I felt my hands free her hair, and she anxiously pulled down her knickers to her knees.

With force, I remembered being in this room just a few days earlier, I turned her around, and bent her over onto the same bed her fella had banged me.

With a sharp tug, I pulled her white panties off, snapping the elastic, and screwing them in my hand. I pulled them up to my nose, and sniffed.

I probed her pussy, perineum and her arse with my dick.
She glanced over her shoulder, arching her pussy towards me, to drive me into her tight clefts.

She pushed against me so hard, that my balls touched her as she literally fucked me, I started to thrust in synchronisation with her.

Her suction pulled me deeper inside her, and there was no momentum of build-up, we just started to fuck each other fast, and furious, the slapping sounds of our bodies echoed around the room. She yelped in pain as she complimented me on my performance, comparing me to her lover briefly.

Anger began to take over as I did not want to touch her, but my hands reached around her hips for something to grip.

"Ophelia was right" She whispered in moments of passion, "You know the business"

"Why did she do this?" I asked, as images of other women appeared in my mind.

She mumbled something as she pushed back harder on my dick. I reached over to her hair, and pulled sharply back.

I ripped her head back by her thick mane, as I rammed deeper into her wet pussy.

She screamed in agony at first, and I continued to pound her harder, and somehow deeper. That pain became pleasure, as she began to convulse with waves of orgasmic satisfaction. I did not care over the pain I was causing her, even when she began to whimper.

I reached under her, and snatched at her pubic hair, pulling roughly at the small wisps, knowingly causing her a pain that she liked.

"I need to know" I whispered, aware that she was getting turned on, and I knew I was ready to release my sperm.

She did not answer me, rather she encouraged me to pull harder at her pubes, and she pushed herself even more firmly onto my pole.

As we began to speed up our rhythmical movement, I felt her hand stroke herself, and her groans became intense. I felt my volley of explosions inside myself, and I released my hot thick creamy cum inside her.

I pulled out instantly, and watched as my final dregs of semen drip off the end. I used her panties still scrunched in my hand to wipe myself, and then I wiped her dripping fanny with them.

"Where is Ophelia" I asked.

"Fuck her" Sian turned on her back, her smooth body, pert nipples and wet pussy smiling at me, if I was in any other position I would have taken her again there and then.

I slid along her body, and placed the panties against her mouth. I pulled at her hair hard once more, and as she let out a scream, I forced them into her mouth.

"Taste that you dirty fucking slut" I hissed as I started to tuck myself back into my shorts.

She gagged as she pulled them out of her mouth, "You're the only dirty fucking slut around here"

She gestured to the window behind me.

I turned to face the balcony, where she was pointing, and something in the window caught my attention.

Outside, watching in, Shannon had watched the whole exercise, with her own fingers inside her pussy.

"Shit" I panicked.

Sian laughed as she stared out at the red-haired girl on the balcony as she continued to touch

She casually placed a negligee on, as I raced to the window, even though I hoped she had not seen anything, it was clear that she had.

"Shannon" I whispered, as I forced open the balcony door.

She glanced at me, and then switched her look to Sian, as she joined us in the cool night air. "This is not what it looks like" I explained.

"On the contrary" Sian announced, as she glided past me, allowing the air to catch the garment to reveal her skin again, "This is exactly what it looks like"

She placed a caring hand against Shannon's cheek, and I realised that she was still fingering herself.

"Your little slut here will fuck anything" Sian explained, as she moved her hand down Shannon's body, and inserting her own fingers inside, "Just like Ophelia and I told you he would"

"What?" I was confused by this.

Shannon finally spoke, "You never loved me"

I shook my head, "No Shannon, I do love you"

"You repulse me you dirty slag" She hissed, "Ophelia told me about the men and women you fucked, she told me you wanked that lad off in his hotel room in Blackpool when she faked her own death to get away from you"

She lurched forward, and pushed me hard against the window. I reached out to stop her from hitting me.

"You deserved everything that you got when she pushed you out of that window, you treated her like a one night stand, and you were not even man enough to send her on her way" She cried, "You didn't love her, and you didn't love me"

"Shannon, whatever these people have said...." I began.

"Said?" She interrupted, "I just watched you fuck my best friend"

Now I was even more confused.

Sian smiled as she made her way back to Shannon's side, and started to caress her, "After you left Mallorca, Shannon and I started seeing each other"

Shannon pulled away for a moment, and withdrew a cigarette from her pocket, as she made her way back to the wall. She perched her cheeks on the brickwork.

"I took Chris from you and now Shannon" Sian explained, "You think that you could step into my world and fuck up my life granny banger?"

I raised my hands, "You will never get away with this"

Sian laughed, "I already have, and I won dick head"

Shannon laughed too for the first time, "She took both me and Chris away from you"

Sian made her way back to Shannon, and reached for a lighter on the table nearby, as she continued, "I always win"

She leaned in and passionately kissed Shannon before me. Anger filled me, and I turned my back on them to walk away.

"Connor" Shannon called.

I stopped and stared at their reflections.

"Are you just going to walk away?" She asked.

I did not answer.

"I said" She shouted, "Are you just going to walk away?"

"Yes" I responded.

"No" She screamed, as she reached over to Sian, stroking her, "You will not treat me like you did with Ophelia"

"Whatever these two poisonous bitches have said about me is untrue" I insisted as I turned on my heels.

"Really?" A question, not a statement, "So in all the time you have been away from me, you have not touched another bit of pussy?"

"Shannon, I..." I began to argue.

"I just watched you fuck my best friend" She added calmly, "Not to mention the fact that I gave you permission to stick your penis into Olivia. Also, did you not get rogered by Chris on the very bed in that apartment recently?"

"Yes I had them all" I confessed, "You wouldn't come near me"

"You and I were a fantastic couple in Mallorca" She explained, "But I was never good enough for you, you were shagging Chris whenever I was stuck at the airport and either of you go the horn"

"Then he fucked Ophelia in a threesome whilst that girl lay dying" Sian added. "You keep your filthy mouth out of this" I rowed.

She pulled a face at me, as she lit one of her cigarettes.

"You broke Ophelia's heart, and you broke mine" Shannon calmly added, as she made her way back to Sian.

Sian casually opened her legs, and I watched as Shannon inserted two fingers into her pussy, causing her to groan in pleasure.

"Sian and I got to know what an absolute bastard you were in Mallorca" She announced, "I knew you bought the shit I said that they attacked me, when the truth was far simpler"

"Tell him" Sian urged, "In fact show him"

With a swift move, Shannon thrust her mobile phone at me, and pressed play on her screen.

The shaky camera took a moment to focus, as the three women came into view in a bedroom, Sian was naked on the bed with Shannon's arm wrapped around her body. Ophelia also sat naked on the bed, as she spoke.

"If you're watching this Connor" She smiled, "By now you probably have been driven crazy by my friends, and the fact that I had faked my own death in a bid to push you over the edge"

She moved the camera herself, and moved it along the two naked bodies on the bed, who were now kissing passionately, Sian had inserted her fingers in Shannon's twat.

"Sian, Shannon and Chris are under my spell now you needless wanker" She teased, "And soon, no one will love you, and when I am pissing on your gravestone, I will rest"

The camera poised for a moment, and the girls started making out for long moments.

Shannon snapped the phone away from me, and concentrated on fingering Sian as she spoke, "Ophelia was my saviour and she taught me how to love, I knew I could manipulate you into believing anything, and lead you here"

Panic set into me now, I knew the way down the fire escape, and this possibly was my only way.

"The ancient Indians believed that every month your blood becomes possessed by the spirits of the dead" She explained, still probing her lover, "And they would ritualistically cut themselves once a month to release demons"

"Are you self-harming?" I asked.

She did not answer me, she removed her sticky fingers from Sian's vagina, and raised them to her mouth, and her tongue darted out as she licked them.

Sian smiled at herself, as she watched.

"That tastes like my man" Shannon announced.

Sian laughed.

Anger shot through Shannon as she lunged toward her, gripping onto her chest. In retaliation, Sian lashed out with her arm, and grabbed her arm, pulling her over the edge.

Together they plummeted over the edge of the balcony. I could hear Sian scream as they fell, and I raced to where they were sitting. It was over in an instant.

Fearfully, I glanced over the edge to the scene below, neither of them were moving.

"Shannon" I cried.

THIRTY ONE

For a moment I had no idea what to do. I was unaware that Chris had entered the apartment sometime between the girls falling and what seemed like an eternity afterwards.

"You have to get out of here" He announced as he too glanced over the balcony. "Shannon...." I began to explain.

Without speaking, Chris took my arm, and pulled me into the room, and began to search his belongings.

I watched as he located a small satchel, and thrust it to me, "You have to leave" "Chris" I did not know what to say.

"They have been after you all along" He explained, "When I told you to trust me earlier, I mean it now. You have to get out of here and quick"

I nervously opened the satchel, and realised that it was full of cash.

"It's her liquidation" He explained, "Go get your passport and leave"

He leaned over to me, and whispered something in my ear. I pulled away, and looked into his eyes for a moment.

I began to panic, and he cupped me in his arms.

"I am begging you" He panicked, "Someone will find them soon and you will have no choice"

I nodded.

"Connor, I meant everything" He explained, "I only ever loved you

"Ophelia" I muttered.

"She is on her way here right now" He worried.

I looked at him square in the eyes and I knew that he was being sincere.

Chris grabbed me by the hand, and forced me out of the apartment, as he explained, "I will tell them I came home and found them over there"

"Why should I trust you?" I asked, "You were part of this all the way through"

"I promise you" He explained, "I hated the fact that Sian disliked you, when I only ever loved you, but I had to stay in the loop"

My hand moved to cover my mouth, "Why does this always happen to me?"

He placed his arm around me, and pulled me closer to him, I felt him begin to get hard in his trousers, "They made a plan to make you kill yourself, and if they failed, Ophelia was going to find you"

I realised he was being sincere as he spoke.

"She's going to be out here the day after tomorrow, and I knew if I hurt you I could possibly make you leave" He explained, "Why do you attract the fucking psycho's?"

"I attracted you didn't I?" I responded.
He smiled, and leaned in for a short, yet lingering kiss, before I pulled away. "You really do care" I whispered.

He nodded, "Now fuck off before someone finds those two bodies outside and puts two and two together"

My head began to swirl, as I took on board everything that happened, and I found myself walking out of the apartment in a daze. I deliberately wandered around to the back of building just to see if the girls were still present. I was not sure as I could not see them from the street.

I somehow made my way back to Lei's apartment, she was out as I stripped, and showered.

Gucci seemed to hide from me as I entered my own room in the same trance I had walked in on.

As if by autopilot, I gathered my clothes in a pile on the bed, and dressed in a pair of combats, and a tee shirt, and then I located my passport from the bedside cabinet.

Tossing my phone onto the mattress, I turned my back onto my room, and made my way to the door. That fucking annoying ring tone begin to sing at me, and I ignored it. Stuffing my passport in the bag. I glanced at the ticking clock on my wall, and realised it was 17:20.

As I entered the lounge, Gucci had changed his mind and come to me for a fuss, I crouched to reach his level, and stroked his mane for long moments, aware that my phone was ringing again in my room.

"I have to leave you mate" I smiled at the dog, and I realised I was talking to him, "And I have to leave your mummy a note"

I made my way to the large oak table, and quickly wrote a farewell note for Lei, I spoke as I wrote.

"Lei, by the time you read this note, you will realise that I have left resort. Sian and Shannon   have set me up big style, and I have to leave. I have left you some money to cover my room until you get someone else in. I'm sorry. Connor. P.S. I will miss you and Gucci"

I sighed as I opened the bag, and withdrew a handful of Lira's, and neatly placed them in a pile alongside the note. I smiled as I remembered helping Beverley last year, and this time I was doing it alone. I knew that I could not fly from Dalaman and had to make the long journey to Bodrum. I had no idea if I was going to get a coach, walk as far as I could or what. I just knew that I had attracted yet another fucking psychotic woman in my life. Two of which were at the bottom of that hotel, and one was one her way to get me.

I felt a tear fall from my eye as I rose, and stroked little Gucci one more time. I heard that annoying phone ring again.

I watched Gucci offer me his paw once as I pulled open the door, as he normally did when he wanted to go for a walk.

"No mate" I was talking to the fucking dog again.

I freely cried as I left the apartment one last time, with just that satchel of cash and a few changes of clothes that would fit in there.

I seemed to have slipped into my trance again as I made my way down the street, as I cannot remember reaching the harbour. Again as if by auto-pilot.

I recognised a couple of the bar tenders trying to entice me into their bars, and I politely rejected their offers for a moment, but then I realised they may be able to help me somehow to get to Bodrum, I had the cash after all, plus the inheritance would see me right once I got home.

I decided to go to back to Idris at the football bar, mainly because he was the only person I could trust, next to Lei, and I could not help but think that she may be part of the vendetta against me. After all, as Chris had said, I do attract psychotic women.

The walk to the bar was long, but I did not care. I must admit, I froze when I saw a police car drive past. Luckily it disappeared as quickly as it had come.

I chose to move off the roadside after that moment, and turned left onto the beach front.

In the horizon, I could see the lights of Icmeler before me, and I concentrated on walking, without looking suspicious.

I must have been walking for about ten minutes, as I heard Lana's voice calling my name from somewhere, I really did not want to see her and pretended not to hear her.

Big mistake really. Within moments, she was racing behind me, calling my name louder, so I stopped, and turned to face her, and pretended to remove some none-existent headphones from my ears before she arrived.

She embraced me, and I could tell she had been crying. "I am so sorry for earlier" She apologised.

"Doesn't matter" I muttered.

"I should have realised I was being foolish, but" She began, and then confusion set in, "What happened?"

"What do you mean?" I responded.

"I have been trying to call you for at least an hour" She continued, "As soon as I heard I wanted to see that you were ok"

"Lana" I placed my hands on her arms, "I have no idea what you are on about"

Her mouth formed a perfect O as she looked into my eyes, "Oh my God, you don't know"

"Know what?" I asked.

"Connor, there is no easy way to say this" She announced, "But there has been an accident"

"An accident?" I repeated.

She nodded, "I don't know what happened, but I think Shannon went to see Sian, and...." The pause was deafening, despite the tuneless karaoke coming from the nearby bar.

"What happened?" I urged.

A single tear fell from her eye, "I think Shannon confronted Sian over what she did to you back in Spain"

I nodded, "Would not surprise me"

"Well...." She spoke uncertain of what to say next, and she struggled to find the words.

"Lana, you're scaring me" I panicked.

"Sian and Chris live on the seventh floor of an apartment in town" She explained, "Shannon and Sian went over the balcony...."

I feigned a panic as she spoke, "I have to go"

Lana shook her head, "The paramedics were there last I heard.... one of them is dead, and the other is unconscious.... I don't know who"

"I have to go" I repeated.

Again, Lana shook her head, "The police are at the apartment, but there is no CCTV or anything, they think Shannon attacked Sian"

Although I knew what happened, I still acted dumb and pretended Lana was telling me something I did not know, I wanted to sit down, and did so, causing the waiter of the bar I was now in to rush over with his pad.

I ordered an Efes, and one for Lana, and began to stare off in the distance.

"Where is your phone?" She asked.

I shrugged, "Chris attacked me after you left, I think it might have fallen out of my pocket"

She placed a caring hand over my cheek, and inspected the bruising, as the waiter arrived with our order, "Olivia and Angie are at the hospital now but the reception is shit, I can't hear what they said"

I took a large swallow, "I need to know if Shannon is ok"

Lana took this as a cue, and tried to dial Angie again. She showed me her screen to prove the dead tone, and I smiled as I noticed the time, 19:37.

Then I remembered.

"I have to go" I announced, drinking the rest of my Efes as quickly as possible.

"To the hospital?" She asked, "Connor, they won't let you see her, they won't even allow Olivia or Angie...."

I took some money from my pocket, and passed it to her, "Lana, I have to do this"

I leaned over, and kissed her on the lips for a moment, before pulling away, and she watched in shock.

"Connor...." She muttered, "That was like you were saying goodbye" I smiled, and rose, and with no further words, I rushed out of the bar.

The sun was still warm this time of evening, as I raced back toward the harbour, as I did so, I could see the boat manoeuvring into the docks. I was sweating like a pig and I could feel the dampness of my patches around my pits and bits as I raced past people. I did not care that I may stink.

I made it to the port in record time, it was before 20:00 as I ran inside. There were barely any people in the port as I made it to the counter.

The Turkish lady seemed uninterested as I approached her.

"Am I in time for the boat to Rhodes?" I enquired.

She nodded, barely interested in me, and spoke in Turkish to her colleague, as she gestured me over to another desk on the opposite side of the room.

I smiled, and walked over to the booth which was unmanned, but with a note advising me that someone will be with me soon.

I heard the door open and glanced over for a moment, watching as a young Turkish couple entered, laughing.

Moments later, the door opened again, and I glanced over again.

"You made it" Chris smiled as he rushed over to me.

"You whispered something to me" I announced, "You told me if I trusted you to meet you here"

I saw his smile crack across his face.

"You told me that you would be here at 8 o'clock, I had to see you" I wanted to know what he wanted.

He smiled, but soon faded to a look of fear, "I am sorry I hurt you"

"You could have warned me" I muttered, as I touched my bruised cheek.

He placed his hand on my cheek and stroked my face for a moment, "When Sian told me that Ophelia was coming, I knew I had to do something"

"I don't know if I can trust you" I confessed.

Sorrowfully, he nodded, and removed an envelope from his pants pocket. I took it, and started to tear at the package, "One of them survived"

"How?" He asked, "That was a seven storey tumble"

"You didn't see?" I questioned.

He shook his head, "As soon as you went I gathered what I wanted, and came over here"

I glanced at the contents of the envelope in my hand. Two tickets with our names on them, flying from Rhodes to Montreal.

"Come with me" He smiled, "I want to start a new life with you"

I glanced at the tickets for a long moment, and thought to myself, do I go home or do I follow him?

I looked into his eyes, and knew what I had to do.

THIRTY TWO

April 25th.

A week had passed since I made my decision and now it was raining in dreary old Manchester. This time last week I was in Marmaris, Turkey, baking in the sun, and now I am here, in the abandoned Churchill's, whilst Justin sold up from his sun lounger in Gran Canaria. I sighed as I could hear the out of tune Curtis warbling in his room across the hallway. He was in my old room, the one I fell through last summer. Well, I say fell, Ophelia pushed me through it, she was crazy like that.

I turned back to the bed, and smiled at the naked woman that lay with her legs open, her pussy smiled at me, as she stirred. Another dirty slapper picked up on Canal Street for the cost of a Vodka and coke.

Curtis continued to sing outside, and I smiled at the sign of the sock on the door. My flaccid member wanted to move as I saw her touch her minge with her own fingers, but there was no hardness forming. I wanted her to fuck off, I could not be doing with another crazy psychotic bird after me. This woman was different. She was larger than my usual type, her black pubic hair flaked with last night's cum, and I knew what I had to do.

Swiftly, I inched toward her, and without introduction, my tongue lapped at her pussy lips. Starting off slow, I moved my tongue between each flap, awakening her in a flurry of shock, excitement and want. I created a slow steady movement of my tongue against her pussy lips and with my tongue flat, I continued to switch between each cleft. I entered her hole with four fingers, then one, now four again.

Soon I found myself putting my entire fist inside her hole. I flexed my hand from fist to palm, and as I stretched inside her, I could feel her insides against my fingers, wet, and her body moved in spasm. I fluctuated my movements between fast and slow, the intensity inside her increased, as I felt the gush of fluid and her satisfying moans increased. My face felt trapped against her pussy, and I heard her swear, forcing me to bury my tongue deeper inside her, and I carried on switching between fingers and tongue against her bush.

My face was wet with her cum as I pulled away for a moment, with my sticky hand I stroked her body with her own juices. I licked again, this time concentrating on her perineum for long moments. Then I stopped.

A flash of lightening interrupted my train of thought, and I rose. "You have to go" I whispered.

"Fine" No argument, as she wiped her mott onto my quilt, gathering her clothes almost instantly.

She wobbled a little as she dressed in silence to the rain outside.

"You were a lousy fuck anyway" She finally commented, buttoning up her blouse.

She sauntered out of the room, and I smiled to myself as I saw her bra on the floor. Moments later, I heard the door close downstairs.

Another flash of lightening hit outside distracting me for a moment. I watched the grey cloud linger over the Manchester street, people outside panicked and ran into shelter, and I turned away, glancing momentarily at the vacant bed. I had not put my quilt back, it was still sketch. My eyes were soon drawn to the photographs in frames next to it, on the bedside cabinet, amongst my hair products, stupid trinkets and my work pass.

The first photo was one of Shannon, Chris and I in Mallorca, granted, she was now scribbled out with a permanent marker, but I could still make her out. I allowed my finger to rub against the glass over her for a moment, and then I remembered.

Turning my attention to the other photograph, I instantly turned it around as Ophelia's face smiled back. I despised her for everything, but it felt good to know that she was thousands of miles away from me, where I should be. I don't know why I had this picture. I suppose I needed it to remind me of my hate for her. I could also see a photograph nearby of myself, Lana, Lei and Gucci during happy times, I think we were drunk, and peeking through the crowd was Sian, looking as devil-like as possible. I kept these bastards close this way. Because a photograph could not hurt me any more than the real thing.

My mind flashed back to the docks, and that moment I was with Chris, making up my mind. I knew I had made the right decision, and smiled to myself. I had deactivated my social media sites, and simply disappeared home. I recalled our conversation. Even now, the pain hurt inside.

My mobile phone started to ring, and I snatched it from its cradle, even though I was starting afresh, I was still uncertain on unknown numbers. I allowed it to go to voicemail, and then listened to the message. Instantly, I rang the number back.

"I am so sorry" I whispered, "But you know I have to screen the calls"

I listened, and felt a joy, and then the phone call ended almost as quickly as it started.

Something was amiss, like I was some sort of dirty secret.

As I raised my head, I felt a tear fall down my face, just hearing those words made me weak. I have endured a lot over this last two years. My parents died, I had a stalker who faked her own death, and then partnered up with my girlfriend to bring me down, I was drugged and raped by my former manager, and the sick bitch covered the fact so that it was I who got fired and not her. Then I walked out on another job, and was now an usher at a local cinema. I wanted one of two people to be here right now. I felt guilty wanting Shannon, but I needed someone to hold. I still did not know who had survived the fall, either Sian or Shannon was still alive somewhere.

The sound of the door creaked, and I realised that Shannon stood in the doorway, in her bikini, her body looked amazing as she posed for me against the frame. Placing her finger into her mouth, she sucked it and then used her finger to circle her erect nipples.

"I have missed you" She teased, as she slipped her breast out to show me, "Can Sian join us as you fuck my brains out?"

She did not wait for my response, she gestured across the room, and I smiled as Sian perched herself on my mattress.

"Whilst you fuck her" Sian purred, "I will suck your bollocks as they bounce on my chin and you will be taken to Heaven"

"No" I whispered.

They both looked disappointed, just for a moment. I blinked and they were gone.

When I raised my head again moments later, Curtis stood in the doorway with the tightest jeans and a half made up face.

"I heard you on the phone" He smiled, as he entered the room, instantly embracing me, before adding with a hint of venom "Was it him?"

I did not answer, I just cradled him in my arms for the longest of moments, daring not to pull away in case I fell apart. Curtis and I had come to an arrangement where if I was horny, we would shag. If he was horny, he can choose me, or go outside and find someone else. I preferred being in control now that Chris was missing from my life, I chose our old agreement of sock on the door means I am entertaining. If not it was a free for all. It worked.

"You have to pull yourself together" He urged, forcing himself away from me, "That slapper from Wilkinson and Co will be here any moment, with another potential buyer, and if they buy, we're both homeless"

I took a moment to gather my thoughts, and nodded. I had not felt like this in a long time. In fact, not since Zoie Dawson dumped me for Peter Nash in nursery. Curtis minced out of the room, and glanced seductively over his shoulder as he knew I was following him.

He paused at the door, and held it open for me, I am sure I felt him sniff my hair as I brushed past. I know for a fact I felt his erection in his pants.

Did not even bother to move, but the dirty smile on his face confirmed it was deliberate.

He leaned in closer to me, his minty fresh breath smelt sweet to me, "Let me take away the pain"

I smiled, "Curtis, no"

"Fine by me" He muttered, as he thrust his groin my way once more, "But you're a massive fool for getting like this, you live in Manchester girlfriend, you need to be out there, fucking anything that moves"

"The last time I went out there" I retorted, "I met a one night stand that just wouldn't fuck off"

"That was your mistake" We heard the door open downstairs, and automatically made our way down the staircase, "You met a woman"

THIRTY THREE

Annabella Rowlands stood in the vacant bar, with her brief case open on the polished bar. She wore a grey suit, with a skirt that barely covered her buttocks, and her tanned legs seemed to go on forever.

"Boys" She greeted with a flick of her wrist presenting a document.

"If you're here to evict us" Curtis began, as I took the paperwork, only briefly scanning it.

Annabella nodded, her blonde hair seemed firm, as though too much hair spray was forever holding it in place. "Justin has sold the bar with tenants, and the new buyers have requested that I serve you with 30 days' notice"

"Tell them fuck off" Curtis insisted.

I nodded, "When will they arrive?"

"This is a thriving night life area, and they want to open next month" Annabella explained, I could tell that she was disgusted at our presence, but she failed to hide it from me, "But they understand that you are sitting tenants, Justin has agreed to pay your deposits on new properties if this will help you to move on"

"Does he know how much it costs to live in this City?" Curtis argued, "I can't afford anything more than a bedsit in a shithole"

"We will find something" I assured, "I still have my inheritance to play with, and if push comes to a shove, we can move into my parent's apartment in Salford Quays"

"You have that family in there" He muttered.

"My parents left me that house and I put it out for rent, and Justin has agreed to find us deposits" I announced, I did not want to think about what I said next, "You can live with me"

A smile crossed his face, "Naked?"

"Shut up" I flirted.

Something about the conversation disgusted Annabella, and she made her way to the door, "You have 30 days boys"

"Who is the new landlord?" I enquired.

"Buyer wishes to remain anonymous" She pulled open the door, and left without any further words.

"If we have 30 days" Curtis announced, over-excitedly "We need to party"

I laughed, "Give me half an hour, I need a shower, and we can hit the bars"

The steam from the water hit me like a blast of wet hot air as I listened to the melancholic music from the radio. The soap was foaming over me and I knew that Curtis was lingering in the communal shower area.

He watched in awe as I allowed the bubbles to cover my manhood, and he became instantly aroused. At first, he tried to hide it by turning away, but the more I ignored him, the more intense his erection became.

Slowly he inched closer to me, and I soon felt him touch my flaccid member, he rubbed it gently until it hardened in his hand.

Within seconds we were kissing, his stubble hurt my lips at first, but we soon became synchronised, he was stroking my cock with fast wet wrist movements, and I returned the favour, causing him to groan a little too loud for my liking.

I pulled away, and flipped him around, he squealed in delight, and I pressed the tip of my dick against his hole. He assisted me by pushing back, and allowing me to enter his tight hole. Soon enough my balls pressed against his arse, and I began to bang him as fast as I could.

I slapped his arse several times, and he begged for more, all the time I was pumping hard into him for several minutes with total abandonment. He squeezed my cock with every plunge, and soon enough I felt that I could not hold on any longer, and I exploded with first one shot, and then multiple shots of cum, and I screamed loudly as each one volleyed. Curtis enjoyed it so much that he continued to squeeze hard onto my dick, refusing to allow me to pull out.

We held each other for a long moment as I finished masturbating him, and as he shot his load, he turned to kiss me, only then allowing me to fall out of his hole.

The rain had long since stopped as we left Churchill's, and there were barely any people about. We crossed the road and as I noticed a coach pulling into the nearby station, Curtis signalled to a few of his friends nearby. He raced over to them, and boasted to them about the shower incident, exaggerating for his benefit, which I ignored. I moved past him, and gestured to the nearest bar.

"Get me a beer bitch" He teased, trying to big himself up to his friends.

"You wanted my dick for so long, you can take that fantasy anywhere you want now" I smiled, as I flicked my wrist in a wanking motion to him.

His friends laughed at his embarrassment, and I pushed open the door to the loud music coming from the Canal Street bar.

He was clearly unimpressed as he joined me at the bar with a face like thunder minutes later.

"So you are telling me that meant nothing to you?" He asked, as he perched on the stool, ignoring the awaiting barman.

"Two pints of lager please" I nodded, and I turned back to Curtis, "You know that I am not on the market, what happened in there was a mistake"

"You will be knocking on my door before we have to move out" Curtis insisted, "You're a slag, and you know it"

I did not respond, and paid the barman who placed our beers before us. Instead, he placed his hand on my knee, which I brushed aside.

I did not get angry with him. Instead, I played his game, and chose a female to flirt with before him, and I smiled as I he became frustrated over me kissing the first lady in the room.

She took my hand and guided me toward the unisex toilets, which annoyed him. I was game for this. But then as she opened the door, I saw someone outside that made me stop. That movement in the corner of my eye, outside, looking in for just a moment.

Neglecting her, I rushed toward the doorway, and raced out to the bustling street outside. Where had everyone come from? This place was empty minutes ago. Frantically, I searched the crowd in both directions, not knowing what, or whom I was looking for.

THIRTY FOUR

It began to rain again and the crowds of people began to disperse into the bars, and the wet streets rapidly emptied. I knew I had seen someone I knew, but I had lost them. I perched on the wall overlooking the canal and I caught a glimpse of two lovers kissing passionately on the pathway below me. I held back from shouting 'get a room'.

I knew someone was watching me, but could not place whom, or where they were watching me from. For a moment, I recognised the girl from earlier kissing another man. I smiled to myself.

In my peripheral, I saw Curtis coming out of the bar with a young man, boy did he work fast, I pretended not to notice, and commenced walking along the street, not bothering with the rain. I did not really want him to move in with me, but hopefully this shag he was taking back could be the one for him and I would be rid of him, unless he turned into a gay version of Ophelia.

Someone caught my attention for a moment in the shadows, but they were not there that long. By the time I had walked to the space between the buildings, he, or she was gone. There was someone pissing against a bin, but he was stockier that the person I saw. It was not the same person who I had rushed out for.

The evening continued mainly alone, but as midnight approached, I had met up with the brunette from earlier. She reintroduced herself as Kate. I made a pathetic apology that I thought I had seen my cousin outside, which she bought. In return, I bought her a few drinks. She was drinking vodka and tonic. I knew someone else who had that drink before, and I pushed it to the back of my mind.

She spent the next few hours with her hand on my dick, or wallet for more vodka, and she pleasured herself in telling me how much she wanted me to fuck her like I hated her. I was happy to oblige, so mentioned I lived nearby.

We were kissing passionately, taking each other's clothes off as we entered the closed bar, locking up instantly behind us. We could hear Curtis and his lover in the throes of passion upstairs causing her to freeze for a moment, but then I noticed it turned her on.

"I want you to treat me bad" She insisted, as she led me to the bar.

Nervously, I was aware that there were two people fucking upstairs, and that anyone passing by may be able to see in, but she was not bothered by either fact.

She lowered herself, and put my dick entirely in her mouth, sucking as hard as she could, which made me groan a little, and I cupped her head, forcing it to take my specimen deep into her throat, causing her to gag.

"Want me to be mean?" I answered her previous comment, and I forcefully grabbed her by the hair pulling her upwards, her almost naked body pressed against the bar.

"Yes" She cried through the pain, "Treat me like a bitch, I want you to fuck me raw, and no matter how much I beg I want you to ignore it"

Despite my grip in her hair, she forced herself closer.

She stroked my penis gently as she anxiously pulled down her pure black knickers to her knees.

With a sharp tug, she pulled her panties off, and made me probe her pussy, perineum and her thighs with my dick. My eyes drew to the pants on the floor, and I wanted them. Reaching for them, I bound her hands together above her head whilst kissing her for a moment. She reached down my body, and tried to enter my hole with her grasping fingers, but failed.

Arching her pussy towards me, I drove deep into her tight clefts.

She pushed against me so hard, that my balls touched her as she literally fucked me, I started to thrust in synchronisation with her.

Her suction pulled me deeper inside her, and like someone else before, there was no build-up of momentum, we just started to fuck each other fast, and furious, the slapping sounds of our bodies echoed around the bar. For some reason, this beautiful woman before me was not as satisfying as I wanted, and for a moment, I remembered Shannon, then Ophelia. But I fought through these images, and she began to use her vaginal muscle to squeeze my dick with every stroke.

Anger began to take over as I did not want to touch her.

She mumbled something as she pushed harder on my dick. I reached over to her hair, and pulled sharply back, kissing her neck, biting it occasionally as I rammed deeper into her wet pussy.

She screamed in agony at first, and I continued to pound her harder, and somehow deeper, meanwhile we could also hear Curtis and his shag getting louder, probably overhearing us. Kate's pain became pleasure, as she began to convulse with waves of orgasmic satisfaction. I did not care over the pain I was causing her, even when she began to whimper.

I reached down, and touched my own dick still inside her, I snatched at her pubic hair, pulling roughly at the small wet wisps.

"I'm cumming" I whispered, aware that she was getting turned on, and I knew I was ready to release my sperm into her chasm.

She did not answer me, rather she encouraged me to pull harder at her pubes, and she pushed herself even more firmly onto my pole, I could see how wet we both were, and we began to speed up our rhythmical movement, her groans became intense. I felt my volley of explosions inside myself, and I released my hot thick creamy cum inside her.

I pulled out instantly, I undid her bound hands, I used her panties to wipe my dripping cock, and then I wiped her dripping fanny with them.

I pulled at her hair hard once more, and as she let out a scream, I forced them into her mouth. "Taste that you dirty fucking slut" I hissed, "You liked that didn't you?"

She gagged as she pulled them out of her mouth, and I recoiled a moment as I realised what I had done.

Naked, she thrust the knickers into my face, and I inhaled for a moment.

Flashes of Sian and Shannon came back to me. I felt sick as I realised that I almost re-enacted the moment a week ago in Sian's room. The bitch before me even looked like her.

"You have to leave" I whispered, still aware of the noises coming from upstairs, I pulled on my trousers without putting on my underwear.

"Thanks for the fuck" She whispered, dressing, and not even maintaining eye contact. The noises from upstairs stopped with the sound of two men satisfying each other, and pretty soon, she was putting on her shoes to leave.

As she made her way to the doorway, I joined her to unlock, "I am not usually like this"

"Honey, I don't care, I needed a dick in me tonight, and well...." She smiled, "Lucky you. I left my knickers on the bar for you"

I cracked a smile, and allowed her to walk out of my life. I instantly closed the door, and collapsed against it. What have I become? I was reminiscing of Sian and that terrible night. I kept on seeing them tumble.

"You ok?" Curtis asked from the stairwell, he was wrapped in just a towel, and his casual shag was tucking his shirt into his jeans.

I realised I was sitting on the floor now, and I rose as his shag approached the door to leave.

"I would have considered a threesome" He commented, as he gently tweaked my nipple upon pulling open the door, giving me a knowing wink as he left.

"Dream on" I hissed.

Curtis smiled, "Did you get off banging that bird knowing I was upstairs?"

"Our arrangement is to shag when we are horny" I concurred.

"Your phone has been ringing all night" Curtis seemed pissed with me,

"Can you not get a better ring tone, it was putting me off"

I made my way to the staircase, and as I placed my hand on the banister, someone knocked on the window.

Someone stood there, looking in. The frosting on the glass made it difficult to see.

"Who is it?" Curtis asked now appearing by my side dressed in just his jeans, and an unbuttoned shirt, and presenting my phone.

Cautiously I made my way to the door, trying to avoid being seen by the person in the window, which was fucking difficult, I tell you.

I opened the door, and the person moved fast into the crowds.

Topless, I ran out to try to chase them, but it was no use. Curtis soon followed, buttoning his shirt, and we soon met amidst the bustling audience.

He passed me my tee-shirt, "It is creeping me out living here knowing someone else is taking over. I think we should take Justin's offer or kick out your tenants soon"

"Keep it off" Someone shouted as I pulled on my shirt, which caused me to blush a little.

"We are not going anywhere until the time is right" I smiled, as I hugged him.

"Good" Curtis laughed, "Now I am gagging for a drink, and I think it is my turn to buy"

"Fucking Hell" I laughed, "If you get your wallet out, the moth will escape"

THIRTY FIVE

April 30th.

   We were awoken early that morning by loud bangs downstairs. We were naked in my bed and we glanced at the clocks on our mobile phones, it was ridiculous o'clock, we had finally drifted off to sleep after a particularly steamy session only a few hours ago. I think, not sure, but there may have been others involved.
   "Is it burglars?" Curtis whispered.
   "Worse" I responded, "New owners"
   Quickly we dressed in the same clothes we had worn the night before, and made our way down into the bar. Two burly removal men were mauling in boxes as we gathered our takeaway paper and cans from last night.
   I could hear someone barking orders outside, presumable to more removal men, and then the door opened. The barker entered wearing shades and a short ladies tee-shirt, revealing his pierced naval.
   "Holy Fuck" He screamed into his mobile phone in the campest possible reaction, so fucking camp, he made Curtis look butch. "Honey, you have to get your arse here now.... No, you will not believe who is pitching a tent with a hottie right now...."
   Anger shot through me again, as I remembered this wanker before me.
   I felt Curtis's hand grip mine, as I lurched forward toward Robin, in his designer gear, no doubt bought for him by his lover. I hated him, as much as my ex agent, and Ophelia combined.
   "You're a dead man Candlish" Robin announced, slamming down the phone, and dismissing the removal men temporarily "When my husband comes over, he will make you pay for stubbing a cigarette out on his dick last year"
   "He raped him" Curtis defended.

"Honey" Robin camply hissed, "You were not there at the party in Mallorca, your little slag here was putting his penis into any hole he could find, male, female, fat...."

He seemed braver than he used to be as he squared up to Curtis.

"Actually where did you go that day?" I asked, recalling that he was not seen, maintaining my grip on Curtis.

To my surprise he confessed, "I drugged that ginger whore up, and planted her somewhere to be found. It was my idea really. I did not do anything to her, I don't do fish babe, and I said to Tommo that we should track you down and fuck your life, and I think we did just that. We just wanted you to pay for abandoning Tommo for no reason, and now look at you"

I held Curtis back, "I proved that I was drugged, and people have already paid for that"

"Yes but you lost your job and came back to good old Manchester" Robin laughed, "Bet you will suck Tommo's cock for your old gig back"

"I told you people have paid, are you not scared?" I asked.

Robin laughed, and shook his head, "Maybe I will let you suck my husband's dick and we can get you some old man's cabaret bar, face it Candlish, your singing career is over"

"People died because of that" I confessed.

"Like your career honey, and now look, you're now living in a crummy bedsit in the bar that my husband bought me for my wedding gift" Robin laughed, "I say living here, we want you two faggots out"

"We were given thirty days" I insisted, "So tell your husband...."

"Tell his husband what?" Tommo asked from the doorway, bemused by my presence, he sure had put on some middle aged spread, and if possible he was more bald than he was last year, and he flounced into the bar area, kissing his lover over passionately, I felt myself heave, he pulled away, and looked back at me, and he was already sporting a stonking hard-on, "You were saying that you can tell me something?"

I did not want to respond, and I felt my own grip tighten on Curtis's hand, I could also see him seething.

"Honey, I need you to go the cash point" Tommo smiled.

Robin tried to protest for a moment, but he could sense he would not win the battle, and snapped the credit card out of Tommo's hand. There was a brief conversation between them, but I did not hear it.

Tommo watched, as Robin made his way out of the bar, and locked the door behind him.

"Let us out" I hissed.

Tommo sucked through his teeth, "I love it when you act all tough"

I noticed that he was now stroking an erection in his tight trousers, and he was beginning to unzip his fly.

"You can fuck off" I laughed.

His solid cock was now entirely out, "Which one of you will take it first?"

I released my grip on Curtis now, aware that he was about to explode with violence, and I was willing to let him attack.

"I still get a burn down there" Tommo hissed, as he drew back his foreskin, stepping out of his trousers, "Remember when you put a lit cigarette out on my cock?"

I did not answer, and I could see the anger build in Curtis, who was trying to hold himself back. Tommo carelessly removed his shirt, and tossed it aside. His middle-aged spread seemed to unfold before us.

"I still think about you when I get that burn" Tommo laughed, "Now for punishment, I think you can suck it better, whilst your little bitch watches"

That was enough to send Curtis into a frenzy, who lurched at the naked man before me. To my surprise, Tommo swung out his arm, and grabbed at him as he approached, taking complete control, and sending him to the ground with force. He lay flat on the ground.

"You" Tommo hissed, pointing at me, as I remained frozen on the spot, "You can watch as I prove to you I will always win"

He lowered himself over Curtis's unconscious body, and wiped his erect cock over his lips, putting it inside the mouth for a moment.

"No" I screamed, finding the courage or the strength to move, to which Tommo moved away from my friend.

I have no idea where his strength suddenly came from, as he was never this strong before, and I felt his arm hit me hard in the face, sending me to the floor too. Dazed, I tried to rise, and I heard the door open.

"Is it time?" I heard Robin ask, as I caught him enter the bar, "I have sent the removal men away"

"Good" Tommo smiled, "Now let's get these two low lives downstairs"

"I could not believe this was so fucking simple" Robin laughed, locking the door behind him, "Right where you said he was as well"

"And worth every penny" Tommo laughed.

I could not even fight back, I was so weak, but I felt my eyes close.

When I came too, I could hear them shagging nearby. I strained, and realised that I was bound to a pillar in the basement, the musky smell really hit me, and I could barely see anything before me.

Their session soon stopped, and I heard shuffling in the darkness beyond, I could hear Robin whispering that I was awake.

I tried to raise my head, but I was sore, "Where is Curtis?"

Tommo and Robin laughed, and I saw Tommo crouch down beside me.

"Suck my dick, or your boyfriend gets it" He laughed.

I could tell Robin was not impressed, but he seemed to obey what Tommo said, and rose. He moved behind me, as Tommo's erect cock probed my lips.

"Try anything and I will slit you from ear to ear" Robin laughed, and I realised he had a blade against my neck, the blunt side was digging into my flesh, and I panicked, "Last time, you hurt him, now this time, you show him love, and taste that salty goodness"

"I would also be tasting the fucking shit from your arse" I hissed.

Tommo took the opportunity to strike my face hard with his palm, "You never talk back you dirty little slut"

I did not have time to respond, as I felt the tip press against my mouth.

"Take it" Robin urged, and I felt his own penis harden beside me.

Tommo pressed, and his cock entered my lips. I gagged as he allowed it to travel into my throat, and he began to mouth fuck me for his own pleasure.

As he thrust, I choked, but with my hands tied behind me I could not fight him off again, and Tommo relished in telling me, "You have a hot piece of tail there, but will you save him, or yourself"

I could not answer as I had his fucking knob in my mouth stopping me from acknowledging, I felt my eyes water, and then I heard a mumble in the distance. I felt bile ride through my throat, and some spilled from my mouth. He seemed to get off on my wretching from his burnt phallus.

"Hear that?" Tommo teased, I could not hear anything, but Tommo was enjoying his shaft in my own wet throat, "He's coming to.... just in time"

He withdrew, and I screamed, anger, and embarrassment by his invasion. I allowed the vomit from inside me to flow freely from my mouth, and through tears, I saw Tommo nod to Robin, who casually dropped his blade. I barely had time to react as I saw Tommo's hot white jizz shoot out of his japs eye and splash into my face, which he found amusing.

His husband licked the come from his dick before Tommo took a moment to dress

"You just have a few minutes" Tommo smiled as he buttoned his shirt.

"You're disgusting" I hissed, aware that Robin was making a splashing noise behind me, I could not twist to see what he was doing but I could smell the fumes of petrol. I struggled to reach for the blade which was just out of my own reach, and I knew that neither could see me move for it.

I could hear Curtis groaning for me, but I could not decipher where it was coming from, possibly above me somewhere?

Tommo laughed, as he fumbled in his pockets for a moment, "You will only have just a few minutes to save yourself, or your fella"

He laughed, as he flicked at the lighter he had pulled from his pocket.

"I have been planning this little bit of revenge since last year" He insisted, "My dick never healed and you need to fucking pay"

"I love his dick and you ruined it" Robyn hissed, seizing a moment to kick at me.

Tommo slapped me so hard across the face, I screamed. Surely someone would hear me.

"Now I'm gonna burn you and your boyfriend" Tommo insisted, as he flicked the lighter once more, and tossed it behind me, "If you survive, I will come back and finish you properly, and if I don't then one of your other enemies will do it for me... you will be surprised what I know about you"

I heard the roar, and felt the heat flare against me.

Tommo slowly lowered beside me, ignoring the intense heat beginning to furrow around the cellar, "When I followed you last week, I had no idea how easy it would be to dispose of you. Perhaps I should start a Connor Candlish hate group, I can invite all those people you have crossed, Ophelia for instance, or Leigh Durber the man you framed in The Gambia. Maybe even that lovely girl from Marmaris that fell over the balcony as you robbed her...."

"You just fucking cum on my face" I insisted, "Your DNA is all over the place"

"Honey" Robin laughed, "We used fake names to buy this place, and there is no trace. It will be an insurance fiddle, and you and your little whore will be in the frame, after all you are squatters, and we gave you thirty days, and you decided not to go out without a fight"

"Shut up" Tommo laughed, as he rose, "Let's see if you can get out of this one"

Tommo laughed and pulled his lover away from me. I watched in horror, and fought against the pillar I was tied to, and in the smoke filled room, I could hear them run up the staircase, but then someone screamed. I could not tell who it was, but these fucking flames were licking at the pillar now, and as I choked. I prepared to die, and waited for what seemed like an eternity.

I tried to call out for help, but nothing escaped my lips, and I was sure Curtis has gone quiet, but I could not tell with the roaring flames.

Then I saw a hand claw at mine. It reached for the blade. "Curtis" I sighed.

"No such luck" Robin gasped as he sliced at my binds.

THIRTY SIX

With a blade in his hand, I did not trust Robin, and I frantically struggled with my binds at my feet. Without speaking, the pathetic queen gestured away from me, and I followed his signal.

The smoke was beginning to get thick inside, and I could hear the sirens already outside. "We have to get out of here" I called.

"Get out" Robin screamed.

I turned to face him, and could see him sitting on the ground, near to where I was just captive, as though he had given up.

"I heard a scream" I asked, almost forgetting that the flames were real around us. He nodded, "I fell"

"Tommo just left you" I guessed.

He nodded again, "We only married at Christmas, and he already has a whole herd of fucks following him, I cannot cope anymore"

"He left you here didn't he?" I already knew the answer.

"I am sorry I was such a twat" Robin sighed, as I became are of the intense creaking of the floor above me, and the room was now beginning to collapse, "I didn't really want to hurt you last year, it was all Tommo, you know how he controls people, me, and you deserve better"

"We have to get out of here" I realised that I was speaking to someone only a small time ago I called a wanker.

"Just go" Robin cried, and he turned his back to me, "I promise I will make it all up to you"

I reached out for him to pull him towards me, but something behind me alerted me, I turned on my heels in time as a fire fighter reached out for me.

As he grabbed me, I heard something collapse, Robin had disappeared, and in his place was a burning piece of timber.

Everything seemed slow as I was removed from the burning cellar, and along the staircase to safety, I saw the hole that he must have fell through, and the fire-fighter expertly manoeuvred me around it. I searched desperately for Robin and Curtis, without success. I screamed, although the smoke made it difficult.

The fresh air outside tasted so sweet as I was escorted to the awaiting ambulance, and I was amazed at how fast the fire-fighters were controlling the building that we had just escaped.

I could not really hear the paramedic as she treated me, I just wanted to know if Curtis and possibly even cock weasel Robin had gotten out, I did not remember seeing him move in the basement, I just had to hope.

The paramedic announced that she was getting me to the hospital, and I tried to talk, it was useless, and I felt pathetic as the door closed. My eyes became heavy as the sirens commenced.

And I slept.

I awoke in hospital, in a private room some time later that day. The clinical whiteness seemed bright against my eyes, but I could make out the shapes of nurses nearby. I knew that I was alright as my dick was already erect and I had not even adjusted to the visions yet.

"Welcome back" A friendly female voice smiled, at least I think she smiled.

"What happened?" I asked, my memory was hazy and I remembered just fragments of earlier in the day.

"You were squatting in an abandoned bar in the City" She explained, "It caught fire this morning and you were rescued from the basement"

My eyes were now clear, and I smiled at the tall blonde nurse before me, "This must be Heaven"

She smiled back at me, "You have some powerful friends out there Mr Candlish"

I felt confused, I seemed to be the only person in this room, in fact it was a private unit as I scanned the area, the nurse was pretty, and familiar to me. I could not place it, but I knew that she was someone I had already met. Mind you I lived in a massive City, so I had probably just seen her in passing.

"How can I afford private nursing?" I queried, a little nervous that the comment was about to see them realise I was not as rich as they may be thinking.

"Someone is paying for you" She checked her notes, "There is a name here somewhere. I am sure it is Mumford"

I felt relieved at her statement. But I after what Chris had told me about his father, something did not sit right. I chose not to dwell on it, "There was someone else in the basement"

"I only know that you and your friend were bought out of that building, he is in the public hospital, I will check on that for you though in just a moment" She spoke, as she made some written notes in my file, the she paused, and looked at me, "You do not remember me do you?"

Realising that I could not genuinely answer her, I nodded.

She gave me a soothing smile back at me, and held out her hand to shake, "My name is Rachel Hambleton, I met you last January, when your parents passed away"

I still could not remember her, and if I offended her she hid it professionally, as I shook her hand.

The silent gap there seemed to last an eternity.
"I was deeply hurt when you left me the next morning at that hotel, miles from my real home"

I wanted to apologise again.

She sighed, "But I understood I was simply a one night stand"

"Don't say that" I insisted.

She moistened her lips with her tongue, "What's the deal with your friend?"

I struggled for words, and I was aware that my erection was on show under the white sheets.

"Maybe when you get out of here, you and I can meet and catch up where we left off?" She smiled, and her hand had reached closer to my bulge, she could see it and I was aware, and uncomfortable.

With a snap of her hand, she pulled away and smiled back at me.

"I am sorry" I think I repeated.

"The person paying your bills is a Mr Mumford" She commented as though I would know who she was on about.

"Chris" I smiled.

"I think his name is Greg" She corrected.

I had no idea who Greg Mumford was. But he had the same surname as Chris, but when I last spoke to Chris he had told me that he was happy back at his parents in Croydon. Probably some relation.

"I have to leave soon" She jotted down her digits onto a piece of paper nearby. She folded it and placed it into my jacket which I noticed now was hanging on the door, "You will need that number at some point"

She paused at the door, and winked at me.

"I work between 9 and five thirty" She continued, "It's difficult to get child care around here after hours, at least on a Nurses wages"

She did not allow me time to respond, and pulled the door open.

"Wait" I called when it was too late.

She did not stop, and by the time I got to the door, she had disappeared into the corridors of the hospital.

My view instantly became blocked by a handsome couple that suddenly arrived from the nearby reception.

"Are you Connor Candlish?" He asked.

I was drawn to his roguish good looks, and I realised he was the father of Chris instantly without introduction, he was almost like an older version, only he had peppered hair that had been dyed some time ago "I am sir"

"Then we need to talk" He insisted, "In private"

He gestured me to the ward, and as I allowed the pretty Italian looking lady in first, I could not help but think that he was paying for my treatment, and yet, I was also in trouble.

Greg instantly took his seat, and motioned that I return to my bed. The Italian lady perched upon his knee, and smiled at me. A total juxtapose to the glare that he was passing to me.

"You and I have something in common Mr Candlish" He spoke with authority. "I take it you mean Chris" I responded.

"You do not mention his name" He hissed, as though I had shat on his doorstep, "That boy is dead to me"

"He told me he was happy" I responded.

"So you have seen him?" The woman questioned, barely concerned.

I shook my head, "No, he called me the other day, and told me everything was fine"

"When was this?" He asked.

"Last week" I responded as though being interrogated.

"And you have not seen him?" He was not asking, more of an accusation, when I shook my head, "He came home alright but we have not seen him since last week, not since he told us that he was packing fudge with you"

"Sir, I...." I began to retaliate.

"You turned my handsome young man, my own pride and joy, into a dirty bum boy" He growled, "And you have angered both me and his stepmother"

The woman smiled at me more, I could not tell if she was condescending or sincere, as she introduced herself, "Eve"

"Where is my boy?" He asked once more.

THIRTY SEVEN

Eve was easily the same age as I was, and I could not help but notice as she adjusted her positioning on Greg's leg. I thought for a moment if she was wearing crotchless panties he would be inside her minge right now.

"I have not spoken to Chris since last week" I repeated, "I called him and he told me how happy he was to be back at home..."

I could now see the anger building in his father's face, but his calmness seemed uncharacteristic. "He went to bed last week after he told me about you, and he has not been seen since"

"If you know where he is you must tell us" Eve insisted.

"I'm worried now" I insisted.

"If you gave a shit about him" Greg hissed, "You would not have left him in that harbour holding those fucking tickets to Canada, and you would have spoken to him more recently than last week"

"He knows why I did not call him" I spoke with urgency in my own voice, "And he knows why I left him in Marmaris"

Anger was now beginning to show in his raised response, "You faggots are all the same, you just fuck and move on to the next one"

I bit my tongue as I did not want to respond to this prick whilst he was being like this.

"Why don't you go and get us some coffee" Eve insisted to her husband, "We will get nowhere with raised voices"

Finally the voice of reason. He glared at her and then me for long moments, before forcefully moving her off his crotch, his semi-on was too obvious, as he gestured to me with his forefinger, "You better get to thinking about who is paying for your treatment and I expect to get some ideas where the ginger tosser is"

"Just go" Eve commanded.

Without any further words, he tore open the door, and marched out, Eve watched the doorway for a moment before turning back to me.

She smiled at me, and she slowly sauntered toward my bed, "Come on Connor, let's be adult about this"

I felt my dick twitch as she perched next to me. It was too obvious to hide.

"So what is it about my step-son that made you think 'I would bang the arse off that'?" She smiled.

"It was not like that" I stammered, aware that her hand was inching closer to my erection than I would normally feel comfortable about, "We were both in relationships, and as friends.... we kind of just...."

Her hand touched the material of my hospital gown, and she stroked it wantonly, as she continued, "Chris told me that you were both fucking women at the same time, I used to do that when I was a dancer, I loved the taste of pussy juice, and cock in the same instance, Greg took a fancy to me, and he bought me this life"

Her hand was now gripping my solid cock under my gown, and was frantically tugging away, I gasped, unsure if it was shock, or ecstasy, maybe even fear that Greg would walk in any second now. How far away was that coffee shop?

Her fast wrist movements began to make my member throb, and I was aware that my balls were banging hard against my thighs.

"I could not care anything about the ginger twat" She confessed, as she used her other hand to stroke my pubis, "But Daddy can't let him be homo, it worries him that he would never be a grandfather. I have done a lot of leg work before we came here, so when Greg offers you a new job, you take it, and forget about him"

I could not respond, as I was already beginning to reach orgasm, and I knew that she knew.

The semen shot through my body, and I yelped a little as I felt it release through the tip.

Teasingly, she raised her hand, covered in my man juice, and licked it, before she playfully covered my modesty with my gown, "Now, forget Chris, and move on with your life"

She moved away from my bed, and used the hand sanitizer before sitting back on the same seat that Greg was sat only minutes ago.

"You know" She commented, "I used to do that with Chris when his dad was asleep, it felt good to have someone of my own age to give a hand job or a blow job to, Chris said it helped him to sleep, though I doubt I could surprise you with any stories of him"

She placed her own finger on her lips, as I was still silent. I don't know how long I gawped at her, but it was soon disturbed when the door opened again, this time, Greg had a smile on his face, as he was accompanied by Rachel, and bearing a tray of caffeine.

Caringly, he placed one of the paper vessels onto my bedside, and smiled, "So, can I confirm you will help me find my pride and joy?"

I nodded, glancing briefly at Eve as she opened her legs briefly.

"If you help me find my boy" He smiled, I was unsure whether he was being genuine, but then again, like father, like son, "I will give you one of the best paid secure jobs in one of my new ventures. You choose, Bournemouth, Blackpool, Edinburgh...."

"Greg owns a chain of nightclubs" Eve interjected, "Dancing bars, you will love it"

"I will help you" I responded, daring not to make eye contact with Eve again.

"And I have some news on your friend" Rachel interjected, "He has superficial burns and will be out of hospital soon"

I was aware that Greg and Eve were making eye contact themselves, questioning my friendship.

THIRTY EIGHT

May 6th

I spent those next few days recuperating at Mr Mumford's expense, and his limousine service taxied me to and from the hospital so that I could see Curtis. His arm was burned badly, but he knew what happened, and had planned to move to his friends in Salford. He also told me that Robin had been found, and was in a coma in another hospital somewhere in Wales. Rachel had become my confidant, and she knew about what I wanted to tell her about what happened in Marmaris, and sworn to secrecy. I could not help but think Greg and Eve would try to find some information. Hell I did not even know which one of those girls had allegedly survived that fall.

Greg and Eve had found me a bedsit in the City, overlooking the canals, and if I looked hard enough, I could see my old apartment nearby. I knew that Greg was trying to buy me for information on his son, but I also knew that Chris would steer clear from me. I knew that I had broken his heart when I said goodbye just a few weeks ago. Part of me wanted to turn back time and just say yes to Canada. Would my life be much different?

However, I could use this situation, and get myself away from Manchester earlier than my original plan. Original plan? I had no idea. I made the decision to return to Manchester as it was my only home. I knew which destination I was choosing when the time was right.

As I moped around my room, something caught my attention in my belongings on my new table. A neatly folded piece of paper. I smiled as I unfolded it, and gently allowed my finger to stroke the words, written by Rachel. Without thinking, I quickly typed in the message, and within seconds she responded.

With a smile, I dressed in my tightest jeans, and whitest shirt, and pocketed the phone into my leather jacket. Hell, if Chris's dad wanted to spend money, let him.

As I pulled open my door, I smiled at the middle-aged lady outside, she stubbed out a cigarette into an over-filled ash tray. She gave me a wink as she grasped a tumbler of whisky. Her perfectly styled blonde hair stayed static as she moved.

"You must be the young tenant" She purred. "Connor Candlish" I nodded.

"Allie" She smiled, gesturing the tumbler to me, "I am your landlady, and I want rent on time stud, or I will come and get it from that sexy ass of yours"

Together we laughed, although I was unsure if she was being legit, or maybe this could even be Ophelia's mother. Shit, I had thought of her again. Why was this slut still in my head?

"It's been a long time since someone played hide the sausage in my pussy" She spoke matter- of-factly, her hand gently rubbing at her fanny. "Would you like to tickle my itch Connor?"

"I will check my diary" I teased.

Luckily, this was the end of the conversation as a passing taxi slowed down enough for me to flag it.

The taxi smelt like sweat and curry and I cracked open a window, making an excuse I was feeling ill. The driver was ranting on about some football match he was missing. Like I gave a flying fuck.

Within moments, we entered a grassy area of Chorlton-Cum-Hardy, and a surprisingly large house for someone on a nurse's salary. The name Cum in the town made me giggle a little. Yes I plan on Cumming this afternoon.

I did not want to touch this driver's money, and all I had was a twenty pound note. Some tip, I thought. I even think he thought all his Christmases had come at once as I was sure he was cheering as he drove off.

The doorway was a large oak door, and as I knocked, I could hear a child inside crying. I remembered something that Rachel had said and I thought for a moment.

That thought was disrupted as Rachel opened the door, still in her nurse's uniform from her shift.

"You only got out hospital today and you wanted to meet up already?" She questioned.

"I know I was an absolute knob head last year" I confessed, "I was grieving over my parents"

"That's the past" She smiled, as she pressed her back against the door, inviting me in, the child had stopped crying.

She guided me into the lounge, which was minimalistic, and I noticed a small grey cat on the chair, who looked at me briefly then went back to sleep.

"So where to start?" She smiled, allowing her hand to wander down my chest, "I think last time you liked nibbling...."

With that she leaned in, and gently nuzzled at my neck. I remembered picking her up when my parents died.

She began to groan as her lips moved wildly around mine, her tongue darting sharply into my mouth. Before I knew it, her tunic was off, and her pants and bra were somewhere across the room.

"I see you're in excellent physical health Connor" She smiled, as she pulled back, "Now if you don't mind, I need to inspect your genitals"

I could not believe it, as she tore roughly at my zipper, releasing my cock instantly, I barely had time to even nod at her suggestion.

"I see you shave" She smiled, as she stroked my erect penis.

I nodded, this is something I had started doing recently, I was bored, and in the shower when I just did it.

"Me too" She confessed, and she began to lower herself, "Back in med school, we were taught that it was cleaner to be bare, and that it improved sensuality, and I have not had a bush for years"

She moved eagerly toward my cock, and licked the shaft with her pierced tongue, and sucked for long seductive moments. Her hands wandered around to my buttocks, and her thumb probed the hole.

Soon enough, she rose, and straddled me without speaking, our lips were used for kissing not speaking. She forced my cock into her tight pussy, and started to ride me, forcing me against the wall. Using her thighs, she gripped tightly, and guided my hand towards her clefts, I began to stroke her wet clitoris, and I felt her minge muscles tighten over my dick and fingers, I felt her nails dig into my back, as my hands now clasped at her hips.

She moved my hands, and held them aloft over my head with one of hers, as she continued to grind my cock, soon she was rubbing her own breasts, and body as I watched. I could see my own dick pounding into her, I felt the back of her pussy with each thrust, and as I felt myself about to erupt inside her, I moved closer to her mouth, and bit her bottom lip, our rhythmical movements intensified, and as she dug her heels deep into my buttocks, her tightening pussy muscles sped up my release, and she lay gasping on top of me, stifling her screams.

I felt my cock fall out of her as it softened moments later.

"Thank you" She smiled, as she clambered off me, "But you have to go soon" "I want to stay the night" I confessed.

"No chance Connor" She insisted, "You missed this opportunity, you were just lucky this time"

"Aw come on" I pleaded.

"My husband will be home soon" She confessed, "What do I tell him? I forgot to give you a bed bath and you chased it up?"

I heard the child stir again for the first time.

She smiled, "Don't worry, it's definitely his"

THIRTY NINE

May 9th

Those fucking words hit me hard. I had no idea how or what I was feeling. I kept thinking that I had misheard her at the hospital that day when she dropped hints that she struggled with a babysitter. I don't even want a child. She was now refusing to reply to my texts and I think maybe it was even blocked. Part of me wanted to get back on social media but the minute I would do that, crazy bitches will locate me.

I spent those nights drunk. Anything I could get, whether it cheap shit cider, or cans of lager, vodka, even Allie's whisky when she was home. That first time she touched me I cringed, but the second time I was numb. I had been pissing myself up the wall for three days, and things were going mental. This morning, I found my mobile phone in the fridge along with a shoe, and my favourite photograph of Chris and Shannon.

Today was particularly rough. It was Shannon's birthday and I was drinking to remember last year. We were mainly drunk and naked in her apartment.

I still did not know what had happened in Turkey one of those had survived. I had removed all contact, by shutting down my social media, and I just wanted out of Manchester, which is why I had decided on which location to go to when the time was right with Mr Mumford. Now I was just waiting for the Cockney arsehole to call me.

As my can of cheap lager was evidently empty, I decided to join my landlady, Allie in her favourite pass-time of whisky. She was very welcoming as she opened her door to my lazy knocks. She inhaled deeply on a menthol cigarette as she leaned against her doorframe.

"I want your minge" I slurred. Charming, even by my standards.

"You are paid up for at least three more weeks" She laughed, as she playfully stroked her own body with her slender arms.

I remained in the doorway, stroking her arm.

"So is this just you wanting alcohol?" She asked, as the moonlight began to shine through her see though negligee, I could see her black pubic hair trimmed underneath her white panties, "Or are you here to give me a portion of your husband bulge?"

She adjusted herself, leaning from one side to another, as her hand gently rubbed down my body, pausing at my belt.

"So, do you want my Wendy House?" She asked, as she lifted up her negligee, before turning and showing me her surprisingly firm arse, "Or my Back Alley?"

I concentrated on my filthy afternoon of fun with Rachel, and I felt the stir in my groin, and I allowed a sarcastic smile to cross my face, I leaned in closer, taking in the stale smoke from her lips, as I pressed my mouth against hers.

"Come to mamma" She muttered into my mouth, and she grabbed my collar of my jacket, pulling me into her room.

I was disgusted by the clutter inside, but as she guided me to the couch, she eagerly removed her panties, and lifted her almost invisible gown revealing her surprisingly smooth tanned skin.

Her pussy seemed welcoming as I allowed my drunken hand to fumble around my groin, as I strained to release my pulsating dick. When I knew I was free, I stroked her hole with the same hand, allowing my fingers to enter her wetness with ease.

"There was some woman here looking for you earlier" She muttered as if this was a normal type of conversation to have when my dick was about to enter her middle-aged canyon gash.

I wanted to concentrate on getting the jizz out of my balls as quick as possible, and her whisky. I needed that son of a bitch.

"Gorgeous bird" She continued to talk. Really? Let me put my dick in you so I can cum already, "She said she knew you from somewhere, but I don't think you have fucked her"

Finally, my knob was probing her lips, and I felt it slide into her hole with ease, "Shut up"

"Looking at the tightness in her jaw" She continued, "You should loosen it, and she will be pathetically grateful....and pliable"

I tried not to laugh as I began to pump into her.

She raised her legs and wrapped them around me, to pull me closer and deeper into her.

"Oh you are good, like my second husband" She panted below me, and as I pulled away from her to admire her body, I smiled as I saw her tits bounce around, I reached, and squeezed, which surprised her. She clenched her pussy muscles, and I knew that she knew business, "Get rough with me you dirty bastard"

I gripped at her dishwater blonde hair, and pulled her forward, she groaned in passion, and with amazing strength, she forced herself closer to me, and kissed my lips, with her wet mouth. Saliva spilled out of our mouths, and I felt her orgasm quickly cascade inside, flooding over my cock, which excited me. So much, it made me cum inside her almost as instantly.

I bucked a little as the moment within me weakened me. I groaned too loud, luckily, I knew there was no one else in the house that could hear us.

"You need to find that woman and give her some of this" She gasped, as she took my dick out of her, still dripping of both of our juices, "You can keep next month's rent big boy"

I smiled, as I knew the money was good, now, where was that whisky I had earned that mother fucker after banging this old bird.

"I think I should come and tuck you in some time" She smiled.

"Anytime there is no sock on the door, you can come any time" I lied, now I had better find a sock to stop the old battle-axe from coming in. Well, unless I was lonely I suppose, "Now, I believe you said there was whisky"

With that, she slapped my arse so hard, that the sound echoed so loud, I felt the sting for several minutes.

We lay naked together for hours on her couch, only getting up occasionally to urinate, and to freshen our glasses. There was no music, just silence, and her golden faked tanned body for company.

As the night went on, my erection returned, and we fucked at least two more times, although her fanny seemed to get more like a well punched lasagne the more we banged, it was like throwing a sausage into a hallway.

It was close to midnight when I made my way back to my room, leaving Allie and her well- worn pussy on that very couch we had been on all evening. I had the half bottle of whisky in my hand, and I placed it onto the top of the small refrigerator I had. I put my finger onto the picture on the fridge, and smiled.

"I miss you" I whispered, I did not know if I was speaking to Chris or Shannon. One of them.

Maybe both, I did not care.

I wanted one of them here. But it was not happening.

The overpowering sense of sleep overtook me, and I felt myself slump against the fridge.

Something disturbed me from my intoxicated slumber. It was early in the morning and I could hear the morning chorus of sparrows outside singing. But that was not what I heard. It was too loud to be outside, but I could not pinpoint it.

Glad I woke up, I needed a piss, and rose. I crossed the room to the small WC I had, and I allowed the dirty stinking waste escape, making the loudest noise as it hit the water.

I became aware of the noise again, but it seemed farther away. I left it at that, and did not flush or wash my hands, I just wanted to curl up under my quilt.

As I made my way to the bed, I noticed the bottle of whisky was open, and a glass with some of the drink inside.

Someone was in my room. With instinct, I switched on my light, and scanned the place. Then I realised the door was locked. I could see the keys hanging from the hole. Instantly I pulled open the door, I ran back down the staircase. Allie's door was open still, and I raced into the room. She lay as I left her on the couch, only this time her hand was tucked neatly into her panties, and I think there was more than double the amount of cigarettes in the ash tray than when I left.

Checking behind me, I closed the door, and quietly stepped toward the sleeping middle aged bird, and dropped to the floor. My eyes remained continually fixated on the doorway. I could hear something upstairs, where my room was, but I could not identify it.

I must have drifted off because the next thing I knew, it was definitely sunlight, and Allie was watching shit daytime television.

"Where did you fuck off to?" She asked.
"I went to my room" No point in lying now, "I needed to check on something" She looked at me confused, "Did we fuck then?"

Perfect. "Yes, a couple of times"

She made a disappointing grunt, and returned her glare to the television, "My fanny does feel a little raw, were you any good?"

"I think someone was in my room" I confessed changing the subject.

"Stop being a massive dick, there is no such thing as ghosts" She judged me.

"No, there was someone in there, I have noticed things moving recently" I remembered again my phone in the fridge.

"Well honey" She choked on her cigarette, "I will pop a camera in there later, and we can snuggle up on this couch watching you masturbating or something"

I blushed. "Thanks"

FORTY

May 17th.

      I barely slept when I was in that room, and Allie would greet me with her open door, and open pussy policy, and for over a week we shagged on the same couch, it was boring and repetitive, and to be honest, I was only going back to her room because I was too scared, and besides, this bitch had whisky. Oh my God, I was having flashbacks to Old Grace in Blackpool. I kept telling myself if she died after sex, then I am surely cursed with the older bird.

      She had been called to her son, Toby's house unexpectedly, something to do with him being arrested, and that morning she shot off to Bristol to sort him out, and once more I was in this place alone. My room had begun to develop a stale smell of something when I opened my door that evening.

      I knew instantly where she has set up the camera, it was above the window, behind the air vent. I tried to ignore it as I entered the room, but the little red light flashed enough to alert me.

      Things were moved, I knew for sure that my phone charger was not in its usual place next to my bed, it was now in the space where the television used to be. This was now in the sink. Unnerved, I sat on the edge of my bed, and waited. I have no idea what I wanted to see. Allie's whisky was still where I left it, and I thought why not, get some of that in me, maybe I will sleep.

      The whisky did not help. Instead, the last thing I remember was pouring the final drop out of the bottle, and then I woke up in the dark.

My refrigerator door was open, and I could see the empty bottle on its side in the door way. My eyes were instantly drawn to the bottom of the fridge. A cut-throat razor lay half open amongst some melted ice. A piece of paper lay folded neatly near it.

I reached for both, one hand on the blade, another on the paper. I opened it, and smiled at myself, noticing the blood note, 'Die'

My head felt heavy and I nodded to myself. I flicked the blade, and scanned my body, thinking of the moment Robin had a blade against my throat not too long ago.

The blunt end felt smooth as it brushed against my arm, and my stomach.

The paper seemed to call to me. I could see the D again, and I nodded once more. I turned over the blade, and stroked gently against my own flesh.

"The ancient Indians believed that every month your blood becomes possessed by the spirits of the dead" I remembered Shannon's sexy accent speak, "And they would ritualistic cut themselves once a month to release demons"

"Release the demons" I repeated.

With that, I buried the blade into the pink flesh of my left arm, and cried in a mixture of pain and euphoria, and I noticed the blood spill quickly. I almost wanted to welcome the sweet taste of death.

"Take me now" I pleaded.

"The hole you need filling is not in your face or in your arse" I could hear Ophelia speak although I could not see her, "It's in your heart"

The last thing I recall is the blade falling to the floor, and I lowered slowly, resting my head into a pool of my own blood, which seemed to spill freely.

I closed my eyes, and waited.

The muffled noises were barely audible, as I blinked uncontrollably when the clinical whiteness assaulted my senses, dragging me awake. I could not detect where they were, but I could hear Allie speaking, and I heard her declare she had found me in my room.

Then for some reason, I felt peaceful, and I found myself back on the docks in Marmaris. It was that last day. I stood there in front of Chris, and I felt as though I could drown in his beautiful green eyes. Instead of walking away, I stayed. We boarded the next flight to Istanbul, and from there Montreal. I bagged that window seat and as he stroked my knee, I watched the world go by. The air stewardess was Daisy, and I was not sure, but I think her colleague was Beverley, I just could not tell from behind.

We landed in the snow, and with just the backpacks, and money, the clothes we wore, we made our way to a log cabin, where by the naked flame of the fire, we kissed. I remember stroking his tattoo of a ship on his chest, it was new, he must have had it when we were apart. The name began with Viv, but I could not make the rest. He moved, and his lips pressed against mine.

May 18th

I was erect, and I allowed myself to touch my shaft, tugging hard for long moments and I felt the orgasmic sensation as I stroked the hardness of my cock.

Starting off slow, and smooth, I soon gained rhythm and began to speed up my pace. Steaming pre-cum seeped into my palm as I shafted myself knowing my own movements. I glanced down at my own manhood, and at that moment I felt that urge of spasm, I bucked, and thrust my hips in the air with the flowing movement of my hand and rhythm, I watched as the first shot of sperm fired from my slit. I bit my own lip as I tried to stifle my moan, and my ivory coloured juice flowed, I soon felt the sensation diminish as I allowed it to fall off my body.

I waited. I could hear the heavy rain outside as I awoke. I was clean, and my left arm was neatly bandaged. It itched, and I scanned my new environment. I saw an empty plastic beaker on the cabinet, and swung my legs over the bed.

Someone had taken a moment to dress me in a hospital issue gown, and I realised I was naked underneath. No pants again.

I crossed the room, and tried the door, it was locked, and I noticed a small buzzer nearby. Instinct told me to press it. There was no noise, but I could hear movement outside. Moments later, a smiling blonde nurse stood outside.

"Mr Candlish" She greeted, "If you can take a step back to the bed, a doctor will be with you shortly"

I nodded, and stepped backwards to the bed, being careful not to let my modesty show. I perched on the edge of the bed, and waited for just a few minutes, as the door opened. The nurse entered first, with a smaller plumper African female doctor close behind.

"Mr Candlish" She greeted, as she pulled a plastic seat from the wall, and placed it opposite me, "My name is Doctor Nnenna Kunja, can you tell me what happened to you last night?"

I struggled to speak, the drink was dancing before my eyes, and the note, and the blade.

She nodded, "Mr Candlish, you were found in your bedroom by your landlady this morning, bleeding, and there was a note, do you remember writing it?"

"Die" I muttered.

"Is that what you want?" She asked, I could see the nurse now scribbling notes, "To die?"

"No" I whispered, at least I think I did, I could not hear myself, but I felt myself gain momentum, "I have just been through a lot and the ancient Indians believed that once a month, your blood becomes possessed by the spirits of the dead, and they would cut themselves ritualistically"

She knew what I was saying, and I saw her nod in agreement, "Under the Mental Health, you were detained under my care under section four, for your own protection, and I have to assess you to see if you are fit to walk out of this hospital and what you are saying, does not bode well Mr Candlish"

"I did not want to kill myself" I protested calmly, "I needed to feel some pain"

Doctor Kunja signalled the nurse, as though something triggered her memory from something she had read. The nurse passed her the notes, and I watched for what seemed like an eternity whilst she studied.

"I have a respected colleague of mine who knows you" She commented, "I would like to consult with her about some of your notes, would you have any problem if I liaise with her?"

"How long am I going to be here?" I questioned.

"Under Section 4, I have 3 days to have you assessed before we make a decision on how best to have you treated" Doctor Kunja announced.

FORTY ONE

May 20th

For the next couple of days, I waited. Mainly in my room, I did not want to socialise with the crazy people that were talking to themselves in the communal area. I behaved, I took my diazepam, and slept. That was pretty much all there was to do here, the magazines were at least a year out of date, and the books were ruined with pages torn, and graffiti inside. The pretty nurse was always popping into my room with my meds, and I kind of named her Sue, she looked like a Sue, but I never made out what her name really was. Like Grace all over again, and I could not for the life of me remember her real name.

Nnenna Kunja made brief appearances in the room, as she came to update me, and this day, I could sense that she was not alone. Her colleague was detained with some security as I waited yet a little longer.

"My colleague will be here shortly" She admitted as she took her seat again, scanning my notes again, "If it all the same with you Connor, I have been conversing with a couple of your close friends, and I would like some clarification on some things?"

I nodded, unsure who she has been liaising with? "I just want to go home" Home? Am I fucking kidding myself? Someone has been stalking me.

"Well, it is clear that you have a stable job and a roof over your head, so it is a possibility" Doctor Kunja continued in agreement, "Are you confused about your sexuality Mr Candlish?"

"No" I responded instantly.

"There was a girl, she told me that you had a relationship with a young man. Can you tell me more about your relationship with Christopher Mumford" A statement straight out there.

"I haven't seen Chris since I left him in Marmaris" I confessed, and who was the girl she had spoken to? "I have spoken to him two or three times"

"Did you cut yourself out of unrequited love for this gentleman?" She asked. Now I knew she was taking the piss.

Why not just say, "Mr Candlish do you take it up the arse?"

"There was someone in my room" I whispered, trying to cover the question, "Someone has been moving things in my room, and trying to push me over the edge...."

"So someone coerced you into using the blade on yourself?" She asked.

"I would rather hurt myself than anyone else" I confessed, unsure if this was the right response.

Before she could respond, the door opened, and I smiled as I recognised the tall blonde nurse that entered.

"Rachel" I smiled.

"Connor" She smiled sympathetically, "I think it is time to talk about Marmaris"

"When you were in hospital after the fire, you confided in me a lot" Rachel continued, as she took her place alongside Doctor Kunja, "And when I saw that you had been admitted, I had to think both morally and ethically whether I liaised with my colleague here, or not"

"Understand, that whatever you discuss in here can help me determine if I can send you home or if you are to stay here for further assessment" Doctor Kunja commented, and for the first time I think I noticed sympathy in her voice. That lovely nurse Sue was outside now, looking in, and judged not to enter with my medication at this time.

Rachel nodded in agreement, "What you told me made me realise what you had gone through, and I am not surprised that you have had a meltdown, and perhaps if you just talk about this, we can source the right treatment for you"

I trusted Rachel, and I had treated her like crap. Part of me wanted to scream at her for giving me the glimmer that the child she told me about could be mine. I had not seen the baby, but I kind of wanted to be the daddy.

"Last year, my parents died" I felt myself speaking. Rachel nodded, "I was on duty that evening...."

I took over, and allowed myself to talk openly. It felt nice, and the time seemed to pass swiftly. I showed no emotion when I referenced the death of my parents, or how I used sex as a comfort blanket, I cried as I spoke about Daisy, reliving that accident in my head, I felt as though I was watching it all play out before me. I explained how Chris and I enjoyed our clandestine relationship despite us both having girlfriends. I tried to stifle my anger when I spoke about Ophelia, Shannon and Sian. I spoke with little embarrassment as I relived my sexual exploits. Some of it was calm, and relaxing, but when I spoke about Tommo I felt the rage burn inside me.

Then I cried once more as I relived those last days in Marmaris. Once again a movie played out as I spoke, and it frightened me. I felt for sure that they were going to throw away the key.

"After the girls took the tumble off the balcony I didn't stay, I ran away" I confessed, "I knew that the police would be out to get me, and I was all set for fleeing to Bodrum for a flight out of the country, when I learned that one of them survived"

"Who survived?" Rachel asked breathlessly, almost as though she had relived some sort of Hollywood Blockbuster love story.

Really?

I shrugged, "I never found out, I knew that I had to locate Chris one last time, I knew he was fleeing via the harbour so I made my way there"

"And then what happened?" Doctor Kunja probed.

I took a deep breath, "Chris passed me an envelope with some tickets to Canada, and I was tempted. I really wanted to go with him. But I could not trust him. I don't know what it was, but I did not know what his plans were for us. For all I knew, he could have lured me back to Ophelia. So I knew my answer was no, so I broke his heart, and left him. He begged me for another chance, but I kept walking, and I eventually made it home. I have spent the last couple of weeks living in a derelict bar with my old friend Curtis, and Tommo burned it down"

I saw Rachel's mouth open.

"They arrested that man a while ago" Doctor Kunja explained, I felt relieved at that comment.

"I hope they throw away the key" I whispered.

"Earlier today, I had met with Mr Mumford's father, and he still believes you know where Chris is" Doctor Kunja explained.

I paused.

"You don't know where he is do you?" A statement I suppose rather than a question.

I felt a tear fall down my face, "I still think I may have made the wrong decision by leaving him there, but I knew not only was there an issue with trust, but maybe it was me, maybe I could not keep him safe"

"Because of Ophelia?" Rachel guessed.

"She was the one who faked her own death, she is the one who should be in here, not me" I protested, "I just wish I could have saved one of the girls, and I wish I went to Canada with Chris"

"Are you confused about your sexuality?" The Doctor repeated her question.

I could sense that Rachel knew the answer, and I raised my head, "I am happy with my sexuality, I like the fact that both men and women want me, some more than others"

"And Chris?" That bitch was probing again, "Were you in love with him?"

I held back my response.

"How many lovers have you had?" She asked.

"I don't know" I honestly answered, "I am in my twenties and have been shagging for the best part of 10 years"

"How many were men?" I was getting annoyed now, she really wanted to know the answer. I shook my head, "It's hard to say, probably half, maybe less?"

"And Chris?" She waited for me to answer.

"I wanted to kiss him until neither of us could breathe anymore" I confessed, "But I knew then there was no way forward. I wish I knew where he was, but I don't, but for just a moment, he made me feel as though it had been pissing down with rain my whole life, but then he made me want to throw away my umbrella and catch some rays"

There was an empty silence for a long moment, as I allowed the tears to fall freely.

"Connor" My thoughts were interrupted by Doctor Kunja. When I raised my head, "I would like to retire and consult with my colleague about your condition"

"You have to let me out of here" I begged. Great, you fucking idiot.

As the door closed, I knew that I had blown my chances, I may as well get comfortable. So I closed my eyes, and thought again. Sian, Shannon, Ophelia and Chris flashed through my mind.

I waited in that room for an hour, it seemed longer. Doctor Kunja entered on her own, and I could not tell from her rock-steady face whether the news was good or bad, but she had a hint of 'you will wait' about her.

"Well Connor" She started, "A few days ago, you took a blade to your arm, and have had five stitches, which will leave a scar forever, and if you decide in the future to hurt yourself, it may be wise that you look at that very scar and think about what you can pull through"

I nodded, "I am sorry" Why the fuck was I saying this?

"Upon the recommendation of Nurse Hambleton, I am pleased to report that we believe that you are of no threat to anyone else, and more importantly, we believe that you are of no threat to yourself"

I smiled. For the first time in what seemed like days.

"That being said" A great big fucking blast of thunder tore through my heart, "I would like you to stay in just one more night, for monitoring purposes, and to ensure you have a safe passage home"

I felt myself nod, and I blocked out what else she was saying as I glanced outside to see the sun shining. I knew I was going to be free.

FORTY TWO

May 22nd

      I faked sleep that night, I had no choice. I knew that nurse Sue would be watching me on Doctor Kunja's orders. When I did sleep, I dreamt a lot about Chris and that farewell. When I had spoken yesterday I did not mention the tears from the both of us. The snot covered kiss farewell, I decided to omit that bit as well. I also dreamt of Sian and Shannon falling. In one dream Shannon survived, in the other Sian survived, both blamed me. I decided not to talk about those dreams, as it may have given the good Doctor scope to keep me in this place.

      Now dressed in a pair of loan cotton trousers, and a baggy hoodie loaned from the lost and found collection, which smelt clean, whether they were or not, I did not care. I sat alone at breakfast, my coffee was luke warm, and my toast was floppy, and undercooked. I scanned the room, and watched the people go about their day, and tried to guess who had gone through what. That old lady in the corner feeding an invisible child, and the topless male supermodel, in his dreams. In reality they could have been me. Thankfully not.

      I smiled to myself as Sue walked into the room, searching for me, and gestured me to make my way to the doorway.

      No one noticed me as I made my way to her.

      "Your lift is here" She smiled, "All you need to do is sign the release papers"

      I nodded, and wanted to kiss her. Why? She had done nothing for me.

Within minutes I had signed my release papers, and waited in the hallway, still in view of the lunatics. Sue had taken my paperwork inside a small office, and told me to wait, whilst my lift arrived, I smiled when the door opened, and Curtis entered in full biker leathers, and tossed me a pink helmet.

"Leave you alone for five minutes, and you go and do something daft" He tried to joke, "Come on, let's get you home"

As I laughed, I felt Doctor Kunja's eyes burn into me. Bet you she thought I was his bitch or something.

We spent that afternoon in a bar near the canal, out in the country. We almost compared injuries, only my bandage was too tight to remove, so I settled to inspecting the scarred burn on his arm. It was not as bad as I thought from what he had told me previously, but he was always a drama queen. Even now, he had a pink umbrella in his cola. I on the other hand was happy with a pint of lager. And another. And much more.

As he came out of the bar walking as camp as ever for the fifth time, some bikers glared at him, not in a menacing way, but he seemed to get off on it.

"You know that they have caught Tommo?" He finally asked as he spilled a little of my beer placing it before me, "And my solicitor believes I can make a lot of money out of it, enough to start somewhere new"

"That's great" I smiled, "I am sorry that I ever got you involved in this"

He brushed it off, "To be honest, I only lived at the pub to save money, now I've met someone, my nurse, and he really likes me"

"Glad you met someone" I smiled, not sure if I was being honest with myself or not.

"Out of interest" Curtis changed his tone, "When I got the call from that Doctor to tell me you were there in the nut house, I was so worried about you, I know that you have been through so much recently"

"You must have been my next of kin or something" I struggled to remember if I had named him previously.

He placed his hand on mine, "Why did you do it?"

I really did not want to go through with this discussion again, "A moment of madness maybe?"

"Then next time you feel like that, you need to call me" He responded, "Maybe I can slip you some of my sausage or something?"

"Thought you already had a boyfriend" I teased, taking a long drink out of my glass.

"You know I always wanted you, I could have you whenever I want, and you were by far the best shag I have had" He smiled, emphasising on the I as though he had always been in control, then his tone changed again, "So why are you staying in a house paid for by Chris's dad if there is nothing between you?"

"Chris went missing and his parents seem to think he will make contact so I thought why not use them and save my own money" I confessed, "I want to get back out of this tin pot country, somewhere nice"

"Canada?" He questioned. I remembered I had told him about those tickets.

I shook my head, "Somewhere hot, where the women wear bikinis and the men wear budgie smugglers"

He laughed, and so did I.

"I am thinking, with the money I earn from Tommo I may open a gay bar in Gran Canaria, or even Australia" He excitedly gesticulated, attracting the attention from some of the bikers again.

"I think you pulled" I gestured.

He smiled, as he glanced back at the flirting butch bearded biker.

"Slut" I commented.

We decided to leave after my eleventh drink, and the afternoon air was beginning to cool. As drunk as I was, I struggled with getting my leg over the back of the motorbike this time, and as I did, I heard the tear occur in the crotch of my cotton trousers, and the coolness of the air as it hit my now on show dick. Pretty sure Curtis knew as we drove back toward Manchester.

Due to where I lived, we had a pre-agreed arrangement that he would drop me off nearby, and like a rhino trying to practice a ballerina rehearsal, I failed to gracefully clamber off the motorbike, but before I could hide my modesty, I fell backwards, and landed on the road with my schlong hanging out.

I heard him stop the motorcycle, as I lifted my head off the ground.

"Now this is too good to miss" He smiled, as he removed his helmet, and placed his lips instantly over my groin. His beard felt coarse against my shaven balls.

My dick sprang to life immediately, and I happily allowed him to suck me, without a care that anyone could see any time.

It was nearly dark when I got back to the apartment. Allie was already nursing her whisky again as I made my way to my room. She acknowledged me with a tilt of the glass, gesturing that I was welcome to join her.

"Give me time to change" I gestured to my loaned clothes, ignoring the cum stain on them. She grunted something, and I made my way up the staircase.

The blood was still on the floor, it looked dirty, the fridge door was closed, but other things were again different. The photograph of Chris, Shannon and I was missing, and my clothes were scattered over my bed.

Locking the door behind me, I took off the clothes I was in, and placed them in the carrier bag that I was using for rubbish. Something in there smelled vile, I almost wretched.

Almost as soon as the hot water from the shower hit me, I felt my dick harden, and I started to tug myself, and I very soon, I felt my own pleasure from within, as the orgasmic sensation shot through me, as I stroked the hardness of my cock, slow, and smooth. I imagined Rachel before me, but within a moment she changed, she became someone else, I could not tell who, but she made me pre- cum, and I noticed that it was Nnenna. Trying to shrug it off, I glanced down at my own dick, and at that moment I felt my spasm, flowing movement of my hand and rhythm, I watched as the first shot of sperm shot from my groin. The juice covered my floor, and I freely groaned out loud.

Being careful to keep my bandage dry, I continued to enjoy my shower, and whilst it only lasted minutes, I just needed to be out of the room, even if it was with the geriatric landlady. Choosing a pair of chino's and a button up shirt, I scanned the room one last time, to remember it exactly how I had left it.

Surprisingly, I enjoyed my evening with Allie, and after the ritualistic thank you sex, she provided me with a cheque for the money that Greg and Eve had already paid into her account.

"I think you need a little holiday" She smiled.

I nodded, "Somewhere hot. I have always wanted to go to Bali"

"I have a sister in Bali, you should look her up. Personally, I have always liked Thailand" She explained, "Cannot wait to get back there in August, and when I go I want you to Skype me some of your penis so I can play with my pussy from the other side of the world"

"I don't think I will be here then" I commented.

"You don't mean you want to ....." She did not finish that conversation and gestured toward my wrist.

I shook my head, "I plan on getting away from Manchester, and I plan on using Mr Mumford as my way out"

I felt her hand begin to inch along my thigh, oh God not again, I only just come a while ago, and I don't think there is anything left in there.

"Allie" I touched her hand, "Has that video caught anything in my room whilst I was away?" She shrugged, "I don't know, I have so busy with Toby's trial, I forgot all about it"

"So are they charging him?" I questioned, trying to get her mind off my dick.

She nodded, "ABH, but the guy had it coming, he grassed my boy up for withholding pills, so I am on my son's side in this one"

"I could do with a drink" I sighed, as I rose, "Shall I call down the garage and get some cans in?"

"Good idea" She agreed, "And I can scan through the video for you, see if I can find anything"

I planted a kiss on her lips, and she seized the opportunity to allow her tongue to penetrate me. It was not all that bad, secretly, I imagined Rachel before me, but I knew I would not see her again after she heard my story.

It was beginning to rain as I made my way to the garage which was only seven minutes from the bedsit, but I wanted it to take longer.

I knew that I was not alone, because someone was nearby. Not as malevolent as whoever was in my room, because this person kept themselves to the shadows. I kind of knew that they did not mean me harm. Perhaps it was my guardian angel, or something. I actually did not fear this person. It could have easily been someone just coincidentally travelling just far enough behind me so that I could not have seen their identity. I briefly remembered the same scenario on Canal Street that night. I smiled at myself, and shrugged the thoughts out of my mind.

The gormless man in the garage seemed one dimensional as I purchased some beer, and cigarettes, in fact I am unsure if he was human with his robotic ways. He seemed to be staring into the distance, as he charged me the mandatory five pence for the carrier bag, and placed my items inside without even lifting his gaze.

As I left the garage, I noticed the shadow of the person that had been following me pull back into the darkness again. Intrigued, I made my way to the darkened side street, and saw it disappear at speed into the blackness beyond. Something glistened on the floor, and I glanced down, I saw a wet flyer for some party, The Vivandier. Strange name. But somewhat familiar.

I chose to ignore this and moved back into the comforting brightness of the garage forecourt, and made my way back to my older woman.

FORTY THREE

We drank most of the beer with the video footage on fast forward when I returned. For the most part, it remained static, with no movement what-so-ever. Well, other than the occasional speck of dust or the spider that seemed to have taken up residency during my hospitalisation. We also, for some reason had candles burning, as if this was some sort of romantic gesture from this woman.

Allie was clearly getting the horn as she wanted my cock more and more. I allowed her to take it out of my pants, and when it hardened, I stroked her hair as she put her mouth over it.

I pressed play on the video, so that I can enjoy her pleasuring me.

She began to lick my shaft, as she worked her way to my tip, I found myself gripping her hair, and I guided her mouth back to my dick, guiding it slowly between her welcoming lips, I let my penis entered her moist throat.

I felt her hand touch me firmly, as I groaned more and her tongue was frantically lapping at my member. I began to shake and moved my hips up and down as she gagged a little for a moment as the sound of my length inside her mouth echoed in the small room.

My groans soon became intense, and I struggled to control myself, but then something caught my eye on the screen.

A shadow was moving across the screen.

"Look" I jerked my dick out of her mouth, and pointed to the screen.

Disappointed, she rose, and joined my gaze at the television. The shadow had moved from the loft conversion above the doorway. A figure in jeans and a black hoodie was in my room.

"When was this?" I asked.

"Today" She explained. "That person knows you are back".

"I need the day I cut myself" I don't know if I was excited, or scared.

Frustrated, she rose, and made her way over to the video collection that she had saved.

I remained fixed on the screen. This clearly was not the person that had followed me today. The person on screen moved over to the fridge, and took the photo, I saw them fold it and place it into the pocket of their hoodie. Then as quick as it arrived, it seemed to be alerted by something outside, and it clambered back into the loft conversion.

Moments later. I opened my own door, and took off my loan clothes.

"They were there when I got home" I panicked, grabbing a candle nearby.

"Oh don't mind me" Allie hissed, still clearly pissed off I stopped her from blowing me, "I will just find that video you requested"
I did not really hear her as I was already running up to my room, candle in hand.

My door was locked, and anger began to take over me, as I struggled with the keys. "I know you're in here" I cried, bursting open the door.

My eyes focused on the loft opening, and grabbing the nearest knife, I prepared for whoever was in the loft. Using a chair nearby I opened the loft cover with force, and allowed it to fall, my little dance as it missed me may have amused some people. I did not care now if they knew I was onto them.

I used the chair again, this time as a hoist, and as I stood on it, I placed the candle and the blade on the rim of the loft. I was aware now that Allie was standing in the door way.

I used my upper body strength, as I pulled myself into the space above my room, and I felt a nail tear at my shirt, grazing my flesh for a moment.

"You be careful" Allie whispered.

I ignored her, and used the candle as light, and I circled the room. I noticed something on the floor near to me, and I lowered to pick up the piece of paper.

The word "Die" was written with blood, and now there was more, presumably mine from my cutting attempt.

"Someone has been living in here" I gasped.

"Impossible" Allie discarded.

"No, there is a pile of shit up here, and...." I paused, as I noticed the mass of belongings nearby, and the open window to the roof inside, "I know how they have been getting in"

I made my way quietly to the window, and I became aware that Allie had used the chair and was hoisting herself into the place.

She joined me moments later at the window, and as we glanced into the night sky, and roof top, a sense of disdain crossed me. I am not even safe in my own fucking safe house.

"This room was sealed off twenty years ago" She admitted, "My father said something had happened here and we were not allowed to come here"

She gestured to a doorway that was boarded up at the far end of the loft. I have to get out of here.

The police came and took the evidence from the loft, and Allie's handyman put a lock on the loft conversion door. That first night, I sat watch and was alerted early in the morning when someone inside the place tried to lift the cover. Realising they had failed they did not stay. I tried to spot them leaving from my window but I could not see a thing. Allie had shown me that the fire exit from the loft was derelict now, and unsafe.

Allie had spent some time looking through the video footage in the meantime, and I sought solace in her arms, when I say arms, I mean we fucked. She got the benefit, and I got the safety. Pathetic I know.

To be honest, I thought she was getting too attached, and I knew that I would not be able to stay here for long. Perhaps I would ask Greg and Eve for their offer of work away sooner. Trouble was they had just flown out to Morocco on holiday yesterday so I was going to be waiting for a little while longer. Oh well. I was getting my dick wet at least.

MAY 25th

It was nice to see Nurse Hambleton again as I turned up at the hospital to have those stitches removed. She did not really speak, other than on a professional level. A second nurse came in to tell me I was allowed to go home.

As I inspected the neat scar, I touched it briefly with my right hand, and I made my way out of the hospital again. It was shortly after one.

I spent the first part of the afternoon at the cinema, firstly negotiating my return to work next week, and then watching some cartoon. My mind really was not there. I just needed something to do, and to stay out of my home. After the movie, I sat in a casino, and played roulette, I changed a hundred pound, and played my own strategy. I loved winning, and walked out of the casino with just over five hundred pound in my pocket.

I knew that the person was watching me again, I was not sure who it was, but I could sense them in both the cinema and in the casino, but both were crowded and dark, and therefore not easy to pick anyone out.

As I left, I had a few missed calls and messages from Allie. Her voicemails seemed urgent, and it seemed she wanted me home for some reason, her sense of urgency usually involved my cock in her pussy, or mouth. My kind of urgency was the shower was broke, or the kettle needed a fuse. Funny how different our emergencies were.

The text message simply read, 'It's her, come home now"

Dialling her number, I began to shake, unsure what she meant, and as she spoke I could sense the frustration in her voice.

"I found the footage of the night you went to hospital, and it is clear" She stressed, "Come home immediately, and we will call the police"

Shit, this time it was not a sex emergency. Slamming the phone into my pocket, I raced home.

She greeted me at the door, with the video tape in her hand, and of course the obligatory cigarette, and I could see more whisky behind her.

"Where have you been?" She asked, presenting me the video, and holding the door for me.

"I had to see my boss" I lied, I could not tell her the real reason I was staying out as much as I was.

"Well, I had poured you a drink, but it was attracting flies" She commented, "So I drank it, and then I drank the next one"

"I don't mind" I responded, as I inserted the video cassette into the machine.

"It's a little grainy at first, but the picture is quite clear" She snuggled next to me, putting her feet onto the table.

The footage of me entering the room was a lot clearer than the other videos. I could see me lying on my bed, and then I started to masturbate for a short time, then I wiped my cock on my sock, and tossed it aside. I could not remember this part. I then started to sleep.

"Fast forward about five minutes" Allie commented.

I obeyed, and watched the fast moving scenes of me in bed.

Suddenly, the shadow started to fall from the loft conversion, and a hooded figure started to ferret around by the fridge.

I could also see my sleeping form, and I must have made some sort of noise as the figure seemed to be startled. It moved closer to me, and then lowered itself, and slithered underneath my bed.

I then moved over to the fridge, and reached inside, I saw me reading that piece of paper, and the blade appeared. I watched, slightly embarrassed as I cut myself, and soon I lowered to the floor, and rested in a pool of my own blood.

"Now watch" Allie commentated.

The figure moved from beneath my bed, and hovered over me for a short time.

It then removed its hoodie, and jeans, and I felt the fear rise within me, as she now began to dance over my body.

She removed her panties, and dangled them over me, then she rubbed her naked body on my back, her fanny was licking at my body as I lay unconscious, she did this for a few moments, before disappearing from the screen for a moment as she moved toward the far wall, just outside of the peripheral vision of the camera, before returning to view, minus those pants.

Her back now clear to the camera, I felt sick, as I noticed "Mrs Connor Candlish" tattooed on her.

"Ophelia" I panicked.

The image turned now, and her face was clear on the screen.

"That's her" Allie pointed at the screen, "The girl that came looking for you"

"The girl with the pliable mouth" I finished her sentence for her.

FORTY FOUR

My head felt full, and empty at the same time as I moved trance-like to my room. I scanned the area where she would have gone during those seconds of absence. Against the wall was a bookshelf, albeit, bare other than a few less than a pound books I had purchased from charity shops. It was the only thing that was not seen on the camera.

Allie was beside me. I inched closer to the bookcase, and scanned the almost barren shelves.

"You are not looking for her knickers?" She asked.

"You saw the video" I responded.

I reached over to the pile of takeaway menus next to some DVD's, I frantically began to move them out of the way. The paper menu's fell to the floor, and Allie started to pick them up within seconds.

I dropped to the floor, and almost felt sick again as I saw the cotton panties in a ball under the entire shelving.

With shaking hands, I reached for the cold underwear, and I withdrew them from their hiding place.

"What is the story about you and her?" Allie asked, as she handed me the menus again, "And do you want me to call the police?"

"A big mistake, she was nineteen when I met her, and she should have been a quick fuck and then I should never have seen her again.... but that slut had other ideas" I whispered, as I placed the balled up cotton panties on the shelf, I was about to continue when one of the menu's caught my eye.

Reaching over to the scruffy pile, I moved the top menu away, and a flyer lay before us. 'Join us on the USS Vivandier this Summer' The invite read.

Allie took the opportunity to lift it from the mess.

"I have heard about this" She smiled, "This woman somewhere in America has won a lot of money somehow and she has invited five random people from around the world to celebrate her win with her and her family"

"Leaving August 15th, Cape Verde" I read from the flyer, "She like a modern day *Willy Wonka*"

"She's got a massive following, how on Earth did you get this?" Allie queried.

I shrugged, I did not believe for one second that I had won a cruise with some rich millionaire, "It was with the junk mail"

"This is legit" Allie insisted, "Let me load her web page"

She made her way out of the room, as I kept scanning the plain leaflet of the USS Vivandier. For some millionaire, no effort was made in the advertising. I also could not help but think I had seen this name somewhere before.

I tossed it aside, and looked once more at the knickers that were on the shelf.

As if possessed my hand reached out for them, and I stroked the lace with the tips of my fingers.

"Why are you doing this?" I whispered, as if expecting an answer.

As if she was listening, the cover to the loft conversion moved, she was in there again.

I moved closer to the hatch, it may have taken me longer than the few seconds I thought it did, I could see that it was lifted up a few centimetres.

"Why are you trying to kill me?" I asked.

She laughed, I knew it was her. I could hear a second feminine laugh too.

"I know that it is you Ophelia, why leave your dirty pants here?" I screamed. Her giggle became silent as we both heard Allie make her way back up the stairs.

"Look behind the fridge" She whispered, and then dropped the hatch with a loud bang.

Allie approached me again, and joined me in looking at the now static hatch.

"She's up there" I whispered. "She just spoke to me"

She glanced up at the stationery loft cover. She did not believe me.

"Come back to my room, I know you are safer there" Allie smiled. She wanted sex again.

"In a minute" I responded, "I have to check behind the fridge"

"I have that site up in my room, and when you come down, we will call the police" She assured, walking away again. She probably did not hear the hatch close after all.

I waited a moment, and made my way back to the fridge. I peered behind it and struggled to see anything out of the ordinary. Gripping the back, I pushed it forward a few inches, and noticed that an envelope was taped to the back of it. I strained to reach for it, but my hand was just beyond touching distance. I forced the object forward a few more inches, and snatched at the paper.

Still shaking, I tore open the envelope, and allowed the encasement to drop to the floor. The neatly folded paper inside opened, and I felt my stomach churn as I read the list.

'Daisy, deceased, Sian, deceased, Shannon, deceased, Connor, deceased, Chris' There was a blank space next to his name.

I could sense that she was still upstairs in the conversion, "What have you done to him?" The silent response frightened me, and I knew what I had to do.

In a panic, I opened my closet, and located the rucksack and smiled to myself, as I noticed it was still filled with the money from Marmaris. My passport was neatly laid on top of the stash. I grabbed my wallet, and bank card, and once more I left my phone on the table. This time, I was leaving again, and I did not care where I went, as long as the psycho bitch in my loft could not find me.

I raced past the open door to Allie's apartment, out into the street. I heard her call out to me, but I ignored her, but I needed to flee. I ran straight forward, daring not to look back for the second time in six weeks.

FORTY FIVE

June 1st

I treated myself to sleeping in a small bed and breakfast for a few nights, whilst I planned my escape. No one knew where I was, and I was a total stranger in Bramhall, which was not too far away from home, but far enough. I had managed to get a small bar job which was also a live in position, and I bought new clothes from a charity shop that sold everything for one pound. My boss, Glynn was an elderly man who sat and farted in the corner of the bar and there was only ever three or four people in maximum. Perfect. I felt hidden. I had even dyed my hair blond in a bid to disguise myself, it was a little bit orange.

My room was about the same size of Allie's and I felt comfortable. At least Glynn didn't want sex every time he saw me in either just my towel or my pants, at least I hope not.

Thing is, he trusted me for some reason, and as I had a spare couple of hours free today, he sent me to the wholesalers with his card to get some supplies for a party that was going to be in the bar tonight. Really? I drove his mini to the nearby outlet, and within twenty minutes I had bought everything for an old farts birthday.

I chose to waste a bit of time in the village. It consisted of quite a few modern bars, I had been to a few on my first night in town, but I spent my time alone, just sitting by the bar, or playing on the fruit machines. Not really socialising.

I chose a nice coffee bar, and sat outside in the sun with my iced latte. My scar was itching, and as I rubbed it, I noticed it seemed to bruise easily. It did not worry me. I finished the drink, and was about to leave, as I noticed a blonde lady standing in the bar area.

No, it really could not be? I made my way back into the coffee bar, and tried to get her attention without being too obvious. As she turned with her hot chocolate, she smiled, and I knew that I was right, Beverley was in front of me, again, and once more in a coffee bar.

"We have to stop meeting like this" She smiled, as she took a seat, "Are you coming or going?"

I ordered another coffee, and joined her, unsure how I was approaching this, not that I needed to worry, because she broke the silence.

"Last I heard" She took a sip of her coffee, "You were in Marmaris with Hibiscus, and something happened"

I nodded, I forgot she knew Oliver, "What was said?"

Beverley shrugged, "I have not seen him since last year, and you are in a lot of trouble Connor"

"If you know what happened, you're in a lot better place than I am" I confided, "Last thing I knew, Sian and Shannon went over the balcony and one of them survived"

I think I must have probed her into letting out some information that she had, "Shannon deleted me from Facebook last year, and I was never close to Sian. And Oliver doesn't work for the company anymore"

"Which one survived?" I asked.

"I honestly don't know" She confessed, "I only hope that you got the revenge that you wanted"

I shook my head, "I ran like a pussy the first opportunity I got"

She placed her hand onto mine, "What are you doing here in sleepy old Bramhall?"

"Me?" I laughed, "What about you?"

"I got promoted to store manager, and I have a job here" She proudly announced, "If ever you want a cheap flight, come and see me, you know I have the discounts"

I smiled, "I am just passing through, until I find somewhere I can call home"

"I know that you are running" She whispered, and her hand returned to mine, "You helped me out once, and I will be indebted to you forever"

"I helped you escape Mallorca with your takings" I smiled, "But maybe you can help me with something"

"Anything" She accepted without even knowing what I would say.

"I keep seeing an invite for a cruise of sorts, the USS Vivandier...." I began.

"That's a myth" She interjected, "Apparently some woman inviting some people she has never met on board her party boat?"

I nodded, "I thought so"

We parted company soon after, and I made my way back to the bar, in plenty of time for the party. It surprised me that we held ten people this time, they must have bought friends. A pretty brunette caught my eye throughout the evening, and she soon introduced herself as Jackie. She was a Veterinary Nurse nearby, and was the niece of one of the oldies.

She watched me all night, sucking on the straw to her coke a little too seductively in front of the old bastards.

As I called last orders, Jackie remained behind, it was obvious that she wanted to see my bedroom, well, when I was the youngest person she had seen in a while, why the hell wouldn't she?

Glynn tossed me the keys to lock up and he went off to his room in the basement, having eyed up Jackie himself for a fleeting moment.

Jackie seductively fingered the rim of her glass, which still had plenty of wine in it, "Do you think I can have a top up?"

I smiled, as I poured her another glass of rose, and passed her a plate of sandwiches. After the ancient canyon that was Allie, I was looking forward to some tight young pussy tonight, and I could hardly disguise my erection, and it was obvious to her.

"My uncle told me there was some young buck here" She laughed, "So I had to come and see you"

"You're the youngest woman I have seen in this town" I smiled.

She smiled, and within seconds, she was clawing at my crotch, "I haven't had a man before, and you're the one who is gonna pop this cherry, now, let me see what Jackie can do for you "

Within a second of her finishing her sentence, my erect penis was in her mouth, and her hands were warm, and gripped against my buttocks, the suction from those lips was so good. The dampness of my perspiring palm slapped the window for a moment, creating a steamy glow around the imprint. I was aware now that she had two of her fingers inside her pussy, poking away with each suck she gave to my cock. Her own knickers, around her ankles.

I felt the semen rush through my groin and shooting into her mouth almost as instantly, she pulled away, and spat the white goo onto the floor.

"I am sorry I will clean that up" She smiled.

"Fuck that" I whispered, as I tucked away, "I am so gonna bang your brains out in a mo"

"So I am staying?" She questioned.

"Give me five minutes" I smiled, "And we can go up to my room" She smiled, as she sucked her finger, "I will be waiting"

I cleared the remaining paper plates, and discarded food into a black bin liner, and made my way to the door.

The night air was still warm as I made my way to the large industrial bin that was already full, and I forced open the lid, and tossed the rubbish into it.

A movement nearby alerted me, it sounded like a bottle being kicked but I could not see anything. Still nervous over recent events, I paused, and peered into the darkness, daring not to speak. I glanced back into the window, and I could see Jackie dancing near the bar. Almost directly below her, I could see Glynn sitting on his bed reading a book by lamplight.

The noise did not happen again, and I presumed that a cat or something had disturbed the peace.

As I made my way back to the doorway, I panicked as a gloved hand covered my mouth, and pulled me to the floor with force.

I tried to scream, but the weight of my attacker was too much as they rolled on top of me.

FORTY SIX

As I struggled against the weight, I wanted to see the identity of my attacker, and I knew who it was almost instantly. It was the shape of the body, much smaller than I remembered, but I knew. I strained, and pulled my hand free, and allowed it to move up toward the hat, and I moved it with an instant.

Chris lay above me, and was sobbing uncontrollably.

I writhed under him, and soon I was free.

Holding my hand out to him, he reluctantly accepted it, and together we rose. "What are you doing?" I questioned, almost too scared to what he would say.

"I have been looking for you for weeks" He mumbled, "It was only by luck I bumped into Beverley in the train station earlier, I was begging for money for a coffee"

"I never told her where I was" I muttered.

"It's a small town, and I just looked until I saw you" He seemed genuine, "I was about to give up today and go back to London"

"Your parents are looking for you" I seemed cold, even I shocked myself.

"No they are not" He insisted, as a matter-of-factly, "May I come in?"

"I kind of have company" I gestured toward the dancing girl in the window.

"Please" He almost begged, "I have spent the last few weeks sleeping rough, eating shit, and all just to find you"

I paused, and even though I did not trust him in my heart, my stupid head was telling me that I needed to give him somewhere to sleep, and something good to eat.

As I looked at him, I was aware that those feelings were still there.

I reached out to him, and smiled, "Come with me"

He took my hand, and together we made our way to the doorway, before I paused again.

"Why did you attack me?" I asked, I was unsure if I wanted to kiss him or kick him in the bollocks.

He shrugged, and gestured to his scruffy clothes, "I did not know how you would take me turning up like this"

I wanted to believe him. I nodded as I pushed open the door, and together we smiled as Jackie continued to dance to whatever shit music was playing on the juke box right now. She stopped as she saw us.

"I don't do anything kinky" She protested before either of us could speak.

"I'm his brother" Chris spoke without hesitation, "Just got in from a yearlong tour in Canada, I kind of landed on him"

"I am sorry" I confessed, aware that she was annoyed with his presence.

"Well" Jackie muttered, almost in disgust, "When your brother leaves, call me"

She gathered her denim jacket, and brushed past me without another word, pulling the door closed behind her.

"Brother?" I asked, as I locked the door.

He shrugged, "It was all I could think of to get rid of her"

"Chris, I...." I began.

He placed his finger on my lips, "I know why you left me in Marmaris, and I forgive you for abandoning me, but you did it to protect me, didn't you?"

I felt myself nod.

"Because of the psychotic bitch you wanted to keep me safe. I went to Dalaman and got the next flight home, I just wanted to be with you" He confessed, as he moved his finger away from my lips, "I told my father and step mother all about how I felt about you"

I guided him now to the bar, because I needed a drink, I poured two pints of lager, as he rested on the stool opposite me.

"You called me" I remembered, I had given him my old number that I remembered from heart. Seemed he did too.

"When I put the phone down to you" He spoke with fear, "My father came to see me, and beat me to a pulp, he could not have a fudge packer as his pride and joy, and he told me before I went to Mallorca that if I ever got shit on my dick he will kill me"

"I am so sorry" I whispered.

"It was not your fault I fell for you" He confessed.

He lifted his shirt, and revealed his perfectly toned stomach, which was covered in faded bruises, but the tattoo from my dream was no longer there. It hurt him to breathe in, I could tell.

I touched his stomach over the bar, and he gently cupped my hand.

"When he hurt me, I lay in bed, and I just wanted to hold you" He confided, "I had to come and find you. I just gathered a few things, and went"

I felt myself weaken again, "I'm here"

"My father is very powerful and won't stop at anything until he finds me" He continued, "Has he been in contact?"

"He paid my rent in the hope I would tell him where you were" I smiled, "But I got the money back"

"If he finds me, he will try to force me back to London" He continued, "But I want to be with you"

I smiled, and took his hand, leaving the two pints barely touched, we made our way upstairs to my room.

We kissed, and I cautiously removed his shirt, kissing his chest, and then we kissed more, as we lay on the bed. Gently touching each other.

In a momentum of fumbling, we removed our trousers, and soon he lay on top of me. His rock hard dick rubbed against mine. I could tell by his moans that he was still in pain as he winced but his hungry lips searched for mine.

We began to grind, and I felt his penis slip between my legs and against my perineum, the pain seemed short, but bearable, as his bulbous head pressed hard, I wanted him inside me, but he was pounding too fast for me to reach and guide.

I started to rub my own dick to his beat, and my other hand ran down to his buttocks, gripping onto it. He started to use his hands to tweak my pert nipples, his lips still fixated onto mine.

"I love you" He gasped, and I knew that he was about to spill his load on me.

I repeated the statement, and watched as he pulled away, his own hand clasped onto his groin, and he furiously masturbated, and I did too.

He came first, and his hot drink covered my entire chest, as though he had built it up since we last saw each other. He wasted no time in smearing it onto me, as I continued to tug at my own penis.

As I gave him my signal that I was about to shoot, he swiftly lowered himself down my body, smearing more of his juice as he did so, and he placed his lips just millimetres away from my tip. My cum spurted, and he placed his mouth over my spilling head, and heightened my satisfaction as he sucked the entire contents from my balls until the insanity took over.

He made his way back along my body, still smearing his jizz, and his lips pressed back onto mine. My own semen spilling into my mouth. I did not mind.

June 2nd.

We awoke deliberately early, the sun had not even risen outside, but I knew that Glynn would be taking delivery soon.

As I stretched over to switch the alarm on my mobile phone from ringing, I glanced over at him, as he stirred next to me. His naked ass looked so smooth and pert.

He was in pain, but happy. And so was I. I glanced down at my scar, and recalled some of those questions in the hospital.

He was awake now, and stroking my back. I turned to face him, and kissed him again, as I joined him laying down.

"I have something to ask you" He smiled, "I have been thinking about this since before we both left Turkey"

With that, he removed a silver ring from his forefinger, and smiled at me. I felt myself blush. "So?" He smiled, as he placed it onto my ring finger, it was too small, but it didn't matter,

"Screw everything, let's get married"

"No" I responded suddenly, as I scrambled out of my bed, gathering my clothes.

I had clearly hurt his feelings, but I was not about to commit myself, he remained silent, as he clambered out of the bed, and started to dress in the same clothes.

"I can't marry you" I commented, "But I do have another plan"

Pulling on his pants, he shook his head, "I love you Connor, and if you don't love me, I may as well go back to London"

I rushed to his side, and gripped his arms to his side, he put up little resistance, "If you love me, then let's do a Hand fast instead"

Now I had confused him.

He stood, mouth agape like the big dumb ginger he was, "What the fuck is a Hand fest?"

I took his hand, and led him gently back to the bed, "It is like a wedding, but it's a Wiccan style wedding, it lasts for one year and one day"

"Why don't we just get married and show the world we love each other?" He questioned, "You hurt me when you abandoned me in Marmaris, all I wanted was to hold you and to let you know everything would be alright"

"I know" I responded, "And that is why I want to make up for it for every day that we live, and if we get to renew our vows every year until the day we grow old and forget each other"

"I will never forget you" He smiled, "You're the only thing that kept me warm at night when I was sleeping in bushes, and on the streets"

He gently squeezed my hand, and I knew I had won him over again, "I want a shower, and then you and I can leave this place"

I smiled, as I took him in with my eyes.

What the fuck had I done?

"The shower is kinda temperamental" I replied with a wry smile.

I could sense that Glynn was not happy as I entered the bar shortly before half past six that morning. He was deliberately slamming down the boxes of delivery that had arrived just moments ago.

"Glynn, I have to leave" I spoke before he could respond, "Something has come up"

"Your arse" He retaliated without glancing over at me, "Fucking dirty little spunk trumpet"

"Glynn" I did not know how to respond.

"You had the chance to deflower one of the finest unplucked pussies in this village" He spat, "And you choose to have some man's meat and two veg crammed into your anus, filling you with his filthy love juice"

The disgust in his voice was scathing, "Glynn, I don't need...."

"Jackie would have been the best thing that could have happened to you" He hissed, as he opened the till, removing some notes, "I watched the CCTV and saw her give you a blowjob and you left the evidence on the floor for me to clean up....It disgusts me to think that man lying with man under my own roof, I want you out"

"Fine" I responded. Well what more could I say?

"That is you paid up to tomorrow" He continued thrusting the notes before me, "Now get out of my house before I call the police"

"I am going" I responded.

"Disgusting" He repeated which echoed as I moved back along the staircase.

Chris was now dressed in my jeans, and my favourite white shirt, which was open, revealing his smooth chest, and the silver chain he had worn since I have known him.

"I heard everything" He whispered.

"Fuck it" I smiled, flashing the cash, "Let's blow this joint"

"Rather you blow me" He smiled, as he leaned in for a kiss.

FORTY SEVEN

June 5th

We made it to Chester, and we used the cash to find a small bed and breakfast in the city. It then took me a few more days to find Maverick. He was still as scruffy as I remembered, seemed like the change he made last year was only temporary. We found him at the site of the old ampi-theatre in the centre, and he took us to a shanty town on the outskirts of Chester after asking around for him for a few days. His hair was rancid, and I am sure there were creatures living in it.

He struggled to remember me at first, and welcomed us to his commune. I gently reminded him that I was once his rep, and the smile returned to his face.

"I remember standing before you, asking if you would worship my cock" He remembered calmly in front of his community, as though they were his disciples, "But this man was strong, and he rejected my penis"

I felt myself blush, and I also felt Chris's grip on my hand tighten.

I decided to break the tension, "So how is Moonbeam?"

The gathering of mutterings from the community rose, and Maverick conveyed silence by just using his arms in a swooping motion.

"Her name shall not be mentioned here" He insisted, "Moonbeam is no more part of this community"

I nodded in acceptance.

He continued, "She has a terminal disease, which would have put this community at risk. So I expelled her"

I nodded once more in acceptance, "The thing is Maverick, I located you to ask you for a favour"

A smile crossed his face, "You now wish to worship my cock?"

"No" I laughed, "I have come to ask you to officiate a Hand fasting"

311

Excitement in the community lifted, and Maverick felt immense pride erupt within, "I have never officiated a Hand fast between two men, this is something new for my home"

"So is that a yes?" Chris asked.

"It's a fucking Hell Yes" Maverick cheered, as he signalled for two women to approach. A brunette took my arm, and smiled at me, as someone who could have easily been her twin took Chris's arm, "Ladies, go and make our boys ready, and if the Brother and Sisters can get the mound ready, with mead and fruit, I will Hand fast you both today"

The hours that we were apart were filled with a bathing in the local stream, and being fed grapes by the girl, who introduced herself as Petal. I mean come on, these names are ridiculous. She spent some time getting to know me and jotting it down in a pad, and then she left me to get ready. A pair of white cotton trousers, and an open topped shirt were laid on my makeshift bed, and I slowly dressed. When I was completely dressed, Petal returned, and placed a gay looking garland around my neck, and styled my hair into a pony tail, using daisies as pins to hold it in.

"Maverick is ready" She smiled, as she removed her gown, I nearly choked on air.

"What are you doing?" I panicked.

"Maverick conducts Hand fasts sky-clad" She whispered, "Be as one with nature"

Naked, she led me out of the canvas room, and we made our way through to the forest area beyond the commune. Chris was already there, blushing as the naked community sat in groups either side of him, and Petal presented me to him.

His female took Petal's hand, and they sat together beside an oak tree.

Maverick appeared from the depths of the forest in his officiating gown, and he instantly dropped it when in full view. His schlong was waving around with every step he took, until he stood before me. Too close I thought, I was already shaking and if he got any closer, I would be touching that stinking penis reaching out to me. Four coloured cords were placed loosely over our held hands.

"Connor and Chris" He began, "When you love someone, you do not love them all the time in exactly the same way, things change, and you grow together in union. We as mankind have little faith in the ebb and flow of life, of love, and of relationships. The only security we have is that of not owning or possessing. Security in a relationship lies in neither looking back to nostalgia, nor looking forward to what may be, but it is living in the present, and accepting it as it is now"

I took those words, and realised their beautiful meaning and simple truth, and that at this moment, I did not need to run, or hide. Meanwhile, he was still going on.

"Chris and Connor have come to us today to incorporate the ancient Celtic ritual of hand fasting in their wedding. This is a declaration of love, where they clearly state that they are marrying of their own free will"

Petal and her twin had risen from the oak tree, and approached us from behind, taking a piece of cord each.

"The promises made today and the ties that are bound here greatly strengthen your union" She explained.

"Do you seek to enter this ceremony?" Maverick asked. I swear his dick was getting harder.

"Yes" Chris and I responded in unison, both trying to maintain eye contact to avoid looking at his rancid cock.

"Then please look into each other's eyes" He instructed, and we obeyed, "Connor and Chris, will you share in each other's pain and seek to alleviate it?"

"Yes" We nodded, and the bind was made, sealing our hands.

"Do you share in laughter, and look only for positives?" Maverick continued. "Yes" And a second bind was made by the girls.

"Will you share your dreams?" He continued.

"Yes" And a third bind was made.

"Do you honour each other as equal?" Maverick continued.

"Yes" We responded.

"Connor and Chris, as your hands are bound together, so your lives and spirits are joined in a union of love and trust, the bond of marriage is not formed by these cords, but by the vows that you have made, for you always hold in your hands the fate of this union. Above you are stars, and below you is the earth, like stars your love should be a source of light, and as earth, form a strong foundation" Maverick continued.

"May your hands be the healer, protector, shelter and guide for one another" Petal smiled.

"The rings?" Maverick queried.

Chris smiled, as he removed my new silver ring from his chain, and I removed the matching one from my pocket.

"You did not advise on vows, would you like to say your own?" Maverick asked.

I nodded, and placed the ring onto Chris's finger, "I promise that I will make you smile every day, and provide you with warmth and love forever. I should never have left you in Turkey, but I am glad that you found me again"

Chris smiled as he returned the gesture, "I slept rough and ate scraps just to be with you, so I promise you this, I too will make you smile, and provide you with the love that you deserve"

"You may now kiss" Maverick concluded.

As I kissed Chris, I could not help but think that Maverick was getting off on the fact, and for the first time in a long time, I felt happy. Nothing was going to stop me.

"Happy birthday" I added as I pulled away.

"You remembered?" He was crying again.

June 11th

We left Chester the next day, and we threw a dart at a map of the UK, and made our way to the winning place. The dart had landed on Hull. Chris knew some people in the area, and we used them to find a small bedsit on Spring Bank, near to the City Centre, which was surprisingly cheap. They even got us work in a gothic bar. We even used pseudonyms of James and Rob Bell.

We kept ourselves to ourselves, our bedsit overlooked a local park, with the entrance in a messy car park, but we felt at home. I had been to the shop directly across the road, and bought a bag full of beers for us. The owner of the shop also owned the bedsit, and she threw in a few extras for me.

Our neighbours were a lovely modern young couple, who liked the party lifestyle, and were constantly drunk or high in our presence. We loved this. I think Chris was keen for an orgy at one point, but he never said. But I caught him looking at them both. Sadie was a tall blonde with hair that went on for miles, and Callum was a smaller dark skinned goon that actually frightened me a little. But their company was immaculate. I loved sitting in their flat stroking their cat.

It was raining outside, and Sadie was sitting in the car park smoking a funny looking cigarette, which she flicked out as soon as she saw me, giving me the "Don't say a thing" smile. She was jovial as flung open her door, and I laughed as I saw Callum in one his weight lifting strains.

Life was really great for us. People knew that we were a couple, and no one batted an eyelid.

As I entered the flat, I tried not to laugh as he lay seductively naked on the couch, with scented candles burning around the place. He was always trying to surprise me.

"Charming" He laughed, as he rose to his feet, and sauntered toward me, "I was thinking, quick bang, and a pizza?"

I barely had chance to respond, before he was kissing me, and fumbling around my crotch, to free the beast.

Pulling me to the floor, I kicked off my jeans, and before I knew it, his cock was before me. I gripped the base of it, and bought it to my mouth, and he was soon noshing me off too, I stroked his balls, and he tugged at mine. The pain was euphoric.

He began to thrust into my mouth, and I returned the favour, our hands gripping onto each other's thighs, and arse, I even allowed my finger to penetrate his anus, and I could tell he was enjoying it as his groans became more muffled by my dick in his mouth.

I knew that I was about to shoot, and I bucked, which encouraged him to suck harder, and faster. Soon enough I came, and my load hit the back of his throat, my cock pulsated, and I continued to suck him. I felt him adjust himself as he released my flaccid penis from his mouth. He stroked my long hair, and I felt his cock flex, and then he released his cum into my mouth. I tried to swallow as much as I could, but it was too much, and soon started spilling down my cheek.

"I love you" He whispered.

"I love you too" I responded, wiping the jizz off my face, and I meant it.

He shuffled down my body, and snuggled next to me, holding me tight. I never wanted to leave this position.

"I'm hungry" He smiled, "I'll order a pizza"

He pulled away from me, and grasped at his mobile phone. After he ordered, he re-joined me on the floor.

"I paid for it on card" He whispered, "That money is for emergencies"

I could tell he was getting randy again as he started to nuzzle at my neck, "We said that about the card"

"If you would have said this time last year we would be a married couple, making love in a shitty old Hull Bedsit, I would have slapped you" He smiled, his cock now erect again. Ready for round two.

And so was I.

I forcefully tackled him, and now I was on top, our lips met once more.

June 12th.

As we had left over pizza for breakfast, we decided to take advantage of the sunshine, and our day off. We went to the harbour, and had coffee. The afternoon was spent at the cinema, where we really did not watch the film, we just kissed, and rested each other's heads on our chests. Some bigot made a comment at one point. We did not care.

We spent the day watching people addicted to social media, and not even interacting with each other. We had left our mobiles at home, we did not need them.

I hated modern living. Perhaps I should have been born a century earlier? No I liked the sex too much.
Taking my hand, we made our way back home, along the almost empty road.

"I think we should dip into the money" He spoke, as he led the way to the side street that lead to the parkway, "Go on a holiday, you and I"

"It hardly constitute as an emergency" I smiled.

"Just think, we can go to Montreal" He smiled, "Think about it, I am just going to get some biscuits to have with our tea"

"What is it about Montreal?" I asked.

"It's a place I want to call home" He smiled.

I grinned, as he skipped across the road and made his way to the shop. I continued to walk around the back of the apartment, and smiled again as I saw some young lovers in the park. He was pushing her on the swing. How sweet?

As I entered the car park, I noticed a new car, a Mondeo in the area, but as we were so close to the centre, a lot of people used it for convenience.

I heard the window electronically open, and a male voice called out, "Connor Candlish"

"No" I panicked.

I could not see who was inside the car, and I frantically jingled my keys in my hands as I wanted to get to the doorway.

"It's him" Another sexless voice announced from the inside of the car.

Without notice, the engine revved, and started towards me.

I panicked, and began to run toward the doorway to our bedsit.

I heard Chris scream my name, and as I turned, I saw him race toward me.

For some reason, I had stopped, aware that the Mondeo was hurtling toward me.

"I love you" I heard.

Chris reached me, with his arms wide open, and pushed me out of the way with seconds to spare. I hit my head on the floor, and could only hear the sound of the car smashing into the wall.

Dazed, I rolled onto my stomach, through the blurred vision from my own eyes, I could see the wreckage of the car, with half the wall covering it. I was aware I was bleeding, but could not see where it was coming from.

The pain was immense, but I strained against it. I also saw those lovers racing into the car park, whether to help, or to see what had happened.

The inhabitants of the car lay unconscious on their seats, and I could hear screams from people inside the bedsits. I am sure I saw our landlady in the window surveying the damage.

Then I saw the hand underneath the rubble. A hand with a ring identical to mine. I screamed, as I used all my energy to crawl toward it

I continued to cry and scream as my hand just touched Chris's lifeless hand. Then blackness followed.

FORTY EIGHT

July 26th.

I dreamed that everything was going to be fine, and Chris and I would finally make it to Montreal. But each time, the dream became darker, like a pendulous rain cloud draining the colour out of life itself. I knew I was dreaming.

The next thing I recall, I came to in hospital for the second time. I was once more in a private room, and almost a week had passed.

A nerdy looking male nurse was already in the room as my eyes opened, and I strained against the clinical whiteness again.

"You have been in a medically induced coma" A familiar voice spoke from my left, almost not caring that I was awake.

I strained to move to see him, and instantly regretted it, as I saw Greg and Eve next to me.

"You took a severe blow to the head when that car drove at you" The nurse explained, "You had to have seven stitches in your head, and arm"

I noticed that my ring was missing, and I croaked, "Chris...."

I sensed the tension in the room. The nurse made his excuses and left, and Greg and Eve positioned themselves closer to me.

"We trusted that you would tell us the moment he got in touch" Greg commented.

"Last week Chris used his card in Hull and we traced it" Eve interrupted, "You two have been together since the beginning of the month"

"I need to see him" I insisted.

"You can't" Greg insisted monotonously, "We need to know why you did not let us know he had made contact with you"

I thought back for a moment, but knew that I had to protect him, after all he did tell me that his own father had beat him, "I went with the moment"

"Fucking faggot" Greg hissed, "You wanted to keep him for yourself didn't you?"

The rant had attracted the nurse back into the room, and I noticed Eve open her purse. She removed something from it, and sauntered toward me.

She did not speak as she passed me two silver rings.

"Where is he?" I questioned.

"I am sorry" She began to cry, "Chris died the minute the car hit him, they could not do anything to save him"

I froze, as I stared at the rings. I remembered seeing his hand, I remembered touching him before I blacked out.

"The funeral is the day after tomorrow in Croydon" Greg announced, "And you could have saved him if you kept to your promise"

"I need to come to the funeral" I insisted.

"I am sorry sir" The nurse interjected, "You have just come out of a coma, and will be in here for some time"

"And I forbid you to attend the funeral" Greg commanded, "I am paying for this treatment because it is the last thing I can do for my son"

"I loved him" I broke down crying.

"Love?" He questioned, "You put your dick into my boy that is just fucking, not love"

"Leave him alone" Eve whispered, somewhat distant.

"And those fucking rings you're holding?" Greg gestured to my hand after a long pause, "Nothing"

He pulled the door open and left the room, as Eve watched in astonishment. "Nurse, can you give me a moment?" She asked.

He nodded, and left the room again.

"I do not have an issue with you and Chris" She insisted, "But Greg has lost his son, you can understand his anger?"

"I need to be there" I cried.

"No I am sorry, we cannot allow that" She comforted, "But I think I can convince Greg to give you that job in one of his bars, like we said before?, this means you can start again"

I did not have time to answer, as I could see the nurse outside again, conversing with police.

Eve noticed too, "This is a murder investigation now, so you have to tell them the truth"

She signalled for the nurse to allow the police officers to enter the room.

The male officer was tall and bald, and introduced himself as Inspector Collins, and his partner was a petite young Asian girl, who barely looked old enough to be out of a school uniform let alone a police uniform, she introduced herself as Inspector Njai.

Eve made her excuses and left the room, I could see her liaise with her husband as the officers took their seats.

"Mr Candlish, you understand why we are here" Collins stated, not even a question. I nodded.

"Mr Candlish, the men in the car were killed on impact, but we found something that may be of interest to you" Collins explained.

Collins pulled an evidence bag out of his pocket, and passed it over to me, "This was found in the vehicle, can you tell me what it means?"

I stared at the writing on the piece of paper. 'Half now, the rest when Candlish is dead' "I don't know" I whispered.

"Look at the signature" Collins nodded to the parchment. I did, and screamed.

Signed, 'O'

"Who is O Mr Candlish?" He pressed.

I stared at the scar on my arm, that bitch had found me again.

"Ophelia" I whispered.

FORTY NINE

I had to be sedated again, and spent the rest of the day in an induced sleep, the officers interviewed me again two days later. The day of the funeral. I still was inconsolable, but I managed to tell them about Ophelia. The police informed me that I was to remain local, in case they found Ophelia. Of course I was adamant that she would get away with it. I stared out of the window, and played in my mind my memories. That fucking psycho bitch kept interrupting my thoughts, but I thought mainly on Chris.

I was released from hospital the day after the funeral, and I had nothing left. As I made my way home, the car park was still cordoned off, and the hole in the wall looked surprisingly clean, as though someone had smartened it up. Someone watched me from one of the flats, and I sensed the curtain close before I raised my head.

Everything in the room reminded me of him, and I cried at the smallest of things. His socks on the radiator, his shower gel in the bathroom, even his book on the table. I knew what I had to do, and it took me a few days, and my neighbours to help and pack his belongings into trash bags. They were kind enough to take them to a charity shop for me, and I stared at the vacant room. The only thing I kept was his ring, which I wore with mine, and his silver chain, which I now also wore. And that book.

That night, I myself packed. Checking the money was still safe in the rucksack, along with my passport, I made my way out in the dead of night, and trekked into the City toward the train station, a single train was waiting, and I was the lone passenger, at least to Leeds, when some rowdy teenagers awoke me from my slumber.

July 2nd

I made my way to his parents' house in Croydon, and considering that Greg was the owner of a chain of clubs, his mid-terrace was not as I expected. In fact, there was fresh dog shit on the pathway just inches away from where my feet were. It took them forever to answer the door, and when Greg did open the white door, I could see the anger in him.

He did not even let me in the house, as he stepped outside, pulling the door closed behind him, "Why are you here?"

"I wanted to pay my respects" I muttered, scared that I was actually saying goodbye.

"You are not wanted around here homo" He hissed attracting the attention of some passers-by. The door opened again, and Eve stood in the frame.

"Please, just tell me where he is buried, so I can have closure" I muttered. "Closure?" He hissed, "You may as well have been driving that car"

His hands now reached for my throat, as the anger within him built up.

"Stop" Eve cried, tearing her husband from me.

"This little arse bandit fucked my son" He cried, as he continued to break down, and also attracting the attention of more of the neighbours.

"At least I loved him" I retaliated, "I never beat him up, or made him run away from home"

Greg turned to look at me, "You do not speak to me like that"

"Tell me where he is" I insisted.

"Wait right here" Eve muttered, clearly annoyed with the attention that our row was bringing.

She returned to the house, taking Greg with her, and I waited, even acknowledging the neighbours with a nod, "Yes I loved Chris"

Someone applauded, another mumbled something about disgrace, and another smiled back, a nice bit of variation out there in this Croydon backstreet. I smiled.

They returned minutes later, and Eve took the lead this time, while Greg lingered behind her disappointingly.

"Far be it for us to deny you memories of our Chris" She explained, as she produced a small show red box, "We had Chris cremated so you cannot visit him, but we decided to scatter his ashes somewhere he loved, so it would only seem right that you take part of him"

My hands were shaking as I took the box. With trembling fingers, I opened it, and I felt a tear roll down my cheek as I saw the ashes within, "Thank you"

I wanted to stop right there, and I turned on my heels to leave.

"One more thing Connor" Greg called, surprisingly calm now.

I stopped, and remained with my back to them for long moments, as I heard him approach me from behind. His hand soon touched my shoulder, and I quivered.

He passed me an envelope, and I turned to face him.

"I don't want you around here" He commented, and as I was about to retaliate he continued, "I cannot accept that you made my boy a fudge packer, but Eve has made it clear that you made him happy over the last year"

I nodded.

"I only wish he remained shagging the Scouse bird from Mallorca, but I suppose I cannot control his...." The pause seemed indefinite, and the word stung him to say, "Urges"

"Sian was not good enough for him" I responded, "She used him, and ..."

"I simply do not care" Greg interrupted, "But you have robbed me of the chance of grandchildren, and you have robbed me of my boy"

"Greg I...." I began.

"You have to earn the right to use my name, you will address me as Mr Mumford. Now, just leave, and look after those ashes, we will scatter the rest of them somewhere appropriate, and I suppose I will have to trust that you will return that favour" He continued, "In that envelope is a one way ticket to Blackpool, and I want you to go there, and run my bar there"

"What?" I could not believe his words.

"The manager we had suddenly left last week, and I need someone there to run things, and if you go there, I won't need to see you face again" He explained, "The Black Orchid is my least profitable bar, and you can earn a wage whilst finding yourself someone else, I know you shag women as well as men, so you can have an open season"

"Thank you" Well what more can I say?

"You have my wife to thank for this" He explained, "Now, please leave, before I do something I will regret"

"Thank you Eve" I nodded with agreement, "And thank you Greg, I promise, I will look after the club, these ashes, and unless it is business related, you will not see me again"

He nodded in acknowledgement, and returned to his wife. "Oh" He spoke, "One more thing"

"Yes?" I asked.

"Chris told me you once set up some bloke when you were a rep" I recollected what he was talking about in one moment, "Keep your eyes on the staff, and if you catch them up to something, get rid, and you may finally have my respect"

I arrived in Blackpool that same day, and started work the following day. The Black Orchid, which was situated in the North Pier area, and as I entered, I realised almost instantly that it was a chain of pole dancing clubs that I had entered into. It should not have surprised me, Eve was hot, and one of his bitches before she married him. On my first day, a tall dark haired lady, dressed in leather, with an assortment of whips and chains on her person greeted me at the reception desk. She was drinking wine by the bottle and smoking cigarettes as though they were going out of fashion.

"So you're the new manager?" She grinned, barely taking her hand off the vibrator she had humming in her pussy, "Name's Julia, but my customers call me The Cock Smasher"

"Pleased to meet you" I tried to hide my embarrassment.

"Come with me" She sighed as she rose, and led me through the black doors, dumping her vibrator on the seat next to her. Dirty bitch.

Even the dancing area was replica of a womb. What the fuck had I entered into?

"Right, we open Wednesdays through to Saturday, and we have our regular doormen on, Stephen and Simon, pair of dicks if you ask me, but you will get to know them" She explained as she sauntered through toward the bar area, "Our bar man is Troy, he's slept with pretty much all the girls in this place, and possibly the men too, I dunno, pissed up tart would probably bang a husky if it licked his bollocks"

"Do you have anything nice to say about anyone?" I jested.

She paused, and turned and looked at me for a moment, "I like your hair" Wow, I asked for that I suppose.

"Right, from my conversation with Greg Mumford, you are to have the keys to his flat and to set up your own wage allowance?" She continued, as she fumbled behind the bar. She located a bowl, which contained lubricant, condoms and keys. She read a few labels on these keys, before passing me over a single key with a red fob, "Ah fuck it, have his car too"

I smiled, why the fuck not?

"So" Julia smiled, "You like your dick sucked?"

"Of course" I smiled.

"Get it out then" She ordered, "First one is free"

Without so much as a warning, she dropped to her knees, and clawing at my crotch, unzipping my jeans, freeing my dick from my pants, and it hardened almost is on command. I felt guilty at first to be honest, but with her moist mouth sucking on my meat, I did not mind.

"Noshing off the new manager huh, you after a pay rise?" Someone spoke from behind me.

"Fuck you" She laughed, as she pulled away.

I turned my head to the direction of the voice, two bouncers stood in the doorway, with the door wide open, and passers-by could easily see in. Nervously I pulled away and put my cock back into my pants.

"Nice one you pair of scrotes" Julia hissed in disgust, then she turned to me, "Next one is free I promise, meet the fucking knob heads"

With that, she sauntered back toward the doorway, slamming it shut behind her as she left. I think I heard her vibrator switch on again.

"You wanna steer clear of her mate" The bald one spoke.

"Yeah" His dumb looking companion spoke, "She may have a mouth like a vacuum cleaner, but her pussy is like a wizard's sleeve"

"I fucking heard that pencil dick" She called from the now open door again, with a hint of laughter in her voice, "The fucking girls will be here in a minute, and that knob head, I think you better get the new guy sorted"

"That new bird on tonight?" The bald guy asked, grabbing his crotch, he turned to me, "You wanna meet her mate, I would split her in two, and order her to make me breakfast immediately after"

"Piss off Si" Julia laughed as she stuck her little finger in the air, "If you went anywhere near her, she would not feel a thing"

"Touch yourself" He laughed, "You weren't complaining when you rode it last weekend"

"Honey" Julia laughed, "I faked every fucking orgasm, and finished myself off with that naked picture of Stephen you sent me from your lads weekend last month, now show him the ropes"

I could tell from her comments, that Stephen was the daft looking one, who seemed proud his image had been sent to her.

"She wants it again Si" Stephen laughed.

"Damn right, mark my words, I will be rogering her before breakfast" Simon laughed, "Right dickhead, you're the new manager, the one who fucked the owners son?"

"You put it so eloquently" I responded, "I know you from somewhere"

"I have one of those faces" He nodded, "Because I am bald, people call me Fester Addams" I laughed.

"Meh" Simon sighed, "We all have secrets, I could not give a fuck, more women for me then" "We all know your dirty little secret ya bald scrotum" Stephen laughed.

"What's that then?" I enquired.

"He's into animals" Stephen joked, as he tweaked his friend's nipple, causing him to squirm like a girl.

"Oh yeah" Simon changed the subject, "I can't work next weekend I have a gig"

"A gig" Stephen mimicked, "Your band is shit, who the fuck will hire you? The Deaf Society of St Helens?"

"Piss off dick breath" Simon bantered, raising his knee in to Stephen's groin just hard enough to disable him, he then turned back to me, "Right, follow me"

I had to laugh, as I followed him up the hidden staircase to my office, overlooking the entire bar. Inside, all the ladies photographs were pinned to the notice board, with their stage names and real names underneath. I smiled as I saw the name Raven, reminded me of a fat ginger bird I used to bone in my home town many years ago.

FIFTY

"So" I sighed trying to take my mind off the pussy on the board, "What do I need to know?" "The last manager left us" He continued, I already knew this, "I have to admit he was a mean prick who got what he wanted by using his position of power. Is that what you are into?" "Nah" I muttered, still scanning the pretty images.

Another girl caught my eye, Anastasia, a petit blonde haired girl with the biggest blue eyes you can imagine, she almost looked unreal, like a manga character.

"Ah, she's the new girl" Simon announced, touching her image as gently as he could, "I would smash her back doors in all night"

"Oi wank stain" Stephen called from downstairs, "The girls and Troy are here"

I glanced through the window, and smiled as I saw a dozen girls gather into the auditorium, and a tall scruffy looking bearded man, wearing a bow-tie stood in the middle of them, he was pawing at one of the girls, I recognised as Raven from the images.

"Show time mate" Simon commented, "And if you want to dick the new girl, I would stake a claim to it now"

"Why's that?" I asked. I felt guilty again.

"Stephen's a massive man slag, he may act like the dumb ass but he can charm the pants off a bird without trying, and between him and bitch with a bowtie, that is what Marty is better known as by us, because of the naff bowties he wears. Well they have porked all the girls in this joint except her" Simon explained, "I have a bet with them both that someone else will get there first"

"Seriously though, where do I know you from?" I asked, realising that it was on the tip of my tongue.

He shrugged, "Never seen you before in my life kid"

"Fine" I muttered, brushing aside his comment, "Give me five minutes and I will make my way down"

He nodded, and I paused for a moment. I waited until I could see him in the auditorium below, before I pulled out my dick, and made my way over to the images of the women on the board. I was in Heaven as I tugged hard, fast, and furious, the woman with the blue eyes caught my attention, and I knew I was about to shoot my load quickly. I shot, and felt the intense bursts of my own ivory coloured juice covered the wall, and I smeared a little onto the image ofAnastasia.

I was surprised by the power of my presence as I entered the bar area, and introduced myself. Two of the girls, and a hairy bloke who I knew was bitch with a bow-tie, kind of ignored me, and were not interested in my presence, and as I spoke, one of them was already down on the bitch with a bow-tie, and it really was a naff black one with some colour splashed on it. Right there in front of everyone. The other one, Raven, had his balls in her mouth.

"Alright, less of that" I instructed.

"Fuck yourself" Bitch with a bow-tie hissed, as he cupped the head of the girl, "You take that drink Victoria, like a good girl"

I gave Stephen and Simon the nod, and they stepped forward. Raven immediately let the ball out of her mouth and raised, as Victoria put up a struggle to two men pulling her away from his dick.

"Everything will be run the same as before" I spoke with authority, trying to ignore the incident before, "Except no staff benefits such as free blow-jobs, you want one Bitch with a bow-tie, you can pay, and we will work out a discount scheme"

"The fuck I am paying to have my dick sucked" He insisted.

"I believe your role here is bar man?" I enquired, and gestured to the stock behind the bar.

Buttoning up his fly, he made his way past me, muttering some abuse, probably about me and the boss's son, I switched off from this knob head.

I could sense Julia approved of my actions, with a knowing nod.

"Ladies, enjoy, and remember my door will always be an open one" I announced.

"Gay" Bitch with a bow-tie sang in the back of the bar.

Anger filled my head, and I turned to him, "You my friend are on a verbal, one more incident and I will kick your ass to the nearest job centre"

Julia cheered, "Stick that up your arse Troy" She used his real name.

"This place would be shit without me entertaining the masses" Bitch with a bow-tie commented matter-of-factly.

"Damn right lover" Victoria smiled, licking her lips and sticking out her breasts seductively.

"Arse bandit there won't be here long, you can suck it in our break baby girl" Bitch with a bow-tie instructed with a point to his cock.

"In the back alley where you belong scum" I muttered.

I could see from the way that she watched my lips, Anastasia's coy smile support my stance on Bitch with a bow-tie and his freebies. In fact, I was sure she licked her lips at me with approval.

"I would like to speak with you all individually, to get to know you, so when you get five minutes, please make your way to my office" I gestured to the room, like they knew where I would be, "Maybe I can start alphabetically?"

Anastasia nodded, and followed me up the staircase, much to the disapproval of Raven and Victoria.

She settled on the chair opposite my desk, as I perched on the edge of it. Her legs crossed at the ankles, as she swung them precariously off the floor.

"Troy won't stand for you ordering him about" She smiled, batting her long eye lashes at me, I felt a familiar stir in my groin area. I felt guilty again, but I managed to hide any movement. "He told the last manager he would shove a banger up his arse if he ever bossed him about"

"I am tougher than I look" I announced.

"So am I" She replied, and I believed her.

"You don't like Troy?" I observed, using his real name.

"Dirty little scrote thinks he's God's gift" She smiled, "You saw the size of his chipolata"

"Wow" I sighed, "No love lost"

"He tried it on with me last weekend, and I kicked him in his Man Cunt" She smiled, "Think he liked it"

"So tell me about Anastasia" I wanted to change the subject, and stop me from laughing.

I glanced at her photo, and realised that her real name was Emily, as she spoke, "Yeah, I am a dancer, but I studied drama at Liverpool, and my ex got me into pole dancing as a form of exercise, when he got sent down, I had to pay my bills"

"Surely there are other jobs?" I enquired, realising that I literally walked into this role.

"Well, yes, but I get to keep the tips here" She announced, "I only started last week and the last manager up and walked, I think Troy thought he would take over"

"Tell me about him" I asked.

"Total prick" She answered honestly, "Made that bitch with a bow-tie look like the pope"

I laughed, "I find that hard to believe"

"Sat right where you are, and said to me I had to suck his cock, and his exact words were I can spit this time, but if I wanted to keep my job I will have to learn to swallow, he was only here a month or so apparently" She remembered, and then she sighed, "If my gran could see me now she would slap me so hard, and take me back home"

"Were you close?" I asked.

She smiled, "She got me into dancing and swimming, I used to do ballet, and was number one in my swimming team. She was so proud of me, I was in so many performances and competitions... when she died, that's when I moved in with my ex... And then we know what happened next, goodbye tutus, hello titties"

"Wow" I smiled as I was aware she was flirting, and thrusting out her breasts to me, "Very impressive"

"So Mr Candlish" She enquired, "Do I spit or swallow?"

"I am not after a blow job" I shocked myself, "Perhaps I could take you out for a coffee?"

She laughed, "I get paid to flash my fanny and tits to anyone who pays, do you really think I could settle into a relationship?"

"I never said relationship" I protested.

"I did" She smiled, as she rose, and pressed her body closer to me, "I can see you have a massive cock, and I want it Mr Candlish, I don't care about flashing my mott and tata's if you don't mind"

I felt her hand press against my leg, inching closer to my cock, and as she cupped my erection, she leaned in for a kiss. I paused at first, and then allowed her tongue to enter my mouth teasingly. Before I knew it, my dick was in her hand, and she began to tug at me frantically.

"You fucking twat" Stephen muttered, as he gormed at me, how long had he been there?

"Put your knob away" Anastasia smiled at him, "I am strictly a one man woman" I then noticed he did in fact also have his knob in his hand, tugging away frantically.

"Let him watch" I smiled, as I turned her around, and allowed my dick to enter her pussy from behind. It felt tight, and wet, and she shuffled to accommodate me. She even moved to assist my hard thrusts.

As I thrust hard into her chasm, he seemed to enjoy his wanking technique, almost admiring himself. I stared down at the dancing arse before me, and spanked it, which not only satisfied her, it also made Stephen more excited. He shot his load on the floor just moments later, and I nodded at him, before gesturing that he fucked off. He had his free show.

Now for mine. My hands gripped hard onto her arched back, and I pushed harder and harder inside her, my balls began to bang against her pussy, and her yelps of passion soon became too loud. I knew that people downstairs could hear us fucking over the music. The sound downstairs soon crescendo.

Throughout the evening, I spoke, and only spoke with three more women before I made my way back to the bar. Shit I needed a drink.

I smiled, as I saw Anastasia with her tits out, dancing around a pole, with her dance partner Raven, I loved how they playfully touched each other's nipples, as they entertained the men of the audience. And some women.

She mouthed something to me, and I knew that I had scored.

I made my way to the bar, and the bitch with a bow-tie remained ignorant as ever, concentrating on Victoria, as she danced. He was rubbing his bulging cock through his jeans,

"Pint mate" I ordered, gesturing to the pump.

He waved it off, and continued to watch. I turned to see what he was smiling at. Victoria was perched provocatively on the podium, with a lolly pop stick jutting out of her mouth, and her left leg raised over her head. She used her hands to raise the right leg high, causing a cheer from the men, as her pussy opened before me, she pulled out the lollipop and sucked the tip with a knowing wink.

A punter rose, and placed a fifty note at her feet, and she took it with one swift movement.

She took him by the hand, and pulled him away into one of the private booths beyond the stage.

I could sense that the bitch with a bow-tie was angry.

"Troy" I called and waited for his response, "Beer"

"That's my wife" He muttered, "I hate seeing her dance for other men"

"So why does she work here?" I asked.

"Because I work here, and she's safe" He insisted, as he commenced pouring my pint.

"Does she fuck them?" I asked.

"If the price is right" He responded, as he finished pouring my beer, "Six pounds"

"Fuck off" I gasped.

"House rules" He explained, with his hand out awaiting the cash. "Put it on wastage" I encouraged.

"No wastage" He insisted, "Mumford rules"

"Half price" I snarled, "Candlish rules"

FIFTY ONE

July 7th

News that Anastasia and I were banging became the bar gossip, and by the end of the week, she had literally stayed every night as I moved into my surprisingly large basement flat near to The Black Orchid. I was also the proud driver of Greg's Mini Cooper, Simon was living in the flat directly opposite me, and he was always alone, but the noises from his room insinuated otherwise. Although, one time, Julia was spotted sneaking into his place, and leaving early the next morning. Denying they were having sex of course.

Raven took an instant dislike to the situation and quit her job on the spot, later that day she had disappeared from her bedsit. I guessed she had gone back home to Essex. Stephen went back to one of the strippers, a particularly leggy red head, knowing that he had lost his bet. Meanwhile, I could not stop Victoria and Bitch with a bow-tie from banging each other senseless in the toilets, I had already lost count on how many times I had called either of them to the office.

Anastasia decided to pay me a visit after another particularly loud argument between Bitch with a bow-tie and I, and as she locked the door behind her, I knew what she was about to do. Lifting her short skirt, she straddled me, and expertly undid my fly before putting my cock inside her clefts.

Starting slow, she soon gained speed, and playfully teased me with her breasts, as she allowed her long blonde hair to fall onto my chest, she bit into my nipples, through my shirt, leaving saliva trails with each gentle nip.

"I was just dancing for some dirty old perve" She confessed, "And I felt my pussy get wet, and I wanted you to fuck me so hard that I can't walk"

I thrust hard, trying to take control, but it was impossible, with her gyrating hips, I realised I was fighting a now losing battle.

I allowed my hands to wander up her body, and I felt her breasts through the soft fabric of her blouse.

She rode me expertly, and I tried to hold back, but her pussy muscles clenched and sucked hard making it almost unbearable for me, I gripped tight onto her back as she forced her mouth onto mine, kissing me.

"Fill me to the brim" She commanded, and I instantly released my load into her, I did not think I would stop but I felt my penis soften once I had drained my babybatter.

She smiled as she clambered off me, and used a tissue from the box to wipe herself. She threw the tissue toward the bin in the corner, and missed.

"So" She smiled, "Can I move in with you?" I paused.

She took me by the hand, and perched herself back on my knee, "I know that you have only just met me, but I think this could work"

"Why do you want to move in so quickly?" I asked.

She sighed, "My ex has sold the house, and I have less than a month to find somewhere else, I should have known really, he told me a few weeks ago about this boat trip he's won or something"

"Boat trip?" I queried, something triggered in the back of my head.

"He's met someone else and is selling the house to fund it" She explained. "What's the name of the boat?" I asked.

"I don't know, I gave up listening to what Oli said when I found out he was knobbing every other cunt he could get his dick into, and it would not surprise me if he went with men too dirty twat" She shrugged, "So, how would you feel about me moving in then?"

"I would need a few days to sort something out" I made my excuse, but I knew I was going to let her do it. She was the best sex I had, in which I was the man at least.

That night, she went back to her home, and I made my way back to mine, I heard Simon in his flat opposite, groaning with pleasure, and his headboard was certainly banging against the wall, and then I heard her screaming with passion inside. Dirty bald bastard had pulled. She sounded like she was enjoying it. Especially as I could hear them going at it with my television on.

Saddened, I pulled out the shoe box from underneath my bed, and gently stroked it.

"I need you to tell me if I am doing the right thing" I whispered, and realised that I was crying again.

I lay down on the bed, and allowed the box to rest on my chest, still listening in to them next door, and I then heard yet another voice. Dirty bald bastard had two women in there.

It made me smile, as it bought back memories of Shannon and Chris, and I turned to the bedside table, and picked up the framed photograph of us. Shannon was now cut out, but I could see her leg in the corner.

"I know that some people may see this as moving too fast" I whispered, "Maybe I should stay single?"

I had been in my apartment for nearly an hour, and Simon and whoever was in there were still banging, who the fuck had given him the Viagra?

Slowly, I moved the box from my chest, and I knew that I had to make a decision, listening to those two at it across the hall, I felt my cock spring to life, and I allowed my hand to touch it, and soon, I was stroking along to their beat. I tugged only just a few times before I felt that beautiful spasm, with the flowing movement of my hand and rhythm, I watched as the first shot of cum from my japs eye. It seemed to coincide with their crescendo of pleasure next door. That sensation of finishing made me smile, and I rose, and wiped the remnants on an old sock near the bed.

I heard the door open across the hall, and I raced over to the peep hole, and smiled as I saw the tallest black lady walk out of the room, and wait for her friend, stroking her black afro that seemed to go on for miles on top of her head. Moments later, I nearly cheered as Julia stood in the doorway talking to someone who was hidden by the door.

She leaned in and kissed, and lifted her leg momentarily as she turned and made her way out with her friend. She took her hand, and they too kissed, and I was aware the door was already closed.

Smiling to myself, as though I had solved a mystery, I turned back to my bed. The box seemed so lonely on there, and I wanted the answer to my question. I glanced down at my wrist, and stroked the scar, and thought to myself, 'Idiot, you did that and now you're talking to a box of ashes'

I made my way back to the bed, and moved the box back to its hiding place, and closed my eyes.

I don't know how long I slept, but it was still dark when I awoke. I really needed to pee, and raced across the room into the bathroom. As I urinated, I glanced at my reflection in the mirror, and realised I hated being blonde. Plus the roots were too long to pull off now. I made a mental note to get something done, and started to make my way back to the bedroom.

Some revellers were outside, and I almost felt the urge to go out again, but I was drained. I paused, and noticed something that I didn't earlier, the wardrobe was slightly open, and with what happened in Manchester, I was slightly unnerved.

Silently, I made my way to the open doorway. Grabbing a knife from the table on the way, I was not taking any chances.

As I inched toward the door, I forced it open, and used the knife to move the hanging clothes. There was a shelf above the clothes, and although small, and no way could someone be there, I still looked.

Near to the edge was a white object, I reached for it, and as I drew it closer to my eyes, I saw a memory stick.

I fired up the lap top, which took ages, and as it loaded, I poured a glass of milk, and returned to the bed, pulling my slow piece of shit laptop closer. It took a few minutes, and when it did, I placed the memory stick into the USB port, and guided my finger onto the pad, opening the menu.

The images were not labelled, other than dates, and as I clicked onto one, an image of Eve and Greg appeared in what looked like this very flat, and the date was imprinted on the bottom corner, as April 15th.

I smiled, as I scanned through some of the images, and even more when I saw Chris again.

But then something startled me.

One image as Eve and Chris with the tower behind them, dated April 30th. The day of the fire, but then something did not ring well, because I am sure that Greg had told me Chris had been missing for some time before he visited me in hospital.

I clicked onto the next image, which was of Chris and some girl, his hand up her skirt, the next one was of him with a bloke looking far too comfortable together, and the dates on both read May 31st. Then another one, of him and Eve. The day before he turned up in Bramhall.

Anger filled the void instantly, and I tossed the lap top aside, smashing it in two.

Frustrated, I walked through the town, toward the beach, holding the box of ashes, and the sun was barely rising. I had tears in my eyes as I tossed aside my shoes. To my right, I could see a drunk young gay man being penetrated by another lad. I wanted to scream at them for being idiots and warn them not to get committed. Like I did.

I made my way closer to the edge of the water, and opened the box of ashes.

As I waved the box in the air, the ash began to dispense into the wind, "I trusted you"

And again I broke down, with the water lapping against my feet. Slowly I lowered myself into the coldness of the Irish Sea, and wept.

"I love you, I hate you, I love you" I chanted for some reason, "I hate you"

Yes Chris did give me the answer to the question I had asked, but I now hated him.

As I turned away with tears in my eyes, I smiled as I recognised the blonde watching me from the promenade. I think that her, the lady that I had met at my parents funeral. I think her name was Sonia?

She gave me a knowing smile and turned. She was nowhere to be seen as I reached the road.

Who was she? And why had I seen her yet again?

FIFTY TWO

July 10th

I told Anastasia that afternoon that she could move in and two days later she had moved the majority of her possessions in. I loved in particular a map of the world she had placed above the bed, she had marked off a few places that she had visited, and those she wanted to visit. I smiled as I noticed Turkey as one of those to go to places. She was not very well travelled.

Out went bachelor man stuff, and in came couple of her large homely items. Stephen and Simon helped her carry the heavy items. The news that we had moved in had caused yet another departure in the form of Stephen's leggy red head, who accused me of favouring my staff. He was still annoyed with me as he was convinced that she was the one for him, but by the very next evening he was balls deep in another stripper called Leona. I had enough of catching Victoria and Bitch with a bow-tie banging away in the toilets, now I had my security to cope with.

Having Anastasia in the flat felt good. I knew that there was no chance Ophelia would locate me, but simply having her there made me realise I was safe.

I knew that Simon could hear me from his flat so I was happy to make as much noise as I could. Passionately, I turned her around, and lifted her short skirt. My hands stroked her pert buttocks, and I gently pulled down her panties, and allowed them to drop to her knees. I teased her pussy with my forefinger, and middle finger, before I entered them into her greedy slit, my thumb played circles with her clitoris.

"Fuck me" She pleaded, arching her bottom toward my erect member.

Ignoring her please, I continued to tease her pussy lips, spreading them mildly, causing her to gasp. She began to buck her hips, trying to force my fingers deeper into her.

She reached out for my cock, and I swatted her hand away. She continued to strain against my hand, and I knew she was about to cum, so I pulled my sticky fingers away, and tasted her juices. Using the same hand, I gripped my cock, and placed the tip against her opening, and stroked it for long moments. Each time she thrust back to force it into her, I restrained, and pulled away, forming full control.

Suddenly, I thrust hard into her, causing her to lose balance for a moment, and to scream with the unexpected force, I pulled almost entirely out, and did again, several times. Each time taking a moment longer to thrust.

After a while, I stopped being forceful, and fucked her as I liked, my hand spanked her buttocks, and my hips were pressed hard against her, and we were soon in synchronisation with our movements. I reached over, and squeezed her nipples hard, and as I cupped her breasts, and still fucking, I forced her into a stand up position.

My hand clasped at her pubes, and I reached wantonly again for the clitoris, but our movement put it out of my reach too much.

I felt her cum, and she groaned loudly, and I forced her back into the doggy position, and I pumped a few more times before pulling out, and urinating my own cum over her back.

My legs felt weak, as I pulled away, and still on her knees, she turned to face me.

"More" She commanded, as she reached for my now softened cock, glistening with our juices.

She used her tongue to lick it until it was hard again, and this time, she forced me to the floor, to which was grateful for now, I was spent.

She smiled, as she sat atop of my dick, and forced it in its entirety into her chasm, and rode, dangerously high, I thought I was going to slip out of her any moment. But she controlled it, and slammed down harder onto my balls, this time, causing me to groan out loud.

July 18th

Within the week, Anastasia stopped dancing, and become a barmaid, much to the bitch with a bow-tie's disgust, he even accused me of sending in a spy. What a prick he was. Although I have to admit, I was happy that she was not taking her clothes for other men for money.

One of the regulars whom we knew as Mr F for some unknown reason had taken a dislike to her transfer, and took it out on Simon, the big dumb bouncer just let him get away with it. Whilst this was going on, Stephen had just removed a rowdy reveller, I watched from the office as he kicked and fought his exit, and Bitch with a bow-tie held onto the naked Victoria. I could see Anastasia enjoying the commotion in the background. She then glanced up at the window, and smiled at me with a cheeky wave of her hand.

I blew her a kiss, and then made my way back to my desk to work on the accounts. I was soon interrupted by a series of knocks.

"You wanking in here?" Simon joked as he pushed open the door.

"I will leave that to you mate" I smiled, "I'm late with the accounts and shit I have to send to knob head"

"There's a lady asking in the foyer, asking to see you" He smiled.

I feared for a moment, thinking that Ophelia was on the case, "What does she want?"

He shrugged, "Dunno, she didn't say. She did say that she doesn't want to come in though"

I furrowed my brow, and used the cursor on my monitor to flick through the cameras until it came to the one in the foyer.

All I could see was a pair of long legs in the corner of the screen, and I manoeuvred the camera to view the owner. A smile crossed my face immediately.

"You know her?" He asked.

"I almost banged her once" I smiled, grabbing a can of deodorant from the drawer, "Tell her I will be right down"

Simon laughed as he pulled the door closed. I quickly checked myself in my mirror, and adjusted my hair, which I still had not had cut or coloured, but it would do.

With a skip in my step, I ran down the staircase, and through the bar.

"Connor, we need to talk" Victoria announced, still showing her box and tits for no reason.

"Not now" I brushed her off, and ran into the foyer, with a smile on my face.

"Hello stranger" She smiled back at me instantly.

"Lana" I smiled as I embraced my favourite Scottish lady in the world.

"Can we talk?" She asked.

As we made our way to the beach, Lana was pre-occupied on her mobile phone, and I took the time to purchase ice-cream, and a coffee each from a nearby vendor. It was too late when I realised that I was almost in the exact spot where I had thrown Chris's ashes, I wanted to move on, but she seemed to remain static.

"When did you get back to the Country?" I asked as she closed her call.

"I left Turkey that day, it was horrible" She explained, "I got back to my apartment, and I decided repping was not for me, I was on the same flight as Chris"

I cringed at the near mention of his name, "I am sorry I left you in that bar"

She shook it off, "No bother, I just did not like it"

"I have to ask about Sian and Shannon" I don't know why, I just needed to know.

"I don't know anything more now than when I left. I never tried to find out" She confessed, "But since moving back, something amazing has happened"

I noticed the smile that crossed her face, "You met someone, haven't you?"

"Yes" She confessed, "His name is Jack and he will be here soon, and that's what I need to talk to you about"

"Sounds like a party" I joked.

She laughed loud, "Oh Connor, I have missed you"

"So no threesome then?" I laughed.

"No honey" She smiled, "Jack's a detective, and has been assigned a case, which involves some activity in your club, and when I saw that you were managing it, I could not believe my luck"

"What do you mean?" I asked.

Serious now crossed her face, "Jack's team has been investigating your girls for a few months, we had a plant in there, but he left all of a sudden, and you took over"

"The previous manager....." I guessed.

She opened her bag, and pulled out a file, she opened it and passed me a photograph, "This is your predecessor, Gavin McLelland"

"I never met him, but he was apparently a massive prick" I smiled, as I studied the black and white image, he was not as I imagined, quite clean cut, and slicked back black hair, "Apparently he just quit"

She nodded, "Gavin was a sleaze, that is why he fitted in so well, but he got too close to the truth...."

She was interrupted by the arrival of a tall slim man with a better pony tail than myself, who kissed her passionately as he reached her.

"You must be Jack" I muttered, almost in disgust my voice upon his arrival.

"Nice to meet you again" He extended his hand, to which I reluctantly accepted as a shake, "You don't remember me do you?"

"Nope" I responded.

"We spoke last year, I believe it was your friend that jumped off the Central Pier last Summer" He explained, "Lana has told me all about you"

I shot her a glance, "Everything?"

"That you two were reps together, at least" He smiled.

"I was just telling Connor about Gavin" She commented as though she too wanted to change the subject.

He nodded, "Such a waste of talent"

"What happened to Gavin?" I suddenly felt a feeling of foreboding come over me.

"Gavin had called through some very important information the day that he disappeared, and we ordered him to abort his mission" Jack explained, "But he never made it back to the station"

I knew instantly what they were saying.

"Gavin's body was uncovered in some wasteland not too far away from where he was staying" He continued.

"What has this got to do with my girls?" I asked.

"Someone in your bar, is dealing Class A drugs, and is responsible for a number of deaths in this area" He continued, "And Gavin uncovered the mystery, and now we need to nail this person before anything else happens"

I shook my head, "No, I cannot have police swarming the place"

"It won't be like that, all we need you to do is to hire Lana as a bar maid or something" He explained, "Have you seen anything suspicious?"

I shook my head.

"Well, if you can let me view the video footage, I am sure that we can find what we are looking for...." He continued.

"Unfortunately, there is only dancing positions" I spoke with concern.

"Honey" Lana smiled, "I can roller skate, and ride them poles better than any of those girls you have in there"

"So" Jack asked, "Do we have you on board?"

Reluctantly, I nodded.

FIFTY THREE

July 19th

The next afternoon, Lana nervously made her way into the bar, I remained upstairs in my office, watching on the camera, as Julia put her through her interview process. I could see Bitch with a bow-tie and Victoria lurking in the back ground watching as Lana expertly skated around the stage, gripping the pole and dancing seductively. Mr F had already entered, and was on his bottled beer.

I felt a stir in my groin as she took her top off, and I was just about to take it out when Simon knocked on the door, with his gormless friend.

Quickly switching over the channel, I gestured them in.

"Where did she come from?" Stephen asked like an excited puppy.

"She just walked in" I lied, "Is she any good?"

"Titties and roller skates?" Stephen squealed, "I would love to split her pussy in two...."

"Perhaps you need to stop banging the girls" I snarled, "Maybe then they will all stay instead of quitting"

"I don't bang all the girls" Stephen moped in the corner.

"He was joking dick" Simon pulled up one of the spare chairs, "It's about Raven"

"Is she ok?" I asked..

Simon shook his head, "She didn't go home as we thought"

"Nope" Stephen was clearly still annoyed by my comments, "They fished her out of the sea by the pier this morning, and now, Sharon has gone missing"

"Sharon?" I questioned trying to scan the photos of my women.

I annoyed Stephen again, "The red head that worked here, she didn't turn up last night for our date, and I am worried"

I forgot her name was Sharon, as she was the only staff member that did not bother to speak with me.

"Ok boys" I confided, "Shut the door, I need to talk to you about something" Stephen obeyed, and made himself comfortable on one of the chairs.

"What do you guys know about Gavin McLelland?" I asked.

"Knob head ex manager here before you" Simon recollected.

"Did you know that he is dead?" I asked.

"What?" Both chorused, almost too high pitched to be manly.

"They found his corpse out of some landfill not too long ago, and now Raven is gone, and Sharon is missing, and what do they all have in common?" I asked, and didn't wait, "Raven was a coke head, and someone here was supplying her"

"I know Sharon liked a bit" Simon laughed.

"So Gavin was supplying?" Stephen queried, still uncertain.

I shrugged, "Nope, but someone here was, and I have to find out"

We were interrupted as Julia entered with Lana, and I could tell that Stephen was already sporting a boner as she playfully jiggled her bottom before him.

"This is Candy" She smiled, knowing that a false name had been provided, "She's got the moves like you have never seen before"

Lana's recruitment was an instant hit. That evening the Bouncers, Troy, Julia and I took a ringside seat as she skated onto the stage, and began to spin at speed around that pole, and I was slightly embarrassed as she removed her cheerleaders top, and her Scotland flag nipple tassels were spinning just as fast.

"She's brilliant" Simon cheered, and I smiled as I recalled how we met, and the circumstances.

All too soon, the night ended, and Candy was welcomed in the arms of the girls, and they all gathered in their dressing room. Stephen had gone off to the toilet, probably for a wank, and surprise, the bitch with a bow-tie and Victoria were shagging in the cellar. Disgustedly, I watched on the camera for a moment as his hairy arse kept pumping into shot on the corner of the monitor.

"Dirty Bastards" I whispered, aware that Anastasia stood at the door.

"I saw you tonight" She smiled, in a friendly way, "You wanted that Scottish Haggis"

I laughed, as I gestured to the screen, "I suppose you would think I found Troy's hairy arse a turn on"

She pulled a face, "I would rather fist myself with a rancid badger"

She perched herself on my lap, and placed a lingering, loving kiss on my lips.

"I love you Mr Candlish" She eventually gasped as she pulled away, "I have never felt this comfortable with anyone"

She knew I could not return the statement.

She continued, almost like she was commanding "You want to fuck the new girl?"

"No" I responded, and I knew this time I meant it, all I wanted was her. Lana was beautiful, but I could not ever betray anyone like I had been with Shannon, Chris, Sian, and Ophelia.

The kiss that followed was the most romantic taste I had on my lips in a long time.

There was a series of raps on the door, and Julia entered without an invite, which angered me a little.

"Anastasia" She looked concerned, "Your ex is here"

She sighed, "I can handle this"

Without words, she sauntered out the room.

"Is she gonna be alright?" I asked.

Julia nodded, "She can handle that cunt of an ex, besides, and Candy wanted a chat with you" I smiled as Candy brushed past her, their hips touching each other's for a moment, I think Julia liked her a little.

Julia moved away, and closed the door behind her, and Candy walked over to the glass overlooking the bar.

"Have you found out something?" I whispered.

"Most of the girls are taking cocaine freely in the changing room" She nodded, "The French girl almost let it slip who was supplying it, but Victoria shut her up"

"Is it her?" I enquired.

"She wasn't taking any" She confided, "But I think it could be a trick, Gavin taught me all about how to spot the clues, and I think it is either Bitch with a bow-tie, Stephen or Simon, and then there is that sleaze ball that was leching on the girls"

I could tell by the pause there was another name to be added to list. She turned to face me, and shook her head.

"Anastasia?" I asked.

"I am sorry" She whispered, "But I have to be suspicious"

"No, it is not her" I responded.

She made her way back to me, "It is one of those"

"It is not her" I repeated.

"You cannot fall in love with any of these girls" She warned, "They get their tits out for money"

"Lana, I have not loved anyone in a long time, and I think I love Anastasia" I smiled. As I finished my sentence, I heard someone on the staircase racing away.

She did also.

Together we ran toward the door, and into the stairwell. I led the way into the bar, as the girls started to emerge from their dressing room.

"Who has just come from upstairs?" I yelled.

Julia made her way back from the reception area with Mr F, as Stephen emerged from the direction of the staff toilets. Bitch with a bow-tie and Victoria made their way from behind the bar.

"Where is Anastasia?" Lana whispered.

The mumbles from the women confused me for a moment, as they became aware of Simon's presence on the stage. He looked haunted, as he staggered into the centre of the platform.

His staggered expression became more daunting as he collapsed on the wooden floor.

"Simon, what is wrong?" Julia asked as she raced over to him.

"The back alley" He stuttered, "I heard something...."

"Honey, what is it?" She soothed.

"Call the police" He panicked, and I noticed he was crying.

I could tell that Mr F was not interested, as he took another drink from a bottled beer.

Without waiting, I raced onto the stage, followed by Stephen and Bitch with a bow-tie, who was barking orders that the girls are to remain.

The doorway was open and as we raced into the dark alley behind the club, I noticed instantly a bloody hand near the skip that we used for the trash. I glanced up at the camera, and noticed that it was facing the wrong way, and as I neared the arm, I realised instantly, it was the red headed lover of Stephen. Sharon.

He screamed.

FIFTY FOUR

Anastasia had returned during the commotion, much to Lana's disgust, and presented me with a threatening letter from her exes solicitor over half of her assets, and I saw them in the foyer on the video footage whilst Simon was on the stage collapsing. Worse still, he had told her that he was joining the USS Vivandier in their conversation. I chose to ignore the coincidence. Mr F had disappeared before the police came but no one noticed when he left.

Stephen was inconsolable as the police interviewed us all over Sharon's final moments, and my camera evidence picked up someone in the alley way moving the position of it on the day that she quit. There was a moment when Bitch with a bow-tie was seen smoking in the area on the day the body was found, but he never went anywhere near the skip, even tossing his butt end the wrong way down the alleyway. Mind you, when he turned Victoria around on the wall and took her up the arse, he was angry that the police threatened to charge him with public indecency. Then we could hear the heavy thud and the metallic slam of something hitting the skip, which caused Simon to investigate.

We remained closed until the police could authorise a reopening, and I could see it not happening any time soon. Greg was fuming at me when he called, but I just closed that call instantly. I could not put up with his moaning old Cockney bollocks. Simon on the other hand seemed full of life. I learned later that he was hitting the vodka much like I used to, and Julia was spending more time at his apartment. It pained me to hear his cries in the night. I kept myself from thinking of Chris in those moments, and often rolled over to hold Anastasia.

July 24th

The sun was unbearable as Anastasia and I stepped out that day with Candy and her friend Jack, and it was killing me to keep the secret. The tourists were out in force, and we spent the day doing as the tourists do, we drank, we enjoyed the tower and the dungeon, and the tram ride down to the Pleasure Beach. As Jack and Anastasia ran to the nearest loo, Lana and I took the moment to make our way to a pre-arranged cafe at the fair, to order lunch.

I ordered Anastasia a large coffee and a waffle with ice-cream, which Lana also had, Jack and I were having hot dogs and tea.

"I know it is not her" I whispered in the queue, "She only started the week before, and she did not like Gavin"

"I just don't trust her" She explained, "She has some secret, and I am concerned that you are being drawn into some sort of danger"

"She is no Ophelia" I smiled.

"I am not saying that, but what is the secret about this ex-boyfriend of hers?" She probed, "Why have you never actually seen him?"

I was interrupted as my phone rang. I struggled to remove it from my pocket as I spoke, "I have never met you ex, the abusive former husband"

I paused as I saw the name on the screen. "What is it?" She asked.

I began to shake, it did not seem possible, but the call stopped before I could answer, and must have gone to voicemail.

"Nothing" I lied, "Just someone I didn't want to speak to"

She smiled, "Ok, I just think that you should be careful with Anastasia"

"Anything you say Candy" I smiled, aware that Jack and my girl were about to enter the cafe. Just in time as well, as our food arrived moments later.

"Remember when we were here last year?" I laughed at Candy.

"I knew you two knew each other" Anastasia smiled, "It was pretty obvious"

"Connor and I were on a course near the North Pier" Candy smiled, I could sense   her   frustration   at   my throw away comment, although I was still distracted by the phone call, "Pure coincidence that he now runs The Black Orchid"

Anastasia went straight to the shower when we returned to the apartment, whilst I made the excuse we needed milk. Keeping my phone close to my heart, I quickly ensured that I was alone as I entered an alley way, I withdrew the phone, and scanned for my missed calls.

His name, Chris popped up on my screen.

Hands shaking, I pressed the voicemail button, and waited. The machine like woman commented I had one voicemail waiting.

I knew I wouldn't hear his voice, but it was his number. There was no noise, just silence. Then the phone call ended.

I listened to it again, and perhaps one more time.

Part of me wanted to cry, but then I remembered those photographs that proved   that he had lied. I listened to it one more time. Then I deleted the message.

Then I deleted his number from the phone. Hopefully then I would not be tempted to call it when I was drunk later. After all, he was dead, what was I going to do, listen to his voicemail to just to hear his voice?

I instantly regretted deleting the number.

I was even tempted to call Greg, or Eve, but I decided against it.

Purchasing some milk, I soon made it back to my apartment, and knocked on Simon's door. There was no answer there.

After a moment, I made my way back toward my own apartment.

"Well, I thought it may be you" A voice commented behind me, causing me to turn on my heels.

Before me, Oliver stood. He had cut his dreadlocks.

"What are you doing here?" I asked.

"When Anastasia told me she was banging Connor Candlish" He laughed and took several steps closer to me, almost as if he was inspecting me, "I thought maybe there was a second numpty out there with the name of the man who bought down that fat bastard in The Gambia"

"I did exactly as you asked" I commented.

"That you did" He agreed, "And the fat fuck is trying to sue me for constructive dismissal"

"And you want me to help again?" I enquired.

"I will call on you" He replied, as he took an envelope out of his pocket, "Anastasia asked me specifically for these when I kicked her out, and I think it is only right she has them now"

I tore open the envelope with little intervention from him, and pulled out two diamond earrings.

"I bought them for her" He confessed, "But now I have a younger model who likes sapphires, I have no use for them"

I placed them back into the envelope, "I will make sure she gets them"

"You do that Connor" He smiled, "And I believe we will be seeing each other in a few weeks on board the USS Vivandier"

"Not if I can help it" I acknowledged that name again.

I presented her with the earrings, which unnerved her at first, so I decided to keep two secrets from her. Firstly, I did not tell her about the phone call from my dead husband's number, and then I did not tell her about Oliver's announcement about the USS Vivandier.

"I did not know it was my former boss Oli" I brushed aside, "But I don't think he will be bothering you"

She sighed, as she tossed aside the earrings, I saw one of them fall onto the floor by the wardrobe, "As long as he disappears, I could not give a fuck"

FIFTY FIVE

It had begun to rain heavily as we made our way out, Candy and Jack had gone ahead, and reserved us a booth. I had to smile as I recognised it as the exact same booth that we had sat in last year.

"There's a duo on tonight" Jack smiled, as the campest man with a glitter waistcoat, revealing his naval I have ever seen introduced himself as our waitress for the evening. He took our order, and he flirted a little too much with Jack. Lana was clearly not surprised.

"Remember when we were here last year?" Candy laughed, taking control over the situation. "And you and that bloke got stripped down to your pants?"

"At least I was in my pants" I laughed, "The other guy went the whole hog and got his schlong out for beer"

"I cannot even remember his name" She confessed, "Calvin?"

I knew she was on about Cameron, but I pretended I did not know.

The waiter had now returned with our drinks, and smiled a little too much to

Jack, but he too did not notice. I think this pissed the waiter off a little.

"These two idiots" Candy explained, "Were ordered to strip down to their pants for the promise of free wine"

"Oh that will be Miss Slut Drop" The waiter smiled, as he tallied our bill, "She has a way to make men strip"

Candy continued to laugh. "This guy sat there with his hairy bollocks out, for some shit tasting wine"

The waiter was clearly not impressed by the comment, and walked away, causing a source of laughter between us, as the compere made her way to the DJ Booth, where she messed about with the microphones during our conversation of Blackpool past. She looked familiar, but I could not place her, she was tall, black, and had equally big black hair piled on top of her head, and she loved herself.

Half an hour past as we gradually drank more and more beer, which was charged at differing prices dependent on which waiter was serving us.

Soon the crescendo of opening music began to blare loud, and we drew our attention to the stage.

"Ladies and Gentlemen, and some people I could classify as variations thereof" The DJ laughed at her own joke, and then pointed to some random punter nearby, "It's time for the best show here in Blackpool, and I want to you put your hands together, stamp those feet for Juicy Jules and Miss Slut Drop in the show stopping show, 'A Night On The Tiles"

The entertaining music seemed to last an eternity, and the girls started to dance to the music, and Jack and I drank our drinks amused by our ladies.

The curtains ripped backwards sharply, and we were entertained by the image of two people with their backs to us, one was clearly a woman with those PVC covered curves, and the naughty school girl had the hairiest of legs, and was bent over with a fake dildo strapped to his arse. The song began, and the woman turned around on her heels to sing, and she noticed us in the corner, we cheered as we recognised our Julia.

Shock seemed to hit her as she recognised us, but she continued her set, "So Miss Slut Drop, I heard you went for a job interview on a farm, have you ever shooed a horse?"

Then the hairy school girl rose for her solo, and we noticed the uncomfortable exchange between them, "No, but I was on the North Shore today and I told a donkey to fuck off"

It was obvious that Miss Slut Drop was a man in drag, and a familiar one to boot.

"It's Simon" Anastasia whispered.

We had clearly embarrassed them as they sang their songs.

As the show ended, Candy, Anastasia and I raced over to the stage to talk to them, and Simon clearly did not want to talk, and ran off into the dressing room at the back.

Julia shook her head, and gestured that we returned to the booth, and she would get him to come over to us after. But warned we may be in for a wait.

It took just shy of one hour before they arrived. Surprisingly still in costume, although they were clearly half cut, and had to liaise with their fans beforehand.

Before I knew it, the DJ was also joining us at the booth.

"So now you know" Simon confessed, drinking more alcohol bought to us by more camp glitter covered waiters.

"Mate, I knew I met you before" I laughed, "We were just saying about when me and that guy got naked on the dance floor"

"I have been dressing up as Miss Slut Drop for the past three years" He continued, "And I hid behind my doorman persona, and to be honest Connor you both were up for it"

"You don't have to hide it" I assured, "I married a man"

"That makes you gay, or bisexual at the least" He started to become defensive, as the DJ began to stroke his hand, much to Julia's disgust "I am perfectly straight, if a man put his penis near my mouth I would rip it off, there is only pussy for me, and only Julia and Karen knew my dirty little secret"

I realised Karen was the DJ now, "Look it is not a dirty secret, I would embrace this" "You will have my resignation tomorrow" He insisted.

"I won't accept it" I smiled, which I felt may have been too much for him, but he smiled back, "I need you to control that knob head Troy"

"Just don't ask me to bring Miss Slut Drop to The Black Orchid" He smiled. Together we laughed.

"Bitch with a bow-tie is a prick" Simon agreed, "Troy fucking hates that nickname" I laughed.

"I promise" I vowed, "This is our secret"

Simon and I became firm friends after that day, and as he only lived across the hall, we'd often sit in each other's house with beer, and converse about our women, and we never touched on the subject of Miss Slut Drop.

Stephen did not like our friendship, and commented a lot on our sexuality at The Black Orchid, and we both laughed it off, and Stephen soon became the lone doorman, as Simon tended to spend time in my office, rather than with him.

Julia and Karen were also pretty much part of our evening drinking crew. But when they started to kiss, it was my cue to leave. Again I could hear the three of them shagging whilst I went back and made love to Anastasia.

It was almost like a race between the lot of us. I was not ashamed of coming second in this case.

July 29th

Victoria was awaiting for me as I arrived in the club that day, naked, as per usual, with the exception of two sparkly nipple tassels that she always wore. She was reading a book, which she placed upside down on the desk as she spoke.

"We need to talk" She insisted, as she put her feet up on the desk, opening her pussy lips showing me her pierced clit as though it was a way of saying hello.

"Do you ever get dressed?" I asked, gesturing to her gown that she had care freely thrown across the bar.

"Don't you like my pussy?" She asked, as she started to stroke it, smiling as she did so.

"What is it you want?" I brushed it off.

"Lock the door" She ordered, "I don't want anyone to hear this"

I did not listen, and sat at the desk, waiting.

"Very well" She insisted, "Troy and I want out"

"Is that all?" I smiled, "You can just leave any time you want"

She smiled, "Oh no, it is not as simple as Troy and I walking through the door into the Big World, with our wages, we can barely afford the bus to Fleetwood"

I knew where this was going straight away, "You don't hold a contract so therefore you won't get a severance pay"

"No" She agreed, "But remember the day Sharon was found in the back alley?" I nodded.

"I had come up here to talk to you about discussing a new act, but you were too busy with Candy..." She began.

"That was you" I realised.

She nodded, "I heard that Haggis lover telling you about the drugs that are being sold here"

"You know about that?" I asked.

She smiled, "I could not let you spoil the fun now can I?"

I did not respond.

"So here is the plan" She smiled, "You give Troy and I the money in the safe, and we take our business elsewhere"

"You want me to give you the takings" A statement rather than a question.

She nodded.

I laughed, "Get out... silly bitch"

"Very well" She calmly announced, and reached for her gown, removing a mobile phone from the pocket, "I am afraid, you have left me with no choice"

"So you are calling the police to turn yourself in?" I smiled.

"No" Calmly she pressed a button, whilst holding a finger out to me, she waited for a moment, and I heard someone answer the other end of the phone, to which she continued, "Remember you told me about Connor being a push over for a fanny? The prick won't buckle, so plan B"

She closed the call.

"Victoria, you are an intelligent woman" I smiled, "I have a crazed stalker who keeps popping up and there are two women in Marmaris that took a tumble because of me..."

"I know all about Ophelia Mason and the lesbians in Turkey"
She interrupted, "Which one of them are dead Connor?"
I did not know the answer.
She sighed and left without another word.

I shook my head, and reached over for the book that she left. The palm trees on the cover seemed to call to me, and I smiled, as I turned the book over, and read the title, "The Last Summer Of Vodka, by Louise Bell"

Louise, my friend from Marmaris, I smiled as I remembered her. She had published her diary about when she started to look for love. I opened it up, and started to read, laughing a little at the dedication to her dog Gucci. For a brief moment, I remembered them both, we were drunk, on the beach in Marmaris again, but these memories were soon interrupted by a piercing scream from downstairs.

FIFTY SIX

The doors were locked, and Candy and Anastasia were bound together on the pole in the middle of the stage as I raced into the room.

Victoria, now dressed in a pair of hot pants, a cowgirl waistcoat and hat, sat casually on the step, and I noticed some of the other girls were now tied up at the back of the stage.

"My husband and I want out" She repeated, "And I just asked our glorious leader for an advance on our wages, and this man slag has refused my kind request"

"Let them go" I insisted.

"Girls" She commanded attention, "This prick here has been on cahoots with the police over mine and Troy's little side line, and we have a snitch amongst us, and you know that Gavin was also a spy?"

"Security" I called, which caused Victoria to laugh.

The reception door opened, and panic took over me as Stephen pushed a gagged Julia through, followed by that Mr F character again "I would have been happy to stay on and continue the trade whilst Troy and Victoria retired in Barbados"

He forced Julia to a seat, tying her hands to the chair, Troy soon entered from the same entrance, Victoria rose from her stance on the stage to join him.

Troy took a long moment to enthusiastically kiss his wife, before turning his back to her. I watched as Mr F casually sat next to one of the girls, stroking her leg.

"The combination to the safe" He commanded, as he pulled a switchblade knife from his pocket, "I have been nice up until now, and I have put up with quite a lot of your shit"

"Give him the code" Victoria smiled, "You know that Troy boy has a way to dispose of witnesses"

He laughed, "Yes, I did like stabbing that tosser Gavin, and when I buried him I felt like I was doing a public service, getting rid of pond scum that grasses on people, and the girls just simply stopped breathing when I crushed their windpipes"

"Enough talking" Victoria commanded, "I think that we should dispose of one of his females to show him we mean business"

Troy laughed, and raced over to the stage, and started to wave the blade singing "ennie meaney, miney mo" to them.

"No" I screamed, "I will do anything"

"Good boy" Victoria smiled, as she sauntered over to me, gesturing over to her husband as she did so, "Baby cakes, wait with the stabbing, just to be sure"

She wrapped her leg around my waist, and thrust her vagina closer to my crotch.

Before anything could be said, Julia screamed out loud, drawing our attention over to her. She had freed her hand and had managed to call the police on her mobile which lay beside her.

"You fucking moron" Victoria screamed at Stephen, as she and Troy raced over to Julia.

"Come to the Black Orchid" She cried, "They're stabbing us...."

Dumbfounded, Stephen frantically tried to apologise as he snatched at the mobile, terminating the call, and tossing it across the room, we heard it smash near the bar, at the feet of Mr F.

"You just signed your own death warrant" Troy hissed, as he yanked her head back with her own hair.

She continued to scream, as he buried the blade into her throat, ripping it from left to right in one swift movement.

The girls and I screamed as the blood flowed freely from her jugular.

"Stop" I screamed, "I will give you the money"

We turned to leave, I was scared for everyone in the room.

It was then that a panicked Simon stumbled into the bar from the smoker's area. "What the fuck?"

Stephen raced over to him, and tackled him to the floor, Simon did not fight back as he stared aimlessly at his bleeding lover before him.

"Keep that bald cunt under control" Victoria commanded, as she walked back over to me.

Stephen nodded as he lay on top of his friend, using his body weight to hold him down, I could tell that Simon was crying over Julia's demise.

Victoria grabbed my hand, "Come on dickless"

She pulled me toward the stairwell.

"If I am not back in five minutes baby" She called to Troy, "Choose which of his sluts are to die first, may I suggest the undercover wannabe cop"

"The police heard where you are" I tried to assure, glancing cautiously at Lana's fearful expression.

"Then you better work fast bitch" She insisted.

I obeyed her and followed her upstairs, and she sat at my desk, as I entered the code to the electronic safe.

"You know, you could come with us" She smiled, I could tell without looking that she had her finger in her box again.

"Just let everyone go" I whispered, taking the money out of the safe, and placing it into a plastic bag.

"Give me a fucking as a send-off" She smiled.

I turned my head to her, and I felt my dick twitch as it sprung to life at the sight of her putting her whole fist inside her pussy. She knew that I liked what I saw, and withdrew in an instant, I watched in awe as her pussy lips slowly retracted back into place.

"If I fuck you, I lose time and your husband will kill either Candy or Anastasia" I responded, trying to hide my erection.

"Ophelia was right" She laughed, as she pulled up her hot pants, "You got me"

"How do you know her?" I snarled.

She moved toward me and snatched the plastic bag of money from me, brushing her stinking hand under my nose, I could smell her fingers waving beneath my nostrils.

"This would have been so much simpler if you just did as you were told in the first place" She insisted, as she turned her back on me.

As she moved toward the door, I paused, and waited for a moment before taking after her.

She started down the stairwell, I lunged forward, pushing hard at her back, sending her down the stairs, her scream satisfied me, but I failed to notice that during the push, I too lost my balance, and landed next to her.

She snarled at me as she rose, and sought the opportunity to kick me in the ribs hard, and I screamed in agony. Blood was pouring out of my nose, but I did not care.

I turned and watched her as she walked toward her husband, with a limp, they kissed passionately, and I noticed Stephen was still struggling to tie Simon to the same chair his dead lover sat slouched.

Gathering my energy, I rose, and walked toward them, to which they ignored for a moment.

"Right baby" She smiled, "Give me two minutes, kill someone else, take your pick of any of these knob heads, we will meet you in the car, call me and tell me who"

He slapped her arse as she walked out of the bar, carrying the bag of money over her shoulder, and shaking her backside as she walked. Mr F followed her.

"Two minutes" He whispered a warning to Troy.

"Goodbye losers" Victoria commented without looking back. "If any of you survive, I will hunt you down and cut you all to pieces in your sleep"

Troy laughed as they left, and waited a moment.

At least with Ophelia I knew she was nuts.

"Right" Troy smiled, I noticed for the first time his sinister smile, "Which one of you pussies do I kill next"

"Take me" Simon sobbed uncontrollably, as he strained to touch his dead lovers hand.

Troy smiled and sauntered over to him.

"No" I screamed, barely with any energy left at all.

"Quit ya whining" Simon screamed, "I have nothing to live for now Ju has gone, If I die, you live"

"What a load of bollocks" Troy laughed, "I will kill each and every one of you mother fuckers"

"Just fucking kill me" Simon screamed.

"Very well" Troy agreed, with a small ounce of sympathy in his voice.

Simon started to breathe hard as the blade reached closer toward him.

"Troy" Lana screamed, "Please don't do this"

Troy smiled, as he pulled out his phone with his spare hand, and pressed the button to call his wife.

He put it on loud speaker as she answered, "I chose the bald cunt who likes to prance around in ladies underwear"

"Do it" She ordered over the phone.

With that instruction he plunged the blade into Simon's neck and twisted as the blood spilled amidst an unidentifiable sound from Simon's throat.

"Kill another" She commanded. "Kill Stephen"

"Wait no" Stephen panicked, as he started to back away toward the door. "You know I will help you to get rid of the evidence"

Troy laughed.

"Please don't" Stephen realised that the bow tie wearing bitch was too far gone, "I did everything you said"

"Shut the fuck up ya dumb fuck" Troy screamed.

"Troy baby" Victoria spoke on the phone.

"I love you" He smiled back, as he toyed with the knife.

"I am sorry" She apologised, "But I am not taking you with me, Mr F can give me a lot more than you can... I am not even sorry, but you will not see me, or the money ever again"

"This is not a joking matter Vickie" He screamed, "I paid for those passports and tickets"

"Did you kill Stephen yet?" She questioned, taking control over the conversation expertly.

Stephen shook his head, as Troy continued to speak, "Not yet lover"

"Then you are not man enough for me" She insisted, and closed the call.

"Bitch" He screamed, as he punched the knife hard into Stephen's chest, and trying her number time and again.

"Troy" Anastasia called, "Let us go"

"Shut up" He ordered, brandishing the knife at her.

I took the opportunity to lunge at him, punching the knife from his arm. The phone fell with a heavy smash at the same time.

"You're gonna pay for this" He screamed, as he reached out for me, clasping at my throat.

I could hear the girls screaming, as his fingers dug deep into my neck, I could see the fire in his eyes. I could also see Stephen, still bleeding lurch forward behind him, grabbing Troy's back.

"I was gonna help you two out of the country" He yelled, reaching for his neck.

Troy's grip on my released, and I fell to the floor, gasping. I could see them grappling before me.

"No" Lana screamed, "You're not a killer"

Stephen took a moment to think, and then smashed Troy's head on the floor, knocking him out in an instant, just as Jack led the armed police into the room. I noticed then, that Stephen had collapsed in a bleeding heap on top of him.

FIFTY SEVEN

Those next few days passed in a blur. We were awaiting our court appearances as Troy was arrested as he came too in hospital, and Victoria and the mysterious Mr F had vanished out of the country. Karen called by the apartment and broke down in the doorway over both of her lover's murders. Anastasia barely left my place, and The Black Orchid once more closed down by the police. Needless to say, Greg was not best pleased with me. I listened to his phone rant without really paying attention.

Stephen was in an induced coma in hospital, and between us, we sat by his bedside talking to him, despite our warnings that he may not come around. Lana had disappeared, and Jack told me she had gone back to Scotland, scared for her life. But her phone was dead.

I had managed to get home before sun set, and Anastasia was lying on her front with her naked arse in the air. She was reading The Last Summer Of Vodka, which I had stolen from the office, mainly because I wanted some connection with my old friend Lei. I must admit, I read it a few times, and laughed out loud, as I remembered her, and her dog.

I felt my dick stir in my pants, as I placed my keys onto the side cabinet, and I took my cock out of my denim prison of my Levi's, and approached her.

Pressing the tip against her anus, I heard her groan and felt her wriggle into her own comfort zone beneath me.

I spat on my dry cock, and rubbed the saliva along my shaft for a moment before using my own lube to enter her tight hole, and pushed so far into her, my balls pressed against her, and before I knew it, she was pushing back, and arching her spine to accommodate my iron-like rod.

Reaching over, I gripped her tits, I pumped hard for several moments, before she pushed herself forward, pulling my dick out of her butt hole. She rolled over, and moved eagerly toward my cock, and licked the shaft before she put it into her mouth for some long seductive sucks. Her hands wandered around to my buttocks, where she moved her fingers between my crack gently.

Soon enough, she rose, and straddled me without speaking, our lips were used for kissing not speaking.

I forced my cock into her tight pussy, as she rolled on top, riding and using her thighs, she gripped tightly. I began to stroke her wet clitoris, and I felt her muscles tighten over my penis and I too tightened my grip on her hips as she began to rise too high, I felt as though I was going to fall out of her minge with each movement.

As she continued to grind my cock, I reached wantonly for her tits again, stroking them, and her body as I watched my own personal show, her blonde hair fell over her face. I felt the back of her pussy with each thrust, and as I felt myself about to erupt inside her, I moved closer to her mouth, our rhythmical movements intensified, her tightening pussy muscles sped up my release, and she lay gasping on top of me, passionately screaming.

I felt my cock fall out of her as I went soft.

"I'm too scared to go to court" She confessed, as she lay breathing heavy next to me, and I realised it was the first time she had said this out loud.

I embraced her, "I won't let them hurt you"

August 2nd

We were awoken by a loud knock on the door that morning. Anastasia was alarmed at the sound of the hammering, and I raced to the spy hole. As I glanced out, I noticed Oliver in the frame.

I mouthed who it was to her, and she shook her head, he knocked again calling out my name this time.

"I am not here" She whispered, as she made her way to the bathroom, aware that he was not going anywhere.

"One moment" I called, trying to make my voice sound further away from the door than I was.

When I was sure she was hidden, I opened the door, and greeted him with his own name. Without making small talk, he thrust an envelope before me, "You're needed in court in London tomorrow for a tribunal"

I opened the envelope, I saw my name on the list, "I can't make this"

Anger hit him, and he forced his way into my apartment, "You have to, you were the one who cried rape, and it is my name that he is dragging down"

"You were the one who asked me to do it" I remembered, "You told me I had to do whatever I had to in order for the fat bastard to get his just desserts, now I can just as easily say that you paid me to do it, and I would walk away with a slap on the wrist.... you my friend....."

"I need you there bell end, I let you sleep with my woman" He explained. "Anastasia is not your property" I insisted.

A hint of madness seemed to cross his face, "She has not told you everything about her life has she?"

"Nothing you can say will stop me from loving her" I insisted, "And besides, I am in court here tomorrow"

"You have to postpone it" He insisted.

I thrust the envelope back into his hands, "No you turn up on my doorstep the day before your own case and expect me to stand up for you against a case you built up against yourself, when I lost two dear friends and could lose another if he does not wake from this coma"

"I heard about the siege" He confessed, and I realised he probably seemed more sincere now, "I suppose I have no choice in this"

"Thank you" I guided him back toward the door.

"Perhaps you and I and Anastasia could recreate that night in The Gambia" I realised that he was flirting with me, and his hand reached out to touch me, "I could not take my eyes off you when you were fucking that rep, whilst we were screwing around you, I remember watching your little man pump hard into her. My big black balls were bouncing next to yours and I know that you liked it"

"All in my past" I insisted, "Anastasia is the only one for me"

"How many men and women have you fucked?" He soothed, as he tried once more to touch me.

"Get the fuck off me" I hissed.

"Have you bought your tickets for Palma?" He asked, trying to change the subject again.

"I am not going" I insisted.

"You have to" He seemed scared, "You can't not turn up, the USS Vivandier is your party"

I chose to ignore him, and continued to guide him out of the room.

"No" He insisted, "It is important that you make it to the party"

"Goodbye Oliver" I continued, and closed the door, I tried to ignore the look of horror on his face.

"You have to believe me" I heard him almost whimper.

As I turned my back to the door, Anastasia smiled at me as she made her way back to the bed, "Thank you for not letting him see me, but did he seem a little weird to you?"

"I never trusted him" I muttered.

"I'm scared" She confessed, "If he turns up again, I think there is something he may try to tell you about me"

August 3rd

Anastasia was not needed as I went to court the following day to give evidence, and she opted to stay home, and I dressed in a second hand suit from the charity shop, and a straight black tie, sat in the dock, giving my statement as clear as I could remember.

The CCTV caught him in the act, and external camera's found Victoria and Mr F abandoning her car in a service station, and their mobile phones and original passports were found in a toilet nearby. That was enough to prove that she was the brains around the siege.

The evidence upset Troy all the more as he screamed bloody revenge on them both before being removed from the court.

I felt emotional as I recalled the stabbing. Luckily there was no more questioning almost instantly, and I was able to leave before lunch. I smiled at the two girls that were waiting to give evidence after me. Stephen's mother, and Karen were also there, comforting each other.

Jack sat in the corridor on his mobile as I made my way toward the toilet.

"Please tell Lana I need to see her" I spoke with sincerity, aware that he knew of my feelings for her.

He shut the call that he was on, and shook his head, "I wish I knew where she was, and why she won't answer her calls"

"Go find her, and love her" I whispered, but in the back of my mind, I knew he was lying to me.

I turned to walk away.

Rushing to the loo, I barely reached the urinal before I started what seemed like the longest piss that ever took place. I had been waiting to go all morning but was not allowed to leave the room unattended, and I did not want anyone watching me piss.

I was unaware when Oliver entered the room, and pressed his back against the exit for a while, he seemed to have been there for some time when I turned to leave.

"It was hard work, but I sorted out a new court date" He explained.

"Send it in the post" I insisted as I approached him, hoping that he would move.

"Why are you being so distant?" He asked, and I realised that he was fumbling around with his buttoned fly, "I need you to tell me you will be there"

"I will be there" I spoke trying not to notice the massive black cock that he pulled out before me.

"Maybe you can touch me for luck" He purred, offering me his dick with his hand, forcing me against the wall.

"I told you" I whispered, "I don't do that kind of thing anymore"

"You don't do anything do you?" He hissed, dick still in hand, and hardening by the second, "When I got you in that orgy last year, you got your dick wet with one girl when you could have had any pussy you wanted, or cock for that fact, yet you were in love with a pair of gingers. Both of whom are deceased"

He was pressed against me now, and grinding a little, "Get the fuck off me"

"I wanted to fuck your tight ass last year when you screwed over that fat bastard" He insisted. His black shaft was now touching my hand, and I pulled away, "My dick scares you"

He laughed and I felt him wrap my hand around his cock, and he began to thrust hard, pressing me against the door with his body weight,

I wanted to scream but the sound was trapped within me somewhere.

"Anastasia could never take me whole, but I bet your hole will be puckering for my meat" His stinking hash breath poured over my nostrils like a rancid snake.

"Last time someone did this to me, I stubbed a cigarette out on his dick" I remembered.

"I like it when you talk dirty" He smiled, leaning in for a snog, "A bit of pain is good for the soul"

"Right" I insisted, as the memory of Tommo flashed through my mind, I forced my hand down his shaft as hard as I could, and I could sense the pain I caused him, as he moved back in pain, but he tried to remain masculine.

"Make me cum" He commanded.

As the pressure of his body weight moved, I seized the opportunity to release my grip on his cock, and to move away from the door.

"Let me out" I insisted.

Annoyed with not getting his own way he put his penis back into his jeans, still a visible bulge, "You will be on that boat if it is the last thing I do"

FIFTY EIGHT

As I walked along the corridor, I heard the judge call for the room to rise, and I crept inside the whole room turned to watch me as I stepped inside the court, and sat next to Karen. Moments later, the door opened again, and Oliver walked in, taking a seat next to me as though nothing had happened.

Troy took his on the dock, as the Judge addressed the room, and I felt Oliver press his hand against my back pausing a moment at my pocket, and I shrugged it off.

"You owe me baby" He whispered, "And you will thank me for it"

He stroked his own dick again through his jeans. Once more, I ignored him.

The judge spoke, and I was drawn to the foreman of the jury, a tall moustached man whose comb over was inappropriately flopping over his brow as he spoke.

"Foreman of the jury" The judge spoke in her commanding voice, "Have you reached your verdict on the charges laid against the defendant?"

"Yes Your Honour" He spoke with a plum in his mouth.

"And this verdict is unanimous?" She asked.

He nodded, "We find the defendant guilty"

The room erupted in cheers, and the judge commanded order, as Troy screamed his innocence in the dock, ordering that his lawyers find his wife and friend.

It took several minutes to quieten the room, and anger filled Troy as he was restrained by guards.

"I will get out and kill every one of you mother fuckers" He screamed.

The heavy rain pounded hard as I made my way back to my apartment. I shook off the water, as I entered the hall way, and I almost smiled as I reached Simon's doorway, as though somehow a little victory had been won.

Hands shaking I felt the jingle of the key at my door, and I instantly started to remove my damp clothes, tossing them to the floor. Almost ready for action, as Anastasia sat amused at my table, sipping coffee.

"Three consecutive life sentences and a further five years for the trafficking" I commented, aware that my nakedness was making her smile wider than before.

"I saw on the news that they think Victoria and that man have gone to America" She smiled, as she rose, and crossed the room, "But I do not care about her, him, or anything else"

She placed her lips onto mine, and stroked my cold naked body as she groaned, and slowly she moved away, removing her blouse.

"You're happy" I smiled, aware that I was now hard, and ready to pound her over the table right now.

She tossed her blouse to the floor, "I found your little surprise"

Now I was confused. She did not react to my silence, instead she took off her skirt, and stood before me in her bra and knickers.

"I think I will start with a blow job" She purred, as she lowered herself down my body, "Then when you are about to shoot your cream, I am gonna stop, and then you can fuck me as hard as you can"

She started to suck hard onto the shaft, taking me wholly inside in one gulp, and I felt the back of her throat with my tip. I grabbed her head, and tried to push it deeper into her mouth, I felt her rough grip on my testicles, pulling hard, in a sharp motion, and I nearly screamed as she continued to take deep swallows of my meat. She moved her hands around my buttocks and she squeezed hard, slapping me occasionally, and I allowed her fingers to penetrate my anus. Her tongue lash against the base of my cock. I began to push my hips up and down as I assisted her mouth movement. My groans soon became intense, she knew the signal, and as promised, she stopped.

I shook my head as I wanted to come, and she laughed, as she guided me down her body, toward her open vagina.

I created a slow steady movement of my tongue against her pussy lips and with my tongue flat, I switched between each cleft as I teased her by not deciding which part to go to next. I entered her hole with two fingers, then one, now four. Soon I found myself putting my entire fist inside her. I flexed my hand from fist to palm, and stretching my fingers inside her vagina, I could feel her insides against my fingers, wet, and her body moved in spasm, as I fluctuated my movements between fast and slow, the intensity inside her increased, as I felt the gush of fluid and her screams increase. She tightly closed her legs, entrapping my face against her pussy, my tongue buried deep inside her, and I carried on switching between fingers and tongue against her hairy mott.

My face was wet with her cum as I pulled away for a moment, with my sticky hand I stroked her body with her own juices, and then I used my dick to probe her pussy, perineum and her arse.

She rolled underneath me, and arched her pussy towards me, to drive me into her tight clefts. She pushed against me so hard, that my balls touched her and I started to thrust in synchronisation with her own frantic movements.

Her suction pulled me deeper inside and the slapping sounds of our bodies echoed around the room. Part of me wanted Simon to hear again. I missed him.

I could hear her groan, and mumble something to herself as she pushed back harder on my dick. I reached over to her hair, and pulled sharply back, pulling her head toward me, so I could kiss her, I was not hurting her, but as I ripped her head back by her thick mane, as I rammed deeper into her wet pussy. Her groans soon became pleasure, as she began to convulse with waves of orgasmic satisfaction and I too was about to fill her with my own jizz.

As we began to speed up our rhythmical movement, I felt her hand stroke herself, and her groans became intense and I released my hot thick creamy cum inside her.

"Yes" She gasped, after several moments. I had no idea what she was on about now.

"What?" I panted, trying to get my breath back.

She smiled, as she rose, and made her way to the beside cabinet. She chose a small box from the draw, and returned to me, presenting me with my own ring.

I swallowed hard, and realised what she had agreed to.

"I know we have only been dating for a few weeks, but yes, I will marry you" She calmly spoke.

"Anastasia, I...." I began, glancing at the ring, and a moment of hatred for the previous owner hit me like a punch in the stomach.

I turned to face her, and she was admiring the ring more passionately.

Without thinking, I nodded, and took the ring from the box, "Emily Anastasia Lewis.... Let's get married as soon as possible, but I have to tell you something"

She took the moment to snuggle up to me now.

"I was not planning on proposing so soon, but it feels right after what we have been through" I agreed, as I stroked her naked body next to me, "Those rings were mine and Chris's, when we got a hand fast earlier this year"

"I know" She smiled, "And it does not matter, you and I both have histories"

FIFTY NINE

August 4th

The Black Orchid was now a shadow of its former self, almost all of the girls had left, with the exception of Anastasia, a Chinese girl, who danced under the name of China, and a tall brunette biker, Diesel. Anastasia had adopted Julia's old role, and was auditioning new dancers as Greg and Eve arrived that day to inspect the premises, and to ensure that I was completing the paperwork accordingly.

After reviewing the footage of the CCTV of the murders, I had a ritualistic bollocking off Greg for letting Victoria simply take the money, no mention of my tumble down the stairs, or the fact some people were murdered in their business, but never mind, I could not give a shit.

Eve sat before me, fluttering her eyes, and I felt as though I wanted her hand back on my dick again for a moment. Then I remembered that photograph, and how betrayed I felt.

"Right" Greg was still talking and I had no idea what he was waffling on, stupid twat, "I will go an inspect the flat, and then we will be off"

"I want to just call into that little boutique around the corner, see if they still have that ring" Eve smiled, as she kissed her husband with a gross like passion.

Moments later he left, and I watched him through the window, he sickened me as he glanced at Anastasia and the girl she was auditioning. I think I saw him with a hard on as he walked past. If he was anything like his son, then probably. I turned, and noticed Eve was still in the room.

"It is nice to see that you have moved on" She confessed. "I love her" I announced.

"Then take her away from here" She continued, "Mr F as you know him has been dealing here for years, and I saw many girls taking his cocaine, hell, I even had a try in my day"

I could not believe that she knew this all along.

"If it wasn't for Greg, it could have been me that was stabbed by that barman here, I am lucky he took me away from this place, my world changed for the better" She continued.

"Yet you still don't love him" I nodded.

"Greg and I did love each other some time ago" She confessed.

"Not anymore?" I pre-empted.

She shook her head, "He has his flings, and I have mine"

"Like his son" I observed.

The shock hit her for a moment, "Chris and I had a thing once or twice, but Greg never knew about it, I suppose you could say I was reliving my youth"

"Why did you lie to me?" I asked.

"I have never lied to you" She commented.

"The day before he turned up in Bramhall, you and him were here" I commented, as I made my way to the desk, retrieving the memory card from the drawer, "This motherfucker was left in my apartment for me to find"

She shook her head again "I have no idea how that ended up in your apartment"

I felt myself fingering the silver chain, "You told me yourself, you used to wank him off and then I find out you two were in Blackpool the day before he turned up at my place, telling me that he had been walking for weeks, and like a dick I believed his lies"

"He didn't lie" She insisted, as she started to close the door behind her, so that no one could hear, "He did love you, and he called me to say he was staying in the flat here, so I came up to him"

She took a seat, and gestured for me to sit.

I knew I was in for a story, but I did not want to listen now, "He came up here to look for you, he had no idea where you were, and I knew that Greg was angry at him. So I had to protect him like I had done for years. I am certain you saw the bruises from the battering that Greg gave to him when he said he was fucking you. I confess what started out as a hand-job soon became a sordid affair, but that is all it was"

By now, I had loaded the photos, and was scanning them without really listening to her, "You had plenty of opportunity to tell me when you were giving tossing me off in the hospital"

"He genuinely thought that you had chosen to move on" She commented, "He slept with a couple of men and women in a bid to move on, but when he heard about the fire in Manchester, he knew he wanted to be with you"

"You're lying" I observed

"No" She shook her head, and I could tell she was being sincere, unlike her prick of a husband, "I have known Chris since he was 14, and I never saw him love anyone like he did you... When I watched him cry at the thought he had betrayed you, I knew I had to get him to you"

I was fingering my chain again, I realised I missed him, but I had moved on. Her words were sincere, and I knew that I had misjudged him.

"I have something important to tell you" I sensed a hint of nervousness about her.

We were interrupted by her mobile ringing, which she took, and glanced at me for a moment. I waited.

When she finished her call she smiled at me, "I must go, but I have something for you" She opened her purse, and presented me with a cheque. I opened it, and smiled.

"Take your woman away from here and start afresh, like Greg and I did.... we left this dump behind" She smiled as she rose, pausing for a moment, "Maybe Montreal?"

"This is too much" I insisted.

"It is from my savings from when I worked here" She smiled, "It is time to do some good"

"Is that what you had to tell me?" I asked.

She paused again, and glanced at her phone before answering, "Yes"

She was lying to me, I was sure of it, but as I glanced at the cheque for £75,000 I did not care.

"One more thing" I asked, still looking at the cheque, "When I found these pictures, I was full of anger, and I threw the ashes into the sea out here, do you think he would mind?"

She laughed, "He loved this place, I think that you chose well"

I watched as she left, via the same way that her husband had left earlier, and I saw the girl that Anastasia had auditioned follow her out, with a spring in her step.

Cheque in my hand, I made my way down the stairs, and kissed my fiancé as she waited at the bar with a pint ready for me.

"Mr Mumford is a prize prick" She smiled. I laughed as I took a sip of the drink.

"I found us a new dancer" She smiled, "She wants the name Orgasma, and from what I saw, she will have all the men dripping their cock milk within seconds"
"Sounds wonderful" I smiled.

"She has a few things to tie up, and will be back at the weekend, and I put her onto the letting agent about Simon's flat" She smiled, "I think this is going to be the start of something special"

"How would you feel about starting a fresh somewhere?" I asked, as I unfolded the cheque before her.

She smiled, as she fingered it, "What with this and the cash you have stashed under our bed in that bag, we can go anywhere we want"

Wait. She knew about the wad of cash under my bed?

I wanted to ask her how, but she simply smiled and gave me a knowing wink.

August 5th

It was a particularly hot Blackpool day as I put the cheque into my account that day, and I explained about the thousands of pounds in Euro's and Lira under the bed in full truth, and Anastasia did not flinch. She agreed that the money should be used in emergencies. We also decided to have another hand fast in Chester, and caught the first train we could.

Maverick was less than pleased when I arrived with a woman, and started to spout off a rant that I had defaced the sanctity of marriage, but as Anastasia explained the circumstances of our union, it softened him. I was sure that I had also seen Moonbeam in the back of his canvas tent, but the girl disappeared as quickly as she was seen.

Once more, Petal became my aide, and her twin helped Anastasia to get ready, and by sunset, we stood at the mound again, with my naked friends. Once more, Maverick stood there with his semi- on as he read from his book.

"A while ago, I officiated a hand fast with this man, and his love, but a tragic accident did sever their union. Since then Connor has found love in this beautiful lady, and they have come to us today to incorporate the ancient Celtic ritual of hand fasting in their wedding. A declaration of love, where they clearly state that they are marrying of their own free will"

Petal and her twin had rose, and approached us from behind, taking a piece of cord each.

"The promises made today and the ties that are bound here greatly strengthen your union" Maverick explained, to which I already knew.

"Do you seek to enter this ceremony?" Maverick asked. I could see that he was lusting over Anastasia. In fact, I think his erection was aiming at her.

"Yes" We responded in unison, my mind was still on whatever his dick was looking at.

"Then please look into each other's eyes" He instructed, and we obeyed, "Connor and Anastasia, will you share in each other's pain and seek to alleviate it?"

"Yes" We nodded, and as before, the bind was made, sealing our hands.

"Do you share in laughter, and look only for positives?" Maverick continued.

"Yes" And a second bind was made by the girls.

"Will you share your dreams?" He continued.

"Yes" And a third bind was made.

"Do you honour each other as equal?" Maverick continued.

"Yes" We responded.

"Connor and Anastasia, as your hands are bound together, so your lives and spirits are joined in a union of love and trust, the bond of marriage is not formed by these cords, but by the vows that you have made, for you always hold in your hands the fate of this union. Above you are stars, and below you is the earth, like stars your love should be a source of light, and as earth, form a strong foundation" Maverick continued, it was a bloody exact replica of my first one, but fuck it "May your hands be the healer, protector, shelter and guide for one another"

We pulled out the rings, I had kept my former ring, and she had chosen a small silver ring from a market that cost no more than a meal from an up market take-away.

I placed the ring onto Anastasia's finger, "I promise that I will love only you forever, making you smile, making you laugh, and making our family"

Anastasia smiled as she paced the ring on my finger, "I will promise that you and I will grow old together, make love every day, and live life to the fullest"

We did not wait to be instructed we were ready to kiss, and a cheer erupted from the audience, I could see again that Maverick's dick was rock solid now, and he was beginning to lower his hand to touch himself.

SIXTY

August 8th

After the hand fast, Anastasia and I made love in the commune tent, aware that people could see through the open flaps, I know for a fact that Maverick was allowing Petal to suck his meat outside the door at one point. That girl that looked like Moonbeam was hovering in the background, waving at me with child-like gestures. It was definitely Maverick's ex-wife.

Finally, we made our way back home to Blackpool to celebrate with our friends. The night was young when we arrived back, and the sun rose when we returned to our apartment.

I could hear movement outside the room just a few hours later.

Struggling with the hangover, I made my way to the peep hole. I could see that Simon's door was open, and I could hear some voices inside, and watched as the door shut.

I was awake now, so I made my way to the bathroom, and released my urine, and I heard something move in the lounge as I finished.

Making my way into the room, I saw an envelope on the floor, I reached for it, I smiled as it was addressed to Mr and Mrs Connor Candlish, tearing it open, and removed the invite.

'House warming, masquerade, tomorrow, signed

Hollie' August 9th

Anastasia told me Hollie was Orgasma's real name, and that she had studied dance in Manchester, and she had split up with her boyfriend of a year. She was looking for a new start, and she knew that The Black Orchid was the way for her. She was like a female version of me.

That evening, Anastasia ironed my shirt as I played around with my mask that we bought from a shop in town, mine was all red, with a pointed nose, and hers was a black velvet with a silver rim.

As she modelled her outfit, she smiled at me, lifting her dress slightly, to show me her pussy.

I walked her over to the bed, and allowed my hand to wander up her leg, my fingers slowly touched her crotch, and I moved my body along hers, kissing her momentarily, lifting her dress, and taking it over her head. Her nakedness was perfect to me, and my teeth soon approached her erect nipples, and as I bit, she squirmed, and inhaled air between her teeth to control the pain I knew I caused. My hand moved from her pussy, and undid my button, releasing my semi-erect penis.

I rubbed my own cock, concentrating on kissing her neck, her lips, her breasts, until I knew I was hard enough for her. Without warning, I lifted her legs, placing them over my shoulders, and I spat onto my own purple head, rubbing the saliva down my shaft, she was wet enough, and I guided my dick expertly into her hole, and I carelessly pumped hard, using my hands to squeeze and tease her rosebud nipples.

Our bodies synchronised in rhythm, and her hands reached for my own nipples, that were just out of her reach, she bit her own lips frustrated, as I took full ownership of penetrating her, and I was aware that our new neighbour could hear me. I knew Simon could, so it was clear that we were putting on a show.

"Turn me over" She urged, "I want to be taken from behind"

"No" I began to speed up my pace, "I want to see your 'O' face"

She nodded, and clenched a little, she knew that was something that would work with me, and I gained momentum, and pushed harder, until I felt that familiar sensation in my groins, shooting my sweet release through my organ.

I encouraged her to join in with her own orgasm and I soon felt my softening cock slip out of her clefts. Collapsing on top of her, and managed to kiss her briefly on the lips for a moment.

She did not say anything, and simply rolled away from me, revealing her naked back, covered in sweat.

"I wish we could stay in bed fucking all day" She smiled, "Perhaps we can use that money that Mrs Mumford gave you to buy a yacht and fuck in the sun?"

"Sounds like Heaven" I agreed, snuggling to her.

We showered together, and dressed each other, I loved slipping her dress over her body, and smoothing it down, and she massaged my dick as she put my trousers on, and then she soothingly buttoned my shirt.

We kissed as we placed our masks on, and grabbed a bottle of wine from our fridge, and made our way across the hall.

Hollie had kept Simon's "Welcome" doormat, and within moments of knocking, a butler in the buff opened the door, causing Anastasia to smile.

"You are the first to arrive" He announced, as he invited us in, leading the way with his bare naked arse.

"Where is our hostess?" I asked.

"Mistress Orgasma is getting ready, and will be with you shortly" He spoke like a rehearsed script, as he guided us to a seat, in the dining area pouring us a flute of wine.

Anastasia took a sip of her wine, and I scanned the room. It was surprisingly bare, and Simon's pictures were still up on the wall. Although our apartments were identical, this one seemed different with the use of spaces.

The butler retired into the kitchen, and I leaned over to my wife, "She has done nothing to the place"

"Give her a chance" My wife smiled, as she stroked my hand across the table, "She is new to the area and is finding her feet"

I could hear her in the kitchen, and moments later, the butler returned.

"Mistress Orgasma invites you to her bedroom" He smiled to my wife, "She would like your assistance with her hair"

Anastasia gracefully accepted the invitation, and took the butlers hand.

"So how many people are coming tonight?" I asked.

The butler soon returned and acknowledged my question with a smile, and he allowed his hand to touch my leg, I could see his bulge increase under his apron, "I would love to be coming any time"

I brushed his hand away, and he smiled back at me, sliding his hand underneath his apron to touch himself. I heard a thud somewhere in the apartment.

"I am not into this type of thing" I insisted.

"Mistress Orgasma said she would like to have a party with you and your lovely wife" He continued as though I had not spoken, as he rose. His erection really protruding beneath his attire, "Would you mind if I watched as you fuck them both?"

"I will not be having a threesome" I insisted.

"Butler" Mistress Orgasma called from her room, "Can we borrow you for a moment?"

He smiled again, I was getting a little freaked out by him now. With that he moved out of the room, probably to have a wank.

He returned a few minutes later, fully dressed, and looking a little flustered. "Going so soon?" I asked.

He nodded, "She will be with you shortly"

He did not even wait, and walked out of the door, leaving me alone again. I was not alone for long, as the bedroom door opened.

She walked out with a PVC cat suit on, and her face covered almost entirely down to the lips with a matching mask.

"Your wife will be with us in a moment" She smiled, as she extended her hand to shake, "I really owe you a lot for offering me the job"

"What happened to the butler?" I asked.

She laughed, "You really are blind to what lies before you aren't you Connor?" I was confused again now.

She tightened her grip on my hand, and licked her lips, "My vagina feels empty without you inside me, it's like an aching feeling deep inside me, wanting you. Sometimes, I feel wet, sometimes I don't. Being here with you now, I have butterflies, starting in my chest, going straight into my pussy, and the heat is intense, I want to extinguish it. Sometimes sensations turn into electric shocks through my body, I want to feel you grind against me, I could die happily with you pinning down, kissing me.... grinding"

I tried to pull away from her.

"Remember that?" She asked, "I loved you, and you treated me like a one night stand that would not fuck off"

"Anastasia" I called.

Mistress Orgasma laughed, "She won't answer you"

Panic struck me,

"What have you done to my wife?"

She laughed more, and gestured to her room, "If you want to see your wife again, you will attend the party"

She laughed even more, as she removed her mask. Ophelia stood before me, larger than life.

SIXTY ONE

She laughed at me as I tried her door forcefully, calling out my wife's name, and I could hear some movement inside.

Ophelia remained in the doorway, "We spent a lot of time tracking you down Connor, and you certainly are a slippery little man slag"

I continued to call my wife's name, much to her annoyance.

"And it would seem that I am not the only one who wants to see you hurt" She explained, slowly walking toward me, "There is that manager of the bar who tried to burn you alive, and then there is his lover who is stuck with life changing injuries because of you"

"Let her out of there" I screamed, I knew I could hear something inside. The movement of material seemed to drift across the room.

She shook her head, "Then you screwed your nurse in her own house, where her husband works hard to pay her way, and what about the old landlady that you were fucking whilst we hid in your loft conversion"

"We?" I queried.

"S and myself" She smiled. "Who is S?" I asked.

She laughed so loud, I genuinely feared for my life.

"You could not even kill yourself when we urged you to" She teased. I looked at my scar.

"You ran like a rat from a sinking ship" She found her comment hilarious, "She was so cut up when you stopped slipping her your pork sword, how can you break her heart when she's as ancient as Old Grace that you fucked to death last year?"

"You killed Grace... you told me" I hissed, still pounding on the door. The silence behind the door was deafening.

"You even went to The Gambia to set up an innocent man, I would not be surprised if he wants your dick in his prized possessions" She continued, totally neglecting my own words previously, "And then you abandoned that lovely young girl to have some bum fun with your Ginger twat...."

I turned to face her, she was only a few feet away from me, "You had him killed because you can't accept I never loved you"

She laughed more, showing no fear, "You broke so many people's hearts on your pathetic little journey, Shannon and Chris both loved you equally and you stole him from that lovely lady Sian, and you did not even pay attention when the girls dropped like lemmings from that balcony"

I realised she knew something more.

She continued, "I have not even mentioned the crazy bitch Victoria and her husband, and that girl you fucked from Canal Street, and all of which want you dead"

"I am sorry I hurt you" I cried, desperate to get through the door, "But I was grieving after my parents...."

"Admit it Connor" She became soothing, "By having a strong word with your wife, I have saved you from someone else who would want you dead"

I began to kick at the door, aware that I was making it bend, "What have you done to her?"

"When you can admit that you belong in my bed, fucking my brains out all night" She smiled, nearing me, her knee was pressing against my cock right now, she was starting to rub it gently, "That night I met you in the bar, you were singing that song that stuck in my head, and we went back to yours, you banged me three times, and left me on Canal Street, but you went off, and put your dick in that yank bitch's mouth"

"You're a sick bitch" I whispered, too scared to think what else to say.

Her knee became move firm against my penis, "I forgive you for being such an insubordinate mother fucking STI case"

She leaned in closer, and I lost my mind, I grabbed at her throat, and squeezed. It frightened me how she seemed to enjoy the experience, she did not even try to defend herself.

"I want you to fuck me like the slut I am" She smiled, "And the dirty little slag you are"

Anger spilled out of every orifice, and I threw her against the wall. The crazy bitch continued to laugh as she fell to the floor.

She rose almost instantly, and she opened her cat suit at her crotch, revealing her smooth pussy before me, "Ravage me raw, and split my fanny....."

I ignored her and started to kick the door off its hinge.

"She will be long gone by now" She laughed, her fingers were now buried into her minge, and she was still making her way toward me.

"Let me in there" I screamed.

"With pleasure" She smiled, as she brushed past me, "It's all I want, you in my bedroom making my beaver look like a well wet drowned otter"

She pulled a key from somewhere unimaginable, and opened her door. "Anastasia" I called, as I barged past her.

The room was a mess, and Simon's pictures still remained in place, including one of him and Julia.

I noticed the window was open, as Ophelia lay on her bed, still stroking her pussy, and reaching for a vibrator nearby, switching it on and plunging it into her cunt.

"Where is my wife?" I asked, stood at the foot of her bed.

"What about the secret your wife is harbouring?" She teased.

"Where is my wife?" I repeated.

"The clues are here" She smiled, "It was Oliver, me or S that kept on leaving you the clues, hiding in the shadows, destined not to be seen"

I glanced cautiously around the room, and noticed some fresh blood on the floor, and something white submerged in it.

Reaching down, I pulled the piece of paper from the pool of blood, shaking, as I knew this was my wife's fate.

Ophelia was still pumping the vibrator into her clunge, "You know what you have to do"

"The USS Vivandier" I whispered.

"Five days, and you will see her again" She whispered, waving the vibrator around as she spoke, "Five days for you to realise I own your dick and every piece of sperm that you ejaculate and for every ounce you have dripped in or on anyone else male or female, you will spend a lifetime making up to me"

SIXTY TWO

Ophelia disappeared again that very evening. The blood was gone, and the police had no trace on Hollie, or Ophelia. My wife's disappearance was reported, and I sat at home crying myself to sleep, and avoiding the phone calls from Greg when I did not open his club.

The revellers outside were enjoying themselves, and I sniffed at my pillow, she still lingered there, I embraced it, and allowed my cock to harden, I soon started to tug hard for long moments and I felt the orgasmic sensation. A slow, and smooth movement for the longest of minutes, I thought of Shannon for some reason, which angered me, and caused me to speed up my wrist movement. I then saw Chris take her from behind, and then Sian made an appearance, lazing it up with Ophelia at the foot of my bed. Anastasia watched from my side, which I knew really was my pillow., Steaming pre-cum soon seeped out of my slit, and at that moment I felt that urge of spasm, I bucked, and thrust my hips in the air with the flowing movement of my hand and rhythm, screaming out as loud as I dared, and I watched as the first shot of sperm shot my jizz followed by bursts of my own juices, I cried to myself.

I swung my legs out of the bed, and used my deodorant on my dick, and decided to go for a walk. I pulled on my jacket, and a pair of jeans, and stepped out into the hallway. Cursing for a moment at the doorway opposite that once housed my friend, and then my enemy. I felt something rectangular in my jacket, and placed my hand in my pocket.

I pulled out a cardboard wallet, and my heart sank as I noticed the airline logo. Opening it, an airplane ticket with my name, and a date only a few days away.

"You win" I screamed, wanting my wife back.

August 10th

I was awaken by a hammering on the door, and nervously, I raced to the doorway, expecting the police, instead, a tired looking Greg Mumford waited for me.

"I don't have the time for this" I insisted, trying to close the door on him.

He forced his way past, and perched onto the table, looking directly at me, "You really are something Candlish"

"My wife is missing, I don't think that..." I began, realising that I was only wearing my pants.

"No" He screamed at me, taking me by surprise, "I have drove all night to get here to see what the fuck is going on, and all I have had is shitty motorway coffee"

Without prompting, I moved over to the kitchen and poured some water into the kettle.

"I knew I was an idiot for even allowing you to run this place" He continued, and I ignored, "The Black Orchid has been dragged through the shit because of you"

I felt a tear well up in my eye, and I started to shake, still holding that kettle. "Why the fuck are you crying?" He hissed.

I did not answer him.

I don't know how long I was there holding the kettle. But I soon felt him behind me, his hand was reaching around my waist, and his fingers started to bury themselves underneath the elastic. His cock was stiffening behind me.

"What are you doing?" I snapped out of my trance.

I felt his lips nuzzle against my neck, and his hand now completely entered into the front of my pants.

I struggled for a moment, as I turned around to face him, his hands cupped my hips firmly, and lifted me slowly. He was surprisingly gentle for someone so tough.

"Get off me" I cried.

"Why settle for silver, when you can have gold?" He insisted, as he continued to kiss my neck.

"Get off me" I screamed, forcing all my energy against his firm grip.

The anger within me shocked him, as he backed off. His penis was erect, and obvious to me.

"You spent all this time hating me for fucking you son, and now you do this?" I screamed, "My wife has been abducted, and you want to slip me your old man?"

Seductively, he turned his back to me, and stroked his own arse, "I will let this open for you if you want to....."

"I loved Chris, and I love Anastasia" I commented, "I would not let you anywhere near my cock if my life depended on it"

"You little bastard" Greg hissed, "I need that bar open tonight"

"Fuck you Mumford" I screamed.

"This is our secret" He commanded, back to his normal self I could see.

August 13th

I packed lightly, and made my way to Manchester Airport again, and hid my frustration at letting them defeat me. I did not tell Eve or Greg where I was going, just that I needed some time away. They did not understand. So far both of them had tried to fuck me, and I was using this against them.

Checking into the First Class Lounge, I watched the planes land and take off from the window, and drank a safe amount of alcohol. Last time I was heading to Mallorca, I was going to see two people I loved. This time, it felt forced just to get Anastasia back.

I checked into a cheap room only that was barely large enough for the single bed. It over looked the harbour. I needed to see The USS Vivandier. I knew that Ophelia would be here, and she would bring the mysterious S and hopefully my wife.

For two days I sat in the window, and watched, I saw nothing but the drunk reveller pissing in the harbour, and drinking. I lived only on water, and chocolate from the nearby shop. My mind was out there wanting an answer. If I could have turned back time, or jumped into that Tardis with my red headed companion, I wish that I could go back to that January night nearly two years ago, and say to Tommo I would not be singing in that bar. I knew it was the day that my parents died, and it was those that sent me in the direction of Mallorca. But I wished that I never met Ophelia, my life would have been different.

Hell if that slut had not turned up, maybe I could be happy in Turkey with Shannon or something? That bitch made my life hell and she was showing no signs of giving up. Maybe I could just push the blonde psycho over the edge of the boat when we are out in the ocean. Knowing my luck she'd survive like she did when she jumped into the sea at Blackpool.

August 15th

I barely slept that evening before the boat arrived in the dock. I remember it was shortly after dawn, and the regular sized boat docked so close to my peripheral I felt I was dreaming. I noticed instantly, although from the short distance, the butler in the buff on the deck, and Ophelia was barking orders at him as usual. I felt that fucking twitch that she gave to me. I hated her. But I was hard.

Ignoring my obstructing erection, I reached over for the invite, that still bore the blood, and I realised the time on it. I had a few hours until midday.
She was there. I needed sleep.

Setting my alarm for a few hours, I closed my eyes, and dreamt of Chris and Anastasia. In my dream they knew each other and were lovers. Like the good old days. He leaned down, and commenced kissing her passionately, throwing her roughly onto the mattress, as I lowered myself down her body, gently kissing her, I slid my hand under her thigh, Chris's hand meandered down her body too, and stroked my hair.

I felt the elastic on her panties with the tips of my fingers, and I pulled them sharply, tearing them apart, and away from her flesh in a swift movement. She allowed my forefinger, and middle finger to enter her moist welcoming vagina. I used my other hand to pull at her skirt, tossing it aside, as her blonde pubic hair glistened in the sunlit room.

I held my cock in my hand, and nodded to Chris as he glanced over at me. I parted her legs with my own, I allowed the tip to gently press against her lips, as Chris straddled her chest, forcing his dick deep into her welcoming mouth. He thrust forward, forcing her to lie on the bed, as I pumped hard inside her.

"I miss you" I called.

I did not know who I was referring to but I miss them both.

He began to lean over to me, his dick still inside her mouth, as he pressed his own lips against mine for a brief moment, he cupped my face, and continued to thrust his member inside her mouth. I reach over to him, and pulled him closer, forcing his penis to fall out of my wife's lips. She struggled to watch, I allowed my tongue to dart in his mouth for a moment, then I pushed him aside, signalling to her.

Chris lowered himself down her back, touching me, or her, depending on how we moved. His cock pressed firm against her anus, and she groaned as she pushed herself onto it, I forced my lips onto her moist mouth to stop her from moaning out loud.

Chris soon felt his own pleasure being climaxed, and he pulled out of her, and held his penis in his own hand, violently tossing himself over us both. His pure white cum shot over the pair of us, and I bit my own lip, feeling the explosion inside my own groin.

I was disturbed by my alarm tone, and I knew what I had to do.

A quick shower later, I made my way out of the room, and made my way to the USS Vivandier.

Butler in the buff, now dressed in Bermuda shorts and a vest smiled at me as I boarded.

"Third to arrive this time" He smiled, as he snatched my invite from me, "Mistress Orgasma has a big surprise for you"

"Mistress Orgasma can die" I hissed, "Where is my wife?"

"Silence" Ophelia commanded from nowhere.

"Where is my wife?" I asked.

"Inside" She gestured, "Set sail Marco, our guests are all here"

Butler in the buff obeyed, and I felt uneasy as the boat moved.

Ophelia laughed as she leaned casually onto the side of the boat, and Palma began to disappear, "Look at you, anyone would think you were about to face a firing squad, when it is me that should be crying, but I am woman and I am strong, and will not let it show to you. It is me that should be standing here, hoping that you could love me"

She turned her back, and allowed her dress to fall down a little, I could see the Mrs Connor Candlish tattoo that I despised.

"How did you afford this?" I spat gesturing at the vessel.

"It's not mine" She smiled, "I think you should meet my guest"

She smiled as she opened the door to the cabin, and sauntered in, where a small bar was being run with another handsome barman with long blonde hair, and I noticed the guest on the stools instantly. Oliver was drinking something clear as he smiled at me.

"I knew you would make it" He laughed.

"Yes, and we know why you are here Oliver" Ophelia laughed, "But I think your journey is nearly over"

"What?" He asked, believing her to be joking.

She smiled, as she inched closer toward him, and slowly inserted her hand into her purse at her side, "You are only here because my husband is sticking it to your bird, and you cannot get over the fact that she left you for a white boy"

He brushed off her comment, "I came here because you promised to make me rich"

"I promised that you will be better off" She corrected, as she pulled a gun out of her purse.

Ophelia gestured with the gun, "Come along now Oliver, let's get some fresh air, before I call security"

Reluctantly, he obeyed, and rose with her assistance, "We are out in the middle of the Mediterranean"

"I doubt there are sharks here" Ophelia laughed, guiding him out of the room, and I followed nervously. The barman just continued his work as though this was normal to him.

The boat had stopped, and we could see Palma in the distance.

"You have the choice" She sighed, "Either jump, or I shoot you"

"You wouldn't...." He began.

She aimed the gun into the air, and fired a warning shot, before bringing the gun to her side. "You crazy assed bitch" He hissed.

"My husband is screwing men and women behind my back" Ophelia screamed, "Don't underestimate what I would or wouldn't do"

He swallowed a little, and peered over the edge.

"If you're a strong enough swimmer, you will make it to the shore before you drown" She smiled, as she inched forward.

"Ok" He panicked, and climbed over the metallic banner, as I heard the door open again behind me, I did not dare to move.

"Now" Ophelia screamed.

I could sense the fear in him, and he obeyed, leaping almost instantly into the sea.

"Someone would have heard that" A voice alerted me instantly, "Your guests are getting restless"

I turned on my heels, ignoring the screams of abuse from Oliver in the ocean, and shook my head as I saw the brunette before me.

Ophelia smiled, as she waved the gun before her, "This mother fucker will be at the bottom of the ocean before we know it"

"Close your mouth Connor" Sian smiled, "You'll get your prize in just a few minutes"

"Marco" Ophelia called, "Set sail again"

The boat started up almost as soon as she finished speaking, and she made her way over to Sian. They kissed for several long moments before me.

Ophelia pulled away, "Sian darling, we can't possibly do this in front of my husband, you know how jealous he gets, and he puts his dick in the next hole he can find"

"Like my fucking grandmother" She laughed, and then leaned in to whisper something to Ophelia.

Ophelia laughed gently, and turned back to me, "I have to tend to our guests, give me two minutes, and then come on down to the hull, and then we can get the party started"

With that she moved back inside the bar. "So you survived the fall?" I asked.

"Your stupid bitch tried to kill me, but she did provide me with something soft to land on" She smiled, "I was out of hospital within weeks, and the insurance I had as a rep allowed me to buy this son of a bitch"

She gestured at her boat, and smiled, like she was demonstrating a show room toy.

"The USS Vivandier" She laughed. "It's an anagram for Sian survived"

I felt sick, and lurched forward, pushing past her.

"Where are you going?" She laughed.

"As your captain has said" I insisted pushing open the bar door again, "Let's get this party started"

Rushing past the barman, who was still ignoring everything going on I followed the sign directing to the hull. I knew that Sian sauntered behind me. I pushed open the mahogany door before me, and screamed.

Anastasia lay unconscious, naked and face down on the captain's table, a butt plug was inserted into her anus, and I raced over to her. As I embraced her, I noticed a bruise on the back of her head, and a white padded gauge on her side, with a small trace of blood on the top.

"You're very welcome for looking after her" Sian laughed, as she stood in the door way.

"The both of you are psychotic bitches" I hissed, as I pulled my wife off the table, searching for something to cover her modesty.

"How sentimental" Sian laughed, "So Connor, do you choose prize number one, or what's behind door number two?"

"You invited me here just to play games?" I asked.

"No dear" She laughed, "We had so much fun making you go crazy in that shitty little bedsit in Manchester, but we thought that things were going far too good for you, so Ophelia and I thought we would give you a choice"

"I just want to take my wife home" I insisted.

Sian laughed, as she turned her head, and screamed, "Ophelia"

"I am coming" Ophelia insisted with a hint of anger in her voice from behind another doorway in the room, "That maggot came too early, like usual"

She kicked open the door, and I could tell that she was struggling with something.

"So Connor" She insisted, "Do you chose your wife?" She heaved, and pulled a large Hessian bag into the room. Something was inside. "Or so you choose this?"

Checking Anastasia was comfortable, I moved away from the desk, "Who is in there?"

Ophelia laughed, as she kicked at the bag, "This mother fucker"

The contents of the bag groaned, and she leaned over it, pulling it off the body. Chris lay before me, nursing his side, barely able to breathe.

SIXTY THREE

I screamed, sure that the thing before me was a ghost. After all I was told that he was dead, and now I had my fucking husband, and my wife in the same room.

"You really should win the Bigamist Bastard of the year award" Sian laughed.

"I was told that you were dead" I whispered to him, ignoring the women in the room as I lowered myself to his side.

"My dad told me you died when the car hit you" He spoke through gritted teeth.

"How sentimental" Ophelia laughed, "Neither of you thought to attend each other's funeral"

"Your mother gave me some ashes" I insisted, and I almost told him about his dad just a few days ago.

He shook his head, as he rose, resisting my assistance.

"I called you not too long ago just to hear your voice" He confessed. The call I had in Blackpool, that day with Lana, it really was him.

"Right" Ophelia sang out loud. Startling me for a moment, "It's decision time lover boy"

"You're fucking crazy" I hissed.

She smiled as she opened her legs a little, and inserted her hand between her legs, "You made me this way you selfish twat"

She withdrew her finger, and placed it next to my lips. I brushed her aside.

This angered her a little, as she withdrew her gun again. Chris panicked, and Sian began to get excited at the prospect something was about to happen.

"Let me tell him our plan" Sian laughed, as she sauntered to her companion's side. I noticed her hand slip under Ophelia's dress, and I could tell by the response her finger was inside her pussy.

"Be my guest" Ophelia smiled, as she allowed Sian's fingers to wander inside her.

"When your stupid bitch pushed me over the balcony, I nearly died" Sian explained, "And I knew that I had to get revenge on you somehow"

"Why are we here?" I pressed.

"Ophelia only ever wanted your love, and you chewed her up and spat her out" Sian explained, as she thrust her hand deeper into my nemesis.

"She was the fucking one night stand that would not fuck off" I laughed, unsure how to react. This angered Ophelia more, and she forcefully pulled Sian's hand from out of her minge,

"You just killed one of your bitches"

Sian laughed, as she licked the juices off her hand, "You get to choose who lives and who dies"

"What?" I whispered.

"Yes" Ophelia laughed, "Bigamy is wrong, and man should only marry one, and you and I both know that I own you "

I turned to face Chris, and Anastasia, who was still unconscious, as Ophelia continued to speak, gesturing wildly with the gun.

"In the eyes of the law, you are married ginger nuts over there, and stripper whore is the illegitimate" She continued.

"Shut up" I insisted.

"You can either stay married to the stripper, or the cock sucker" She teased, "The other one will be full of lead before you know it"

"You won't kill either of them" I spoke.

"You have less than one minute to choose, or I will choose for you" Ophelia laughed, "And then I will give you until September 30th and then I will kill the other one"

"Consider it a birthday present" Sian interjected.

"You're mad" I panicked.

I turned to Chris, and I saw him shake his head.

"Tick fucking tock" Ophelia mocked.

"Choose her" Chris mouthed to me, and gestured to my wife.

"I won't let you kill any of them you crazy bitch" I screamed, as I turned back to her, "You should have died when you jumped off the pier last year"

Anger filled her face as she rose, and screamed for Marco again.

"When will you learn?" She screamed, aiming the gun at me, "You belong to me, and no fucker else, I am giving you a gift"

"A gift?" I cried, as the door pulled open, and Marco entered.

"You have just over a month to fuck the brains out of one more person, someone you said you loved" She insisted, "And now you haven't made a choice, I get to choose"

"No" I cried.

"Remove him" She ordered to Marco, as she waved the gun between Anastasia and Chris.

I barely had time to move, as I felt Marco and Sian grip at me, and the last thing I saw was Ophelia move closer to Chris, who was still struggling with his injury.

"You should have chosen" Ophelia laughed.

They pulled me out of the room, and Sian laughed as I fell to the floor outside. She swiftly slammed the door closed, and I heard the bolt lock.

I rose, and frantically tried the locked door.

"You should have chosen" Marco repeated, as he pulled me further away.

Angrily, I turned to him, "Whatever she is paying you, I will double if you just get me inside there now"

Marco shook his head, "I love her, and will do anything to make her happy"

Before I could respond, I heard the gun shot from the room behind me, with a sexless grunt and then a heavy thud of something falling, quickly followed by the second shot.

"Chris" I screamed, "Anastasia"

"You chose their destiny" Marco smiled as we exited the bar area, this bell end was stronger than I gave him credit for, although it must have been him I could hear in Ophelia's room when Anastasia disappeared, "I am surprised you say his name first, when I recall that day we met in Mistress Orgasma's place in Blackpool...."

"You have to let me in there" I knew I was fighting a losing battle.

"What? ... so you can mourn over one dead shag?" He teased, "And fuck the other one senseless whilst she watches?"

I felt his grip begin to slacken on me, and I realised how close I was to the edge of the boat, this fucker was going to throw me overboard like Oliver before.

"You treat people like toilet paper, you just use them and throw them away" He shook his head, "You upset her and now you pay"

I heard the bolt move in the distance, someone was coming out of the room. I strained to look over for a clue.

"She told me all about how you seduced her with vodka that night in the puffters bar in Manchester" He continued, "How you shagged her brains out, then tried to abandon her. All she ever wanted was to love you... she followed you all the way to Mallorca..."

"After injuring someone" I interjected, "She's a psychotic nut job"

This angered him a little, "Why she loves you, I have no idea... I could provide her with love, sex and treat her like a princess. Both Anastasia or Chris would be better off when your body is found, and you can reunite with whomever is dead in Heaven"

"You said you love her" I tried to negotiate, "Then let me in that room, so that I can stop her and you two can sail into the sunset together"

He laughed, "One of your partners is dead in there"

"There may be a chance...." I began.

"You see" Marco laughed, "Ophelia won't fuck me until your corpse is rotting in the ground, and the disillusioned bitch still thinks that you will run back to her eventually"

Shit, straight from the fucking frying pan and into the fire.

"So if your body washes up on a beach somewhere soon, I win" He smiled. With that, he lifted me with all his might, and I tried to fight back.

He used his strength to push me over the edge of the boat, the back of my legs hit the metal barrier, and the pain shot through me.

As I fell through the air toward the Mediterranean, I saw a shadow approach him, but before anything else could be revealed, I saw something unidentifiable being tossed over the side, and then the effervescent salt water splash I caused distorted my vision, and those few moments I was underwater was long enough to realise that I had somehow drifted far enough out to sea that the boat seemed quite a distance away.

"Help" I screamed, at the great vastness beyond.

SIXTY FOUR

Choking on the salt water of the Mediterranean, I struggled to maintain my float. I had only been in the water for a few minutes, and the USS Vivandier was close enough. I did not dare to approach it for fear that Ophelia was there again with that fucking gun.

I barely knew how to tread water, and I was aching. I needed to swim for it. I knew Mallorca lay the way of the boat, but why had it stopped.

From the rear of the USS Vivandier, I could see movement. Marco was backing away from someone, but I could not see from whom.

I could tell from the commotion that someone was bleeding heavily. But those were the only words I could make out.

"Connor" Someone screamed.

The water in my ears could not identify the owner of the voice, but it was concern.

Taking a deep breath, I lowered myself beneath the surface of the water, and I swam forward, I had no idea if I was swimming into danger or safety.

As I neared the vessel, I heard a splash in the water from somewhere ahead, and I felt my heart leap into my throat for a moment.

I could hear the dull call of my name again, and I felt the sting oh my own desperate want to breath begin to burn inside me. I was nearing the surface and I knew fear was setting in.

As I burst through the surface of the water, I realised that I was only metres away from the boat. I scanned the ocean to see who or what had caused the splash I heard just moments ago.

Nearby, I saw the naked back of Marco, lying face down in the ocean.

Frantically, and silently I waded over to the body, and rolled the body over, his throat was cut deep and the blood flowed angrily in the salt water.

I hoped nobody had seen me, and quietly swam back to the port side of the USS Vivandier.

This was my only salvation, and I had no idea who was dead or alive on board.

Shit what had I done to deserve this? Oh yeah she was on board this boat with my wife, husband, and the barman, oh and the other psychotic bitch from Liverpool. It would be quite easy for me to give up now and let the ocean take me, like Marco had said moments ago. Maybe then Ophelia can move on to her next victim?

"Connor" Someone called from above, had they seen me? I was still deafened by the water in my ears, I did not trust the voice. Not until I could identify it.

I panicked as a rope hit the water behind me. "Grab it"

I glanced up the rope, as the barman leaned over.

"Climb it" He commanded, his long blonde hair billowing over the rail of the boat.

"I don't trust you" I called.

"You have no choice" He retaliated.

"You killed Marco" I gestured over at the floating body.

"And you will join him if you don't climb on board" He yelled, "What are you going to do grip on the plimsoll line until we reach Mallorca?"

I felt myself reaching for the rope, and heaved myself out of the water.

As I reached the deck, I prepared for a new battle. The blonde barman took a stance, and waited for me to strike first. Neither of us moved.

"Who are you?" I asked.

"Someone sent to look after you" He commented as though I should know. "Stop dicking about" I insisted, "Who sent you?"

"You may call me a guardian angel Connor" He spoke, as he gestured to his pocket, I could see the rim of his wallet sticking out a little. With one move, he grabbed it, and tossed it over to me, "Earlier this year, my brother did something bad to you, and I felt it my duty to help you out"

The wallet landed just away from my feet, and I reached for it, without taking my eyes off of the barman. As I opened it, the drivers licence identified him as Cavanagh, and as I glared at the photo next to him, I nearly screamed at the camp looking fairy smiling back at me.

"How do you know this twat?" I asked, tossing the wallet back to him, which he surprisingly caught.

He nodded, and could not hide his smile, "That's my little brother Robin, he told me what he did to you last year, when him and is partner drugged you and got you fired from your job. I also know that they deliberately started that fire in your bar. He made me promise to repay you, he told me about her and begged me to protect you"

I could sense his hatred for Robin and his partner, and I did not know what to say, "How is he?"

"He is undergoing therapy for the burns, but he will pull through" He retracted his stance, "Do I have your trust?"

"I saw you throw something over the boat" A statement, not a question or comment.

"I had to slam the door shut so that no one could get out of that room" He commented, "I threw her spare keys overboard, only Marco had the spare set"

I hesitated, "How do I know you're not working for Ophelia?"

A sour cringe crossed his face, "Mate, I had to bang her so much just to get this job, let's just say that it was like shagging a sack of spuds"

I wanted to laugh.

"Look Connor" He controlled the conversation now, "Two shots were just fired inside there, and we have to find out who has been hurt and who needs our help"

I nodded.

The walk back through the bar seemed longer than I remembered. Cavanagh led the way, and I soon saw the barricade he had made against the door, made entirely of bar stools.

Without words, he shoved several aside, and produced the set of keys from his back pocket.

He smiled at me as he inserted the key into the hole, "Whatever lies in there, you have to hold it together"

I nodded.

The key twisted, with a loud sound produced from the latch inside.

The silence beyond seemed deafening as he cautiously opened the door, and led the way inside.

I followed, and felt the moistness underfoot of something that made a squelching noise, I did not want to look down.

Anastasia was not on the table where I had left her, but her binds and the butt plug, were nearby on the floor.

Ahead lay a hand on the floor, palm upwards, hidden by the corner of the table. I raced over to it, and felt a sense of relief as Sian lay face down with her blood-stained back showing no signs of life. I felt a smile cross my face, but I hid it before Cavanagh saw me.

"She's dead" I whispered. Cavanagh gestured to the doorway.

Ophelia was sat upright, her eyes closed, with a bleeding gash on her forehead, and glass ash tray lay at her side. Next to her, a pool of blood was forming, and I realised the reddened face and hand before me.

Fear set in, and I screamed.

Book 2. – Spurned Lovers.

Book 3 – Journal Of An Unloved Woman.

Book 4 - Masquerade

Printed in Poland
by Amazon Fulfillment
Poland Sp. z o.o., Wrocław

50277009R00247